A FALSE EXILE

Keith Nalumango

Copyright ©2022 Keith Nalumango
All rights reserved

The characters and events portrayed in this book are fictitious. Any similarity to real persons, living or dead, is coincidental and not intended by the author.

No part of this book may be reproduced, or stored in a retrieval system, or transmitted in any form or by any means, electronic, mechanical, photocopying, recording, or otherwise, without express written permission of the publisher.

ISBN : 9798819687321

Cover design by Art Painter Library of Congress Control Number: 2018675309
Printed in the United States of America

To Dr. Ed and Diane Buckner,
for the warm friendship, and for making me
see the world as I see it now

TABLE OF CONTENTS

COMING BACK 1
Chapter 1 3
Chapter 2 10
Chapter 3 18
Chapter 4 24
Chapter 5 29
Chapter 6 35
Chapter 7 39
Chapter 8 43
Chapter 9 46
Chapter 10 51
Chapter 11 55
Chapter 12 60
Chapter 13 62
Chapter 14 65
Chapter 15 69
Chapter 16 77
Chapter 17 81
Chapter 18 87
Chapter 19 93
Chapter 20 96
Chapter 21 102
Chapter 22 108
Chapter 23 112
Chapter 24 114
Chapter 25 121
Chapter 26 126
Chapter 27 131
Chapter 28 133

Chapter 29	141
Chapter 30	147
Chapter 31	155
Chapter 32	164
Chapter 33	168
Chapter 34	174
Chapter 35	180
Chapter 36	185
Chapter 37	190
Chapter 38	194
Chapter 39	197
Chapter 40	200
Chapter 41	204
Chapter 42	210
Chapter 43	215
Chapter 44	220
Chapter 45	228
Chapter 46	233
Chapter 47	237
Chapter 48	242
Chapter 49	255
Chapter 50	260
Chapter 51	263
Chapter 52	267
Chapter 53	274
Chapter 54	277
Chapter 55	284
Chapter 56	287
Chapter 57	291
Chapter 58	295
Chapter 59	298
Chapter 60	306

Chapter 61 313
Chapter 62 318
Chapter 63 324
Chapter 64 329
Chapter 65 333
Chapter 66 338
CHAPTER 67 342
SIX MONTHS LATER 347

COMING BACK

I open my eyes. Only darkness. And the pain in my throat? Ah, I've been screaming, yes. I want to stand up because I need to pee. After that, I'll leave this place, even though I have nowhere to go. My body feels so weightless, if it wasn't for this fatigue, I would lift it by myself, for myself, and take it away. Anywhere.

Am I still in prison? I know I'm in bed. The bed covers. Ugh! They smell of blood.

I remember the dream.

The prison cell was tiny. So tiny, sometimes I feared that the walls were about to crush me into ground beef. At times, it felt as if the air had been sucked out of the room.

Well, the sun was up when the short prison guard finally brought in the food. Finally, because it had been a long, uneasy wait. Someone had said the hanging would take place at dawn. So, I nibbled at the bacon, egg, sausage, and chilled baked beans. Soft bacon—just the way it used to be served in the university dining rooms where I first met her.

The pastor came in next, what he called 'The Word' dangling from his left armpit, his lopsided eyes focusing on two different parts of me at a time. It was as if the man was seeing a dead body and a living person at the same time.

"Leave me alone!" I screamed.

"You don't want a prayer, my son?"

"I don't want your prayer if it's going to save my life. I want to die because I killed my wife and my children. My life is worthless without them."

"So be it, son. Let endless pain descend upon you from above. May you suffocate forever and never die, and may that spectacle be shown live on your TV."

I had opened my eyes then.

I have a better view of the room.

With difficulty, I stand up. Unlike the prison cell in the dream, this room has a low ceiling.

One baby step at a time, I get to the door. I find the handle and turn it.

Outside, the reflection of the sun against the white walls of the building across the garden hurts my eyes. I retreat into the smelly room and conclude that I must be in a motel, one like those you see in the movies. Probably in the Mojave Desert. In the distance, I hear the sound of eighteen-wheelers pounding the highway.

Then I remember Rebecca and the room service: The French fries and the T-bone steaks on white plates. Vegetables…

CHAPTER 1

"Are you aware of the concept of polarity management and polarities of democracy?" Norman Tau, the flamboyant and most powerful of the four VPs of the corporation, asked.

Patrick shook his head. He knew the question was leading somewhere.

"Do you ever read?"

"Sir, if you don't mind, my production team is waiting for me downstairs."

"Two great minds," Norman spoke as if Patrick had not uttered a word. "Doctors Johnson and Benet. The concept is simple. While not every dilemma can be solved, it can be managed."

The telephone on Norman's large desk rang. He abruptly picked up the receiver and listened.

What was that about unsolvable problems? Of course, Patrick knew that not every problem could be resolved. But could every problem be managed? He thought about the secret he could not share with anyone—not even with Denise, the wife he doted on. He wished he knew someone, other than his wife, he could talk to about the burden he carried.

"No, no, no!" Norman screamed into the receiver. "And I mean a big *no!*"

A happily married father of three, Patrick Kanya was six feet two inches tall with an athletic body and a charming appeal. Those he worked with knew him as the handsome, jovial go-getter, the unsung celebrity Hollywood was yet to discover. As head of television production, Patrick was a mid-level manager at the Zambia National Broadcasting Corporation, commonly known as ZNBC, a state radio and television agency. The job paid him well, so he enjoyed the kind of material comforts not many of his former university classmates could ever dream of. But the responsibilities the corporation had placed on him in a politically charged atmosphere sometimes seemed insurmountable.

"I really don't care," said Norman.

Patrick looked at his cellphone. He had been in Norman's enormous office for fifteen minutes, and he could tell that his boss, who was very good-looking and about six feet tall, was engaged in a bitter quarrel with Alex, the diminutive marketing director. For as long as Patrick could remember, the two directors had been at loggerheads over what airtime marketing could sell.

Norman put his feet up on the desk and said, "We'll see about that, Alex!" He hung up and gave Patrick a stern look. "I run radio, television, and the news, idiot! Bloody Napoleon complex eating this guy!" Norman removed his feet from the desk that, only the previous week, had replaced a larger but less expensive one. "Okay, next item, the driver's death. What happened?"

"Sir, I don't have anything new to report."

"Hey, I want to hear it again!" Norman roared. "Last time I checked, I was the boss, right? Come on, Patrick, you know my management style. I get things done, and this is how I get things done."

Patrick's problem was that Norman was not his direct boss. His boss was the controller of television, a man Norman had made irrelevant by going directly to mid-level managers to "get things done." Patrick had long concluded that Norman cared about no one except himself. But Norman was so well connected in society, it was rumored he was more powerful than the corporation's CEO. Norman pandered to politicians' whims by meddling with television airtime to accommodate ruling party propaganda programs, even against the advice of operatives on the first floor. Rumor had it that Norman spent weekends with politicians hunting game.

"I want to hear your story over and over again until you lose your mind and quit your job, you hear me?" Norman quickly turned on that infamous plastic smile of his. "That marketing bastard is tempting me, Patrick…Look, tell me the story again. Maybe I forgot."

"With due respect, Norman, why are you so confrontational? Everyone here complains about you." Patrick wished he hadn't said those words. Up on the wall, behind Norman, hung the head of state's official portrait. It was rumored that Norman was on first-name terms with the man in the portrait.

Patrick hated politicians.

Norman grunted. "You know I don't care what people say about me. They don't call me Mr. T for nothing."

Mr. T? Patrick almost laughed. Five years ago, when Norman assumed the ever-so-great position of VP, he had embarked on the great project of getting everyone to call him Mr. T. No one had listened.

"Patrick, tell me how Nathan, a company driver, lost his life while you and Larry were looking on. Look, Larry told me in confidence that you ordered Nathan to keep driving even when it wasn't safe to do so. What am I hearing here? A plot to kill a poor driver, just because he's a driver?"

Patrick glanced at the clock on the wall. He wished he would leave. Twice during the past few days, he had been called to Norman's office to explain the circumstances leading to the death of one of the drivers in his department.

"The car stopped," Patrick spoke with deliberate ease. "I was in the back seat, Larry was in the front passenger seat. The traffic lights turned green. I asked Nathan why we weren't moving. I didn't know some drunken driver wasn't going to stop. In any case, Nathan was the driver."

"Hey, hey, hey, show some respect for the dead," Norman snapped, his right-hand forefinger pointing at the ceiling. "The man was obeying *your* instructions. Now he's up there, dead, waiting for us to pay lots of money to his family."

Norman's cellphone rang. He picked it up, looked at it as if it was some strange object, and said, "This marketing idiot is testing me. Patrick, this is not a dilemma. It's one problem I can resolve." He pointed at the door. "Talk later." Patrick stood up quickly and got to the door. "Patrick!" Patrick stopped in the doorway but didn't turn to face his boss. "The first thing you do

5

when you get to your small office, send me an email. The subject will be *People Who Hate Norman in this Company.* Your name will be at the top of that list. The longer the list, the better because I want to enjoy seeing each one of those bastards suffer."

"Thank you, Mr. T," said Patrick.

"Are you making fun of me?"

Patrick hurriedly closed the door behind him, waved at Norman's two executive assistants, and headed for the elevator. He liked the war between Norman and the marketing director. Anything that made Norman uncomfortable was welcome.

As Patrick entered what he had just been told was his small first-floor office, Jennifer, the personal assistant who served both Patrick and his colleague, the head of operations, pressed the telephone receiver in her right hand against her chest and whispered, "The minister of information and broadcasting services."

Oh, not again, thought Patrick. "I'll take it in my office," he said. "And where's my team?"

The boys and girls who constituted Patrick's senior production team should have been there half an hour ago. Had they left because he had taken too long responding to worthless queries in Norman's office?

In his office, Patrick sat behind his medium-size desk, constantly straightening his necktie. Many times, he had been tempted to leave his job. Okay, he loved the job. There was great satisfaction in sitting at home watching television programs he had created. But that sense of fulfillment always came at a price. Working for politicians wasn't an easy job.

"I believe he hung up," Jennifer said from the door. "Should I call him back?"

"No. Let him call if he needs me. Why don't these people ever call Norman?"

Jennifer gave Patrick a long, hard look. "Larry called to say the team will be late."

Patrick studied the ceiling. A stainless white. If only his life and the rest of the world could be like that, life would be devoid of pain, he thought.

He lowered his gaze to the mess on his table and slowly shook his head. Loose paper. Folders facing up, facing down. A black shoulder-mount video camera. Camera batteries. A boom microphone headset.

Jennifer had left, and Patrick folded his arms across his chest. He remembered a time, not so long ago, when his table used to be neat. That was before the secret, the incident he could never share with anyone, had taken place and began to haunt him. Since then, he had become so forgetful, his wife had noticed, but Jennifer, who believed in free speech, hadn't said a word about it. Why hadn't she? Did she know? Could she be that one person to whom he could open up and share the secret?

To his right, he saw the unmarked folder he hadn't touched in many days. In there was a board resolution that gave him sleepless nights. About fifty of the corporation's five hundred employees worked under him. If the resolution that called for a reduced employee count and the merging of the functions of operations and production were to be implemented, one of the heads would have to give up his position. Neither he nor his colleague liked that, of course.

Through the window, to his right, he saw the FM and television antenna. If the antenna tower and all that it supported were to collapse, chances were, they would reduce his office to rubble. He would die while on duty. The corporation would compensate his family in the same way Nathan's family was going to be compensated.

He thought about Nathan. Nice guy. Nathan always had a joke to share. And Patrick knew that Nathan's unemployed wife had just given birth to the couple's first child. Maybe Nathan was in a better place. No secrets to hide, no bills to pay. But how would Nathan's widow and the child survive? Every child needs a mother and a father. He would see to it that the agency hired the widow.

The sound of the telephone startled him. "The honorable minister on the line again," said Jennifer.

"Okay, the usual."

"Of course, I'll listen in."

"Young man, must I beg to speak to you?" the minister asked in that hoarse voice Patrick had come to hate so much. Like Norman, Honorable Marvin Boti was a difficult man. He was the government spokesperson and member of the cabinet who always issued statements that needed to be retracted and tweaked by the newsroom every so often.

"I'm sorry, honorable minister. And how are you, sir?"

"You expect me, an African bull, to be ill? Listen, I want you in my office tomorrow at ten hundred hours."

"Honorable minister, I won't be available tomorrow, sir."

"Yes, you will be available."

"Sir, I'm leaving for the United States at midday tomorrow."

"*You* going to America?" The minister chuckled. "And at *our* company's expense? No, I want you here, young man. You want to join the CIA? Otherwise, go to America to do what that you can't do here?"

"It's the second phase of a workshop on HIV-AIDS, sir."

"We don't have AIDS here," the minister snapped. "Tell me if you have AIDS, and you know I have the power to speak to a very good doctor to treat you. See you tomorrow."

The minister hung up.

"Can we talk?" Jennifer was standing in the doorway. Patrick had not seen or heard her open the door.

Fondly known by everyone in the corporation as "BS," for "Big and Small," Jennifer had a mind of her own. An only child who had inherited her father's huge estate which he had allegedly acquired corruptly, she had no fear of losing her job. Patrick envied her for that.

Patrick motioned Jennifer to sit in any of the many chairs in the office.

"Don't worry about them," said Jennifer, pointing at the telephone receiver on Patrick's desk as she sat down. "Many people thought my father was a fearless man when he was a cabinet minister. No. He was a scared man. I know politicians. They always test the waters. You go on your trip tomorrow. Surely, you should be used to that by now. Patrick, you have something weighing you down. Oh, yes, I can tell. Maybe the departmental reorganization? The threats from government ministers? Or your trip to Atlanta, being away from your family for two weeks?"

Patrick smiled, and Jennifer stood up. As she opened the door, she stopped and turned to face Patrick. "You know, I saw you leave the newsroom as a young man to come to this office. Did you think ruling party politics wouldn't follow you here?" She stepped back into the office, closed the door, and lowered her voice. "Ah, I hear of a problem upstairs. It's about Norman. The marketing director, small, stubborn, gave him a black eye."

"No!" Patrick said, hitting his desk with his palms like someone playing the African drum. "I just love that short fellow." He shrugged. "Well, not really. But if Alex can do that to Norman, I love him. Just for that."

"Yes, just after you left his office, I hear. Norman started the fight, but I know the marketing director is going to be fired. Norman has too many connections to lose his job."

"I know."

Patrick wished he would reschedule the weekly meeting with Larry and his team to later in the day. Above all, he wished he could find someone to confide in before he left for Atlanta. Someone who would listen to the burden he carried with an open mind. Over the years, he had immersed himself in his work, and he had lost the few friends he used to have.

He had less than twenty-four hours.

CHAPTER 2

Some women needed more than one point of attraction to be considered beautiful. Patrick's wife, Denise, had many such high points, and each one could stand by itself to propel her to a global beauty contest.

Back in his village, Patrick's people would refer to Denise's teeth as "white as unspoiled milk." From the first day he saw her, he had wanted to run his tongue across her large upper incisors that were shiny white and purer than African ivory. He loved her heart-shaped chin, deep-set brown eyes, and model's body.

Denise hadn't changed much over the last eighteen years the couple had been together. Her laughter and her broad smiles continued to excite him. Above all, she had always been a good listener.

Over the years, she and Patrick's only sibling, Rebecca, had become close. When Patrick's parents died, Denise mourned them as if she had lost her own parents, who had died much earlier. She was everything a career man needed in a woman. Although he spent more hours at work than he did with her and the kids, she never complained.

"Oh, baby, you shouldn't have!" said Patrick, his right hand making a circular movement over the many plates of food on the table. "It's like a feast. We should have invited the servants."

The dining room was an extension of the living room in the open-plan house the couple had designed with the help of an architectural assistant. The main bedroom was spacious, but money allowing, the couple would extend its bathroom. They would also build a half-bathroom for guests near the front door.

"You're right about the servants," Denise said from the far end of the table for eight. "We'll give them a plate."

The couple had a large dining table because they had hoped they would be entertaining friends and relatives quite often. As it turned out, they hardly had the time to do so. Patrick worked long hours, so the family rarely ate together.

"I think this is the best cooking I've tried in my forty-three years," said Denise, displaying the smile that never failed to thrill Patrick. "And only because I want you to remember, while in the US of A, that there's home cooking where you came from."

Patrick saw his only daughter, Alice, conceal a smile. He had named the seventeen-year-old after his maternal grandmother.

"What?" fourteen-year-old Chris said to his sister.

"Feels like the last supper," said Alice.

Alice was as beautiful as her mother, and as independent as young people her age were in the new millennium, and Patrick and Denise often worried about that. What could Alice be doing behind their backs?

Patrick wanted to concentrate his attention on the family, but he kept thinking about his trip to Atlanta the following day. There was no way he could be at the honorable minister's office at ten and catch the plane at midday. He couldn't see anyone firing him for traveling on company business, anyway. He thought about staying in a hotel for two weeks, and he hoped the facility would be as good as the local Lilayi Lodge, where the first part of the workshop had taken place.

"Except it isn't, Alice," said Denise.

"I said *it feels like the last supper*, Mom."

"No, it isn't," said Patrick. "You know we're not religious."

Alice stared at her food.

Like many of his colleagues at the radio and television station, Patrick had many times been tempted to receive "gifts" from wealthy people who badly needed television exposure. He had politely turned down every offer. He and Denise had used their resources to build the house in the Meanwood area, a new suburb not far from the Lusaka International Airport. Of course, the couple had taken a small bank loan when they needed money for plumbing, electrical wiring, and finishing touches. Patrick never understood why Norman, his bad-tempered boss, had gone out of his way to elbow grease the deal with a mortgage manager, so the couple ended up getting favorable lending terms. He remembered Norman boasting, "It's whom you know, and everyone who matters in this nation comes to me." It was Norman, too, who had insisted that Patrick, and not anyone else, should attend the Eastern and Southern Africa Media Managers Workshop on HIV-AIDS Reporting. "The second part of the workshop will take place somewhere in the US," Norman had explained. "And you'll love America."

"Dad, you look...lost," said Alice.

Patrick smiled. "Just thinking about my trip," he said.

Alice had just been dropped home by the MacKinnons, who were the family's former neighbors, after a tennis training session at Lusaka Club. She still wore her tennis gear, and Patrick thought his daughter's white skirt and white top were too revealing. For a year, he had supported his daughter's dream to become a world-class tennis star like the Williams sisters by paying for her coaching even after his daughter had shown no talent for the game. He hadn't yet told her that he intended to reduce the training sessions from twice to once weekly because of the high costs. If he were to get a promotion to the position of controller, which was unlikely to happen on Norman's watch, his dependents' club membership and training would be paid for by his employers.

"And how's the training going, Alice?" asked Patrick.

"You have a third Williams sister in the house, Dad," said Alice with a smile.

"Listen, children," said Denise. "Your father worries when he travels."

"We know, Mom," said Chris. It was as if he was singing, not talking.

"Honey, let me share a secret with the kids before you leave," said Denise. "A secret I've never shared with anybody."

Patrick's pulse hastened as the kids looked at their mother with great expectation. *Does she know?* was all Patrick could think of. He was sure she didn't. Besides, if she did, she wouldn't discuss his secret with the kids.

"First, your dad is going to celebrate his next birthday in the US of A."

"No secret," said Alice. "We already know that."

Patrick smiled and bit into his tasty chicken curry. He stole a glance at his wife's alluring smile and her deep-set brown eyes, and he knew he would always love her. Those who didn't know her well believed Denise was a very private person, and yet she talked a lot when she was with family.

"How old are you, Daddy?" asked seven-year-old Junior, the child Patrick and Denise secretly called "The Accident" because he was unplanned for. Then again, so was Alice. Their first child was born before they got married.

"Forty-two, son," said Denise.

"Yeah, you guys are about the same age, right?" asked Chris, the son who talked so much that both parents had constantly cautioned him to learn to listen. "Yeah, some siblings have many years between them, a sizzling gap that makes one of them think they're superior and senior..."

"What's the *point*, Chris?" asked Denise.

"Sorry, Mom," Chris said and turned to look at Patrick, who smiled broadly. Chris had taken so much after him, looking at him scared Patrick sometimes. While Alice looked more like her mother than Patrick, all the kids had taken their good looks from each of their parents. The straight noses came from Denise, whose great-grandma was a mulatto.

"You keep saying you're sorry, but do you actually mean it?" asked Denise.

Chris shrugged. Patrick had too much on his mind to intervene. While he hoped that Denise wouldn't reveal anything that would make him uneasy, he tried hard to concentrate on the tender chicken, which was broiled in oil and spices, mostly curry. The vegetables went well with the brown rice. He wished, though, that Denise had served their traditional *buhobe*, a thick cornmeal porridge cooked in plain water. Above all, he hoped he would find the courage to discuss the burden he carried with Denise before he left for Atlanta the following morning.

"Great cooking," said Patrick, looking into Alice's piercing eyes. "You're right. Really feels like the last supper."

"I feared you were going to say it was too heavy for dinner," said Denise. "Your daughter here helped me prepare it."

Alice wiped her mouth with a white napkin, a way to conceal a smile.

"No, this is great," said Patrick.

"Thanks, Dad, but no, Mom. I merely suggested the brown rice, the curry, went to the club to play great tennis, and you put the ingredients on the fire."

Patrick believed Alice was going to be a great public speaker, hence his hope that his daughter would be a television personality and not a tennis star. And Chris? Maybe he would be a rapper.

"She's right," said Denise, looking in her daughter's direction and nodding.

Patrick hoped that someday, Alice would make someone a great wife, even though he wasn't prepared to give his daughter away to a stranger. As far as he knew, she didn't have a boyfriend. Yet.

"She's always right," said Chris.

Denise smiled without showing her teeth. Strange. She rarely did that, Patrick observed, except when she was feigning it to please the kids.

Patrick cleared his throat and rubbed his hands together. "I have to be at the airport by ten tomorrow, and you all know I'm lousy at choosing presents. So, why don't you write down a very, very short list of the things you want? Junior, you have been very quiet tonight. What's going on?"

Junior said, "I want a new...uh. Thinking."

Patrick was saddened by the fact that he was going to a country his family had always wished they would visit someday.

Denise said, "Okay, kids, you write down something on a piece of paper, each one of you. As for me, you know I don't need any gifts. I have enough clothes, shoes, you name it."

Patrick was touched by his wife's selflessness. The love she had for him and the family. Her calm manner. Her beauty. Her youthfulness. Her great cooking. And her great lovemaking. He would miss all that—except the lovemaking. The couple hadn't enjoyed sex in the past few weeks, and yet Denise always said, "It's okay, baby," even when the act hadn't gone so well. "I know it's the long hours at work, the politics."

"I don't want a gift, Dad," said Alice.

"Wow, you guys make me feel rotten," said Chris. "Is it okay if I ask?" Patrick nodded. "Oh, you look sad, Dad. We'll be okay. We're likely to live longer than you who's flying over an ocean where some of our ancestors perished on slave ships."

"Chris, please!" Denise sounded upset.

"Sorry, Mom," said Chris. "I mean, flying can be…"

"I said, just ask," said Denise, her voice lowered. "What do you want Dad to buy for you that you can't buy from here?"

"A drone. I mean, a simple drone. Maybe worth fifty dollars? I don't know." Chris maintained his composure. "Or maybe not. Maybe I don't need anything from the US, Mom."

Alice chortled. "But you can buy drones from here. And where are you going to fly it? We live near an airport." She sounded like a big sister who was in charge of things, and Patrick loved that. He waited for the others' responses. Denise always managed such challenges better than him.

"I mean, we have them here," Chris spoke with his hands. "But, hey, they're expensive. *Out there beyond the seas expansive, I see expensive drones that drove me insane, and without signs of science, there's no sense.*" Patrick clapped his hands while everyone looked on. "Thanks, Dad. You appreciate art. And Mom? Dad could be driving me to some remote place, blast the drone thing into the air, we have fun. We eat out, too. I get tired of Alice's cooking. Maybe, when you get back, Dad, we eat out more often, by the Kafue River, maybe? We fly the thing and come back to the city." He looked around the table. "Doesn't that sound reasonable?"

Denise shook her head. And suddenly, it was as if something had tickled her so much that she had to cover her mouth with her left hand as she laughed.

"What now, honey?" asked Patrick.

"Just the way your son talks, darling," said Denise. "Endlessly. He should be a television soccer commentator. He would be talking about goals before any team scored. Will you consider hiring him?"

"And me, Dad?" said Junior. "I want a drone. I don't want to share with Chris. He hates me."

"No, he loves you," said Denise.

"But..." Junior whined.

"Okay, okay, kids," said Denise. "Alice, the dessert, please."

Alice served a sponge pudding with apricot jam. "My South African friend taught me how to prepare this one. Not even Mom knew about it."

"This is great, darling," Denise addressed Alice. "This friend of yours, you two seem to be very close, and yet you never bring her home."

"She doesn't have to come home to remain my friend, Mom," Alice said argumentatively.

"But you've been to her home, Alice," said Denise. "The point I'm making is, friendship is special. But never trust your friends with your secrets." She addressed Patrick, and he didn't like that. What was Denise about to say? "As you grow old, you lose friends instead of gaining friends."

Patrick nodded, and somewhere, a phone was buzzing.

"It's your phone, Mom," said Chris. "In your bag. Why do you keep it on silent? Do you guys...?"

Denise gave her son a stern look. "Chris!" she said as she picked up her purse from under the table, took out her cellphone from there and looked at the screen. "It's Aunt Gertrude. She can wait. And Chris, your father and I are not your 'you guys,' okay?"

"I'm sorry, Mom," said Chris.

"Okay, kids, let me tell you about friendship," Denise was elated. "There was a small crowd at the wedding of Mr. Patrick Kanya and Miss Denise Neo. Of course, we didn't have the money for a big wedding. Alice was still a baby, and milk was expensive. Many of our friends from the university were there. They are the ones who put a few pennies together to make that event possible.

The late Uncle George and his wife, Gertrude. The late Uncle Albert. Mercy. Your dad and I haven't made real friends after our friends just…died. Our family members. Uncle Ben and Aunt Rebecca. There were some very beautiful women in the room. And I said to myself, *he chose me.* Your dad chose me. Yes, out of all those beautiful women, your dad chose me."

The kids turned to look at Patrick, who smiled, before they turned back to face their mother.

"And I cried. Yes, I cried. You know why a woman cries at her wedding? It's all about her past, the terrible things she's gone through, and it's about comparing yourself to your friends, some of whom are not yet married, or are in terrible marriages." Denise paused. "That's why I cried. Without friends, you can't get far in life. Look, we now have a great dessert on our table because of Alice's South African friend. However, friends, family, they can let you down, too."

Chris clapped his hands and whistled.

"No, you won't whistle in this house!" Denise snapped.

"Sorry, Mom," said Chris. "You speak well. You should be on television."

"Your Dad won't hire me."

"Seriously, Mom," said Chris. "That's very moving—about women crying? I didn't know that. It's just that that's very moving. Look at dad. He looks really sad."

"I told you, that's what he does before he goes on a long trip," said Denise. "Hey, Junior, what's going on? You look lost, honey. Talk to Mom."

Junior said, "So, is Daddy going to buy me a drone, Mom?"

"Oh, sweetheart, you know dad will buy anything you ask for," said Denise. "Dad wishes he would take us all with him to America."

"Yes!" Junior jumped off his chair. "Let's go and change, and we go!"

"How about school?" asked Alice.

"I don't like teachers, Daddy," said Junior. "They want you to do stuff you hate."

CHAPTER 3

He woke up, and Denise, her head resting on her right shoulder, was looking down at his face. Slowly, she got on top of him.

"I'm sorry I pestered you last night," she said as she stroked his ears. "Are we going to have a memorable goodbye?"

The warmth and wetness of her breath on his left ear made her so irresistible that he wished they would make love. But he was tired, having spent half the night wide awake.

"Sorry, just not feeling well. And you know what? I suspect one of us at that workshop was a spy."

"Under this regime, honey, almost everyone is a spy. Just don't do it."

"I don't get it."

"Never cheat on me. Not even with a condom."

There was a loud, rapid knock at the door.

"It must be Junior," Denise whispered.

"We go to the airport, Daddy," Junior said from behind the door.

Patrick looked at his phone. 6:00 am. "Okay, be there in a second, son."

On the wall, facing the bed, Patrick stared at his daughter's decoupage of family photos and newspaper reviews of the television shows he had created. It was a masterpiece. Alice's talent was in the creative arts, and not in the tennis that she loved so much. Memories of the accident in which Nathan, his departmental driver, had died, flashed in his mind. He remembered his two most dependable subordinates also dying in the prime of their lives. Only, the two hadn't died from an auto accident, but from AIDS, so their deaths had been slow and painful. Nathan had died in Patrick's arms.

They had a hurried breakfast, and even though their home was not far from the airport, they were ready to leave by 10:30.

Patrick was at the front door when he heard Junior scream, "Don't touch me, I'm going with Daddy!"

"No, you're not," Chris retorted.

Patrick lifted his youngest child and got to his white Jeep Cherokee. The gardener, Wisdomtooth Banda, and his wife, Martha, the maid, were waiting by the vehicle. Patrick hugged both, and to Wizzie, he said, "Take care of the family as always." Wizzie grinned. To Denise, he said, "Honey, got a hundred?"

"You need some money?" asked Denise.

"Yeah, to give to Martha for the kids."

"Of course," said Denise, and Patrick saw his wife take out a few bills from her purse and give them to the maid who had been such a great asset to the family. "Two hundred."

"Good," said Patrick.

Using three different cellphones, the gardener took several photos of the family. Patrick felt dizzy as he opened the driver's door. He placed his right hand over his heart. Maybe, when they got to the airport, he would speak to his wife in private. It just wasn't right for him to leave without telling her what was bothering him.

"I'll drive, honey," said Denise. She was standing behind him, and she was the kind of woman who always got what she wanted.

"No, darling, I'll drive." He was surprised to see her walk reluctantly to the other side of the vehicle.

Patrick drove slowly, thinking about the very important issue he should have discussed with his wife. Chris and Junior did most of the talking. Would Dad send photos? If it was very, very cold when Daddy got to Atlanta, could he bring some snow to their house?

Patrick listened. He would miss his family, and he was worried about the minister who must have been waiting for him at that very moment.

"Something on your mind, honey?" asked Denise. They were approaching the Airport Road junction, and the Cherokee slowed down to yield to the highway traffic.

"Do I look like I'm not okay?" asked Patrick.

"Maybe you shouldn't go." Denise put the back of her right hand on Patrick's forehead. The feel of her hand made him shiver. "No temperature, but suppose it's malaria? I'm told they don't have malaria over there, so they may not have a cure for it."

"Mom could be right," said Alice.

"No, baby. Sounds silly, but there's this TV program my team has been working on," said Patrick. "Anyway, I trust my team. They'll do a good job." How could he tell his family that he couldn't tell them what he knew and that he was lying to them about not knowing what was bothering them? "I'll be all right."

Junior said timidly, "Better if we go together. Maybe?"

"No!" Chris screamed, and Denise turned her head to face the kids. "Sorry, Mom."

Patrick found a parking space. "Here we are!" he said, trying to sound cheerful. He remembered the unfulfilled promises he had made to take his family across the southern border to Zimbabwe and further down to industrialized South Africa.

"Come on, guys, let's go," said Denise. To Chris, she said, "Get Daddy's case from the back and shut up for a change."

His hand luggage on his right shoulder, Patrick led the way to the terminal building.

"It's like you're really in a hurry to leave us, hon," said Denise with a chuckle. "Are you okay?"

"You tell me. You keep saying I'm not."

He saw her shake her head, and he felt rotten. Really rotten. He should have told her about the secret. But how could he?

There was endless chatter in the large lounge that had an imposing staircase leading to the second floor. The family sat down, and Patrick wondered why the man at the far end of the row of chairs was alone. Didn't he have a family? Was he going on a long trip like him? Did he, too, carry the burden of guarding a secret he couldn't share with anyone?

"Dad, don't die like Boyd's grandpa," Junior broke the silence.

"No, son, I won't die like Boyd's grandpa."

"Who is Boyd's grandpa?" asked Denise.

"He died when the plane fell in the water," said Junior. "He was going to play football. Then the plane refused to fly. That's what he told me, and he didn't bring Boyd a drone when he died."

"Okay, baby, you told me the story once," said Denise. She massaged her son's left shoulder. "And how is your friend, Boyd?"

"The teacher shot him," said Junior with a straight face.

"Lying again!" Chris said mockingly.

"Yes, you, the teacher pointed fingers at him and said, I'm shooting you. Bang! So, he died."

"Okay, Dad's not going to play soccer, and he doesn't have a teacher who shoots, okay?" said Chris.

Junior looked angrily at Chris and gruntled. "I'm talking to my daddy. Daddy, do people go to heaven when they fall in the sea? It's not their fault. The plane fell, and they fell, and they..." He shrugged.

As Patrick listened to his family's blather, he wondered if he should take Denise's arm, lead her away from the kids and reveal the secret to her.

"Last call for Mr. Patrick Kanya, a passenger traveling to Johannesburg," a lady's voice filled the hall via the public address system.

"Last call?" said Patrick, and he jumped to his feet. "Just as well we came early."

"Wow! When was the first call made?" asked Denise. She rose, picked up her purse from the seat, and yawned.

"Well, guys," said Patrick. He hugged Alice first. His daughter had been unusually quiet. Patrick avoided looking in her eyes, for he didn't want her to see the fear and the sorrow in his eyes. All he wanted was to get on the plane and leave.

"Have a great trip, Dad," said Chris, who flashed a mischievous smile. "But listen to this: *When I'm twenty-two/No longer a teen/Like a twin/I'll do it too in between...*"

"Do what?" asked Alice.

Denise chuckled and said, "Alice, what do you want him to say, dear?"

"Mom, you're always on his side."

"No, big sister, she's never on my side," said Chris, and he started to sing: *"Mom's always on Junior's side, and when the jury decides, I could replace 'decides' with 'besides.'* A failed rhyme, don't you think, Dad?"

"I like it," said Patrick. As he hugged Denise, he realized just how much he loved her, and it hurt to hear her whisper in his ear that she loved him very much. He remembered their love-making that morning, but only after Junior had left the door. He had felt his virility come in full force for the first time in weeks. "I love you, too, baby," he whispered, and their lips met. Again, he felt compelled to speak to her about the issue that was weighing him down. Instead, he lifted Junior and held him in his arms.

"I also want a kiss, Daddy." Patrick kissed his youngest child on the cheek. "No, here," said Junior, pointing at his mouth.

Everyone, including a couple that stood close by, laughed.

He kissed Junior on the other cheek.

Junior, in turn, made faces and said, "Yucky!" He wiped his left cheek with the back of his right hand.

"Son, the plane won't fall into the sea, okay?"

"So, will it fall on the very tall trees?" asked Junior. "Isn't it painful on the trees and rocks?"

Denise disentangled Junior from Patrick's arms and made him stand on the floor. Kneeling before her son, she said, "Listen sweetheart; no, the plane won't fall."

"Not even in the water?" asked Junior.

"Not even anywhere, fool," said Chris.

With clenched fists, Junior approached Chris, only to burst into tears. "Alice said I'm going to die."

Denise looked at Alice, who shrugged and said, "I was just saying last night that I don't see the need for you guys to build a new bedroom. I mean, I'll be moving out soon, so even if you intend on having another child, I don't think you need a new bedroom."

"*You*, moving out?" said Denise, and she took a few steps toward her daughter. "And when is that going to happen?"

"I'll be going to university soon, Mom," Alice said quarrelsomely.

"I know, I know," said Denise. She looked at her husband.

"Well, honey, we know you'll have to move out someday," Patrick said abstractedly.

"That's what I meant, Dad," said Alice. "Life is full of structures of dying creatures. Mornings die into afternoons, which die into evenings, nights become mornings. I'm home today, the next time, I'm elsewhere, creating my little world without you."

"My philosophical daughter!" Patrick said. He looked around the large hall. There were more people then than there were when the family got there, and everyone seemed to be in a hurry.

"Yeah, everything changes," said Chris. "I like what you said there, big sister—*structures of dying creatures*. Can I use that in my new song?"

As Patrick started to walk away, he heard Denise call his name. The kids were standing at a distance, she was hastening toward him, and he was afraid. All he wanted was to get on that plane and go. "Honey, are you going to leave me in suspense, not telling me what's been bothering you? Did I do or say something wrong? And what was that talk about a spy at the workshop?"

Patrick passed his tongue over his dry lips, turned, and hurried to the check-in counter. "A spy, yes," he said. What would be the point in telling her the secret? Knowing about it would only scare her and make things worse for everyone.

"Patrick!" This time, it was his sister calling, but he walked on.

The air was filled with the smell of disinfectant, and he looked at his phone: an hour and a half after he should have reported to the minister's office.

"Mr. Patrick Kanya?"

A tall man came out of a door, a fried chicken breast in one hand. Patrick's heartbeat quickened, and he felt slightly dizzy. Had the minister ordered that he be stopped from traveling?

"I know you from TV. Hurry on, sir; you're almost late."

CHAPTER 4

The details of the Airbus aircraft he was flying on didn't matter. Neither did it bother him that this was the first time someone had taken the window seat he had booked. He wasn't worried about traveling economy, either. He always traveled business class on company business. But his ticket wasn't bought by his employers. The American nonprofit organization that had sponsored his trip had chosen his mode of travel. He could have asked his employers to upgrade the ticket, but that didn't matter. There were bigger issues to worry about. Like calling Denise and telling her that she was right about his state of mind, but that he couldn't tell her what was bothering him.

Just thinking about the secret made him feel feverish. He hoped to find a solution to the problem in the next two weeks.

He thought about the tall man, the one who was eating chicken against the background of the smell of strong bleach. Patrick hadn't appeared on television in a long time. So, how did the man know who he was?

He opened his eyes. The aircraft was taxiing, and the man seated next to him held on tightly to the seat in front of him as if his life depended on that grip. The man closed his eyes, while his mouth moved as if he was praying.

Patrick thought about his job. He couldn't remember how many popular programs he had initiated, and yet it was always the person who appeared on television who received accolades from the viewers.

He thought about his only sister. Five years older than him, Rebecca had become the head of the family when, a decade ago, both their parents died in a bus accident that had reduced their bodies to ashes.

Known in the family as 'a woman of substance,' Rebecca was strong and reliable. He had ignored her at the airport because, at that moment, all he had wanted was to leave. Still, he knew that his sister would help Denise manage the family while he was away.

A crackling sound awakened him. "You can undo your seatbelt, sir," a cabin attendant said. Her thin lips and those deep-set eyes reminded him of Denise.

Denise. The woman he would love all his life. Had he done the right thing by not telling her his secret? He recalled how, for a year, he had admired her from a distance. Every time he saw her in the university dining rooms, in the library, and at the university's splendid gardens and lakes, she was in the company of her three female friends. It was love at first sight.

One evening, he was with his best friend, the late George Tabo, in one of the dining rooms. As usual, she was with her friends, and they were seated at a table that sat eight. After picking up food trays from the serving lines, Patrick and George made straight for the girls' table.

"I believe we have been invited to sit here?" Patrick addressed Denise. She ignored him, but one of Denise's friends, whose name Patrick later learned was Gertrude Cheelo, said, "Of course."

"Is the lady with the great teeth also welcoming us?" George addressed Denise, who smiled bashfully.

Patrick and Gorge had done that many times. They would share jokes between themselves as if they were oblivious to the girls' presence. George, who was a mathematics major, had a theory: if the girls laughed at the jokes, the probability was high that eventually, they would become friends. He was right. Before long, the boys and girls were sharing a study table on the fourteenth deck of the university library, right at the point where the large water fountain gave in to gravity and sent the spray of water back down to the pool below.

When Patrick and Denise started dating, once in a while, they found time to sit next to each other in the lecture theaters, even though he was a mass communication student, and she was an English major.

In the Clifford Little Theater of the School of Education, he listened to a Ugandan professor's lecture on how European Christian missionaries to Africa served as agents of slavery and, later, colonialism. That lecture was to shape how he viewed religion. He was later to miss several of his own lectures to listen to the same professor. Denise, in turn, listened to a lecture on truth and public accountability in journalism, and she wished she was studying mass communication.

In his room, one evening, at the older part of male students' halls of residence, fondly known as "The Ruins," or "The Monastery," she expressed great alarm when he tried to make love to her.

"We have known each other for only a few weeks," she said.

He was taken aback by her response, but he understood her position. Many girls wanted to play hard to get to show that they had high morals.

A month passed, and the university closed for a two-week vacation. He hoped she would spend the vacation thinking about where the relationship was going. She stayed in the city, and he went to visit his parents at a rural school near his hometown, where his father was the headmaster.

The truth was, unlike Patrick, Denise was a virgin, but she didn't want even her closest friends, Gertrude and Mercy, to know about it. Patrick was later to learn that during the short vacation, Denise learned a lot about relationships from a former high school classmate who already had two kids.

After the vacation, Patrick gently walked Denise through their first lovemaking. While he aimed at not hurting her, he ended up doing just that. A few days later, she put aside her fear and embarrassment, and he escorted her to the university clinic. It took a while before they could try again.

In the evenings, they loved to walk by the university lakes, and both believed that it was there, amidst the exhilarating fear of being caught by security men, or even by fellow students, that Alice was conceived during Denise's last semester at the university.

Upon graduation, Denise got a job as a teacher. But she hated the job. Teachers put in too much work for which they were not well compensated. Students were rude. He had persuaded her to become a journalist, as anyone who could write well could become a successful journalist. She had said no; she would find a job she loved someday.

"A juice for you, sir?" a cabin attendant, the one who reminded Patrick of his wife, said with a smile.

"No, thanks," he said, yawning. He closed his eyes. Maybe he could take a nap before they landed in Johannesburg. Sleep refused to come.

Six months into his first job at the radio and television corporation, Patrick was ready to quit. The work hours were long. Production tools were scarce. The money wasn't good. Stress was killing him slowly. He hated the politicians most. Chances of politicians denying the words they had said were very high. Above all, there was the case of Judge Goodwin Hove, who had taken thirty minutes to reprimand the family of a rape victim in a case before him. Judge Hove had even passed down a six-month prison sentence on the wailing family members for contempt of court. Outside the courthouse, Patrick had faced a television camera, a microphone in his right hand, and said, "The sentence was shocking, the accused left with a smile, while the family was shepherded to jail for contempt."

He was later to learn that the judge had not taken kindly to that commentary.

Patrick was always in trouble with his assignment editor, too, and soon, he began to fear that he wasn't born to be a journalist. But when, on the orders of a senior ruling party politician, his assignment editor was fired, Patrick's new boss gave him a chance to try his luck in current affairs. He produced half-hour documentaries that captured large television audiences and invited positive commentary from the nation's most unsympathetic television reviewer.

A year later, Patrick applied for the middle management position of head of television production.

Patrick loved his job. He loved the idea of creating something with pictures and sound, and that something was electronically relayed to people's homes, and the viewers enjoyed what they saw and heard. That was how he had once described his job to

Grandmother Alice, who had lived to be a centenarian and spent all her life in an African village where no one had ever owned a television set.

"Ladies and gentlemen, we shall soon be landing at Oliver Tambo International," a lady's voice announced.

Patrick was so tired, he fell asleep as soon as he sat down at the departure lounge of his connecting flight. When he woke up, a strange lady, who was about Denise's height, was asking him where he was going.

"Atlanta," he said.

"Sorry, but that flight has already left."

CHAPTER 5

He opened his eyes, and he didn't know where he was. Ah, he had spent the night in a hard chair, and his neck hurt badly. He had never missed a connecting flight before, and he wondered what Norman would say about that lapse.

"Sir, I would run to get to the other gate to board your flight," an airport official told him.

When he got to the gate, he called the workshop coordinator in Atlanta. She didn't pick up, so he left a message.

The seventeen-hour flight to Atlanta was tiring, but the lady who met him at Atlanta's Hartsfield-Jackson was personable. She was in her fifties, with big bones, and her blonde hair was tied in a ponytail which she touched every so often. Her flowery dress was long, touching the feet, and her sweater was loose and flowery, too.

Patrick studied the arrival area. He wasn't surprised when he didn't see golden tiles and diamond walls at an American airport.

"I'm sorry I missed the flight," he said.

"No problem, I got your message. The name is Anne May. Just Anne will do. We made sure the workshop took place after the winter. The only bad thing is, the pollen is here, but it's not that bad this year."

Patrick had no idea what the talk about the pollen was about, and he didn't ask, even though he felt comfortable in Anne's company. For weeks, he had received communication from her about the workshop. He noticed that she smiled a lot and even stole glances at him.

"I heard a lot about you. But seeing you is different." She turned to look away from him. A group of soldiers was walking away from them. "Don't get me wrong, but you're a very attractive man." She grunted. "No, that's not right. Forget I said that."

"No problem," said Patrick. He was used to receiving such compliments from both genders. Again, he looked around the large hall. He knew what he was looking for, but he wasn't going to ask.

"It's much bigger than you think," she said. "The airport, I mean."

"I guess it is."

They talked about the weather and Africa as they waited for his small case to appear on the carousel. Had the bag been put on the flight, or had it come on the earlier flight? He didn't want to spend money on clothes, only to receive the case a few days later. "So, the other two gentlemen from Zambia will be arriving later in the day," said Anne May. "That means I'll have to drive back here. Did you see them at the Lusaka airport? The two Js—Justin and Jacob. You Zambians got the lion's share of this workshop. Three of you."

"No, I didn't see them," said Patrick. He realized then that because of the family drama about his plane falling from the sky, he had forgotten to look for his colleagues who would be with him at the workshop. "Are the others already here—let me think. From Botswana, South Africa, Kenya, Tanzania, Uganda? Did I get it right?"

"Yes, Mauritius, too. They all arrived yesterday. Tired? Time change, of course. Jetlag?"

"No, I slept well on the plane," he said, even though he was feeling disorientated. He picked up his luggage; a midsize bag with wheels. "Time change, yes. You people live in a different world from Europe and Africa."

As the two sat on the shuttle bus that was taking them to the parking lot, Patrick thought about the television programs that would begin showing while he was away. He trusted his team. Everything would be all right. And yet he could never understand why he cared. He knew he was a good worker, but if just one ruling party politician were to call for his dismissal, no one in management, least of all Norman, would stand by him. They wouldn't even give him a farewell party. He had seen good men and women before him leave the corporation that way.

They found their way to Anne's Dodge Caravan in the massive parking deck. He sat in the passenger seat, and on the righthand side, which he considered to be the wrong side for the passenger.

"Are you okay?" Anne asked after a while.

Patrick realized that he had fallen asleep. He remembered that he was, at long last, in America. He wished Denise and the kids were there with him. Ahead, tall buildings were approaching. They looked like a postcard photo, the kind he intended to mail home the following day. Using his cellphone, he took several photos of the Atlanta skyline, and suddenly, he realized there would be no need to send a postcard.

He had no idea whether they were heading north, east, south, or west, but he loved the fact that he was in America. He looked forward to the workshop, to meeting the friends he had made at the first one, seeing as much of Atlanta as he could, taking more photos, and posting some on Facebook, while many would go to Denise's inbox. He had so much to think about, so much to achieve.

"Yes, I'm okay, except it felt scary, back there, you driving on the wrong side of the road. But it's okay here, seeing that the other lanes are so far away from us and everyone is breaking the law." He chuckled and counted the lanes on their side of the road. Eight. Wasn't that too, too many lanes? Okay, he had seen that in England and Germany. He saw what looked like hundreds of cars in each lane. Did people in Atlanta hate trains and buses? Did they ever rest during weekends?

"I know," she said. "We also think that you people drive on the wrong side of the road. So, we're on what we call Interstate 75 stroke 85. Two highways merge at one point. Seventy-five runs from Florida to the Canadian border."

Patrick wished there were other people in the vehicle, for Anne seemed to be the chatty type, and he was the only one who had to respond to her questions and comments. All he wanted was some quiet to think about the family he had left home. What if some crazy man knew that Patrick was away, and he climbed the wall at dawn, broke into the house, and caused harm to Denise and the kids?

"I like it here in Georgia. We have lots of trees," he heard Anne say.

He opened his eyes when she said, "We're finally there, Mr. Kanye."

"I'm sorry, but I don't blame you. Kanye West is a superstar the world over. The name is 'Kanya.' It means 'light' in my African tongue."

"*Kanya*," she said. "Did I get it right?" He nodded. "Good. So, this is the hotel. The Marriot. I hope you find it comfortable here. It's not far from I-285, a busy highway, and we're not very far from Cumberland Mall, for those of you who want to do some shopping for the family." She undid her seatbelt. "I guess you'll be sleeping for a while. You can grab a snack now if you're hungry."

He hadn't expected the workshop to take place in a first-class hotel, even though the first workshop had taken place at a first-class lodge. He looked forward to meeting his friends from other countries. In particular, Peter Obong'o from Kenya had become a great pal. After the first phase of the workshop, Patrick had twice spoken to Peter by phone.

"No, I'm not hungry," he said. "We had so many meals on the flight, I couldn't tell which one was lunch, breakfast, or dinner."

Anne laughed, and he wondered why she had so many gaps in her mouth. Were false teeth that expensive in America?

They got out of the vehicle at the same time. "Once more, I apologize," she said.

"Apologize? For what?"

"What I said about you at the airport." She avoided his gaze. "About you being a special person? It was inappropriate, and I apologize."

"I didn't take offense."

"Lord mercy, I'm relieved to hear that."

They got to the reception desk, and he felt her body close to him as he signed for his room.

As they walked down the long corridor, with its fresh smell of clean carpets, and the whizzing sounds of ice stations and vending machines at every turn, Patrick was wondering what Denise and the kids were doing at that very moment.

"I love the smell of apple scent in the air," he said.

"I'm glad to hear that," said Anne May.

In his room, she inspected the bed, the windows, the bathroom, then the table and chairs. She turned to face the window, where a bird incessantly fluttered its feathers on a nearby tree. She turned on the television. A detective movie was on. "I'll see you tonight at dinner."

He watched the door close behind her, and he lay on the bed, staring at the ceiling, thinking about his family. He found the wi-fi connection on his phone, and using WhatsApp, he sent a message to Denise: *Arrived safely, sweetheart. I miss you all. Love you. Can't wait to come back already.*

He wondered what the minister had said and done about his no-show at the office. Maybe he should have told Norman about that. He stared at his phone, and finally, he pressed some buttons. He had to reveal the secret to Denise. He just couldn't keep her in the dark.

The ringing tone came on. Three times. Four times. He began to sweat. "Hello, darling," he heard her say, and he feared he was going to break down.

"I'm so sorry, Denise. I should have told you...Look, can we go video? Are the kids around?" He wanted to see her face. He wanted her to see his face. Tell her the truth.

"No, sweetheart, I'm alone. You want us to make love?" she chuckled. "The unfinished business?"

"Between the two of us, who's the crazy one?"

"Not me, Mr. Kanya."

He missed her so much, he wished everything was different, that he had told her the truth, and that she was there with him. "I got here today and they call me Kanye West here. They think I'm his brother."

"Did you say *today?*" she sounded alarmed.

"I missed my connection flight in Johannesburg. I could claim it wasn't my fault, that my flight was delayed, but no. I fell asleep.."

"Seriously, Patrick?" Denise was whispering, and he wished he would hang up on her, but no. He had to be man enough and tell her what was bothering him. The matter couldn't wait. "What *is* going on, Patrick? Please?"

"Can we do video?"

He found the video button and pressed it. Bleep…bleep…bleep. The phone showed 'reconnecting.' Four times, he called her, and this time, without the video. She didn't answer.

Tears welling out of his eyes, he got off the bed, slowly crossed the room to the bathroom, and standing by the toilet bowl, he masturbated.

He washed in the sink and got back to the room. Standing at the window, he counted the cars and trucks that were sprinting in both directions on a highway not far from the hotel. Twenty-seven…Forty…Sixty-eight. There were so many trucks, he wondered what kind of goods they carried.

He had a busy schedule ahead of him. Two weeks seemed like a long time, but he couldn't wait until the last minute to come up with a plan that would free him from the burden of the secret that shadowed him day and night like an invisible ghost only he could see. He sat at the table under the hanging television set, and using his phone, he googled one place after another.

When he woke up, his neck hurt, the clock by his bedside showed midnight, and he was sitting in the chair, drooling. He had missed dinner.

CHAPTER 6

The first time Patrick saw Peter Obong'o in the restaurant during the first part of the workshop in Lusaka, he had experienced something he had never felt toward another man. It was as if the Kenyan was the brother he had never met.

That morning, at the Marriott, six workshop participants sat at the same breakfast table. Patrick and Peter sat opposite each other, and Peter dominated the conversation. A few years older than Patrick, Peter had a very dark complexion. Tall and slender, he was graying and balding prematurely.

"We in African television can talk about love and hate because we know some politicians sometimes see us as enemies," said Peter. "Unfortunately, I see that polluted stratosphere making its way into American politics, and very soon, who is going to observe whose elections?" Patrick noticed that everyone was attentive. "All of us here must be prepared to lose our jobs. So, when I'm not managing television programs, I'm growing maize and rearing cattle commercially. As a Kenyan, farming is in my DNA."

Peter kept talking, and when he said, "I look humble like an abandoned African dog," Patrick's ribs were already hurting from laughter. "That's how you defeat hurters. Politicians hurt when they know you're not hurting because you're smarter than them. Always look humble. Brother Patrick, I'm inviting you and your family to my *shamba* in Kenya. If you can't come by an African flying basket, I'll buy you a ticket. But a basket is better because you don't need a passport. Ah, our distinguished hostess wants us to go."

Wearing a pair of jeans and a white T-shirt that displayed a large black map of Africa, Anne May stood at the far end of the dining room, talking to a hotel staffer. The participants finished their meal and trooped down the hallway.

Although workshop participants had been advised they could wear smart casual, Peter wore a suit, but without a tie. "Better be formal than not," Peter told Patrick, who was dressed in a sports jacket and baggy, khaki pants.

"Yeah, I get it," said Patrick. "Peter, did you say at the Lusaka workshop that you had a cousin here in Atlanta?"

"A cousin?" Peter seemed to be thinking hard. "Ah, yes, yes! Nicholas. We share a surname, yes. He and his very, very beautiful wife have lived here for a very long time. If these Americans don't show us around Atlanta, Nicholas will take us as far as Alaska, my friend."

At the end of the hallway, a brown padded door led to a conference room with a high ceiling. The soft lights that looked like little windows to the skies made the room feel as if it had natural light and was bigger than it was. The tables were arranged in a horseshoe format and were covered in a white tablecloth. Patrick could see, in his mind's eye, Denise arranging something like this. His wife could be detail-oriented to a fault. The first thing Denise always whispered in Patrick's ear whenever the couple attended a function was a comment about the arrangement of the room and its décor. He could see her expertly arranging the large supplies of bottled Dasani water, apples, oranges, chocolate, and bananas in the many baskets that reminded him of Grandma Alice, who was known for making the best baskets in her neighborhood. He missed his wife and regretted that he had not opened up to her and told her his secret. Maybe he would call her later in the day and tell her?

"Please, find a desk where your name appears and take your seats," Anne May said from the front of the room, in front of the large video screen. "So, welcome to the second phase of our workshop. I'm so pleased to see you all in Atlanta. We're all one, happy, global family. And, please, call me Anne."

The participants hastily found their desks.

Anne introduced her assistant, a young African American woman who sat in one corner of the room.

"Her name is Kacondra," said Anne. "And from where she is now, as you can see, coffee, tea—I hear you love your tea hot. Those will be served during our breaks."

Kacondra smiled and waved both hands, and the participants gave her a standing ovation.

"In Africa, we believe in tribalism," said Peter. "So, we welcome our sister."

There was laughter, and Patrick looked forward to cementing his friendship with Peter, who, as at the first workshop, seemed to be the natural leader of the group. Maybe Peter would turn out to be the person he could trust with his secret?

"This is a much larger workshop than the first one, which was so successful, we decided to add more countries from the region," said Anne. "Where's Rana from Mauritius?" A tall, light-skinned young woman raised her hand. "Ah, yes. So, Zambia has three delegates. Kenya has two. Lesotho, South Africa…"

Anne spoke at length about the workshop's program.

Before long, the participants were referring to Patrick and Peter as "The Two Ps" because each time one of them said something, the other supported the friend.

The first break came, and the workshop participants gathered in the corner where Kacondra had sat earlier in the day. While his friends were taking snacks, Patrick stole himself away from the other P and waited until Anne May, who was talking to several participants, was free.

"Hi, Patrick!" said Anne. "You and Peter are making this workshop so enjoyable. Did you sleep well?"

"Yes, thanks."

"Can I get you something to eat?" Already, Anne was turning to face the snack table.

"No, I've already had a soda, as you call soft drinks here. I was just wondering, is Emily going to be here?"

Anne sharply turned to face Patrick, and he wondered if he had said something wrong.

"Ah, Emily," she said, regaining her composure. "Your friends were asking about her, too. I'm not surprised she made such a great impression on everyone in Lusaka. Emily's young and vibrant, but unfortunately, she won't be conducting this workshop. It would have been great if she did, as she would have seen a direct connection between where you guys are now and where you were during the first workshop."

Thandi, a female journalist from Zimbabwe, who had been standing close by, said, "I was going to ask about Emily, too."

Anne said, "I'm glad to hear that." To Patrick, she said, "She left suddenly a week ago." Turning to Thandi, she said, "Young people have the freedom to flee whenever they want to fly. You're from Tanzania, right?"

His head lowered, Patrick walked away without excusing himself. He had hoped to meet Emily.

CHAPTER 7

It was the third day of the workshop, and while Patrick and many of his colleagues struggled to stay awake due to the time difference, it was amazing to see how Peter, whose time zone was an hour ahead of Patrick's, managed to keep awake and alert all the time.

There was ululation when Anne May announced that the hotel's shuttle bus would take the participants to Cumberland Mall for shopping on Friday. That evening, Patrick spent long hours on his phone's internet.

Friday came, and Patrick sat next to Peter as Derik, the hotel's shuttle bus driver, a chatty, elderly black man, talked about the history of Cobb County. "The white man grabbed it from the Cherokee tribe in 1832. Oh, man, the Europeans grabbed the world from everybody. Africa, Asia, Australia."

"Don't you see a bit of a Samuel L. Jackson in him?" Peter whispered in Patrick's ear.

Patrick couldn't see the resemblance, but he nodded.

From his seat on the bus, Patrick didn't think much about Cumberland Mall. It looked so tiny. But once he and Peter were inside the building, he appreciated the creativity of the people who had designed the complex. It was as if the entire building was built underground, and yet from the food court, Patrick saw that the parking lot was on the same level as where they were.

Back home, Patrick had a busy schedule, so he always did his shopping hurriedly. His friend Peter, on the other hand, seemed to have a lot of time on his hands. The two men spent most of their time at Macy's, where Peter bought a suitcase full of presents for his wife and children. He seemed to have thousands of dollars in cash.

"Funny. We have all these things at home," said Peter, "but when you come to America, you must prove to your family that you were with Obama and that you were loaded." He laughed, tipping his head to the left, a characteristic Patrick had noticed about his friend.

. "I'm afraid I'm not buying anything," Patrick said, thinking about the drones his sons had asked for. "I'm saving to build an extra bedroom, one away from the other bedrooms so that when you come to visit with your wife, I'm thinking that's the room you should be sleeping in so that we don't hear you make noise in the night."

Patrick felt he and Peter were bonding so well that soon, they would be sharing secrets.

"Oh, yes, my wife would love that," said Peter. "We must express ourselves freely during the greatest moments of our short lives."

In The Last Act section of Macy's, Patrick offered to pay for a bra that was selling at five dollars. "For Mrs. Peter," he said.

"No, my friend. No man allows another man to buy a bra or nickers for his wife." Peter said, laughing. "Besides, my wife hates clothes that are on sale—only joking. And are you telling me my bedroom project in Zambia is on hold?"

To Patrick, Peter's response was rather brash. He cautioned himself to tread carefully from then on. Still, he couldn't resist asking, "When will your cousin show us around?"

"Now you're talking, my friend."

It took Pater several attempts to reach his cousin by phone, and an hour later, Patrick met Nicholas, a reserved, heavyset man in his early forties. Patrick put Nicholas's height at about five feet eight, and his oxbow legs seemed to be his most prominent physical feature.

Like Peter, Nicholas wore a business suit. Driving an old but comfortable Mercedes, he didn't say much during the drive home because Peter, who sat in the front passenger seat, asked many questions, but didn't give his cousin a chance to respond.

"Patrick, Nicholas is an accountant," Peter said proudly. "A very good one."

"Until I came here," said the soft-spoken Nicholas. "I used to think selling insurance was an impossibility. But when you speak with an accent, you have no choices. You do what the African lion does—eat grass. And like the lion, we never fall in love with the grass. I would say, we make money, even though, sometimes, living on a commission, you have to get a night job to supplement what you don't get during the day. Ah, we're here."

Located in a cul-de-sac, Nicholas's multistoried house was massive with a four-car garage. He ushered his guests into a huge living room whose ceiling was so high that Patrick wondered how the family changed their light bulbs. The leather sofas were so comfortable, Patrick wished he could surprise Denise with a similar set. Denise! He had to share his secret with her.

"My wife works long hours as an RN. She'll be home soon," Nicholas announced. "We're hardly together." He showed his guests around the house—four bedrooms, three and a half bathrooms, a finished basement which, for millions of people back home, would pass for a full house. "We have a couple that wants to move in, but we haven't agreed on the rent yet. They have offered six-fifty monthly. My wife wants eight hundred dollars. They have two jobs each, but they want this place for almost nothing." He cleared his throat.

Patrick had heard about Americans doing two jobs at a time. He knew of no one back home who held more than one job at a time.

"This life is hard," said Nicholas. "We leave our great jobs in Africa and come here to work as laborers. We have good academic qualifications, but the Americans don't even look at our diplomas. Maybe the British would look at our degrees because they are our former masters. I don't know. Anyway, you get hooked to this place. Like my former tenants, they lived here illegally for years."

Not long after the men had settled in the living room, Nicholas's wife, Kezia, got home. From the moment Patrick first laid his eyes on her, he found it hard to stop staring. A stunningly beautiful woman who was much taller than her husband, Kezia was to Patrick what an Ethiopian queen should look like. Despite her fatigue, which was obvious to Patrick, she prepared the evening's meal for her visitors—*ugali*, which was the equivalent of Patrick's *buhobe*, a thick cornmeal porridge. They sat at a small table in what Patrick noticed was a second dining room that was not far from the kitchen. Using their hands to eat, they ate the *ugali* with T-bone steaks and vegetables.

"Let me speak like an African grandparent, even though I'm not one yet," said Peter. "When are you two having children?"

Patrick noticed how husband and wife instantaneously stopped chewing, and Kezia's left-hand thumb pressed hard against the dimple in her left cheek. The long silence that followed was most disquieting. Had Peter said something wrong? Looking at his plate of food, Nicholas cleared his throat and whispered, "I thought you knew."

"What?" Peter asked. Rather thoughtlessly, observed Patrick.

"We had two kids," said Nicholas. Like a child, Kezia's chin almost touched her plate of food. It was as if she wanted to hide from everyone. "They were abducted by criminals in the night. They have never been found. Five years ago. That was back home when we went on vacation."

Patrick could smell and feel the ominous presence of pain in the room. He imagined his home being burgled, Denise raped, and the children abducted, never to be found.

"How come I didn't know?" asked Peter, as if someone, and not him, was to blame. Patrick didn't like the way his friend was conducting himself.

"It's alright," Kezia whispered. She stood up. "Tell them, Nicholas." She hurriedly left the room.

Patrick had noted earlier how Kezia had mastered American English, while Nicholas had retained a heavy East African accent.

"They did something to her," Nicholas whispered. "Raped her." He sniffled. "We have vowed never to go back home again. Never. That's why we're here, despite the harsh working conditions."

Patrick wanted to say something to soothe the stranger who was his host. But what was there to say? He was glad, though, that he had met his friend's cousin.

That was according to plan.

CHAPTER 8

It was the last day of the workshop, and Patrick was awakened by the constant vibration of his cellphone. Denise was on WhatsApp video.

"Happy birthday, darling!" she managed to say before Junior's face filled the screen.

"Daddy, happy birthday, my daddy," said Junior.

"Happy birthday, son," said Patrick. A few days before, he would have asked the kids to leave their mother so that he could speak to her alone. He probably would also have chastised Junior for grabbing the phone from his mother. But not anymore. He had made up his mind about how he was going to resolve his problem. He had no intention of encumbering his wife with his secret.

"You see, Dad, I told you we would be safe," said Chris. He, too, must have grabbed the phone from someone. "So, how big is my drone, Dad?"

"Hello!" Patrick spoke into a dead phone. He had forgotten to put the phone on the charger the previous night, and the juice had run out, especially since he had spent so much time on Google.

The hotel phone rang. "Everyone here is saying they can't have breakfast in the absence of the other P," said Peter.

He took the most hurried shower he ever had, but by the time he got downstairs, the workshop session had already started, and Anne May was saying, "I'll miss you all."

Two hours later, Kocondra unveiled a cake.

Happy Birthday, Patrick.

Everyone clapped their hands and sang *Happy Birthday, dear Patrick*, while Patrick covered his face with his hands and asked, "How did you know?"

"Of course, I have everyone's bio on file," said Anne.

"Will you allow me to speak, Madam Anne?" asked Peter, and there was laughter. Patrick wished he could be half what his friend was. Peter was a natural leader. He was funny, sometimes brash, but personable, still.

"Of course, my Lord," Anne said sweetly.

Peter touched his neck. "Oh, I have no necktie to straighten. Many of us here cemented the friendship we had started during our first workshop back in Africa. Last night, I was telling my friend, the other P, about the two things my parents told me about friendship." Patrick felt uneasy. He had confided in Peter that he carried a secret that was affecting his sanity. "One, never trust your friends because your friends may know something about you that they shouldn't know about."

Like everyone in the room, Patrick nodded and clapped his hands.

"Two, always treasure your friendship. Are you with me, Patrick?"

Patrick nodded.

"Good," said Peter. "But can anyone tell me why, after I've been told that my friends could be the source of my failure, I should still treasure friendship? Patrick?"

Patrick wished he would rush out of the room and take refuge in the restroom. "Well, my people have a saying that a tree cannot stand by itself," said Patrick. "A tree needs soil to support it, rain, water, and friendly winds. So, while all these things could betray the tree, it's only a *could*. Everyone needs a friend. Peter and I agreed last night that friends should never share secrets."

"I'm not sure about that," said a female voice.

"And I'll tell you why," Patrick continued. "You don't want to burden the people you love with secrets, and you don't want your friends to blackmail you." He feared he was going to break down. He wished he would tell the group that he should have discussed his problem with Denise. Maybe, knowing what the problem was, she would have known what to do. "That's all."

He watched his colleagues devour the cake that bore his name, and he was glad that none of them knew that he hadn't been fair to his wife. He watched them sip tea, coffee, and sodas, and as soon as he saw that Anne May was free, he dashed over to her and said, "May I speak to you in private, please?"

"Of course." He noticed that this time, she didn't look alarmed.

She led him to the farthest corner of the room. "Now, I'm scared," she said. "Is it what I said at the airport?"

"Anne, I just want to ask about..."

"I know what you want to say." Suddenly, Anne sounded—almost stern. "Look, Emily no longer works here. I've told you that before, okay? What do you want from me?"

"It's not what you think," said Patrick, feeling slighted. He had never heard Anne speak to any of his colleagues in that tone. "I'm afraid I owe her some money." He saw that Anne was listening. "I don't think it would be respectful for me to give you the money and ask you to hand it over to her. It's...it's a cultural thing. In Africa, a married man never borrows money from a strange lady and then lets other people get involved in the transaction."

"I understand. But even if I were to accept the money, I wouldn't know where to find her."

"I thought just as much. I've called her many times, but the number she gave me isn't in use. You see, I had an urgent problem that needed to be resolved. I discussed it with her, and she said I could pay her back when I came for the second workshop." Anne nodded. "I also have a message for her from my wife. The two got along very well. Our kids, they just loved her. She came home. Twice."

"I understand," said Anne. Then raising her voice, she said, "Everyone, the final part of the workshop starts in three minutes."

Patrick stood still, and from the corner of his eye, he saw his colleagues take their seats.

CHAPTER 9

During the workshop, Patrick had spent very little time with his two fellow Zambians, Justin and Jacob. Both men came from the press side of the media, so he didn't know them well. He had found spending time with Peter, the Kenyan, more profitable, and for a good reason. After so many years in the television business, Patrick had learned to gain from every human relationship.

The workshop's closing ceremony began with the issuance of certificates of attendance, followed by emotional speeches from participants who had bonded so well, they called each other friends. There were even rumors of love affairs among participants.

The ceremony had come to an end when Anne asked to have a word with Patrick. He was going to miss her. Every morning, she had asked everyone how they were doing, and that seemed to come from the heart.

Again, she led him to one corner of the room, where they sat at a table, facing each other.

"It's a small issue," she said. "I'll miss this group. You Africans are a very warm people. So, you told me you owed Emily some money. Well, Emily had a little problem with our auditors. Something to do with rooms at the lodge where the first workshop took place. But that's not why she left. I'm sorry, I told you earlier that I didn't know where she was. The fact is, I do. I called her yesterday, and I told her about you wanting to pay her. She said no, you can keep the money."

Anne stood up and pulled her chair away from the table. "I thought that would put your mind at ease. You don't owe her any money now."

Patrick wished he could say that he wanted to see Emily. "I'm so relieved to hear that," he lied.

Patrick didn't sleep well that night. He had hoped to meet Emily, for his survival depended on meeting her.

The following morning, he missed breakfast. His room phone rang off the hook, and he ignored it. He didn't want to talk to anyone. Not even to Peter.

Later in the day, he was among the last participants to leave the hotel, as his flight to South Africa was leaving in the evening. He made sure that his small case was the first to go in the belly of the bus. Anne May stood by the shuttle bus door and shook hands with everyone. "I'm sure our paths will cross someday," she said to Patrick.

Patrick got on the bus with his colleagues from Zambia and neighboring countries and sat in the rear seat. He wished he had said goodbye to Peter, who had left earlier in the day, as he had to fly Ethiopian Airways from New York.

While everyone talked excitedly, Patrick sat in silence, watching the bumper-to-bumper traffic on Interstate 285. Derik, the shuttle bus driver, took advantage of the wait time on the highway to talk about his days in the military. "Vietnam was horrendous," he said. "Came back home a young man, and what's next? I'm accused of violent crimes I never committed. Incarcerated for years. And I can tell you, I loved it down there in the Motherland. We once docked off the port of Mombasa, Kenya, and I wish we had spent more time on land to get to know the people."

"You should visit South Africa," someone said.

"Someday."

When the bus stopped at the international side of Hartsfield-Jackson International, Patrick was the last to disembark. By the time he got his case out, all his colleagues were in the terminal building.

He watched men, women, and children come in and out of the building, each one with a plan that took him or her to a specific destination. He had read about the millions of people who passed through that airport every year. He was just a tiny fraction of those numbers, but from then on, he could boast that he had twice been to the world's busiest airport.

"You sure know how to travel," Derik said. The old war veteran was closing the bus's luggage bay door in a lackadaisical manner; sort of a routine procedure, one he could do with his eyes closed after many years of practice, perhaps.

"I'd rather carry the money than luggage," said Patrick.

Derik seemed to be much taller than Patrick, and he didn't have the usual potbellies men in their late seventies were infamous for.

"A soldier always has something to carry," said Derik.

"Yes, sir," said Patrick.

Through the glass wall of the terminal building, he saw the last of his workshop colleagues disappear into a crowd. Cars and buses came and went, and Patrick wished he was free of burdens.

"Be prepared, young man, be prepared," said Derek. "Whatever you do, do it right. If it's something you must defend, you got to have the tools. Finding happiness isn't easy."

"Yes, sir," Patrick said sheepishly. "Who would be happier than a soldier who's about to see his wife and kids after being away in a foreign land for two weeks? I'm just...just scared. The aircraft..." He had used the term 'aircraft,' as opposed to 'plane.' "It flies over water for twenty hours. No land below us, just the water and the ocean bed. Isn't that scary?"

Derik chuckled. "I like the way you people say 'water.' Sounds so romantic." He looked down as if he was searching for something sensible to say to an intelligent television executive. "Are you scared of flying?"

"No, sir. But life scares me, yes."

"One thing, it's safer up, up there..." Derik pointed at the skies in a sweeping manner. "Think of all the accidents on our roads that happen every day, then think about one plane crash every five years."

Derik had used the term 'plane,' too. "That's because we have millions of cars and thousands of planes," said Patrick. Behind the glass wall, he couldn't see any of his workshop colleagues. "Time for me to leave this foreign land." He shifted his hand luggage from the right to the left shoulder.

Derik shook his head slowly. "You got time, I know. I come here often. Look, America has never been anybody's foreign land, son. Some of my ancestors, they came from Africa. Many Americans, they came from everywhere else. This is no one's foreign land. That's why it's called the melting pot of the world. No other country is like this country. Let's just say, the Native American lost his land."

"I'm glad you see it that way," said Patrick. "I saw it on TV here, people saying immigrants are the cause of your problems. Of course, immigrants are the source of America's problems. Why? Because the owners of this land, the only ones who're not immigrants, are not in charge." He picked up his case. "I have to go."

"I see you have the true fighting spirit of Kunta Kinte."

"I had this dream last night," said Patrick as he again moved his carry-on, this time back to the right shoulder. "A nightmare. I couldn't sleep after that, so I'm tired. Anyway, I'll sleep on the plane. Thanks for everything. Can I tell you a secret?"

Derik looked at his phone. "I have five minutes."

As Patrick moved closer to the older man, he wondered if it was worth it to share his secret with a man who would probably not find it easy to put the problem in its correct cultural context.

"I wet my bed, sir, but my wife pretends it's not an issue. What do you think?"

"Incontinence? I'd say it has come rather early, but it's not a strange thing." Derik looked at his phone. "Why is it a bad thing for her to understand? That's what spouses do."

Patrick smiled. "I've got to go."

As he entered the terminal building, he felt as if he was losing something. He wished he had seen Emily. That would have made a big difference in his life. He stopped and looked behind him. Derik had said he had only five minutes to spare, but the old man was still standing where Patrick had left him. Patrick waved. Derik didn't wave back. Instead, Derik made a ninety-degree turn, as if he was on the drill square, and walked to the other side of the bus. Within seconds, the bus was driving away. Patrick felt as if a part of him was being stolen from him. He had a good time in Atlanta with his colleagues. But everything had its time. Everyone had a home to go to, whether America was a foreign land or not.

He turned to face the crowd in the building, and he knew exactly which way to go.

CHAPTER 10

Denise couldn't sleep. In just a matter of hours, Patrick would be home.

She propped her pillows so that she could sit upright and continue to read James Baldwin's *The Fire Next Time*. She had last read the book in her university literature class. Now, she could read it casually, away from her professor's watchful eye. She had recommended the book to Patrick, who had read it twice and recommended it to her.

A sudden burst of gunfire in the neighborhood startled her. It was 2:30 in the morning. Her breath labored, she remained still, holding her cellphone in one hand, the book in the other, knowing there was nothing she could do. She wanted to go to the boys' bedroom, though. If the criminals broke into the house, they would have to kill her with Junior in her arms. She waited. She would call the police if the exchange of fire got closer to her home.

The shooting continued for five more minutes before she heard the squealing of car tires, followed by what sounded like a car chase and some distant shooting after the car sounds had faded. There was nothing strange about that. Shootings were so commonplace that in the morning, no one bothered to ask their neighbors or their children about the incidents.

A soft knock at the window made her spring to her feet.

"Madam, they have left."

It was the night guard Patrick's employers had sent to make the family think that all was safe while her husband was away. The guard wasn't armed, and he came to the house only during the night, sometimes drunk.

"Thank you," said Denise. "And be careful."

Denise badly wanted to fall asleep, so she put the book on the nightstand, just as the door swung open. She turned on the bedside light. It was Junior.

"Are you scared, my darling?" she asked.

"Chris said Dad is waiting at the airport." Like a statue that was designed to look convincingly bored, Junior had planted himself at the foot of the bed.

"It's not even three yet, and Dad's plane hasn't even touched down in Johannesburg, honey. Go back to sleep."

"I can't sleep," Junior spoke with bitterness. "May I sleep with you, Mom?" Already, he was walking to his dad's side of the bed.

"Of course," Denise said as she rolled the bedding down, revealing her husband's three pillows.

"I can't sleep, Mom. Chris, he snores too much, that boy."

Junior jumped into bed, and soon, Denise felt her son's arms around her. She yearned for her husband, and she was glad he would be home tonight, and hopefully not too tired for them to make fulfilling love. As for Junior, he was getting too big to be sharing a bed with her.

She had missed Patrick. They were a perfect couple. A few glitches here and there early in the marriage, but they had overcome those. Many of her university contemporary couples had separated. She would never leave him.

"So, he's not coming now, Mom?" asked Junior. "Chris said he was sleeping with you now."

"I thought *you* were sleeping," Denise said, chuckling. It was the way Junior had said, 'sleeping with you.' "Didn't you say Chris had said Dad was waiting at the airport? Okay, son, do you remember Daddy's flight to Johannesburg? That's the same plane he's catching to get back."

"And he has my drone?"

Denise didn't want to break the bad news. Patrick had said he wasn't going to buy any gifts, and she believed he meant just that. The money he had saved would go toward the master bedroom project. She knew he was committed to that. But she would leave that to him to explain to the boys.

"So, Mom, you don't answer me, and why don't we just go to the airport and wait for Dad now?"

Denise raised her head and turned to face her son. "Are you crying?"

"I don't want Dad's plane to fall in the big ocean. If Dad dies, I will die."

"Come on, Junior! I've told you before, Dad is going to be back with us in one piece, okay? I don't want to hear you say that again, you hear?"

"Thanks, Mom. Sorry. I just want my own daddy."

Within seconds, Junior was snoring.

Denise tried to catch some sleep. None came. She stole herself out of bed and eased to the kitchen, where she removed T-bone steaks, fresh fish, beef, and pork sausages from the deep freezer. She put these in one of the sinks to defrost. She saw that there were enough potatoes and vegetables for the welcome ceremony. When Patrick got home, he would be greeted by sizzling sausages on the grill and a table full of plates and cutlery in the garden. The maid, the gardener, and their children were welcome, and they would even have to-go plates that would feed them for the rest of the week.

It was 9:45 am, and Denise concluded that everything was in the right place. The servants would be cooking the food while the family was away at the airport.

There were two more hours before the flight's scheduled arrival time, so when Alice saw her childhood friend, Alec MacKinnon, the two talked for a while before they disappeared somewhere in the airport complex. Chris also took Junior away. As she sat alone, Denise feared that Patrick had forgotten to save money and had, instead, bought the two precious drones. The bedroom project had been on hold for years; it would be nice to finally get it done. He probably had bought the drones. Patrick loved to surprise her.

She was glad he would be home tonight. Not only would they make love, but her anxiety over the family's safety would be assuaged. The shooting in the neighborhood the previous night had frightened her. But then, what if the criminals had knocked on her window, and she had a gun? Would she have had the courage to open fire on them? Neither did Patrick have the capacity to stop anyone from attacking the family. She and Patrick hated guns. Guns were dangerous. Many couples they knew owned guns, and some had used them to shoot fellow family members. She wasn't going to ask him to buy one. She was sure, though, that even if they bought one, Patrick would never use it on her. There were times when the couple had considered moving to their hometown in the west, where crime wasn't much of an issue. But how could Patrick leave his job? To do what in a small town? To become a cattle rancher, perhaps? Cattle rearing was their people's main source of wealth. Well, maybe they could do that after his retirement? And what about her job? While she didn't like working for her boss, the job paid her well.

She remembered the days when Patrick was a young man working in the newsroom and always coming home late and stressed out. She remembered him looking for a job elsewhere and not finding any. She also remembered asking him to ask for a departmental transfer.

Junior joined her. It was as if he had dropped from nowhere. He sat close to her, his head resting in her armpit.

"It's boring, Mom," he whined.

"And why are you bored?" Denise snapped. There were times when she wished she would be alone.

"I want Dad to come, and then we can go home, and then he'll show me the drone plane he bought for me before we eat the sausage."

Over the public address system, the announcement the family had been waiting for finally filled the hall. The South African Airways flight from Johannesburg had landed. Denise looked at her phone. 12:25.

The flight was on time.

CHAPTER 11

For returning residents and citizens of Southern and East African states, customs and immigration procedures were always speedily completed at the Lusaka International Airport.

Denise told Junior not to talk so loudly as he counted each person who came out of the baggage collection area.

"That's Daddy!" he exclaimed.

"No, that's not him, fool!" said Chris.

Junior covered his face in his hands. "I hate this boy, Mom," he whimpered.

Twenty minutes. There were no more passengers coming through the exit from the luggage pickup area.

"Dad is not here," said Alice, who rarely exhibited impulsive behavior. Denise inhaled deeply. Calm down, she told herself. Patrick is taking his time.

"Denise, where's the American?" It was Rebecca, and she was approaching fast.

At five feet eleven, Rebecca looked as tall as her brother. Sporting a blue blouse, a long calico loincloth that was tied around her waist and touched her highly-priced crocodile skin high heels, and a matching headdress that partially revealed her dreadlocks, she had her brother's handsome face, but in a feminine way. Denise believed her sister-in-law would look even prettier without the heavy makeup she wore every day. She seemed to be clinging to her Kira Chevron shoulder bag as if some bulky man had threatened to snatch it from her.

"We haven't seen him," said Denise.

"Have you been to the desk?" asked Rebecca. "Maybe he missed the connecting flight? So, he'll catch the next one?"

"The next flight is not today," said Denise. "Something must be wrong. Patrick is a stickler for time. Maybe..." She squinted and rubbed the back of her neck. She didn't like it when things went wrong.

"Go on," Rebecca said reproachfully. "*You* tell me. You're his wife. What's happened to your husband, dear?"

Denise excused herself. As she walked away, Junior screamed, "I want Daddy!"

She walked towards a short man she had earlier seen come through the exit door and was speaking to another man. She had seen those faces before.

"You didn't answer me, Denise, my dear," Rebecca shouted.

"Excuse me, sir, my name is Denise, Mr. Patrick Kanya's wife. Did you attend the workshop in Atlanta with him? Did he get on the plane?" She felt a little choked; she didn't want to break down. "Please!"

"Justin," said the man. "My friend here is Jacob Mando. I'll be honest with you, madam. Your husband just ignored us at the workshop. A very unfriendly guy. Sort of a loner. He had a friend from Kenya. Jacob, any idea what those two were up to? I mean, seriously."

Denise couldn't believe what she was hearing. Patrick being unfriendly? He had told her about his Kenyan colleague, yes.

"Even at the first workshop, those two were always together," Justin said and got so close to Denise that she felt her space was being violated. She took a few steps back.

"He didn't do any shopping," said Justin. Denise looked behind her. Rebecca was approaching. "You know, that was strange behavior because Zambians love shopping abroad."

"I know, sir, we have a project to..."

"What project are you talking about, Denise?" asked Rebecca. "The problem is, you two have too many secrets. Where is my brother?"

"Please, help me, sir," Denise pleaded.

Justin said, "He came with us on the bus."

"Yes," said Jacob. "The bus to the airport. I mean, Justin, did you see him get off the shuttle bus?"

"Oh, yes, I did," said Justin. "Only, he sort of...waited—you know, like he was waiting for someone?"

"Waiting for someone?" Rebecca sounded alarmed. "A woman, you mean?"

Denise wished Rebecca would shut up.

"He didn't have a big case," said Justin. "Maybe he got lost between the bus and the plane?" He threw his hands up. "It's a big airport. Or maybe he was arrested."

Denise didn't know for how long her children had been standing close to her. Did they hear Aunt Rebecca say their father was waiting for a woman?

Jacob yawned and said, "People do crazy things. Madam, can you lend me three hundred dollars? My family didn't show up. These customs morons are asking me to pay an arm and a leg for things I bought at fifty dollars. Idiots! Do they think they will get a salary raise from my customs money? I'll pay Patrick as soon as I can." Turning to Justin, he said, "That's the problem with us black men. When a basic white woman shows you her clear-white teeth, she becomes an asset, an obsession."

Denise feared she was going to pass out. She needed something hard, like a concrete pillar, to lean on, and she wanted to tell the man to stop it! Patrick would never cheat on her. Why should he? She had never cheated on him. Okay, she had a few problems with him when they were at the university. But that was then; the couple was still young. Patrick had matured and never cheated on her since they got married. She knew that for a fact.

"Will you shut up?" Rebecca shouted. The man called Jacob opened his mouth but said nothing.

Junior had stopped crying, and Rebecca led the kids away.

"Didn't you say he fired your cousin?" Jacob asked Justin.

"Yeah, over some silly political TV documentary. Please!"

Denise turned and followed her family.

"Will you lend me the money?" said Jacob. "Fuck! What a family!"

Rebecca was on the phone, speaking softly to someone as a lady should do. Denise dialed Patrick's number. The call went to voicemail. She remembered that the last time she heard from him, he was still at the hotel in Atlanta.

Aunt Rebecca had always been close to her niece and nephews, and Denise feared she would need her more because, somehow, she had calmed Junior, who was standing between her aunt's feet, drying his cheeks with his hands.

"So, Mom, Daddy, his plane fell in the sea like my friend's grandpa?" asked Junior.

"Shut up!" Chris yelled. "The plane left him. He'll be here tomorrow."

"Don't shout at your brother, you hear?" Denise said irritably.

"And don't you shout at my nephew like that!" Rebecca snapped. On the phone, she said, "I'm just tired of this Patrick stroke Denise bullshit, honey. Okay, talk later." Turning to Denise, she said, "I'm sorry, girl. Let's not lose direction. Let's ask the airline where your husband is."

Denise wished she would sit down and think. But she thought about her kids. They all looked up to her for strength. Patrick was safe. He would be coming on the next flight from Johannesburg, and all would be well.

They all hurried to the information desk, Denise leading the way, and she was surprised to see how Rebecca effortlessly carried Junior in her arms.

"Excuse me, I want to enquire about Mr. Patrick Kanya, a passenger from Johannesburg." The lady at the service desk looked disoriented. Denise understood that many jobs weren't as easy as many people thought. "Was he on the flight?"

"Give me a moment," said the lady. She pressed some keys on the computer, and her eyes searched the screen. "Patrick...Kanya...Ah, he didn't board the flight." She looked up. "I'm sorry."

Denise felt weak in the joints. Since his promotion, Patrick had traveled a lot, and not even once had he missed a flight. However, there was a first time for everything. "Not your fault," she said.

"Then whose fault is it?" asked Rebecca.

Again, Junior started to wail and wriggle in his aunt's arms, attracting the attention of the many people in the large hall. Denise was getting upset with her youngest child. But she knew that Junior was innocent, that it wasn't his fault that her father had missed the plane, and that he had the right to know where his father was. But where was Patrick? Did he have malaria before he left home?

"Instead of standing there like a statue with an open mouth, why don't you call your husband?" asked Rebecca.

CHAPTER 12

By the time Patrick got to the self-check-in terminal, all his colleagues had left for the security check lines.

"Do you need assistance with checking in, sir?" asked an elderly African American lady.

"No, I'm okay," said Patrick. "Waiting for my colleagues."

"Have a nice trip," the lady said and moved to the next terminal, where she spoke to an elderly white couple.

As if he had never been there before, Patrick admired the high ceilings, the bright lights, and the hundreds of people crisscrossing the hall without bumping into each other. Over the past two weeks, he had googled everything he needed to know about the airport. Facing what he believed was the west, he walked hurriedly. He saw carousels, he walked through doors and kept walking until he found a shuttle bus that took him miles away to the domestic side of the airport. It was a long trip, and he spent the time usefully by carefully plotting his next move.

The bus made the last stop, and he came out. He remembered that the underground public transportation system had the Red Line, the Blue Line, and the Gold Line. From a vending machine, he bought the Breeze card, which was the ticket to all metro Atlanta transportation systems. If he could find his way around the web that constituted London Transport, with all its underground, road, and tram systems using the Oyster Card, surely, he could find his way around Atlanta, which was a much smaller metropolitan.

He got to the train station and hoped to get safely to the Extended Stay America hotel that he had googled. The hotel was in Cobb County, which would not be far from Cumberland Mall, which, according to his calculation, would not be very far from Nicholas's home. Patrick would need a roof over his head for a few days or weeks. Nicholas would show him how to survive in America. The brother would understand that there was no way he could go back home. Not with the secret that had made him come this far after choosing to miss his flight back home.

He approached a friendly-looking elderly man and asked, "How do I get to Cobb County?"

"Catch the Red Line to the Arts Center." Speaking with a heavy accent, the man had confirmed what Patrick already knew. "Ignore the crazy Five Points station. I mean, I'm a rural Georgia boy, and that place is crazy. The Arts Center comes after Midtown. Catch bus number 10 on the yellow-and-gray bus system known as CobbLinc to Cumberland Mall. Got it? Bus number 10."

Patrick nodded.

"From the train, you go up to the end and find the bus," said the man. "One thing, you won't need to buy another ticket; the one you have now is good."

"Thank you," Patrick said with a smile. He knew what he was doing was wrong. He could even be arrested. Wasn't missing that plane back home like jumping bail? But he had no choice. He had to stay in America, and he had to use public transportation, for he couldn't afford a cab. Again, he looked around him. He didn't see anyone pretending to be reading a newspaper when, in fact, they were watching him. Rather, everyone, young and old, was looking at what had become man's most precious possession—the cellphone.

Suddenly, he felt his heart pounding in his chest. He understood why. He was breaking the law. What he didn't understand was where and how he got the courage to do all the crazy things that had led him to that moment.

He waited for the train.

CHAPTER 13

From the airport's information desk, Denise walked slowly as Rebecca led the family to her spotlessly white Range Rover.

Five years older than Patrick, Rebecca had entered the university five years before Patrick, and four years before Denise. She had left the university after her first year in law school to become a secretary at a law firm. A year later, she became a full-time businesswoman. She loved the limelight, dressed elegantly every day, and spoke loudly, always demanding full attention from everyone.

"I want all of you to ride with me," said Rebecca.

Denise chose not to disagree with her sister-in-law. Maybe it would do her good to drive home alone and think? And what had happened to Patrick? Did that nasty man suggest that her husband had eloped with a white woman with clean teeth?

Alice was holding Junior tightly in her arms, and she was walking past her aunt's vehicle and heading for the Jeep Cherokee. Everything looked surreal to Denise. She wanted to be alone, and yet she needed her children by her side.

"Okay, go on," Denise heard Rebecca say bitterly. "Go with your mother, child. All I want is to protect you from meeting with an accident. Your mother is not in the right frame of mind to drive."

Denise got to the Jeep, and Rebecca was standing next to her.

"Talk to me, Denise. Tell me how a tall, intelligent man, could miss a flight, and he doesn't send a message home. I've been in this world long enough to smell a rat."

As soon as the kids were seated in their father's Jeep, Denise slammed the driver's door and followed Rebecca to the Range Rover. "Rebecca!" she called.

"I'm calling for a family meeting to discuss this mess, Denise."

"What mess? Just what mess, Rebecca?"

"You better not call me 'Rebecca,' girl. We had agreed that you would call me 'Aunt Rebecca.' It's for the good of *your* children. Not many kids have aunties, and if they do, the aunties don't care. Have some respect. I'm eight years older than your husband, remember?"

Rebecca was lying about her age, but that didn't bother Denise. "You seem to be enjoying the fact that he's not here, don't you?" Denise stared at her sister-in-law without blinking. "To you, this is some scene in a bad drama, right?"

"Mom, please, let's go!" Alice called from the Jeep. "Junior is very tired and grouchy."

"Coming, honey," said Denise.

The sky was overcast, and a distant thunder warned of a coming storm so late in the rainy season.

"I smell a rat, Denise."

"Rebecca!" Denise screamed. Already, tears were welling up in her eyes. She wanted to continue telling Rebecca off, but hadn't she said enough?

"You will live to regret this, Denise."

Denise raised her hands and got in the Jeep. Junior was sleeping, so no one said a word as Denise drove slowly, thinking about Patrick, and thinking about her sister-in-law's erratic behavior.

Denise had first met Rebecca at a family meeting that was called to discuss Denise's five-month pregnancy. Five minutes into the meeting, Rebecca had paused one question that had ended the meeting prematurely: "You're talking about some kind of reparations, but did my little brother take his dick out of his tight pants and force it into your girl's tiny body?"

The next time the two families met, it was to discuss the wedding.

Over the years, Denise had come to accept that Rebecca was the family's drama queen no one could change or challenge. She had come to understand why Rebecca never survived in corporate life. Rebecca was too proud to take orders from anyone. After trying several jobs, she had ventured into rearing chickens for sale in her backyard. Next, she had opened a ladies' clothes boutique in downtown Lusaka. She also reared cattle and engaged in commercial fishing on the Zambezi River, back in her hometown of Mongu. She had married Ben Mate, her agemate and former law school classmate. To show how independent she was, Rebecca never changed her last name to Kanya-Mate.

After graduating from law school, Ben had joined a private law practice, but after twice failing the bar exam, his employers had given him an administrative position that included managing clients' funds. Soon after, auditors discovered that Ben had been embezzling clients' money. His employers chose not to prosecute him because the publicity would do their reputation more harm than good. A long spell of joblessness turned Ben into an alcoholic with a short fuse. He stayed home, and yet he had the privilege of scolding Rebecca over her temperament in the presence of anybody.

They had arrived home, and Denise muttered, "Me, regret it?"

"Don't worry about it, Mom," said Alice. "Let's concentrate on Dad. Forget about that crazy woman."

Wisdomtooth, the gardener, a grilling coil spring in one hand, rushed to the Jeep. "The boss, he's not here?" he asked.

CHAPTER 14

The train was neither full nor as fast as he had expected. Patrick spoke to two other people on the train about where he should get off, and both were so friendly that he almost broke down. How could people be so good to him when he was such a bad person, one who shouldn't have been on that train, but on his way back home to his family?

The train stopped at College Park, and a man wearing a heavy coat and a big hat got on board. He sat opposite Patrick and seemed to be lost in thought. He had heard that, like the British, Americans on public transportation minded their own business. That wasn't the case back home where, the last time he traveled by bus, he saw and heard everyone speak to everyone.

The train went underground, and suddenly, it picked up speed. He sat still, his luggage tucked between his legs, the carry-on bag dangling from his left shoulder, and a brochure of the transportation system on his lap. He held tightly to his seat as if he expected someone to push him off the train and steal his belongings.

Occasionally, he looked up. The route map on the car wall opposite him tallied with the one in the brochure. So far, so good. And yet he still wondered how safe he was. Could the people around him sense that he was an alien who was about to break their land's immigration laws? Was it normal for passengers to look at the maps on the walls so studiously, the way he had been doing? Was there a way of doing things that was exclusively American? Determined to find out everything he needed to know, and not lose the battle he had chosen to fight, he sat back in his hard seat and took a deep breath.

The sight of "the crazy Five Points" underground station, as the man at the airport had called it, was eyepopping. There were bright lights, people of all colors going up and down, trains whistling, arriving and leaving. It wasn't London's King's Cross or Waterloo, but it was close. Soon after, his train stopped at The

Arts Center. He couldn't tell which way was north or south, but he knew that the CobbLink bus to Cobb County would be upstairs, to his right as he came out of the staircase.

He picked up his cases and followed a trail of passengers. At the height of the high staircase, men and women went in different directions.

"Excuse me," he asked a black woman who seemed to be the same age as himself. "Where do I find the bus to Cobb County?"

"Bus number ten," said the woman. "Come with me. That's my bus."

About a dozen people were waiting for the bus, so Patrick sat on a bench, his case by his side. Back home, chances were, someone would grab the bag from him in broad daylight.

The woman sat next to him.

"You're not from here," she said.

"No."

"Let me guess."

"Yes?" he turned to look in her face. A pretty woman. One who was probably not eating too much takeaway, for she wasn't obese.

"New York?" she asked, her smile exposing a good set of teeth. He wondered why Anne May hadn't corrected her dental geography.

"I wish," he said, returning her smile. "Another guess?"

"Now, I get it. From the islands."

"I wish I was from the land of Bob Marley. No, I'm from Africa."

"Africa!" Did she look—alarmed? Was she once mistreated by an African lover? Or was she FBI?

"Yes, Africa," he said, and the bus arrived. Everyone leisurely stood in a line that led to the front door of the bus.

"I'd love to go there someday," the woman said and started to walk toward the passenger line.

Because he had to pick up his case, by the time he got to the line, two other passengers were standing between him and the woman.

When he got on the bus, the driver didn't ask him for his ticket, but he showed it, anyway. All the seats had been taken, and he couldn't see the lady he had been talking to. He put his case on what he believed was a luggage hold near the driver.

"No, no, no, my man, you can't do that!" the driver, a bulky black man, snapped. "Remove it!" His mouth wide open, Patrick stared at the driver. "I said remove it, *sir!*"

Patrick pulled the case down, and it hit the floor with a thud. The driver shook his head. Back home in his land, Patrick would have asked the driver why he was being so nasty to a passenger. Maybe passengers were not supposed to talk to bus drivers in the US? The truth was, he didn't even know how drivers behaved towards passengers back home, as he hadn't used public transportation in a long time.

He looked behind him. The lady he had been talking to was seated at the back of the bus. He wished someone would get off the bus soon so that he could sit down. No such luck, for he knew that the next stop would be Cumberland Mall.

The pain of the memories of his shopping expedition with Peter hit him hard. Peter was going to be with his family the following day. Again, he was sure that his decision not to go back home was in his best interest.

Through the window, he recognized the mall, but he felt panicky when the bus seemed to be going back to the city. He felt relieved when it stopped, and the driver announced that the bus would be proceeding to Cobb County after the stop. He didn't have to get off here. The motels he had seen on Google were on Cobb Parkway, also known as Highway 41. He wasn't going to stay at the extended-stay facility because he would have to use a debit or credit card, and he had cash only.

He remembered that every time he went to London, he had to learn where to ask the driver to stop the bus. 'Request Stops,' the British called them. Was it the same in Atlanta? Half the passengers got off the bus at Cumberland Mall, so Patrick sat next to the lady he had spoken to at The Arts Center.

"Where are we now?" he asked.

"Cumberland Mall. Do you know where you're getting off?" she asked.

He wished she wouldn't speak so loudly. He didn't want to speak loudly. Not with his accent. And neither did he want anyone on the bus to know that he didn't know where he was going.

"I hope you can show me," he spoke softly. "I need to book a room. Not too expensive."

"Okay," she said, her lips pressed together as if she was surprised he didn't know where he was going. Hey, everyone is a stranger wherever they have never been before, he thought. There was a good reason why he was where he was.

"I think you get off here," the lady said several bus stops down the road. "Here's my business card. You may need it someday when you want to travel. You made the right decision, coming to Atlanta. If a black man doesn't make it here, they never make it anywhere in the US."

CHAPTER 15

"Not even a debit card?" the woman at the motel's reception desk said, looking extremely surprised. "We don't take cash."

After going back and forth, the woman made a lengthy call to her boss. "I'll take the cash," she said, a sneer in her voice.

Patrick hated the room from the moment he stepped in it. The smell of tobacco and decaying matter was forbidding, the bathtub was discolored, and he wondered how he would get himself to sit on the toilet. He hesitantly sat on the frayed bed linen and broke down. What had he done to himself, to his family? What did Denise think when she learned that he wasn't on the flight from Johannesburg? Did Junior cry?

He studied the business card from the lady on the bus. Kimberly was in the business of selling cruise vacation packages. If only she knew, thought Patrick. He wasn't in the United States to be in the business of traveling but to survive. He could not go back to his country because it was not advisable to do so.

He helplessly watched a roach dash from one corner of the room and disappear under a chair. Reluctantly, he put his head on a pillow and wondered if there was a better way he could have approached his problem instead of finding himself in that overly unpleasant situation. He thought about the secret he had kept for months. He wished he had discussed the matter with Peter.

He missed Denise and the kids. Oh, Denise! He was lucky to have her. Many of their friends from the university were divorced. Victor had been married three times and was currently divorced. Richard had remained married to the same woman even after his wife had discovered that he had three children out of wedlock. There was talk about Richard not being the father of the kids he called his own. George. Poor George. His best friend had died too early, leaving his wife, Gertrude, childless and ceaselessly grieving. Gertrude never remarried, and as far as Patrick and Denise knew, she had never dated anyone. She was a special woman and a great friend. Denise would find comfort in her company.

He thought about what he was about to do, and he was afraid. Suppose he was denied asylum? He had learned during his Google search that the asylum path wouldn't be easy, even though he was a journalist. Still, he would give that a shot. He had marketable skills that would easily land him a job. He could marry a good woman. That would be an easier solution, but was he ready to get into a relationship? No. He could never fall in love again. What wasn't on the table was going back home.

He woke up the following morning wondering where he was. The motel. It was hard to reconcile the fact that the motel room was filthy, and yet he had slept like a log, and not under the filthy sheets but on top of the bedcovers. He was glad he didn't have to wake up in the night to use the toilet. He had paid for a whole week, so he couldn't cancel his stay at the motel without losing money.

Through an opening in the blinds, he saw cars in the parking lot. Unlike him, some people owned cars and houses, and they had families to go to after their stay at the motel.

In the bathroom, he washed his face and looked at himself in the mirror. He hated the lines of fatigue and the sunken eyes he saw. It was as if he had gained ten years overnight. As he walked to the reception window, he told himself to be a man and use his management skills to carve out his future. He was born a winner.

The same receptionist he had met the previous day was at the desk. "Did you sleep well?" she asked. At last, she was friendly.

"Yes, thank you, did you?" he said. "Did you work overnight?" He needed to prove to the world that even he could make conversation.

She smiled broadly, exposing a gold tooth. "You wore the same clothes last night," she said laughing.

"Ah, yes." He examined his clothes and the shoes he hadn't taken off the whole night. "I need something to eat," he said, looking away from her staring blue eyes.

"We don't provide dining facilities here," she said and yawned.

"I know. Where can I buy a phone? The cheapest kind?"

"Ah, just around the corner, this way," she said, pointing and smiling. "You can walk, right, Mr. Handsome?" she whispered.

She was flirting with him, and for the first time, he noted that she was a very attractive middle-aged woman with big boobs.

"And your name is?" he asked.

She was sitting on a stool behind the window, and he was standing outside, so he was sure the wall between them made it impossible for her to see the bulge in his pants. He missed Denise.

"Debbie!"

They stared at each other.

"Great name. I gotta go, Debbie."

Walking in the direction Debbie had pointed, Patrick suddenly felt feverish. He needed to move his bowels, and it was urgent. The more he thought about the toilet in his room, the faster he walked away from the motel, and yet he knew he would have to go back to the motel. He had no idea whether he was heading north or south, but what he knew was that he had never imagined he would find himself in his current mess.

The sound of a jet plane made him look up. It was a military jet, noisy and fast. Had he caught that flight to Johannesburg the previous day, he would have been home by then.

He was the only customer at the phone store, a small craggy building by a road junction. The cashier, a young man who said very little, recommended a Motorola Consumer cellphone and a twenty-dollar phone card. As he walked back to the motel, he opened his home cellphone, removed the sim card from it, and stepped hard on it. The instrument that had connected him to his past was no more. He could now plan his future without worrying about communicating with anybody from the past.

He was tired when he got back to his room, and he could tell that someone had just been there, for the mixture of a strong stench of tobacco and old carpet grime had been upgraded to an overwhelming smell of disinfectant.

He found the business card the African American woman he had met on the bus had given to him. Kimberly did not answer.

Just like Denise. Denise would never answer a call from a strange number.

He called another number, this time, one with many digits. There was no reply. He called again, but he couldn't even leave a message because the system didn't ask him to. He was tempted to call Denise—just to hear her voice and then hang up. But what purpose would that serve?

He lay in bed, looking at the white ceiling, and it dawned upon him that he had turned into an animal, one without remorse, a lion that had abandoned its lioness and calves because all that mattered was finding food and survival. Tears blinded him, and he found no peace in the fact that, considering what was at stake, he had no choice but to leave his native land. But what if he had plucked up the courage of a real man and talked about it?

He eased to the toilet, lifted the lid, closed his eyes, and sat on the dirty toilet bowl—deliberately so, to inflict emotional pain upon himself for being a horrible creature. It was a good bowel movement.

He got back to bed, and sleep came to his rescue. When he woke up, it was morning, and he couldn't believe that he had slept another full night without getting up. He felt an urgent need to pee and move his bowels. In the bathroom, he stared at the discolored toilet seat. He had peed and even sat there the previous night, but he couldn't get himself to spend another minute there.

Debbie was not at the reception desk, and the man who sat there looked angry. He strolled to the road, hoping to find a supermarket and buy himself some food and disinfectants to wipe the toilet down. He had no idea where he was going, but he kept walking.

He got to a gas station. There were all sorts of snacks, including sodas, and cookies on the shelves. He badly needed to move his bowels, so he asked the gas attendant—the equivalent of a petrol attendant back home—if he could use the toilet.

"It's not locked, man," the man said with some measure of hostility. "In the rear."

Patrick stood still, wondering why the attendant and the man at the hotel were so hostile. Did it have something to do with the way he spoke?

The little room Americans called the restroom was no better than the one at the motel. But Patrick had no choice. Using a lot of paper, he wiped the toilet seat, and he had another good movement.

He bought himself a hotdog, and by the time he got to his room, he had devoured it. And once in his room, he called Peter again. There was no reply. Again, he was tempted to call Denise. Five times, he called Peter's number until he realized that Peter would be sleeping at that hour.

His body reluctant to go there, he got in the shower. The water was hot, and it felt good. He got under the sheets, but sleep never came. At 3:00 am, he called Peter. No answer. He closed his eyes, counted 1 to 10, and called his office number. On the second ring, Jennifer, his assistant, said, "Hello?" and Patrick cut the connection.

An hour later, he called Peter's cell number.

"What? *You* calling from Atlanta, Georgia?"

Hearing Peter's voice made Patrick so miserable, he fought hard not to cry. There was so much to remember and say about the good times the two men had at both workshops.

"What's the African bull still doing there?" asked Peter.

"Peter, can you call me? Please? I don't have enough money to stay on the line much longer."

"A man can sense trouble when he senses one, my friend. I'll call you in a moment."

Five minutes passed. Ten minutes. Patrick was getting restless. Twelve minutes. He called Peter again. His friend didn't answer. Patrick knew then that although he didn't have a choice, he shouldn't have abandoned his family. He had hoped everything would go smoothly, like immediately finding help to settle down. He admitted, though, that this was merely the beginning of the long battle he had chosen to fight alone.

The phone rang. "Hello, Patrick, my brother." Patrick missed his friend's boisterous laughter. "So, you marry some beautiful senorita in Atlanta, and you don't tell me? We didn't even say *kwaheri* – goodbye in Kiswahili."

"Peter, I need to speak to Nicholas."

"I can hear the urgency...Hello? Patrick, are you there? Hello?"

Patrick could hear Peter, but it was obvious that Peter couldn't hear him.

"If you can hear me, Peter, please, I need to talk to Nicholas."

"Hello, Patrick...Ah, looks like he can't hear me."

The line was cut. Patrick cursed Africa for being who she was—the child who had inherited so much gold and diamonds from her dead parents but didn't know how to turn them into wealth.

He called again. Peter didn't answer.

Although his phone was very basic, Patrick was able to google. He looked up the white pages for the name 'Nicholas.' But Nicholas, who? He couldn't remember the last name. During the past two weeks, Patrick had come to learn that Atlanta had many cities around it. For instance, his motel was in a city called Marietta. The Marriott hotel where he and Peter had stayed was in Atlanta. He had read that cities were found in counties. That was the same as in England. He knew that his motel was in Cobb County, and so was Cumberland Mall, from where Nicholas had picked him and Peter up the other day. And Nicholas hadn't driven far before they got to his home. So, Nicholas lived in Cobb County. But in which city? Other than Marietta, there were cities like Smyrna, Austell, Mableton, Kennesaw, Powder Springs, and Acworth.

Looking at the location of Cumberland Mall on the map, Patrick concluded that Nicholas lived either in Smyrna or Marietta. On the other hand, he could be living in Atlanta itself. Or Mableton. It was frustrating.

Patrick called Peter every day, but the Kenyan didn't answer. On the fifth day—two days before Patrick's stay at the motel would end, and he would have to pay for another week to stay there—Peter called.

"I'm sorry, my brother," said Peter. "You know how we television people are kept busy. But I think it must be your line. The Kenyan telephone system is the best in Africa."

Patrick missed that laughter. "I'm here in Atlanta, my friend," he said. How could he tell his friend that what he had done was the best alternative any person in his situation would have chosen? "I need some help. I want you to talk to your cousin, Nicholas. Tell him I need somewhere to stay. I'm running out of options. Tell him I won't be at his home for long. Soon, I'll find my feet."

"Yes, yes, I hear…"

"Please, text me his full name and phone number. Will you do that, please, sir?"

"A man can tell that when a brother is calling a brother 'sir,' he's desperate. That's not you speaking, brother. It's the danger in you pleading with me for help, and yet you don't have to plead. Do you remember what we discussed the other night about friendship? You followed the rules. Never encumber a friend with your secrets. But I think you should have spoken to me, and you should do so now."

"Thank you, brother."

"I don't need to send you my cousin's number. His name is Nicholas Obong'o, remember? Same last name as mine. I'll speak to him and ask him to call you. As Africans, my home is your home, but my wife is my wife." Peter chuckled.

"It's political, brother."

"I guessed just as much. We in television, we're the endangered species. Those guys who work in radio, not so much. So, I'm inviting you to come to Kenya. I think, politically, we're more tolerant than you people. Your family can come here right away. Anyway, I'll still text you Nicholas's number."

"Thank you, brother." Patrick looked at the phone. Had Peter cut the line, or was it another case of Africa's telecoms systems at work?

He sauntered to the bathroom, stood by the toilet, lifted the seat, removed his wedding ring from his finger and threw it in the open toilet. He pushed the water cistern handle and watched the ring disappear into America's sewer system.

CHAPTER 16

It was Monday morning, and Denise got up early. She could choose to stay home and impatiently wait for Patrick to show up, or she could go to the office and avoid Junior's constant questions about his father's whereabouts. To make a statement about her state, she wore a black long pants suit she hadn't worn in a long time and some low-heeled shoes. As usual, she wore very little makeup.

She was at the front door when she heard Junior say, "Mom, you, you said Dad was coming. You lie!"

Denise stood still and closed her eyes. She had counted the number of times she had called her husband. Fifty-seven. She had sent WhatsApp messages. Eventually, the phone stopped ringing. Why? If Patrick was dead, wouldn't his phone still be ringing? She still hoped, though, that he would come back home soon. Maybe he would be back that very day or the next day. But what if he had fallen ill and had been admitted to some expensive hospital, since his colleague, the one who had desperately wanted to borrow money from her at the airport, had said he had seen Patrick at the airport? If he wasn't ill, was there something she didn't know about him? Some big secret? No, she and Patrick never kept secrets from each other.

She turned to face her son and stooped to caress him. "Sweetheart, I didn't...Dad will be here."

"Mom, why do you keep lying to him?" Alice had appeared from nowhere, and Junior started to cry. Denise felt tingles in her chest. "And where are you g-o-i-n-g, Mom?"

Denise turned slowly to face her first-born child and only daughter. Alice wore pajamas and a sulky face. Like the other kids, Alice had decided she wasn't going to school.

"I'm going to work, sweetheart." Junior freed himself from his mother's embrace and fled into the house.

"Dad is not here, and you're going to work? Is there someone more special than Dad at your office?"

Denise's jaw dropped. What could she say? She understood her children's fears. "He will call," she said, hoping that even if her words didn't soothe her daughter, they would turn out to be true. "During the day, perhaps. I know that."

"You *know* that? How? Did you and Dad plan this—that he should not show up at the airport so that we can have sleepless nights? Did you?"

"You don't need to shout, child. I have to go to work. You know what kind of man I work for."

Their eyes locked, and Denise wished she had something sensible to say to her daughter.

"Do I know what kind of man you work for?" Alice said sharply, took a few steps back into the house and closed the door.

The tears in her eyes blinding her, Denise got to her Honda Civic. *Damn!* The left rear wheel was flat. Their cars rarely had flat tires, and when they did, Patrick, and not her, always changed the tire. She saw that the gate was still locked. The night guard hadn't come since Saturday, the day Patrick should have come home.

"I saw the tire, madam." It was Wisdomtooth, the family's gardener. "I'll change it. Then today, the boss will come."

"Thank you," said Denise. She couldn't conceal her grief, and she was aware that the gardener had seen her tormented face. She handed the car keys to the gardener and watched him change the tire. So easy. She would do it the next time she had the misfortune of having a flat tire. Patrick would be home before the end of the day.

Denise got to the office half an hour late, and Matilda Chanda, the petite executive assistant to the company proprietor, was busy on the computer keyboard. She looked up and smiled at Denise, but she didn't say a word. Denise had accepted that the love-hate relationship between her and Matilda would never end until one of them left the company. Denise was responsible for all the administrative, simple bookkeeping and payroll functions. Matilda answered the phone, took notes, kept the office diary, and made tea. The source of the problem seemed to be that Denise received a far bigger paycheck than Matilda.

"Hey, hey, my girl, she looks great!" Maxx Mandallo, the short, pot-bellied owner of the company, stood in the open doorway, the massive office he called *the palace* behind him. "I know. Young African bull came from America, he keep you awake whole night. He fill you up with good, good stuff. Did he bring me American chocolate? This baby needs American chocolate." Maxx took off his shades and blinked rapidly, the tip of his unlit cigar in his mouth swiftly shifting positions.

Denise believed Maxx was a baby in a man's body. When she started working for him as an office manager and personal assistant, she was hopeful that her boss would eventually become a gentleman, or that she would get used to his bad manners. She was wrong. But the money was good, so she said very little about Maxx's bad manners, even to her husband.

It was no secret that the man who was fondly known by the nation as 'Big Maxx' was a playboy. He spent his money lavishly on concubines and vacations. Denise wrote the checks, so she knew that for a fact. What the public didn't know was that Maxx was legally married to one woman and secretly married to several others under African customary law. Over the years, Denise and Matilda had kept a list of Maxx's concubines. Six on average at any given time. Some of the relationships never lasted a month, and it was shocking to see that some of the women were married to men in high places.

Denise ignored her boss and proceeded to her office, sat down and waited for Patrick to call. He was going to call. Soon. But suppose he didn't? Suppose he didn't come back? Suppose he was dead? Or arrested? She had heard that it was very easy for a black man to be arrested in America. How could she place bail? How would the family survive? Emotionally. Financially. Maxx was a very influential man, but only in Zambia. Would he ask the government to intervene? Would he, in the meantime, raise her salary? Maxx had the means to pay her a better salary. He wasn't as dull as many people thought. He had a knack for making great business decisions, though without much analysis. Despite his humble formal education, he had invested wisely in real estate, ending up with more than fifty residential and office buildings to his name. Some of the residential buildings were occupied by some of his concubines. Maxx even promoted amateur boxing, which wasn't a profitable venture. "To look big in eyes of the nation," Maxx often boasted.

Denise couldn't think straight. She had never faced this kind of problem. Could she be exaggerating the seriousness of the issue? Was Patrick in trouble? Should she discuss her concerns with Maxx? Patrick got along well with Maxx. It was Patrick who had secured her current job. At the time, Maxx was said to be an egoistic former drug dealer who had invested his ill-gotten money in a trucking and property company. His love for the limelight had attracted him to Patrick, who was then an investigative reporter. Patrick had done a television story on Maxx, and soon after that, Maxx had offered Patrick a bribe to run another story, but this time, to portray Maxx as a great philanthropist. As far as Denise knew, Patrick had never taken bribes from anyone. Not even after Maxx had offered her a job.

Denise's office door opened wide and Maxx, his broad smile exposing a perfect set of false teeth, said, "The whole world, it's for me." And as if he was cued by an unseen prompter off the set, he laughed uproariously until tears filled his eyes.

"Sir, are you laughing at me?" Denise asked. She wasn't going to let anyone laugh at her. Patrick would be back home soon.

CHAPTER 17

It was a week since Patrick had not shown up, and Maxx escorted Denise to Patrick's employers, where Norman and a lady from HR met the duo in the boardroom.

"What do you tell your kids?" asked the HR lady.

"They haven't been to school since," said Denise, and she hoped she wouldn't break down. "I tell their teachers that the whole family has the flu." Her best friend, Gertrude, and her cousins had been of great help. They constantly called. "Of course, I'm running out of answers."

"Well, our wireless provider, Airtel, has confirmed that his phone is no longer functional," said Norman.

"You people send my boy to America," Maxx stated. "Find him."

Having Maxx in the meeting made Denise nervous. She had never known her boss to have the patience of a diplomat. But since he and Norman were said to be great pals, she was hoping Maxx would be an asset.

"Yes, we sent him there," said the HR lady. "But we don't know what has happened. We will be writing to foreign affairs to help us find him through our embassy in DC."

Norman's phone rattled, and he rose. "We'll get back to you," he told Denise. "Hello, he spoke into the phone. "State House? Yes, I'll be there." Addressing the HR person, he said, "We could get back to Mrs. Kanya in a few days, maybe?"

Denise was disappointed. The meeting hadn't achieved anything. If anything, it had buttressed Patrick's argument that Norman was an unsympathetic person. She was glad, though, that Maxx was on the phone the whole time the two drove back to the office. She didn't want to answer any more questions from her boss. So far, what she had heard from Maxx seemed to suggest that he believed she was responsible for Patrick's disappearance. Twice, he had asked, "Were you nice to him, like give him everything every night?" and the other day, he had said, "Men sometime, they want to break from bad women."

Back at the office, Denise remembered Patrick saying he feared someone at the workshop could be a spy. Could that have a bearing on his failure to come back home? Had he been recruited as a spy? By whom? Had he become privy to some information he shouldn't have known about, and if so, had he been eliminated? By the Zambian government? The American government? She dismissed that theory. It sounded like a story from the movies.

She had been at her desk for less than a minute when her phone rang. "Hey, it was great to see you here," said Norman. "Feel free to call or pass by."

"Thank you. How is Lisa?" Denise immediately regretted having inquired about Norman's wife. The rivalry between the two women went back to their university days.

"She's fine. Hey, how about you two getting together soon? I believe you have so much to talk about."

"Sure."

Denise got home early because she had requested the family to meet and discuss Patrick's disappearance.

"Good to see everybody," Rebecca shouted from Denise's front door. "Sorry, Uncle Ben couldn't come. Sloshed as usual. What do you expect from a genius?"

All Denise's three first cousins who lived in the city were already seated. Edward, who worked for a multinational auditing firm, was Rebecca's agemate. Edward's sisters, Brenda and Christine, were mid-level civil servants.

Rebecca bounced in, walking as if her high-heeled shoes were sinking into soggy soil. "You need to do something about these carpets," she said. "People don't use carpets anymore, Denise. Everybody agree? Hard floors. Parquet." Everyone, except Denise, laughed. "I don't care how I said that word— par, whatever. I'm not Congolese, I'm not French."

Alice sat opposite her mother. Even though the boys rarely left their bedroom, Denise had told them not to come to the meeting. Rebecca sat in Patrick's favorite chair—the rocking one he had bought from a garage sale years ago.

In one corner, the large-screen television, property of Patrick's employers, was on mute.

"Turn off that thing," Rebecca ordered. "It reminds me of my little brother."

No one responded.

Denise took a deep breath. "I called this meeting to talk about my husband's..." She paused, shrugged, and lowered her voice. "Is Patrick still there? And where's 'there'?" She looked in Edward's direction. She had expected him to open the meeting. Instead, he was staring at the ceiling, and her other cousins were looking at Rebecca.

Edward said, "I'd like to offer suggestions."

"Just a moment, just a moment, Edward," said Rebecca. "First, we better speak loudly so that everyone can hear everyone. Now, my brother goes away for a little while, and already, there's no drink in this house?"

"Alice, bring some drinks," said Denise.

Alice reluctantly rose and left for the kitchen.

Edward said, "I was going to say that..."

"Actually, it was me who called this meeting," said Rebecca, and Denise's eyebrows shot up. "Remember how he ignored me when all I wanted to say was goodbye to him at the airport?"

Alice came back, wearing a sullen face and carrying a heavy tray of sodas, tea, cups, spoons, and cookies, which she put on a side table next to Aunt Rebecca.

"You didn't have to make it so—what word is that?" Rebecca momentarily put her right hand on her niece's right shoulder. "They use it a lot in government. Yes, ceremonial. Is there a beer, my dear?"

"Uncle, what will you have?" Alice asked Edward.

"Serve the ladies first," said Rebecca. She stood up and hurriedly poured herself a cup of tea. "Your grandfather loved tea. *Any time is teatime,* he used to say."

As everyone was serving themselves their choice of snack, Edward suggested that Denise should go to the American Embassy. "They will use their sophisticated system to find him."

"Good idea!" said Rebecca with great excitement. "Why didn't I think of that?"

"I could come with you," said Christine. "Edward, too. He has connections in high places."

"May I say something?" asked Alice.

"Of course," Brenda addressed Alice. Heavyset like Edward, Brenda wore a long dress that touched her sandals. Denise considered her a free spirit. "You're a big girl now."

Rebecca sipped noisily from her cup of tea. "I want you to say what you know, Alice. Remember, you were crowned queen when I gave you my grandmother's name."

Denise winced. She remembered giving birth to Alice seventeen years ago and suggesting that the baby should be named Noria, which was her mother's name. The couple had settled on Patrick's grandmother's name. So, was it on Rebecca's insistence that her daughter had been named Alice? She didn't like the fact that Patrick had been disingenuous. She would have to raise the issue with Patrick when he got home.

"I have a theory," Alice stated. She looked around the room and at everyone's faces. "It's only a theory. I don't think Dad is dead. I saw a change in his behavior in the last few weeks before his departure."

"Now you're talking, little girl," Rebecca said and poured herself another cup of tea. "So, he changed from *what* to *what*?"

Denise lowered her gaze to her manicured fingernails.

"Dad used to be a very cheerful, loving man. He continued to be loving, but he was reserved. Very reserved. It's like he was here, but he wasn't here."

"I know, I know, darling, please don't cry," said Denise.

"Let her talk," said Rebecca. "Cry, my dear, cry."

With one hand, Alice wiped tears from her face, and with another, she rubbed her chest. "Something happened, auntie," she said tearfully. "I don't know what. Maybe, Mom, you know what happened? You said the other day that you knew he was coming back. When is he coming back? The boys and I want Dad back." Denise wished her daughter would calm down. She didn't want the boys to be disturbed. "I'll be going to university next year. I want Dad to take me there. In his car. I miss him."

Denise flinched as she bit the inside of her left cheek. What was that about Alice wanting her dad to take her to the university? Patrick wasn't her only parent. She too could take her there. What was important was to find Patrick. It didn't matter who drove which child where, when, and by what car.

"Go on, child," said Rebecca. "I like what I'm hearing."

"Mom, I have to say this." Alice faced Denise. "I used to hear you and Dad argue sometimes." Denise wanted to yell that her daughter was lying. She and her husband were the best of friends. "You used to argue a lot in the middle of the night while the boys were asleep. You know, I used to stand by your door and I would hear you argue. I remember hearing Dad say, *Keep your voice down. I don't want the kids to hear us.* And you would say, *How about you? You're shouting.* I swear, I used to hear that."

"Child!" Denise snapped.

"You will not harass a witness, Denise!" Rebecca said, only to burst out laughing. "Oh, dear! Anyway, you can't hide the truth. You just can't. Denise?"

Edward said, "No, first, Alice, I want to…"

"No, let me explain," said Denise. "Yes, like any couple, we had disagreements."

Rebecca exclaimed, "Heavens above!"

"Will you let me finish?" Denise raised her voice.

"Are you getting upset?" Rebecca shouted, half rising from her seat. "It's your daughter revealing the truth, not me."

"I'm sorry," said Denise. "But those were not the kind of disagreements that would have made him leave the family. Besides, if he wanted to leave me, he could have divorced me. But leave his children because of me, Aunt Rebecca? No. The Patrick I knew wouldn't do that."

Rebecca said, "Well, it seems to everyone here that the Patrick you knew is not the Patrick you know now because he hasn't come back to his children. What type of differences did you two have? Financial?"

Brenda stood up and said, "I don't think we're getting anywhere."

Christine stared vacantly at Denise.

"I've been thinking," said Denise.

"No, I asked you a question," said Rebecca. "What kind of differences did you two have?"

"Ladies, please," Edward said calmly.

"I've been thinking, the day he left, and the previous night, he wasn't feeling well," said Denise. She was thinking hard. She didn't want to tell the story of the spy. Patrick wasn't certain there was a spy among the workshop participants. "Yes, there was something strange about him. He even said that in the car."

"Yes, I remember that, Mom," said Alice, who had calmed down, and Brenda resumed her seat. "You even said he shouldn't go. What if he had malaria?"

"So, Alice, are you changing your statement now?" asked Rebecca, who stood up to pour her third cup of tea.

"So, Dad is in heaven now?" asked Junior. He was standing in the arch leading to the bedroom area.

"How long have you been standing there?" asked Denise. "Go back to your bedroom. Now!"

Junior wiped his eyes, turned, and disappeared into the depth of the house.

"Be kind to the poor child," said Rebecca.

Denise feared she was going to break down in front of Rebecca. If Patrick planned to leave, why didn't he say so? What was he scared of that she didn't know about? She had asked herself that question so many times that it no longer seemed useful to keep asking it.

"I guess I'll have to travel to Atlanta," she said.

CHAPTER 18

Nicholas came to the motel the day before Patrick's stay was to expire. Patrick noticed that the heavyset man was either upset, distracted, or both.

"Excuse me, my brother, but I'm tired," said Nicholas. He picked up Patrick's luggage and put it gently in the trunk of his old Mercedes.

"I'm grateful you still came, despite that," said Patrick.

"Two jobs. That's hard. I was an accountant back home, yes, and I had my *shamba*—you know, a small farm where I grew maize, groundnuts. I can't get a job as an accountant here."

As the two men drove in uneasy silence, Patrick would have loved to ask, merely as a way of making small talk, why Nicholas had two jobs, but he concluded that wouldn't be wise. He had heard that many Americans had more than one job at a time and that many immigrants never wanted to say what jobs they did.

They stopped at a supermarket. It was the first time Patrick was seeing the inside of an American supermarket, and this particular one wasn't any different from the supermarkets back home in Africa. What surprised him were the amazingly low grocery prices.

"Yes, the prices are low, but..." Nicholas shrugged.

When Nicholas stopped the car in his four-car garage half an hour later, Patrick said, "I have no sense of direction. Where are we in relation to Cumberland Mall?"

"The mall is not very far from here. This place is known as Smyrna, Georgia."

"Thanks."

"No problem, brother. I just want to say you should have consulted us before you made this...this drastic decision. It's not easy to live in this country right now." Patrick stared at the windshield. He wished then, as he had many times before, that he had flown back home. "It used to be easy ten, twenty years ago. Without papers now, you're in...you know, in shit, brother. I'm just being real. Mr. Trump doesn't like immigrants, legal or illegal."

"I'm sorry, brother, I don't want to mess up your life," Patrick said sheepishly. "I'll just leave, go back to..."

"No, no, no. Go where? Peter told us you have a political problem back home. Right now, you're still in what they call 'immigration status.' In other words, you're not illegal yet. Another six months, and yes, you'll have to watch your back. So, what I would suggest is, you apply for asylum and arrange for your family to come and join you. But had you asked me that time you came here with Peter, I would have told you, no, no, no, please, go to Canada."

There was a knock on Nicholas's window. It was his wife, Kezia.

"Ah, you two have met," said Nicholas, this time wearing a broad smile. He opened his door.

"*Karibu,*" Kezia welcomed Patrick in Swahili.

Patrick got out of the car. "I'd love to learn."

Nicholas showed Patrick his temporary bedroom at the far end of the passage on the second floor.

During dinner, Patrick pitched his case. "It's political, yes," he concluded. "If I went back home now, chances are, either I wouldn't have a job, or possibly, I could be killed."

"We should take him to see the pastor," said Kezia, who hadn't said much during the meal she had prepared so well. "You could send word that you want to see him after the service, Nicholas."

"It shall be done," said Nicholas.

As was the case the Asaw her, Patrick felt guilty for being attracted to a lady whose husband he constantly referred to as 'brother.' Kezia's skin was smooth, and her teeth were a perfect shiny set. She probably wasn't aware that she was meant to be a movie star and not a nurse. Patrick couldn't understand how he could feel that way toward Kezia and still be deeply in love with Denise.

After dinner, Patrick retired to his bedroom. It was as large as his main bedroom back home. The bathroom was much smaller, though, but that night, he took the best bath he had in a week.

Patrick's wish was to apply for asylum. At the same time, he would be looking for a job in the electronic media industry.

But at breakfast the next day, Nicholas dampened his hopes. "Unless you're an IT guru, no one will sponsor you for a work visa here. Your only hope is political asylum, brother."

The days passed by, and often, Patrick would have breakfast alone, as his guests sometimes left for work early. One Sunday morning, Patrick, who had no say in the matter, escorted the couple to church. On the car speakers, soft gospel music almost sent him to sleep. He stayed awake and decided he would not tell his hosts that he wasn't a believer.

On the lower floor of the massive church building, Nicholas introduced Patrick to a smiling bearded man. "Brother Patrick Kanye is from Zambia. And Brother Isiah Kariuki here is Pastor Felix Gawo's righthand man."

The large church was full, and Patrick had never heard any of the hymns sang by a lively choir accompanied by a jazz band. He was about to ask Nicholas if church songs were still called hymns, but like the many excited and chanting people around him, Nicholas started to speak in tongues.

"The best church I've ever been to," Nicholas whispered after the holy spirit had left him. Patrick nodded. "I used to think my father was the greatest reverend on earth, but Brother Gawo?" Nicholas shook his head.

It was time to collect the tithe, and Nicholas gave Patrick a hundred-dollar bill. Patrick escorted the couple to the altar and deposited the money in a large basket.

Sounding like an African American, Pastor Gawo's breathy voice eloquently spelled out, partially in song, body movements, and speech, what would happen to those who refused to tithe. He said a special prayer for the great men and women of God who tithed, and the congregation went wild, shouting and screaming.

Yet again, for the general collection, Nicholas generously gave Patrick fifty dollars, and twenty for the building fund.

Soon after the service, Nicholas led Patrick to a small office in the basement of the church.

"Sit down, brothers," said the self-assured Isiah. "Before you meet the man of God, I want to hear what your problem is."

"The problem was that there were people in my company who were spying on me," Patrick spoke with a lot of confidence. "They were feeding the intelligence service with lies that while I held a strategic position in the company, I didn't like the ruling party. So, a credible source informed me that I would be killed upon my return home."

"Yes, Brother Nicholas whispered that to me last night. We'll get you a good asylum lawyer." Isiah shook his head slowly. "Africans!"

"No, brother," Patrick disagreed. "No, it's not just us. It's human nature."

Ten minutes later, Patrick met the fifty-year-old pastor in a lavishly furnished office. The pastor was a short man, almost too tiny to be considered a full-grown man. Patrick couldn't tell if the man's head was too big for his body, or was that because he had a big Afro? His nose was bell-shaped, and his lips were thick and red like raw meat. He had a squint in the right eye. Add to that a light stubble and a permanent sneer, Patrick feared that the small man was the type that didn't believe whatever he heard from anyone.

"Brother, I woke up this morning, and the Lord told me you're one of his very loyal servants." Patrick couldn't believe how the pastor's American accent had vanished. "I wish we had met before you made that decision not to go back home."

Patrick was now sure that he had made a mistake. But it was too late to consider going home. He would find a job. Unlike the many immigrants he had read about online, he was highly skilled, and he would overcome every hurdle.

"Things are hard here, brother. You see, America looks good on paper, in the movies, on CNN. It's not the promised land, uh-ah! It was good when our own man, Brother Obama, was in the

White House, and Clinton before that. George W, too, was kind to our type. We felt safe. It's all about bills here, brother. Racism at work. Bills. No time to relax, like back home, weekends, you go fishing, get some vegetables from your *shamba,* or milk the cows, uh-ah. And the beef here is different, brother. That beef back home tastes special with *ugali.*"

"I can't go home, brother."

"We'll pray for you, and God will stand in the way of your enemies. I have helped many brothers like you." Gawo left his executive chair and sat in one that looked like an antique so that the two men faced each other at close range. He rubbed his hands as if he was preparing for something big. "Now, tell me nothing but the truth about yourself. If you lie to me, remember, you're lying to God, in his house, he who told me you're his humble servant."

Patrick took a deep breath. "I'll tell you the truth." Gawo listened with his eyes closed as Patrick told him nothing but the truth, not because he feared God's wrath, but because he wanted Gawo to help him settle down. "I'm sorry I didn't tell Brother Isiah the whole truth."

"My brother, life is a shopping mall," said the pastor. "Sometimes you go there to do the shopping, but oftentimes, life does the shopping, and when it does, it gives neither the change nor the right product. Brother, learn to be the shopper, not the one for whom life shops."

He closed his eyes, and he heard the pastor take a deep breath. "In the name of Jehovah, I'll be honest with you. This kind of problem can only be resolved by God himself, and in one second flat, through the blood of his only son, Jesus Christ. I wish I could tell you that the solution is as easy as in John or Mark 1st, 2nd, or 3rd. But it's not." He opened his eyes and stood up. Patrick did likewise. "Okay, I had this young man. He was in a similar situation. He came to see me on Sunday, and on Monday, he was dead. He took his own life. Be strong, brother. When you die, you either go to heaven, or you go to hell. *For every man shall bear his own burden,* Galatians 6, Verse 5. The world is God's garden, which he has leased to us to till portions of, and after we harvest, we must give him a tenth of the harvest to appreciate his love. But as we sow the seed, we make mistakes. We err. That's where you come in, brother. You're tilling God's soil. You must be courageous enough to make hard decisions in order to harvest plenty so that you can pay back what you owe God. No one, brother, is going to pay that debt on your behalf. Go back to your family. Amen?"

Patrick stared at the high and recessed ceiling. To his right, a vase full of fresh flowers seemed to be waiting for him to respond to the pastor's chanting. Should he say, "Amen," when he didn't mean it? He knew that what he had done back home was wrong. But now that he was in America, he had a chance to start life afresh. He had made the right decision to stay.

"I see that you need to join our Bible study group."

CHAPTER 19

Denise and her cousin Christine were ushered into what looked like a conference room at the United States embassy in the Ibex Hill area. The stocky lady officer listened to Denise's story without interruption.

"So, I'm sorry to hear about your husband," the officer responded in a very calm manner. "We hope he's safe, and that he'll be coming back home soon. Your husband is a household name, of course. I'm aware of the great work he does at the television station."

"Thank you," said Denise. She felt safe, sitting before the embassy officer, a fellow woman who seemed to understand her difficulty.

"Oh, yes, I've met him on several occasions. So, tell me something—anything that you think could help. Was he feeling well when he left? Did he hint to you about some problem he was battling with? Work-related, perhaps?"

Denise remembered Patrick complaining about fatigue and the possibility that he could be unwell. No, it was her who had expressed the fear that he could have malaria, and Alice had said something similar. No, she wouldn't tell the officer about the spy story, and neither would she say that Patrick wasn't feeling well when he was leaving, as that would suggest that he wanted to go to America at all costs.

"Madam, I've spent hours, day and night, thinking about what could have gone wrong, and I can't come up with an answer."

"I understand, and again, I'm sorry your husband hasn't shown up yet and is not communicating." The lady paused. It was the kind of break in a conversation that made Denise think that maybe the lady suspected she wasn't telling the truth.

"So, over half a million people go missing in the US every year." The lady had a kind face, large eyes behind horn-rimmed tortoise eyeglasses, and she wore very little makeup. Denise liked her. She reminded her of Miss Hill, her white high school principal. "So, it's very difficult for the FBI—that's our federal police..." Denise nodded impatiently. "Of course, you know that. So, some of these people voluntarily go missing. Your husband may fall under that category, but the truth is, we don't know. It's difficult for us to follow up on every case, of course. There are more than ten million illegal immigrants in the US, give or take. Some of them end up in detention centers."

Denise resisted the temptation of blurting out that she didn't want to hear about detention centers. She couldn't imagine her Patrick being handcuffed and taken to jail. "I know my husband," she said. "Patrick wouldn't do that to us—voluntarily going missing, I mean. Madam, he must be in some kind of trouble."

The officer nodded. "So, Mr. Kanye is a fine man, I know."

"*Kanya,* not Kanye," said Denise.

"I'm sorry. I hope he comes home soon."

"I don't think you understand," Denise said, rubbing the back of her neck. Feeling weak, she put both hands on the table. "He hasn't come back, madam, and that's why we're here. Your government is very powerful. You can find him and bring him back."

Christine put her left hand on her cousin's right shoulder.

The officer's large, green eyes opened wider. She blinked rapidly, sat back in her chair, and rubbed her hands. "So, I can only hope that he isn't ill or in trouble. He has a good job here, even with the challenges that come with it."

"Madam, is there a possibility he could be in one of your many prisons? I mean, I can't see Patrick breaking any laws, but I hear it's very easy for a man who looks like him to get arrested there in your country."

She remembered the man who had asked him for a hundred dollars at the airport. He hated the man. How could he suggest that Patrick was with another woman? Patrick would never do that. "How easy would it be for me to get a visa to America?"

"You want to join your...?

"I have no intention of living in a foreign country," Denise snapped. "I want to go and find my husband."

"Well, you would have to apply," the lady said calmly. "Each case is considered on its merit, but the key issue is meeting visa requirements."

Tears in her eyes, Denise stood up. "Thanks for your help," she said.

CHAPTER 20

Patrick had been at the home of his Kenyan hosts for more than a month, and no word had come from their church about the legal representation they had promised him. He accepted the fact that no one was obligated to do him a favor. Or maybe, because Patrick had found an excuse to miss several church services, Pastor Gawo was having second thoughts about helping him?

At the breakfast table one Monday morning, Nicholas cleared his throat in that special way Patrick had come to associate with his friend's way of saying, *I'm about to say something I've been ignoring, but now is the time to get it over with.* "I've taken the day off from work to attend to your case, my friend." As usual, beautiful Kezia had served a full English breakfast. "We're going to see an immigration lawyer. He's from the great nation of Nigeria, a member of the church, so he will take your case free. I hear he came here as an asylee when he was young, and his parents were politicians."

Patrick wondered if this was the time to tell his hosts the real reason why he had missed that flight back home. But wasn't it too late to reveal the truth after he had lied about it to the couple that had been so good to him? He regretted telling Pastor Gawo the truth. Could the man of God reveal his secret to one person, who would, in turn, tell another person, and soon, Nicholas and Kezia would learn the truth?

Several hours later, Patrick and his host entered Emmanuel Musa's law office on Windy Hill Road, not far from Interstate 75. It seemed to be a one-man practice without a receptionist.

"I have another appointment in half an hour," the short, bespectacled young man who wore a half sleeve sweater and looked like a professor said, and for ten minutes, Patrick spoke uninterruptedly.

"Sir, you have given a very good narrative about your fears, but your case has to be credible," said Emmanuel. "Do you have any evidence, such as documents, to support your claims about threats from politicians? Newspaper clippings, official letters, specific instances of threats to show genuine persecution?"

"I'm sorry, I don't," Patrick said with a sense of hopelessness.

"I'm sorry," Emmanuel said, and he stood up. "I believe any credible lawyer will tell you the same. Let them not get your money just because you're vulnerable."

Patrick looked at his hands. They were resting on the table, and they were not trembling. But deep inside, he was scared. How would he build a life in America without being granted asylum? He had read about people who lived in poverty, under the shadows, and were eventually deported. What excuse then would he give to Denise and the kids, to Rebecca, and to everyone who cared to listen? Chances were, he would be divorced, jobless, and without family or friends.

"I understand," said Patrick. "And thank you for telling me the truth."

Later that evening, during dinner, Patrick felt a strangely powerful attraction toward his hostess. He tried to concentrate on his problem. He had left Denise and the kids, and the consequences that came with that hit him with such ferocity that he fought hard not to shed tears in the presence of the couple.

"There's no point in seeing another lawyer for a second opinion," said Kezia, her teeth glowing like stars in the night. "Why don't we talk to Kunta?"

"Oh, no," Nicholas grunted. "Kunta has a great name, Brother Patrick, but I don't like his business. It works, but it's illegal. He finds you an African American woman to marry, and you get your papers. No. You could go to jail, and then you're deported. What's the point? Besides, his fee, it's very high. Brother Patrick wouldn't afford that."

"Still, maybe he knows something, a way we don't know about," Kezia insisted.

Nicholas dismissed the issue with a wave of his left hand.

During the weeks that followed, Patrick was restless. He slept little because he had several dilemmas. First, he didn't want to be seen to be putting pressure on his hosts to do more than they seemed to be able to do for him. Second, he didn't want to be seen to be a leech, living off the sweat of his hardworking hosts. Third, every single day, he felt that he was being drawn into an emotional pull that would end up calamitously. He had wet dreams in which Kezia was his willing partner, and when he was awake, he couldn't stop thinking about her. So, when Kezia was home and Nicholas was at work, Patrick avoided being home alone with Kezia. Despite the cruel heat of July, he took long walks in the neighborhood admiring the houses in the cul-de-sac where his hosts lived. Wouldn't it be great, though, if the houses were made of concrete, the way houses back home were built? Wouldn't it be even nicer if he was walking side by side with Denise at that very moment, and the kids were in their large house down the road, one just as big as Nicholas's? What had he done? How had he ended up like this?

One afternoon, after a long walk, he locked himself in his bedroom, hoping he would watch the news or watch a movie, but he couldn't concentrate on anything. He still loved Denise. About that, he was sure, and yet he was infatuated with Kezia. While he believed he had greatly harmed his family with his recklessness, he still thought that, given the circumstances, leaving his family was the only option he had. He needed to find peace with himself so that he could think straight. He had hoped that he would get asylum, find a job, and change his name. The reason behind his stay in America dictated that he would never see his family again, and that was a hard pill to swallow.

For hours, he cried until he fell asleep.

Later that evening, Patrick was sitting in the living room, and Nicholas had just come from work. "I was wondering, brother," Patrick said. "The man my sister talked about the other day. Kinte?"

"Ah, Kinte?" Nicholas snarled from the bottom of the staircase. "No!"

"My apologies, brother. I'm in a desperate situation."

"I understand," Nicholas said and walked with heavy steps to the upper level of the house.

Patrick wished he would pack his bags and leave for the airport. Instead, he hurried to his bedroom and slumped into the loveseat he very rarely used.

The following afternoon, Patrick was alone at home. He knew that there were four bedrooms in the house, and he had been to three of them—the one he slept in, the main bedroom, and the one in the basement. He wondered why, even when he and Peter were shown around the house, the tour had excluded the bedroom next to the main one. He stood by the bedroom door, slowly turned the door handle and pushed. The door opened wide, and so did his eyes. His abdomen fluttering, he squinted and rubbed his eyes, trying to drink in everything he was seeing. He stood still, a weakness in the knees rendering him motionless and wondering if he should make an attempt to enter the room or walk away. As he slowly recovered from his initial shock, he tried to understand who his hosts were. They never missed church service and claimed to be born-again Christians.

Downstairs, the grinding noise of the garage doors made Patrick realize that he wasn't supposed to be where he was. He turned quickly, and as he scurried down the stairs, his heart in his mouth, he felt as if he was floating, but in a moment, he was in the living room, where he sat on a sofa, staring at the muted large-screen television.

Kezia was home much earlier than usual, and Patrick felt uneasy. He wanted to talk to her about his feelings towards her, and yet he knew that wouldn't be right.

"Good afternoon," she said and proceeded upstairs, and when she came back down, she was wearing a tight-fitting tracksuit. Was she telling him something? Wearing no makeup, she was the natural African woman he had longed for every day. He wanted Kezia so badly that he concluded the answer was to take a walk. But how could he? The bulge in his groin would certainly show if he stood up.

Kezia stood at the foot of the staircase, the same position where her husband had stood the other day, and said, "Brother

Patrick, in case you move out, there's something I want you to learn. Come!" She beckoned and strode to the kitchen.

Patrick closed his eyes and wished his erection would terminate. He stood up. *Que sera, sera.*

By the time he got to the kitchen, he believed he was doing fine. He stood as far away as he could from Kezia, his body facing away from her.

"Do you have a dishwasher back home?" she asked.

"No."

She showed him how to operate the dishwasher.

In the laundry room, she said, "I see that you need a woman." She giggled and looked away.

"I'm so sorry." He knew she had heard the tremor in his voice.

"No problem. Nicholas and I have discussed that." She turned to face him, and in her face, she saw a deep sorrow. An ache, perhaps? "He cares about you, your brother. He wants me to find you a woman among my workmates." She chuckled. "You're a very good-looking man, Sir Patrick. God will give you a good woman soon."

Feeling relieved, he said, "Thank you, Kezia. You're so kind." He touched her shoulder and felt his hands tremble, but still, he had no erection.

"We're here to help you, brother."

He was glad when the lesson on the use of appliances was over, and he rushed to his bedroom, sat on his bed in a facepalm posture and cried. Minutes later, he dried the tears and wished he could find fault in Denise. She was a rare woman, the most trustworthy person he knew. She had never abused him emotionally, the one reason for divorce he had heard many times from his former male university contemporaries.

He eased to the bathroom, and imagining he was making love to both Kezia and Denise, he masturbated.

That evening, Nicholas said to Patrick, "You and your sister Kezia seem to be getting on well. She wants me to talk to this man, Kunta. So, to Kunta, I will introduce you, brother."

Instead of getting some relief at the new development, Patrick didn't feel comfortable about meeting another stranger to narrate lies about himself. How could anyone forgive him if he told the truth about why he had chosen to live in America?

Nicholas took Patrick to Kunta the next day. In his mid-twenties, Kunta was of medium stature. He had stormy eyes that gave him an African warrior's look.

"Is that your true name—Kunta?" Patrick plucked up the courage to ask the self-assured man who lived in a basement that had a comfortable living room.

"Yes. The famous Kunta Kinte, he was my ancestor. One of those who were kidnapped from my family. Hey, I like meeting people from Zambia. I'm from *The* Gambia."

Patrick was beginning to feel good in Kunta's company. "And do you know how your country added the *The* before its name?" he asked.

"Because some of your letters were sent in the mail to us, and some of our mail ended up in Zambia. Okay, big man, I'll not betray you. This is something I do many times. To me, it's confidentiality, Mr. Patrick. I hear you have no money. No problem. I don't want money, just to help brothers and sisters in this white man's land. The woman who can help, she's African American. Age, sixty-five. Her name is Aretha. Questions?"

"Isn't she too old to...?" Nicholas sounded alarmed.

"Leave it to me," Kunta spoke with a high degree of confidence. "Have I ever let you down before?"

Patrick felt an urge to pee. What had he done to Denise and the kids?

CHAPTER 21

To get to Aretha's townhouse, Nicholas drove down a hill to the subdivision's cul-de-sac and parked next to a Cadillac Seville.

"I love these cars," said Nicholas. "But American cars have one problem—bad turning angle."

As Patrick followed Nicholas to the front door, he wondered if he would ever get used to living in a house that didn't have a security wall around it. Back home, you had to have a wall, or else…

At the front door, a message on the storm door read: *Come in. Your welcome.*

The floor of the small kitchen to the left was littered with food cans. Ahead was a vast living room with a glass door facing a flower garden at the back of the house. The part closest to the kitchen served as a dining place. On a wooden bookshelf to the right, close to a staircase, a bookcase exhibited a large collection of books—African and African American history, philosophy, cooking, biographies.

"No, no, Patrick, sit down, brother," Nicholas whispered harshly. "Don't look at her books."

The two leather sofas in the room were threadbare. On the walls, African paintings reminded Patrick of home. He had seen similar paintings on the streets of many African cities: excessively tall and lean women dressed in calico dresses with matching headgear. On their backs, they carried babies, and the bulky loads that were perched on their heads looked burdensome.

"Must be very Afrocentric," Nicholas whispered.

No, I don't belong here, Patrick thought as he saw Aretha walk down the staircase, a red, yellow, green, and black scarf dangling from her overly exposed fair-skinned neck and chest. Dressed in a loose African calico shirt and black tight-fitting leggings, Patrick thought the lady looked much younger than her sixty-five years. She sat down across from him and constantly passed her fingers through her short dreadlocks. And Patrick got it—she somewhat reminded him of his sister, Rebecca.

Aretha constantly smiled and seemed to be warmhearted. Her stares made Patrick even more uncomfortable, though. What was she thinking about? That she had found herself a young, handsome husband? She talked about the great empires of Africa, from the Zulu in the south to Songhai in the west, and the Mali empire in the north.

"Patrick, I understand you're from western Zambia," she said. "I read about King Lewanika and how he signed treaties with England. Before that, the Basotho people came from the south. And there was this king who banned slavery. I'm ashamed, I forget his name. He's my favorite king." She laughed.

"I can't believe you know all that," said Patrick.

"Come with me," said Aretha, and she stood up to head for the staircase. Nicholas and Patrick stood up. "Not you," she said to Nicholas.

As Aretha opened the door to a bedroom, Patrick remembered, with great premonition, what he had seen in his Kenyan friends' second bedroom. As soon as he had opened the door, he had faced two gigantic black dolls, one male and the other, female, and both were placed in a sitting position on a bed. On the bed, the nightstand, the windowsill, the floor—everywhere—were dozens of candles and crosses of various shapes, colors, and sizes.

He had recalled the story about the couple losing their two children while on vacation. Did the two dolls represent those kids? And how old were the kids when they were abducted? Patrick would never know, as he intended not to ask. But what the scene had done to him later in the night was to make him cry as he remembered his kids.

The bedroom was large enough to provide the comfort he would need—if, under his circumstances, he would enjoy any comforts again. A farrago of old books, copies of *Ebony* and *Black Enterprise* magazines, broken picture frames, canned foods, and other items littered the double bed, the floor, and even the windowsill of the large window that faced east. The place reminded him of Alice, his only daughter. She had that decoupage of family photos and…He didn't want to think about it.

Patrick liked the view from the window. Beyond the well-tended garden was a thicket of tall trees. He thought about the bedroom he and Denise had wished to build after the workshop, and…he didn't want his landlady to see the sadness on his face. There were African paintings on the bedroom walls as well.

"I'm an honest black woman, and I must say, you are a very attractive black man," Aretha said, looking him straight in the face. "So, you may find many women being attracted to you. I have to approve before you can invite a female companion for the night."

"I don't see myself doing that."

"Don't worry about it. If you pay me twenty-five dollars, I'll get my friend Delores to work on this," she said, pointing at the hotchpotch of items in the room. "So, you agree to pay five hundred a month? You have free cable, free utilities. I know you don't have a job, but I discussed that with Kinte…uh, Kunta."

"Agreed."

Downstairs, she showed him the television. "You can watch when I'm not watching. Otherwise, I live in my bedroom. The TV in your room is small. You buy your own, a large one, and I'll give you a box."

Other than the jumble of items on the kitchen floor, about a dozen king-sized bananas, most of them turned black from over-ripening, sat in a bamboo basket that, once again, reminded Patrick of Africa; Denise kept her fruit in a similar basket. Tiny bugs danced around the bananas, landing and taking off abruptly as if they were fleeing from something invisible and ominous.

"You have ants in Africa, I know," said Aretha. "Once you open your cereal bags, clip them. I hate to see ants in my food."

She showed him which sections of the refrigerator and storage space he could use; not much space, but he didn't intend to eat much. He would always miss Denise's cooking.

They sat in the living room, and Nicholas said to Aretha, "He wants to move in tomorrow."

"Yes, and my son will give him a job," said Aretha, and she burst out laughing. "The rules are simple." She picked up a piece of paper from a side table and looked at it as she spoke. Patrick wished he would wake up to find he was only dreaming. He nodded. "If I approve of an overnight visitor, you pay fifty dollars the first night, seventy-five the next night. You'll use my gas stove to cook. You'll use my washer and drier once a month. You'll never enter my bedroom. Never, unless I ask you to, or there's a life-threatening emergency. You'll terminate this agreement after giving one month's notice in writing."

Moments later, Nicholas said, "Thank you, sister. Thank you."

As Patrick got to the front door on his way out, he wished he would never meet Aretha again. Tomorrow morning, while his hosts were away at work, he would catch a cab and head for the airport. He would stay there until he was able to catch the next flight back home.

The following morning, after Nicholas and Kezia had left for work, Patrick called the airline on his hosts' landline, and he learned that his air ticket had been invalidated. He was angry with himself, with Anne May, and he was angry at the world for being so unfair to him. He was a good man. He loved his wife and kids. He had done great things for them. He knew then that he had no choice but to move to Aretha's place.

That evening, Patrick embraced Kezia as Nicholas waited in the Mercedes. Once more, he felt guilty for the feelings he had toward her. It was wrong to feel that way, and he was glad he was leaving. He quickly freed himself from the long embrace, and he heard her chuckle. He hoped she was not trying to tell him something.

"We'll miss you, brother," she said. "Please, feel free to visit."

He knew then that she was sending him a hidden message. He didn't intend to visit. He didn't even intend to live long. What was the point? There was no way he could find happiness away from his family.

"Well, we'll be seeing each other every Sunday at church," said Nicholas.

In the car, Nicholas said, "You know what I don't understand? A country like Zambia, it has lots of mineral wealth. Copper. Cobalt. Gold. Emeralds. Water. I googled it, brother. You have The Victoria Falls, one of the natural wonders of the world. You have wild animals like us. Why are you a poor country?"

"It's a long story, brother," said Patrick. "It would probably be the same answer to the question of why Kenya is not a developed country."

Nicholas nodded slowly.

"May I ask a question—and forgive me if it offends you."

"No, no, ask Brother Patrick, please."

"My good friend Peter. How are you related?"

"Ah, why do you ask?"

"He didn't know about your…children. So, he asked that question about…"

"Ah, that!" Nicholas lifted his hands and then let them fall on the steering wheel while he stared ahead of him. "We're not blood relations. You know, we Africans! Everyone is a brother, no cousins. We were together at Lenana High School, one of the best in the nation. A family from Switzerland paid for my schooling there. Peter and me, we competed very well for the best cadet position in school, so we became brothers. But over the years, after I came here, he made friends with other people. Kezia and I have very few friends here, except the few at church. In this country, you make no friends because you're always working. Anyway, to answer your question, Peter didn't know about our kids."

"I thought as much."

Nicholas wiped his nose. "An interesting man, Peter. One time, they say he killed someone. You know how people talk. They say he had a quarrel with this brother from Ethiopia. So, Peter grabbed the brother's car keys and tried to throw them in a well. You know, that kind of well back home that has a concrete structure. So, the man dives to get his keys, and he crashes his skull against the concrete wall. Well, the police, they said it was an accident. Then another time, he had a girlfriend. He dropped her near her home, and as she was crossing the road, a big truck ran over her and killed her instantly."

Patrick turned his head to face his former host. "Are you making this up?"

"No, people, his enemies, maybe they made this up. Peter gets along with everybody. But even he, he has enemies, brother. So, be careful. Watch your back. It's WYBA. Watch Your Black Ass."

CHAPTER 22

Denise's day at work began with an emergency meeting with his boss. Three of the company's truck drivers had problems with the police in Zimbabwe. It wasn't that this was the first time the company's trucks had been impounded in that country. The new problem was that the three drivers had been charged with offering bribes to the police.

Denise sat still in *the palace*, listening to Maxx speak to someone on the phone. "I'm no politician, me, no. But I say, we always bribe traffic police in Zimbabwe, in Zambia, even when we have no traffic offense. Now, because my drivers, they refuse to offer big bribe, my trucks are in prison?"

Maxx listened for a long time, and occasionally, he winked at Denise, who sat patiently, thinking about her family.

She couldn't remember the last time the entire family had sat at the dinner table to eat and laugh like they did the night before her husband's departure. She wondered what Patrick had for breakfast that day, or if he was still alive. She felt like screaming: *Patrick, where are you?*

The kids had resumed school, so while they sometimes talked about their school friends and teachers, the one question Denise dreaded most was hearing Junior demanding to see his father's body. "My friend, he say when Daddy dies, you see his body, you visit his grave, you cry."

Alice had proved to be the most difficult to calm down. Denise understood why. While Patrick was very close to all his children, he and Alice had a special bond. He liked to address his only daughter as *my grandmother*.

"Thank you, I wait," Maxx and hung up. "Junior officer from high commission. They say situation it's so bad, even diplomats, they are stopped by police. Brother President Mugabe, he messed up country before he died. Denise, tell Zulu to deliver goods to Olympia Park late today. No one at home now. Jesus, these women can kill you walking—uh, alive."

Gilbert Zulu was the company driver whose daily chores were to deliver groceries to Maxx's concubines during the week and even during weekends. The stories about his adventures with the women never failed to amuse Denise. Otherwise, working for Maxx was a challenge. The man displayed a variety of characteristics ranging from unpredictability, funny, silly, annoying, kind, petty, and moody. Sometimes, Denise wished she would stay home and wait for her husband to come back. But coming to work gave her some relief from facing her predicament.

"Look, my girl," said Maxx. Denise listened intently. So far, Maxx had been very supportive. He had promised—only promised—to raise her salary, and twice, he had given her cash to buy groceries. "A good girl like you, you go wasted sex-wise?" Denise's heart skipped a beat. "You know me. I'm Big Maxx." His right-hand fist hit his chest. "I'm big. In bed, the best. Big Maxx will make you forget small Patrick, I swear."

Raising her brows, Denise tapped her fingers on the desk. The man before her, a tacky, potbellied fool with gray hair sticking out of his nostrils, had just insulted her.

"I'm a married woman, Mr. Maxx Mandallo."

"Okay, okay, put your husband here." Maxx's fist hit the desk. "I see him on table, I know you're married. If not, you're just like any woman on the market. Any man can buy you."

"Really?" Denise rose.

"Forget, Denise. Sit down. I just want to see reaction from you. But a man like me, I'm very, very good in bed. Oh, forget."

It wasn't the first time Denise had heard Maxx use inappropriate language, but not to that extent. She turned, and in a moment, she was at the door. She opened it with a lot of energy and stepped into Matilda's office, only to close the door gently behind her.

"Oh, my God, did he touch you?" Matilda's eyes and mouth were wide open.

Denise shook her head. She got to her office and picked up her bag.

It was the peak hour, and the drive from the light industrial area of Lusaka to her home in Meanwood usually took an hour. This time, she didn't count the minutes. She didn't even know how she got home. But she was home, thank goodness, and a text message from Matilda came through: *Mr. Maxx wants you back. Says he was only joking. Come back, Ms. Denise. What about me?*

Denise went straight to bed, and lying in the fetal position, she cried herself to sleep. Before long, she was dreaming that Patrick was making love to her in a way she had never known him to be capable of.

She was awakened by an annoying sound. It was her phone.

"Mrs. Kanya." It was a man's familiar voice.

"Yes?"

"Did I wake you up?"

"No. I mean, it's okay. Who's this?"

"It's Norman."

Denise sat up. "Have you found him, Mr. Director? Have you found Patrick? Please?" She started to cry.

"I'm sorry, Denise, but no, I wish I had. I'm really so, so sorry, Denise. Mind if I call you Denise?"

"I guess..."

"In which case, call me Norman. Look, Denise, I can't pretend I know what you're going through. No, it wouldn't be right. But it's about our friend Maxx. You know, he and Patrick were business colleagues, if not friends. Maxx sponsors a lot of our television shows. Are you listening?" Denise blew her nose into the tissue she had been keeping by her bedside since Patrick's disappearance. As if Norman could see her, she nodded. "He asked me to speak to you. Says he's very, very sorry, and he wants you to go back to the office. Please, Denise."

"Did he tell you why I left?" She feared she was going to cry again.

"You know, Denise, Maxx was merely being Maxx. That doesn't make him right, of course, but..."

Denise hung up and wished she would die. Just die. With or without pain. If Patrick had ditched her, what was the point in continuing to live? How had she offended him? How could she find out? Or had an American gun killed him? But where was he killed? In a busy airport terminal building, and in the city where CNN had its headquarters, and there was no news about his death? No. Patrick had dumped her in the same way a man forgets about the prostitute he slept with an hour ago.

The next morning, Denise didn't go to work. She instead made a big decision—she was going to sell Patrick's Jeep Cherokee.

CHAPTER 23

Patrick's first night at Aretha's home was not so comfortable. Although much more comfortable than his motel bed, his new bed was hard and squeaked with every slight movement he made. Above all, the pillow was hard as a brick and bumpy like most roads back home. It was good, though, to have a room he would be paying for, one he would call his asylum room. Between nightmares, two of them about being so sick that he was losing his hair, he woke up, his neck hurting, and it took him some time to remember where he was.

In the morning, Aretha asked Patrick downstairs and said, "Breakfast will be a scrambled egg, two slices of bread, butter, grits, and a cup of coffee. That will be three dollars only. One more meal at three, and that one will be five dollars. Ah, D'Angelo. That's my son. He'll be here at twelve to talk to you about a job."

Patrick wasn't hungry. "Sounds good," he said.

D'Angelo came two hours later than the appointed time and sat next to Patrick on the sofa. He seemed to be about the same age as Patrick, but he was slightly shorter. He had a lighter complexion than his mother, who was of about the same shade as Denise's. D'Angelo looked so emaciated, back home, in Patrick's village, people would nickname him 'Long Bones.' Some people would even conclude that he had AIDS. AIDS! Patrick knew so many people whose lives had been taken by that deadly disease, sometimes he wished he had become celibate like an honest priest at an early age.

"Patrick, this is between you and me, not the both of you," Aretha said as she walked slowly down the staircase. She wore a loose, multicolored dress that touched the knees but had a long slit that revealed her legs. "D'Angelo, he thinks he's my firstborn," she whispered and sat opposite Patrick. "No. I had another son before him, but I never told D'Angelo." She burst out laughing. Patrick stole a glance at D'Angelo, who didn't seem to be concerned about what his mother had just said. "I don't know what happened to my firstborn." D'Angelo sighed and stared blankly at the television set whose audio was a mere whisper. "I have a daughter. Her name is Nubia Makeba." Again, she laughed, and this time, Patrick got alarmed. Was Aretha all there?

His feet jiggling, D'Angelo said, "Okay, my company has always been a one-man thing, man, black-owned, of course. I keep my lawn equipment in great condition, so when I go out to work, I work fast and efficient. Now, you can work with me. I don't need no white man's papers from you. I'll pay you in cash. It's just that right now, I don't have a contract. But don't worry, soon, you'll be able to pay Mom three hundred dollars a month for the room."

"No, Dee," said Aretha. "I already told him it's five hundred, and he agree."

"No, Mum. He can't afford five at my rate. I pay what I can pay, Mum." D'Angelo turned to address Patrick. "See what I mean?" Patrick felt as if there already was a bond between the two agemates against the female, who happened to be much older. "I'll pay him three hundred every two weeks. A man needs food. You know, a drink? Like when I take him out, he must buy me a drink."

"Dee, I told you, Patrick, he agree to five hundred."

"Mum, you don't understand a man's nature. A man must find a girl and buy her a drink. You see what I mean, my man?" Patrick was in an awkward position. Whom was he to agree with? "You start working as soon as I have some job lined up, my man. I'll show you the works."

"Thank you," said Patrick. To Aretha, he said, "I appreciate you accommodating me."

Aretha looked up, constantly crossed and uncrossed her legs, and pulled at a silver chain that carried a tiny cross under her scarf.

"Let me say one thing," said D'Angelo. "You leave that room, you lose your job. My mother needs the rent money. Deal?"

Patrick wished he would say what was on his mind: that he didn't intend to stay in that house for long, for he would soon get a great job.

He wished he knew how he would achieve those goals, though. Something would come up soon. A foolproof plan.

CHAPTER 24

The ad appeared under *Motor Vehicles For Sale* smalls in one daily, and by 7:00 am the next day, five people had called Denise's cellphone to enquire about Patrick's white Jeep Cherokee.

"You say five thousand dollars or nearest cash offer," said one caller, a man with a melodious voice. "I'm offering four."

"Sir, by nearest, I mean something like, uh, maybe two hundred less," said Denise.

The man hung up.

Another caller said he would love to see the vehicle. "I'll pay five," he said, and suddenly, Denise was afraid. Was selling Patrick's vehicle the right thing to do? What if the caller was a criminal who came home, raped and robbed her and harmed her children? She wished she would find a man to sell the car for her. The gardener, maybe?

"Can I call you back?" she said.

"That's okay, baby, but..."

She hung up.

She wanted to go back to bed because she was always exhausted, for she rarely slept well, and she ate very little. Being awakened by a nightmare at 2:00 am had become routine. Often, she sat in the bathtub and cried. If she knew that Patrick was dead, she would readily accept that she had become one of the millions of widows in the world.

When sleep eluded her, she put on a gown and walked to the dining room. The two letters she didn't dare to open the previous day were still on the dining table. One was from Patrick's employers, and it was addressed to him. She opened it. Patrick had been terminated for desertion. Her husband had been fired. Sacked. Her throat feeling dry, and her fingers shaking, she cursed the day she first met Patrick. She should never have been deceived by his great looks. She could have married an ugly guy and found the happiness a woman craved for.

She continued to read: *And in view of the fact that you did not ensure that staff under your supervision did not retire imprests amounting to a figure yet to be determined, as of now, you have no terminal benefits. However, due to the uncertainty of your case, management may reconsider this decision to suit future circumstances.*

In a simple twist of fate, Denise had become the man of the house, the role she had always dreaded, as that would have meant that her husband had died. No wonder, Patrick's check had not been deposited in their account that month.

She put the letter on the table and studied the envelope it had come in. It was just a white envelope. Couldn't Norman have waited until there was definite information about what had happened to Patrick before he ordered his termination? *Desertion!* Really, Norman? Patrick would never desert anyone.

In the morning, she called the servants. Martha worked inside the house, sweeping and mopping the floors, doing the laundry, and cooking. Martha's husband, Wizzie, worked mainly in the garden and ran errands for the family. The couple had been working for the family since Chris was a baby. They were hardworking and loyal, so they had become part of the family. For practical purposes, Patrick had given the nickname 'Wizzie' to Wisdomtooth Banda. He was a smart man with a high school diploma. Denise had heard that he and Martha had met in middle school. Martha had become pregnant and left school in the eighth grade. They later got married when Wizzie completed high school. The couple lived with their three children in the servant's single bedroom quarters behind the main house.

Wizzie came in and stood at attention away from the dining table.

"Join your wife at the table," said Denise. Wizzie sat next to his wife, and Denise understood why the gardener had taken so long to come inside the house. The cologne he wore informed her that he had taken some time to wash the sweat off his body. How civil!

"As you know, my husband is not here," she said and avoided their eyes. "So, I can no longer afford to keep you in employment."

It was hard to continue talking, as the Bandas were a great couple, and Denise was hopeful that Patrick would be back home soon before another family grabbed them.

"We understand, madam," Wizzie said without consulting his wife.

Denise knew that if she and Patrick were to find themselves under similar circumstances, Patrick wouldn't have spoken on her behalf before consulting. That was how great Patrick was as a companion.

Denise couldn't find the courage to tell the couple that she needed them out of the servant's quarters soon, as she needed to rent out the place.

The phone rang. It was Norman.

She answered, and to Wizzie and Martha, she said, "You can go."

"Go where, Denise?"

"Sorry, sir, but I was talking to the servants. How are you?"

Norman chuckled. "Please, don't call me 'sir.' Aren't we friends? We agreed on first names, remember? Patrick would approve, I'm sure."

"Approve of what, sir?" She lowered her voice. "What can I do for you, Norman? You have been calling me often, but you never mentioned you were firing my husband."

"That's better," Norman chuckled. "I mean, you calling me 'Norman.' Can we have lunch? We can talk about things. Like why Patrick was terminated. Face to face. You know, like if he's dead, you'll inherit a small check in the form of his terminal benefits. Life insurance and things like that. You would get more if he hadn't allowed his subordinates not to retire their imprest. Look, this is a dilemma."

"Okay, let's talk." She tried not to sound combative. "So, when and where do you want the talks?"

"Today. I'll pick you up at midday."

She wondered if she was doing the right thing, having lunch with Patrick's former boss, but when Norman came at the appointed time, she was ready for a showdown. As she approached the maroon 2017 Lexus RX 350 SUV, she saw a woman seated in the passenger seat.

"Long time no see, Denise," said Lisa, Norman's wife. "I'm sorry to hear about Patrick."

"Thanks."

Lisa Daka, as she was known before she married Norman, was Denise's senior by two years at the university. Undoubtedly one of the most beautiful girls on campus, Lisa seemed to get along with everyone except Denise, whom many students considered to be the most beautiful girl in the university. Seeing Lisa brought back the bad memories of Denise finding out through a student newspaper that Patrick had cheated on her with Lisa. Patrick had apologized, and Denise had forgiven him. Sitting in that expensive vehicle behind Lisa, Denise wished she had used that opportunity before Alice was conceived to break her engagement to the man who had just been terminated for desertion.

Denise was surprised to see how short the trip to the Bonanza Golf Club Restaurant had been.

As they entered the dining room, Norman announced, "I want the usual table."

"Yes, sir," said a young lady who wore little make-up.

It was Denise's first visit to the restaurant, and she liked what she saw. When her pumpkin soup arrived before anyone else's, Lisa said, "Eat, Denise."

Denise slurped the soup so fast, it was gone in minutes. When she looked up, she realized that Lisa was gazing at her.

"I'm sorry," said Denise. "I didn't realize how hungry I was."

"That's okay," Lisa's smile showed off her curved lips and snow-white teeth.

Suddenly, Denise felt rotten. How could she eat so gluttonously when her kids were eating basic foods?

Two waiters brought the remaining two bowls of soup and the three main dishes at the same time, and again, Lisa said, "Eat, girl." "I know Patrick will be back soon."

Denise didn't like it when people said that. Who told them Patrick would be back soon?

Instead, she said, "Sir, you said there could be some terminal benefits?" said Denise.

"Yes, of course. But I have to check with HR."

"Norman, can't you do more than *just* checking?" asked Lisa. "You're the boss. Can you assure my friend here that you'll ensure her financial comfort? Like giving her what a widow would be entitled to?"

"The problem, honey, is that you, yourself, just said Patrick would be back soon, and then you call her a widow. Show me the death certificate, and we'll cut the check."

Lisa shook her head slowly.

"Damn!" Norman hissed. He looked around the room, as if he was searching for something that shouldn't have gone missing.

"What?" asked Lisa.

"I hate this," Norman angrily pointed at his bowl of soup.

"Tomato soup, right?" asked Lisa with a frown. "That's what he ordered, Denise, didn't he?"

"Yes, but they should have told me it was tomato soup, *this* type."

"What type, dear?"

"Forget it, okay?" Norman snapped.

After a prolonged silence, Lisa asked, "Tell me, Denise, what happened between you and Patrick?"

"What *happened?*" asked Denise.

"Yes. When a husband goes missing, the first person the police talk to is the wife, girl."

"Are you saying I killed Patrick?"

"Then who did?" asked Norman.

Denise's stomach hurt. She covered her face in her hands.

"No, no," said Lisa. "Let's forget about it."

An hour later, Norman and Lisa dropped Denise at home. The lunch meeting had accomplished nothing.

Standing at the front door, Alice asked, "Is that your latest boyfriend?"

"No, honey. That was your father's boss and his wife."

"You're lying!" Alice shouted. Denise rolled her eyes. "There was no woman in that car. I saw a man. You know, I just don't feel like living here anymore. Not without Dad. Did you call Dad last night?"

"Child, you will not speak to me like that!"

Alice slammed the door. Denise tried to open it. It was locked. She knocked, and Martha opened the door.

"Where's this young lady?" Denise asked, her stomach heaving. Martha walked away. Denise got to the dining table, where she stood still and concluded that her daughter had every right to be angry at the world. Of course, Denise had stopped calling Patrick because there was no point in calling when the phone was no longer in service. She knew she was a good mother and wife. She had never cheated on her husband. She had continued to love him even after he had left her and after he had confessed to cheating on her with Lisa and with Hazel Omei while they were all students. She considered the world to be a nasty, ugly, angry, and annoying place.

"Martha!" she called.

"Madam."

"No more flowering the plants inside the house until the boss gets here. Ah, I forgot you won't be working here anymore."

"I work few days, madam."

Denise sat down, and the phone rang. It was Rebecca.

"I want us to sit like family and talk like friends," Rebecca said without the usual chitchats. "I've been thinking, did Patrick have a girlfriend? Maybe she traveled with him to America, and together, they decided to start a new life."

"You know, Patrick has his faults, but do you think he's capable of abandoning his children?"

"Well, my little brother has become capable of doing what he just did. Okay, Denise, how are you doing financially?"

"Honestly, we're broke. Patrick and I never made enough to save. Besides, we had the house loan to service."

"I don't need the details. I'll bring some food for my niece and my nephews."

"That would be very kind of you, Rebecca."

"Yes, and you can starve." Rebecca chuckled. "How could a woman as smart, intelligent, beautiful as you not make money? And I hear Maxx didn't fire you? You just walked out? Do you have someone in mind who will feed you?"

Denise chose not to respond to that. Besides, Rebecca had hung up.

"Madam, what do we do, madam?" It was Martha. She was standing in the archway leading to the kitchen. She and her husband had decided to work a few days a week without pay, provided they stayed in the servant's quarters. Buying time until they found jobs, Denise was sure. "What do we eat now?"

Denise wanted to say, *How selfish of you! You've got your family. My husband is missing, and all you think about is not having a job?*

"I'm so sorry, Martha."

Somewhere in the house, Alice was shouting at someone, probably her younger brother, Chris, who had become a recluse.

That afternoon, Denise put a sign on the rear windshield of the Cherokee that read: *SUV 4 Sale*, followed by her home phone number.

"Mom, you lied to me." Junior was standing not far from the dining table. "You said Dad's plane didn't fall in the big ocean."

CHAPTER 25

Two months had passed, and D'Angelo rarely called. But when he did, it was to confirm that he hadn't secured a landscaping contract yet.

Although his only expenses were the monthly rent and the food bill that came with the rent, Patrick feared that he would soon be running out of money. Sometimes, he skipped meals and drank water with sugar for energy.

Patrick was dreaming about Junior having been expelled from school when he heard a knock on the door.

"Hey, it's D'Angelo. Open up."

Patrick reluctantly opened the door.

"Mum didn't tell you?" asked D'Angelo.

"Tell me what?"

"If you don't want the job, I could find someone else." D'Angelo chuckled. "Only joking. Put on some work clothes. Fast."

From then on, Patrick's work day started at 7:00 am, Mondays, Wednesdays, and Fridays, when D'Angelo picked him up in his red F-150 truck which sounded to Patrick like it needed either an engine tune-up or replacement. The important thing was that it was capable of pulling D'Angelo's lawnmower trailer to distant workplaces.

The Monday job, which Patrick performed at a low-scale apartment complex, was easy, and the manager was friendly. He didn't like the other two assignments, where the managers practiced micro management.

Often, D'Angelo dropped Patrick at the work site, saying he was going to look for more business. "You know, together, we can make big bucks," D'Angelo often said before he disappeared for the day, only to come back hours later to pick up Patrick after he had been waiting for a long time.

Patrick soon got to understand his employer's situation. D'Angelo was in poor health. He constantly yawned and sometimes said he couldn't see well. He said he had no appetite, and often, he stopped the vehicle to use a portable urinal.

"Brother, I think we need a different approach to the way we do this job," Patrick suggested one morning.

"Stop right there, my man!" D'Angelo raised his voice. "You think I don't know what I'm doing? Okay, why don't you run your own company?"

"I apologize, brother."

"You better be."

They didn't talk to each other, but as they parted, D'Angelo said, "Hey, you and me, we're good, right?"

"No problem."

The following day, Patrick waited for longer than usual before D'Angelo, looking pale and exhausted, showed up and said, "Sorry, I should have told you, bro, but this was our last day here, bro."

"You mean...?"

"What else do you want me to say?" D'Angelo snapped.

Patrick put his work tools in the truck's trailer and sat in silence in the passenger seat as D'Angelo drove slowly. A few houses from Aretha's house, the truck stopped.

"Tell Momma not to ask for rent because it's not your fault you lost the job," said D'Angelo. "She has an angel's heart, bro."

"So, we lost the other contracts, too?"

"Yeah. That's what I said, bro. They wanted to revise our contract to slave wages, man. I said, no, my black ass, I still got my pride."

"Tell me something, bro," said Patrick. "Your mother."

"What? You like her?" D'Angelo wore a broad smile.

"Is she okay? I mean, the things she says."

Patrick felt as if D'Angelo's red eyes were boring into his face. "Did I hire you to analyze my Momma? You was a shrink in your country?"

"I'm sorry, bro, but..."

"I haven't said what I wanted to say," D'Angelo screamed. "Did I ever ask about your mother, your father last week, yesterday, today, tomorrow? Mind your own business, man." He covered his face in his hands. "I don't know, man. Sometimes, you annoying."

"I'm sorry."

D'Angelo smiled, extended his right hand, and said, "We good, right?"

The two men shook hands.

His limbs shaking, Patrick got out of the truck, and at the same time, the truck's engine spluttered and stopped running.

"What are you looking at?" asked D'Angelo. "Just go, okay?"

Patrick wished he would leave. But go where? Aretha didn't seem to be all there, and was D'Angelo okay?

Aretha was waiting inside the house but by the front door.

"Waiting for him," she announced. "My man. He's a good man, but he married to a jealous white woman. He not even as handsome as you, Patrick, and yet this motherfucker don't show up. I been waiting here three hours. The water bill is high, but I even had a shower. Never trust a black man married to a Miss Anne."

It was the first time Patrick had heard an adult use the term 'motherfucker' away from the silver screen. "Miss Ann?" he asked.

"A white woman. The only time I been having a shower is just before my man comes to see me, and before I go to church." Aretha said bitterly.

Patrick had never heard Aretha talk about going to church.

"I'm sorry to hear that, but there's gas smelling in here, Ms. Aretha," Patrick said and he quickly got to the kitchen. The stove was hissing, and he turned off the gas.

"Do you think he coming, Patrick? Think like a man."

Through the window, Patrick saw an Amazon truck and a man carrying a heavy box walk toward Aretha's front door.

"I love shopping online," she said, her tone more positive than before.

Patrick already knew that. Aretha received several parcels from Amazon every week. The other day, while she was away, Patrick had counted Aretha's coats in the cloakroom by the entrance. Ninety-nine.

"I'm afraid D'Angelo lost all his contracts, ma'am."

"My son, he always gets new contracts," said Aretha with a great sense of assurance. She opened the door and said to the delivery man, "Bless you." When she came back in, she had a large parcel, which she put on the floor by the front door. Through the transom door, she continued to watch the front of the house. "And his truck, it always breaks down, D'Angelo. He bought it on Craigslist, and it gets badder and badder every day. He's dying, my son is dying. I'm his mama, and I know he dying. So, tell me how you going to pay your rent?" She smiled broadly, her dentures white as snow. "Okay, there's a black woman out there my age, and they desperately need tall, handsome, young black men like you. She'll give you a shelter and a bed."

Patrick saw no point in saying that he would never be forced to sleep with any woman.

"I need the rent," Aretha sounded agitated. "If I had a man, I wouldn't need a tenant. And this motherfucker tells me never to call him, but *he* calls me."

Patrick got to his room and sat on the bed. That evening, he didn't go downstairs to eat, and that night, he had trouble falling asleep. He was used to the rough bed and the physical work he did for D'Angelo. But the night's thunderstorm was menacing, and knowing that he could no longer pay his rent scared him. Was it too late to fly back home? And was there a storm menacing the Meanwood home at that very moment? Junior was scared of storms.

It was 2:30 in the morning. The rain continued to pound the window, while the wind ceaselessly thumbed the roof and the trees outside. Patrick wished he had friends to talk to. He wondered who had taken his place at the television company. Larry, the executive producer stroke director extraordinaire? Was Jennifer still in her office, answering calls and reminding Larry of his daily chores? Had the company reorganization taken place?

He went to the bathroom. From there, he could hear Aretha's loud snoring. When he got back to bed, he opened Captain

Theodore Canot's *Adventures of An African Slaver,* a book he had picked up from Aretha's large collection downstairs.

He heard Aretha's door open. For a minute or two, she attempted to lock the door. When that was done, she walked noisily down the stairs, mumbling to herself. A minute later, he heard her heavy footsteps as she climbed the stairs. It took her a minute to unlock her door. He heard the door close, the lock click, and her loud laughter was irritating. She went through the same procedure three more times—opening the door, locking it, walking downstairs, coming upstairs, locking it, and laughing.

He was awakened by a loud knock on his door. It was 3:30 am, and he opened the door. Aretha was dressed as if she was leaving for a formal function.

"Have you seen the sea?" she sounded anxious.

"You mean, have I ever been to the sea? Yes, the last time I was in England, a colleague took me to see the famous white cliffs of Dover. I read about them in elementary school."

"The sea. It's come to our door."

"Yes, ma'am, I saw it. We're safe. We're on the second floor."

"If you say so," she said, looking relieved. "They say they're going to shoot all the black men tomorrow…Why you look surprised, Patrick? Like you don't believe me? I just saw it on TV."

He believed she had seen something on television. After all, the television in her bedroom was on 24/7.

"Okay, I thought I should warn you," she said and went back to her room.

Slouched on the squeaky bed, Patrick stared at the ceiling. If the world was some object he could punch and stab with a knife, he would kill it.

"I'd love to go back home," he said aloud. "But I can't."

CHAPTER 26

So far, only one out of the eleven people who had called to enquire about Patrick's SUV was a woman. Given a choice, Denise would sell it to another woman. Men were a dangerous species.

"They are here, madam," Wizzie reported, and as usual, he was standing in the arch, away from the dining table that had become Denise's office.

"Remember, if you sell it, I'll give you a hundred dollars."

"Thank you, madam."

She followed him to the garden, where the vehicle's white body sparkled in the bright sun after Wizzie had given it a thorough wash.

It was a family, thank goodness. A small man with a round face and a clean-shaven head, a lady who wore expensive clothes, and a smiling baby boy. They drove a white Acura SUV, meaning they had the means to buy another SUV.

"Madam, my wife called. The name is Debe. Call me Mark."

"Glad to meet you, Mark," said Denise. "Yes, I remember her calling." Already, she was feeling uncomfortable. Mark was staring at her. That was the story of her life, though, one she could never get used to.

"What a beautiful baby you have," said Denise. "What's his name?"

The woman smiled broadly. "His name is Mark, Jr. Thank you."

"So, this is the beauty," Mark walked around the Jeep, studying it as if he knew a lot about cars. "Did you say 2012 model, madam?"

"Yes."

"This doesn't look like a twelve. It looks like a 2010."

"It's a 2012, Mark," said the woman, and her baby smiled.

"Are you paying for it, or am I?" Mark retorted. "Okay, can you start the engine?"

Denise didn't know her hands were shaking until she turned the ignition key.

"Madam, listening to the engine, we'll offer three thousand dollars."

"No, Mark, as you can see..."

"Then there's no deal."

"Surely, this is a good vehicle, sir," Denise pleaded. "My husband used it to drive to work and back. In five years, it has done only thirty thousand kilometers."

"Very good car," said Wizzie.

"That's not the point," Mark addressed Wizzie. "The point is, we can only offer three thousand."

"Then we have no deal, Mark," the words thoughtlessly came out of Denise's mouth.

Mark took another look at the vehicle. "Okay, four-wheel drive, the seats look new. So, who's coming with me on the test drive? I'll leave my wife and baby as collateral." He burst out laughing. "If I don't come back, you have them for dinner."

A sickening joke, thought Denise, and suddenly, she didn't like Mark and his short beard. Besides, she had never been able to relate to short men.

With Wizzie as his passenger, Mark drove the vehicle out of the yard. Denise invited Mark's companion inside the house, where she served her a cup of tea.

"I hope we have a lot of rain this year," said the woman. "My name is Monica. We live on a farm."

"Monica? That was my aunt's name. I'm Denise."

"I must apologize," said Monica.

"Apologize?"

"My boyfriend, Mark. He has a short temper, no manners. I mean, I'm being honest. I saw the way he was staring at you. But it's hard to blame him, madam. You're a very beautiful woman. How could Mr. Kanya leave a woman like you?"

Feeling heaviness in her stomach, Denise avoided eye contact with her late aunt's namesake. "So are you. You're really beautiful."

"No, I don't mean it that way, Mrs. Kanya. You're actually beautiful."

"Tell me, how do you know me?"

"Your story was in the papers, on television."

"Uh, I see...Look, they're back."

"A beautiful vehicle, madam," Mark's attitude seemed to have changed after the test drive.

Monica pulled Mark to the side. The two whispered for a while, and when they got back to the SUV, Mark said cheerfully, "Okay, we'll pay forty-eight hundred. Cash."

"Sounds good." At long last, someone was paying good money. So far, the highest offer Denise had received was $3,500. Considering how broke the family was, she had almost given the vehicle away at that price.

Mark took a large briefcase from the back seat of his SUV. He put the case on the Jeep Cherokee's hood and started counting the money. The bills were old, so Denise believed they would be genuine US dollars.

"Just make it five thousand, Mark," said Monica.

Mark nodded and finished counting. "Would you like to count it, madam?"

"No, I was watching you count," said Denise. She picked up the money and put it in her leather purse, which was a gift from Patrick on her fortieth birthday. And now, she could plan her life.

"Can we have the spare keys?" asked Mark.

She had forgotten about the spare keys. Of course, they were in her bedroom, on Patrick's nightstand.

She quickly got to the bedroom, and suddenly, she wasn't too sure she was doing the right thing. If it was okay to sell the vehicle, was the price right?

She had found a buyer, but where were the spare keys? After a frantic fifteen-minute search, she concluded that she had searched everywhere.

Outside, in the garden, Mark said, "In that case, we have to reconsider..."

"It's okay, Mark," said Monica.

"It's her car," said Mark. "If someone steals it?" He opened his arms wide. "Okay, deal. Can we have the title?"

Denise felt worthless as she walked back to the bedroom. She should have thought about the title. And it was where she had expected to find it—in the old briefcase that was under the bed, the one Patrick valued so much because it was the one he had carried to his job interview at the television station. In it, the family kept all the important documents, such as birth and educational certificates.

She pushed the purse full of money under her bed and hurried back to the front of the house.

As if he was shortsighted, Mark held the title close to his eyes. "Is this your name?" he asked.

"Yes, that's my husband's name."

"So, it's not your car?" Mark sounded hostile.

"It's *our* vehicle, my husband and I."

"Then where is your husband? His name appears on the title, and it's him who should sell the vehicle, isn't that right?"

"I'm sorry, my husband is not here."

"Then I'm sorry, there's no deal. Can I have my money? I'm being polite. You wasted our time."

Denise looked at Monica, who was looking down.

Just after the couple had driven away in their Acura, Denise's home phone rang. A man said he loved her voice so much, he was in love. "Can I buy your car and sleep with you?"

She watched helplessly as the receiver fell to the floor. She was not going to pick it up, but she found enough strength to get to the dining table, where she slumped into her favorite chair. Tears blinded her, and she quickly dried them with the back of her right hand. She was glad the kids were at school.

That night, she locked her bedroom door, sat on the bed she had shared with her husband for many years and mourned him. She concluded that Patrick was dead. She knew it. She could feel it. Patrick was a good man. There was no way he could have let her and their kids get to this. Broke. Selling properties. Yes, the spy story Patrick had talked about made sense. He must have come across a state secret that had cost him his life. Something to do with his work. State agents had made sure he died in a foreign land. Maybe if the people who had killed Patrick found out that she knew about the secret, they would kill her, too, and the kids would be orphaned.

She would never tell anyone about it.

CHAPTER 27

He heard her struggling to open the front door. Grudgingly, he got out of bed, rubbed his hurting neck, and rushed downstairs to help, but she had already opened the door.

"Good news," Aretha said, running out of breath. "The HR manager at Welcome Supermarket, she's my friend's cousin, the pastor. You can work there using my son's name. But you can't work many hours because D'Angelo, his health, it's poor, so he's going to apply for disability. Sit down." she pointed at the dining table.

"You say you were a manager, Patrick. Use your manager's skills to find solutions to your problems. You working there, how do you avoid getting my son into trouble? All I want is my rent paid on time."

Patrick remembered the many problems he had solved at the television station. Those were company problems. He had never faced a personal challenge as immense as the one before him.

"First, thank you, Ms. Aretha," he said and sat at the table with her. "I'll think about it."

That night, he tossed and turned in bed, paced the room, and repeatedly visited the bathroom before he sat at the study table by the window.

Hours later, he had just fallen asleep when he heard a consistent knock on his door. "Are you going to take the job? D'Angelo, he wants to know if he should bring the papers."

It was 2:00 am, and he said, "I have a plan, Ms. Aretha."

He dressed quickly, and again, he and his landlady sat in the same dining chairs they had sat in the previous day.

"What's your plan?" Aretha asked.

"I'm still thinking."

"You have no time. Do you have money to pay the rent?" She stood up.

"I want to see two things from D'Angelo. His ID and his social security card. How much does this job pay?"

"Very well. Eight dollars an hour. You talking to me like you're my manager."

Patrick had read intensively on the job market and wages in the Atlanta metro area. He knew that there were scores of people who made less than eight dollars an hour. Even if he were to work only twenty hours a week, he could pay his rent and still have some change to buy food. After all, Welcome Supermarket was only a walking distance away.

By the end of the following day, D'Angelo hadn't brought the documents Patrick had asked for.

"I forgot to ask him," said Aretha.

Patrick continued to work on his plan during the night. At 4:00 am, he concluded that there was no point in worrying endlessly about his family. Leaving his wife and kids was the only thing any reasonable man in his position would have done. He would find happiness without them, and they would manage without him.

CHAPTER 28

"I'm so grateful to you, Martha," Denise said. As usual, Martha said little. She stood obediently away from the dining table, the frozen chicken Denise had given to her in one hand. The couple had continued to work a few days a week, and because Denise wasn't paying them, she helped them with food whenever she could.

"You are our mother." Martha was almost in tears. "The boss will come."

Denise hated it when people said Patrick would come back home soon. The man had ruined her dream of one man, one family.

She heard the gate open and looked outside. It was Wizzie. She had sent him to put up signs by the roadside reading: *Garage Sale. Everything must go!* She was going to sell all the dresses, shoes, blouses, sweaters, shirts, coats, and jackets she hadn't worn in the past year. She and Patrick had planned to do that for years, but there had never been enough time to hold a garage sale. Patrick had always been busy. Had she missed something there? Was it true that he was always working? Maybe he was having an affair all those years. But how come he always answered when she called his office number? Was he having an affair with one of his coworkers?

"You can go now, Martha," she said, and Martha hesitated. Denise didn't want to hear Martha say one more word about the boss coming back home soon. "You don't have to work today."

That evening, at the dinner table, Chris said, "Mum, you're not eating?"

Denise feared she was going to break down. "Children, I want to talk to you. I have a feeling we may never see your father again." Unlike that evening, the one before Patrick's departure, Denise didn't stand up at the table to address her kids. She paused to look at each one of them. Alice was staring at her without blinking. How did her daughter manage to do that? Chris was looking at his food. Junior was almost in tears. "One thing I want us to learn from this is to be honest with everyone we deal with. Look them in the eye and tell them the truth. Another thing, you'll all have to learn to attend government schools."

"So, Mom, are you saying Dad was lying to us about something?" asked Alice.

"Did I say that?"

"Then what are you saying?" Alice asked, and she stood up and left. Chris followed. Junior broke down and left without looking at Denise.

It took another hour before Denise could leave the table. She felt weak, tired, and worthless, and yet she couldn't ask her kids to wash the plates.

The next morning, Denise woke up feeling groggy from lack of sleep, but she still found the strength to visit several public schools, looking for school places for her kids. Yet finding places in government schools wasn't as easy as she had thought.

"Not everything comes easy, Denise," Rebecca told her later in the day. "I'll talk to a few people in high places."

A week after Chris and Junior had started classes at two different schools, Junior said he had made friends among his classmates, and he seemed to like his female teacher a lot. "She says I look like Dad, so I'm a very, very handsome boy, Mom. But the toilets are...yucky!"

Alice came from school one afternoon and announced from the doorway that she wasn't going to leave her private school.

"Come, sit down," Denise pointed at the dining chair next to hers. Alice didn't move. "Okay, where will the money come from, child?"

"The principal said I just can't leave my school when I'm in my senior year. What stuff do they teach in government schools, anyway? So, maybe my aunt will pay for me? Just maybe?"

"Your aunt will pay for you?" said Denise. "I said, come sit here. I'll call your Aunt Rebecca now."

Alice gave Denise a long, angry stare before she walked away.

Rebecca didn't answer. Denise called again, and Rebecca said, "You better have a good reason for calling me night and day. Is my brother back?"

"No, Aunt Rebecca, but your niece says you're paying her school fees?"

"Is that a way of asking me to pay for her, Denise? If Alice found a means to pay, she's merely doing what *you* should be doing—being objective, practical about life."

"I'm sorry, but..."

Rebecca said, "Be strong, Denise," and cut the line.

Denise didn't take offense. Rebecca had her own problems, so she could afford to be naughty sometimes. Besides, everything that had gone wrong had gone wrong because Patrick had caused everything to go wrong. She looked at the pile of letters on the table. For days, she had avoided opening them because she wanted to stay away from bad news.

She opened the one from the bank. She and Patrick had obtained a small loan to complete their house, and the bank wanted to know when Patrick would pay the two-month arrears on the account. *Unless the money is paid by the end of the month, the bank will have no choice but to begin proceedings to repossess the collateral*, the letter read.

With the sound of her heart pounding in her ears, Denise wished she could sell the Cherokee the very next day. If she could not sell it, she was going to have to sell her blue Honda Civic. But even that was in Patrick's name.

The next morning, Denise was about to call a company that was advertising an open clerical position when her cellphone rang.

"It's me," a man said.

She had heard that voice before. "Excuse me?"

"Mark Dube, madam."

"Yes, of course. How is...?"

"Monica? She's fine, I guess. We're no longer together. She wanted to be my boss. Always arguing. Anyway, the Cherokee, is it still available, madam?"

"No, but my husband is still gone."

"No problem, madam. I know a senior police officer who can help. Easily."

"Oh, how easily?"

"Do you want to sell the Jeep, madam?"

"Yes, I do."

"Okay. The price. The police officers want something for a Coca-Cola, madam. Two thousand dollars. Because of that, I can only pay three thousand."

"I'll take it," Denise responded instantly. Now, she could pay the bank, and the kids would still have a roof over their heads.

When Mark came to pick up the Cherokee the following day, Denise said, "Our house is up for rent."

"Sorry, I'm not in the real estate business, madam," said Mark.

"I was hoping you would know someone."

"You were wrong. We have to go."

It was sad to hand over the keys and see the vehicle being driven away by the young lady Mark had brought with him for that purpose.

Denise put the money on the dining table and called the bank.

"My name is Denise Kanya. You wrote to me, saying I should call you on this number. Is this Mr. Kenneth Lloyd?"

"Yes, this is Kenneth. I knew your husband well. The bank advertises on television, so...Anyway, are you paying the full amount today?"

"No, Mr. Lloyd, I was hoping..."

"I'm afraid I cannot say anything new or different from what's in that letter, Mrs. Kanya. It's either you pay in full, or our lawyers will be talking to your lawyers."

Denise looked at the dollar bills on the table, and the thought of giving any of them to the bank didn't make sense. Before long, she would have to sell something else to service the loan. "I will call you back," she said.

"You have until the end of the month, Mrs. Kanya. And do you know when Patrick is coming back?"

Denise cut the line. She found Wizzie in the garden and gave him a hundred-dollar bill.

"Thanks for selling the car, Wizzie."

Wizzie held the bill in his hand and stared at it. Denise walked back to the house and called Rebecca. "I didn't want to say this, but it looks like we're losing the house. We have no money."

"Denise, Denise!" Rebecca shouted over the line. "You say you went to the university and got yourself a degree, right? Me, I dropped out after two years. Put your four years to better use, girl. I'm putting my two years to good use."

"I'm sorry I called."

"You should be."

For a week, Denise looked for a three-bedroom house or an apartment in relatively decent residential areas, but the rent was prohibitive. None of the properties went for less than $300 per month. Using her university education, she concluded that it would be folly to think that she could sustain a decent living anymore. She turned to the compounds. Wizzie found a small, two-bedroom house in KK Square, a compound by the busy Great East Highway. The house had the advantage of an internal bathroom so that the family wouldn't be leaving the house to use the toilet or the cold-water shower.

Denise took the kids with her to view the house.

"That yellow house looks nice," Junior said, pointing at the house next door. The yellow house had a small flower garden in front.

"We can't afford it," Denise whispered. "Besides, it's not up for rent."

"When it's for rent, Mom, can we go there?" asked Junior.

Poor kid, thought Denise. Her baby had no idea how broke the family was.

She opened the front door of the house, and Alice said, "Mom, do you want to raise your family here? Look at the roads! So much dust. There's no ceiling." She swept her hand over the entire living room.

"Honey, the money we raised from the garage sale isn't enough to guarantee rent for more than three months. The landlord was good enough not to demand a deposit. Wizzie negotiated for that."

"How about the money from the sale of Dad's Jeep?" Alice was confrontational.

"That's what we'll be using to pay the rent, dear. The food. It was an old vehicle. Alice, do you have a problem with trust?"

"I have a problem with you giving away Dad's house and car."

"Alice, did you say *your* dad's house?" Denise realized that she was shouting and her fingers were trembling.

"Yes."

Denise shook her head.

The next weekend, no one said much when Denise's cousins, Brenda and Christine, hired a truck and assisted the family to move to KK Square. At the end of the day, many of their household items were broken, and as not even half of their belongings would fit in the new home, Denise left some in the old house.

After Denise's cousins had left, Alice said, "I'm spending the night at my friend's place."

"What friend?" Denise asked, and her phone rang. "A moment."

A man introduced himself as a representative of the bank from whom Denise and Patrick had borrowed money to complete the Meanwood house. "I'm here, talking to your servants. I told them they can stay in the servant's quarters until we get security people here."

"That's fine," said Denise.

"I'm going, Mum," said Alice, clumsily carrying the folded decoupage of family photos and newspaper cuttings in her hands. "This is for me and Dad."

"Please, will someone here give me a chance to breathe? Sorry, sir. Talking to my kids."

"No problem," said the man, and he hung up.

"Not my fault that you chased my father from here, Mum," said Alice.

Denise didn't make an effort to stop her daughter from leaving. She was too tired to think, let alone remain standing. She collapsed into a chair and wondered if she would ever get used to the stained toilet—the only one in the house, which she would also have to learn to share with her kids. The landlord had not kept his promise to fix the bathroom door lock, which made it difficult to open the door. The small size of the rooms made her feel as if there wasn't enough air to breathe. Probably the entire house was the size of her former living room and the kitchen put together. Her body ached from the time she had spent scrubbing the floors and the walls, and yet a foul smell still lingered in the air.

Denise was saddened by Chris's understanding of the family's predicament. He didn't complain about the tiny bedroom he was going to share with Junior. Generally, the boys seemed to have accepted their fate. It seemed to Denise that learning that they would never see their father again had hurt them more than having to move into a tiny compound house. Maybe things wouldn't be as bad as Denise had feared.

Their first evening at the new home was cruel. The family used a two-plate stove for cooking and boiling water for a bath, and they ate from the tiny living room. The night was even worse. Denise would have to share a bed with Alice when her daughter came home—if she ever did; and, of course, she would. Parting with the big bed she had shared with Patrick and replacing it with a much smaller one hadn't been an easy decision to make.

Before she retired to bed, Denise pushed the all-important old briefcase under the bed.

In the night, she expected to hear people shouting, "Thief! Thief!" but all she heard was distant laughter, Congolese music, and a ceaseless flow of cars. At times, she sat up in bed as if she was waiting for something to happen.

And something did happen.

It was 4:00 am, and Wizzie called. For a long time, all he could say between sniffles was, "Madam...Oh, madam!"

"What is it, Wizzie, you scare me. Is Martha okay? The children?"

Slowly, Wizzie calmed down. "Six men, madam. They pointed guns at me, and they told me to put your things in a big truck." He sniffled again. "Then they...they slept with my wife, madam. Sorry. All of them, while I looked. My teeth, they are shaking. The police, they haven't come. No transport."

"I'm so sorry to hear that, Wizzie."

She listened intently and her body shook from a mixture of fear, anger, and helplessness. She concluded that just like there was no point in hoping to see Patrick again, there was no point in calling the police. Neither Patrick nor the police would ever show up.

Soon, the sun was up, and the boys were still sleeping. She knew they were exhausted from lifting household items the previous day, so she let them sleep. But a peep through the boys' window revealed a large group of people standing in front of her house, talking in whispers. She scurried to the front door and opened it.

She felt a squeeze in her heart.

CHAPTER 29

Feeling as if the air was being siphoned out of her lungs, Denise leaned against the door and steadied herself. An aggravating sound made her quickly bring the cellphone to her right ear.

"It's me, Denise." It was the neighbor across the road from the Meanwood house Denise had just lost. "Are you okay?"

"Yes, I'm okay."

"The police are here now. Imagine, I called them four hours ago. What do we pay these bastards for?"

Denise stared blankly at the window. Her Honda Civic was sitting on stones. "Can we talk later?" she spoke into the phone and hung up.

She sat still in the living room, staring at a white wall. The kids were still sleeping. Had they died in the night? If they had, she would have no choice but to take her own life, too.

Her cellphone rang again. She ignored it, but when it rang again soon after, she answered it. "Do you know that Maxx would get you back into your house and protect your family? What do you have to lose, madam? Your husband is dead."

Denise couldn't place the voice, but it sounded as if the woman on the line was reciting lines. No, she would never offer her body to Maxx. She would fight this war and win it.

"Who are you?" she asked, but the line was dead.

Minutes slowly turned into hours, and Alice came home later in the day. She kissed Denise on the cheeks and hugged her brothers.

"How did you come?" asked Denise.

"I didn't want my friends to see this embarrassing place, Mom." Alice looked around her and at the roof. "Mom, you're doing your best."

"Thank you, child. That's going to be our bedroom." Denise led her daughter to the room, where they both sat on the small bed. "I gave the larger room to the boys."

"Mom, if you didn't drive Dad away, then who did? Not me. Not Chris. Not Junior. Not Aunt Rebecca."

"Alice, I don't know if your dad was driven away from us or if he was taken away from us."

"So, do you think he found a white woman? Aren't black men crazy about white women?"

Mother and daughter were facing different directions. Denise shifted her position and hugged her daughter. "I wish I knew, child. I've thought about everything that happened between us during our last few weeks together, and I can't find a clue." She remembered Patrick's spy story; the one that never made sense to her.

"I can't see Dad with another woman. So, maybe you're the only one who knows the truth. That's what my friends think. Would you tell me if you knew?"

Denise wished she had the right answers to her children's questions. Patrick, her sweetheart, the love of her life, had done this to her. Were Alice's friends right? Was Patrick in another woman's arms at that very moment as she held their daughter in her arms? She wished one of these mornings, she wouldn't wake up. The kids would suffer without her, but they would survive. Many orphans survived the wrath of the world and even became stronger.

She remembered the day she first spoke to him in that dining room at the university. She had seen him many times before that, and she had considered him attractive, but too attractive to marry, the kind of guy women fought over. And she had fights with two of her former university contemporaries, Hazel and Lisa. She considered herself an idiot. All these years, Patrick had been planning to leave her and the kids, and she never suspected anything.

"Mom, I have to go," said Alice. "I have school work to do. I'm writing an essay on parents."

"So soon? And won't you tell me where you live?" Denise was too scared to ask what her daughter was going to write about Patrick and herself.

"Won't you tell me where Dad is?"

Alice was about to leave when Gertrude called, and asked, "Anything new?"

The two friends hadn't spoken much since Patrick's disappearance, for Denise was too busy wading off insanity to visit friends, and Gertrude had kept to herself for years since her husband's death.

After speaking for a while, Gertrude said, "That's so, so gross, you not having a job and losing your home. Look, I'll talk to people I know about a job. But for now, how about you and the kids coming over this weekend? Please, don't say no."

Junior was elated to hear the news. Even Chris managed a smile, and Alice agreed to come.

On Saturday afternoon, Gertrude sent a cab to shuttle Denise and the kids to Sunningdale, an upscale Lusaka suburb.

"You look great," said Denise. And she meant it. Gertrude, who had a great job with a United Nations agency since she left the university, wore dreadlocks, a pair of denim jeans, and a matching shirt that showed off her petite figure.

Gertrude's well-furnished living room, the large windows, and the smell of fresh air, sadly reminded Denise of the home she once shared with Patrick.

"Come, I'll show you around," said Gertrude.

The three bedrooms, each one well furnished, could have accommodated Denise's entire family with great comfort. But even if Gertrude had been her sister, Denise wouldn't have asked to move there. She had never begged anyone for anything in her life. She also decided not to talk about the many photos hanging from the walls of every room, mainly of Gertrude's late husband, George, family members, and their friends from the university. Denise counted the number of times she herself appeared in the photos. Fifteen times. Were those photos always displayed there, or had her friend put them up as a show of sympathy, even when the two hadn't seen each other for long?

Gertrude had cooked oxtail, fish, chicken, vegetables, rice, the traditional *buhobe*, and French fries, and everyone, except Alice, ate more than they should have, for Gertrude kept urging them to "have some more."

Alice had a room to herself, and the boys shared one. As Denise tucked his youngest son in bed, Junior said, "Mom, can I stay here forever with auntie? I hate sleeping in that house. It's not even Daddy's house."

Denise turned to face the door and escaped to the nearest bathroom, where she dried the tears off her cheeks.

Sharing a bed, Denise and Gertrude spent half the night discussing politics and reminiscing over their university days. None of them brought up the issue of how they had met their husbands.

The following morning, Gertrude said, "Girl, you talk in your sleep."

"Don't tell me what I was saying because I don't want to tell *you* what *you* were saying."

Gertrude was standing by the bed, and Denise was still lying in bed, her body refusing to get up. She felt so comfortable, all she wanted was to go back to sleep and forget who and where she was.

"Me? Talking in my sleep?" Gertrude grunted. "Maybe, yes, you heard me. You know, I haven't shared a bed with anyone since...since he died."

Denise regretted mentioning that Gertrude talked in her sleep. How was she to know that the topic would lead to old memories? "Hey, you held me like a man holds his woman, and you called his name."

"I'm sorry I disturbed you, sweetheart," Gertrude smiled broadly, her left hand covering her chest, and the two friends laughed together. "I can never forget the campus dining room culture."

"It was the meeting place, the theater away from the theater halls," said Denise. She wished her friend hadn't brought up the subject. Patrick's disappearance had hurt her more than anything she could remember. Whereas Gertrude had seen her husband's body, Denise didn't know where Patrick was.

Gertrude sat next to Denise. "I wish human beings could have standby spouses. I mean... You know, like the kidney, the lungs, eyes. A pair each."

"And the head?"

"Poor head," said Gertrude. "It stands alone and lonely."

They laughed together again, and Denise was touched to see her friend shade a tear. "I meet men sometimes," said Denise. Gertrude's large eyes opened wide, saying a lot without words. "Men I've never met before. And, oh, they're so good in bed."

"Denise, are you serious?" Gertrude repeatedly hit her thighs with her hands. "You know there's still AIDS out there?"

"Oh, no, I mean in my dreams. They make love to me in strange ways. Mainly young men."

"Ah, *that!*" Gertrude's voice was soft. She sat in a bowed posture, looking away from Denise. "It used to happen to me a lot. Not anymore."

"I find it strange. Disturbing."

"No, Denise, you're just being human. Hey, did I tell you I met the chairman of the ZNBC board? You know he's married to my aunt, right?"

Denise sat up. "No. What?"

"He said Norman had told a board meeting that Patrick wasn't a good guy, that when Patrick was at the university, he had to be institutionalized for weeks because he had washed his library books in the sink."

Denise felt a flush of heat through her body. "Norman said *that* to the board?"

"You and I know it was that short guy who had an endless crush on you—what was his name again? Danny. He's the one who washed his books with soap and water, stood on the rooftop of his hall of residence and shouted, 'I want to die like Jimi Hendrix!' Remember?"

Denise slumped back into Gertrude's soft pillows and closed her eyes. How could Norman be so spiteful, so petty? Neither she nor Patrick had ever liked Norman, anyway.

Denise's cellphone rang, and without thinking, she answered it and listened. "No, I wouldn't do such a thing," she said and hung up. "Talk about the devil. One of Norman's TV girls wants to interview me about my situation."

"I think you should, Denise."

"No, I won't."

"It may heal you."

"No, it won't."

"Denise, suppose he appeared today, which he could, would you two get back together again?"

Denise sat up. "No, no, no, Gertrude, my girl. Not after what he has done to us. I wouldn't even look in his direction or say his name."

"Sweetheart, listen," Gertrude cleared her throat. "You know, my boss, the country director? He's looking for a domestic assistant. The wages are higher than average."

"No, I can't be someone's house servant. I've had servants before, Gertrude."

"I'm sorry. I'm just trying to help. It's like you run his errands, pick up his kids from school, that kind of thing."

"Thanks, but no."

It was Sunday afternoon, and the time to go back home came too early for everyone. Gertrude wanted the family to stay one more night, Junior said he wasn't leaving, but Denise didn't want to be spoilt by her friend's kindness. When the taxi Gertrude had called arrived, the two friends hugged and kissed each other's cheeks, and Denise was saddened to note that her friend's hand tremors had become more frequent since the two had last met.

CHAPTER 30

Standing in the front doorway of the small house she now called home, Denise stared at her Honda Civic. She hadn't replaced the stolen tires because she couldn't afford them. Besides, each night the car sat on those stones, someone was vandalizing it. The taillights had been partially yanked out. The body had dents and scratches. The windshield had dings. She blamed herself for that. She should have sold the car after realizing that she couldn't keep it safely in her new neighborhood. Maybe Mark, who had bought the Jeep at a song, would have bought the Honda as well before it was vandalized? She even blamed herself for Patrick's disappearance. Maybe there was something about her that wasn't right, and she wasn't aware of it?

From the boys' bedroom, she heard gales of laughter. Alice, who had not shown up for weeks, had come to visit, and only she could make Chris laugh. Denise still didn't know where Alice lived. She wished she knew how to handle her daughter. It was time for lunch, and Denise called her children to the table. It was the first meal all the four of them were going to eat together at the new home.

As the plates were being passed around, Denise said, "Alice, I have the right to know where you live, honey."

"Mom, I can't say." Alice stubbornly looked at Denise from the chair directly opposite. "If Dad was around, I wouldn't have left. I have to continue my tennis lessons, Mom. I'm doing this for Dad." Denise noticed that her daughter was continuing to stare at her, and without blinking. She hated that. "I have to pass my exams, too, and I can't do that from *this* home."

Alice rose and took several steps away from the table. Her arms crossed by her chest, she leaned against the wall. Denise sat still, her elbows on the table, and her hands covering her face. "My trainer is giving me free lessons because he had a lot of respect for Dad. I spend nights at my friend's place. You know, the one who is training with me? Dad would have approved."

"And who is your friend?" asked Denise.

"Aunt Rebecca has no problem with that."

"Alice!" Denise screamed and her fist hit the table.

"Okay, if it makes you happy, I live at Aunt Rebecca's place."

"You know you're lying!"

Junior covered his face in his hands and started to cry. Chris stopped eating.

"Mom, you're being unnecessarily unreasonable," Alice spoke with annoying calmness.

"Go to Mom's bedroom, baby," Denise said to Junior. "I love you."

Junior reluctantly stood up and ambled to Denise's room.

Denise looked up. A group of people, probably a church choir, was singing. Chris picked up Junior's plate and his own and went to the kitchen. Outside, the singing was getting louder, and Denise saw a large group of men and women congregating by her front door. "What do they want?" she asked. At the same time, she heard plates breaking in the kitchen. She sat still. If God was there, how could he allow this to happen to her family? How could he allow so much hate, so much strife? And why was God said to be a man and not a woman? A woman would have better understood the needs of her children, and the marginalization of women and people of color. Patrick was right. There was no god. He was right, and yet he was wrong when he left her and the kids.

"Do what makes you feel good, Chris," Alice shouted above the singing from outside. "Mom, we're not opening for those morons. Dad wouldn't have approved. We'll remain silent, and they will get the fuckin message and go away."

The food had not been eaten, and Denise was scared. Alice had become daringly domineering and rude. She stood up.

"Sit down, Mom!" Denise was alarmed by the tone of her daughter's voice. "I know this tiny house is full of shit, but this cleanliness is a sickness." Alice's eyes had turned red, and she was throwing her arms about. "Dad wouldn't have approved of you coming to live here. No, Mom, let me finish. Do you know how gross, embarrassing it is to belong to this family?"

"Alice, it's because your dad isn't here that it's *gross*—whatever you call it."

"He isn't here because he's dead!" Alice snapped.

Denise felt a sense of complete loss, an emptiness, a heaviness in the stomach that made her feel exhausted and nauseous. "Maybe you can tell me how he died?"

"Mom, all I'm saying is, cleaning and cleaning this place all the time won't change things. You can't clean shit, Mom!"

Junior came out of Denise's room and dashed for the boys' room.

"How dare you speak to me like that?" Denise pointed a shaking finger at Alice, who grabbed a piece of paper from the table, shred it into tiny pieces, and scattered those on the shiny floor.

With her heart pounding in her ears, Denise got closer to Alice and slapped her across the face. Seeing that Alice continued to stare at her in arrogant silence, Denise slapped her daughter again, and her hand hurt.

"Go on, kill me. You killed Dad, didn't you?"

"Child..." Denise sat down. The little girl she had carried in her womb had turned into an animal. She wished she could simply disown Alice and die. Outside, the choir was even louder, and that was so infuriating.

"Mom, I want Daddy," Junior said from the doorway of the boys' room.

One more plate or glass fell to pieces in the kitchen. Outside, the singing crowd was getting hysterical, singing a hymn or song Denise had never heard before. She sat still in a chair, Junior's head resting on her lap.

"Alice, my child," Denise had calmed down. She needed to show leadership. "I've never wanted to lay my hands on any one of you. You know that. But this nonsense must end today." She noticed that Junior was dozing and that the choir outside had stopped singing.

No longer in combative mode, Alice pressed various parts of her face with her forefingers. "You hurt me. But I forgive you."

"Your dad is not here, and you still must respect me. I'm your mother."

"I know. But you hurt me."

"Alice, listen to me. Do you want to see me dead?"

"Again, you're shouting, Mom. You're a violent woman." Hearing the anger in her daughter's voice made Denise wish she would lock herself in her room and stay away from life. She would never hit any of her children again, for they too were suffering intensely from the trauma of the loss of their father.

"Mom, were you cheating on him? Just asking."

"How dare you?"

"I'm sorry, Mom. I'm just...you know, confused."

Junior sprang to his feet. "I want Daddy!" he said groggily, arms spread wide apart as if he was pleading to be protected from an invisible enemy.

Denise lifted Junior and took him to her room. It had been a long time since she had lifted him, and he felt heavy. It was always Patrick who lifted their children when they were toddlers.

She put Junior on her bed, walked past Alice, and got to the kitchen door. The choir outside had disbanded, and Chris was staring at the sink, broken China and glass on the floor.

"You have something to say?" asked Denise.

Chris shrugged.

"Son, I want to hear your voice."

"Nothing."

Denise noticed that her son was beginning to sound like Patrick—a deep, smooth, and confident voice. "Only to say that the human race lacks humor, full color, no grace but rancor, no social welfare, just rage and societal warfare."

Denise managed a smile. "That sounds like my boy." She walked back to her bedroom, where she lay next to her son. She hoped Alice wouldn't follow her there, for she wouldn't know how to be civil.

Rebecca called. Why did people always call at the wrong time?

"Hello," Denise whispered.

"What's wrong with your voice?"

"Junior is sleeping."

"Denise, be smart. If Junior sleeps now, he won't sleep in the night. What's your next step?"

"Next step?"

"Yes, about your husband. Or have you forgotten him already?"

"You know you're being unfair."

"Don't interrupt me when I'm talking about my only brother. Have you ever lost a brother? Have you? Now, calm down. We need to come up with a plan. A beautiful girl like you, you can't suffer in a city where half the rich men are hungry and cheaters."

The line was dead. Denise grunted and shook her head slowly. She was beginning to hate Rebecca, And she felt rotten for hitting her daughter. She had never done that to any of her kids. And Patrick was to blame. Patrick had left not because she, his wife, had done anything wrong.

She got back to the living room, where Alice sat in a chair, lost in thought, her fingers pressing parts of her face as if she was looking for ways to build a tight case against her mother.

"Alice, will you promise you and I will never fight again?"

"Mom, I'm sorry."

Denise wished she and her daughter would hug and become friends. But Alice had always been Daddy's girl, and Denise never understood why.

Chris came out of the kitchen and scurried to the boys' bedroom.

"Won't you say something, Chris?" Denise asked as the boys' bedroom door closed gently behind her elder son.

"You miss him, don't you?" Suddenly, Alice was calm. "Talk to me, woman to woman. It's the sex, isn't it? You miss it, I know."

Denise felt a tightness in the chest, and for a moment, she feared she was going to have a heart attack. She tried to swallow, but without success. What had happened to the world?

"Alice, what's wrong with you?"

Alice stood up and walked around the table, and before her mother, she went down on her knees.

"You have disrespected me, Alice." Denise wished she had never married Patrick. That would have meant not having the kids whom she loved so much. But maybe having Alice wasn't a blessing? No, she still forgave her daughter. It was Patrick she couldn't forgive. "I'm your mother, but I'll not embrace you, you hear?"

"I'm sorry," Alice whispered and sat in the chair next to Denise's. "I know about sex, Mom."

"You *what*?"

"I'm having sex. It's great sometimes. It's, uh...confusing."

"So, who's this...this guy?"

"Alex."

"Alex MacKinnon?" Alice nodded. "But he's white, Alice!"

"*But* I'm not a racist. Why, you have white blood in you."

"No, Alice, I'm black!" Denise realized she had raised her voice. She didn't want the boys to hear her and Alice talk that way. "Okay, honey, I don't want to hear you talk about white blood ever again. It wasn't out of choice. It was about slavery. A white Portuguese man or whatever, he came from Angola and raped my great-great-grandmother, and...I don't want to talk about it, okay?"

"I'm just saying, Mom, you and Dad speak the same language, but here you are, talking to us in the white man's language." Shaking her head, Denise gave her daughter an angry look. "Why didn't you teach us *our* language, and now you don't want me to marry a white boy whose language is English like me?"

For the first time since the family moved to the compound house, Denise wished her daughter hadn't come home. She didn't like the topic before them. She thought about the MacKinnons. They were a nice white family and neighbors when Patrick and Denise lived in a company house in Olympia Park which, before the country's independence, was a whites-only suburb. Alex, who was merely a year older than Alice, was the MacKinnons' only child. He and Alice had known each other from childhood, playing together in both family homes and in the yard, unaware that there was racism out there in the world.

Alice clicked her fingers. Denise stared at the empty ketchup bottle that faced upside down on the other end of the table. She wondered how Patrick would have handled their daughter.

"Every mother has a dream for her children. Finish high school, go to college, play professional tennis, maybe, and promote the family name. No parent wants to see her children end up as housemaids. Never." Denise's breath quickened. "So, you guys are practicing safe sex?"

"Me and Alex, we don't believe in condoms," Alice said assertively as if she had made the most important statement of her lifetime. "Alex says that's from the sixties. We believe in nature. Like you, I don't want to talk about it. Alex's parents are paying my school fees."

Denise's wide-open mouth felt dry. The MacKinnons were paying Alice's school fees? Without consulting her? Alice was lying. "Child, you know about AIDS, STDs, pregnancies?"

"Me and Alex, we know about all that, Mom."

Seeing no point in pursuing the issue, Denise said, "Okay, your dad told me something I never told anybody." Alice was listening attentively. "He said he suspected one of the workshop participants was a spy. Just suspected."

Alice stood up. "Why didn't you tell me? I'm his firstborn child, Mom." She looked at the roof and held her head in both hands. "So, the spy killed Dad?" She covered her nose and looked around the house. "Where's your toilet?"

Denise pointed in the direction of the toilet. The bathroom was so close to the kitchen, she had asked the landlord why that was so, especially when the ventilation in there wasn't so good. The landlord had said that's how the house was planned.

Alice got to the bathroom door, grabbed the door handle and pulled.

"It's a problem lock," said Denise. "Just like everything else in this house…Wait, Alice, don't tell me!" She stood up, hands drooping to her side.

Alice fell to her knees by the door and vomited. Denise gently rubbed her daughter's back, saying, "Oh, my goodness, Alice! Don't tell me."

"I'm sorry, Mom. This place and our lives makes me sick."

"*Make*," said Denise.

"Who cares about your school grammar?"

Her entire body shaking and feeling cold, Denise concluded that life had no meaning. She found a curtain from the old house and went down on her knees to mop the floor as Alice vacantly looked on. The door to the boys' room opened slightly, only to close gently.

"It was an accident, Mom," said Alice.

Again, Denise wished she would drop dead.

CHAPTER 31

Alice left for her new home, but that night, Denise felt emotionally drained, and sleep eluded her for hours. How could her daughter, smart as she was, allow herself to get pregnant before she could carve out a career through a college degree? How could the MacKinnons accept someone else's daughter in their home without talking to the girl's mother?

Denise eventually fell asleep, but not for long, for she was awakened by a soft knock on her window.

She sat up, and without thinking, she said, "Who is it?"

"Come to the window, Mrs. Denise Kanya."

It was a strange man's voice. She wanted to stand up and run to her boys' room, but she couldn't move. Her heartbeat was racing, and she wished she would sink into the concrete floor under the bed.

Slowly, she got her strength back and crawled to the window, where she knelt and raised her head to the window level. With difficulty, she created a little opening in the curtains and peeped outside.

Although visibility was poor, she believed she saw three men. Two of them were putting tires on her Honda Civic, and another was at her window. She thought about her parents and Patrick, and she questioned God's existence.

"We need the car keys," the man at the window said casually. It was as if he was asking his girlfriend to pass him a beer. "You scream, we shoot your sons—Chris and Junior. I know your girl is not here. She's beautiful."

"Please, don't. I'll get the keys."

"Call the police if you want," the man said in good English. "They won't come."

"No, I'll get the keys, sir."

"Better hurry. We don't have time for lazybones." The man laughed.

Denise felt the warmth of her urine trip between her thighs.

Outside, a car engine started. "Forget it," said the man. "We don't need the keys."

Denise remained still, hoping the man wouldn't shoot her boys through the window. But before long, the car drove away, its fading sound replaced by the sound of barking dogs mingled with those of the other cars that ceaselessly pounded the rugged roads of the compound.

"Sister Rebecca," she said into the cellphone.

"You're calling me at this hour? Has he come?"

Denise cut the line.

Rebecca called back after the sun had come up. "I'm sorry about everything. I never mean it when I say you should find a rich man. You know that, don't you?"

"That's fine," said Denise. "I'm not a whore. Anyway, we are all suffering. We've lost a loved one. We all think he's dead, and yet none of us can produce his body. So, we're entitled to bad behavior, but not all the time."

"No, no, no, don't say that, my dear. His *body*? No, Dee. I don't think Patrick is a *body*, no." Rebecca cleared her throat. "My baby brother is there somewhere, alive and kicking like a strong horse. I can feel it in my bones."

Denise wanted to say that her car had been stolen, but she changed her mind. "By the way, I received a call from his former employers. They want me to talk about my situation on TV. What do you think?"

"A TV interview? It's okay if you want to be a celebrity, that's fine. Just don't say anything negative about my family."

Junior was knocking impatiently on the bedroom door, so Denise excused herself and ended the call.

"Where's the car, Mom?" asked Junior. He jumped into bed, where his father was supposed to be. Denise had no intention of telling the boys about the men who had come in the night. Neither would she tell the boys that their sister was pregnant and eloping with a boy whose parents she knew well. In any case, Junior was already snoring.

Hours later, Denise called the television producer who had contacted her the previous day. "I'll talk to you, but on my terms," she said.

The car from the television station came much earlier than she had expected, so she told the driver that she wasn't ready.

"My boss told me to wait, madam," said the driver. He waited for an hour, and as Denise got in the passenger seat of the company's Toyota Corolla, she saw a man peeping through one of the windows of the yellow house. She stared back, and the man left the window.

Facing the imposing redbrick building in which Patrick had worked for years made her wonder what it was that Patrick had been doing behind those walls that got him into trouble, ending with him running away. How much spy work was done behind those walls, if any?

She had put on a business suit and just the right amount of makeup, but the show's producer insisted that the television makeup artist should redo Denise's face. She was pleasantly surprised by the result. Perhaps Aunt Rebecca was right; Denise was still as beautiful as she had always been.

Fondly known as 'Gina' by the nation, Georgina Mopane was ZNBC's most celebrated show hostess. She sat with Denise before the planned recording of her popular prerecorded primetime show titled *The Woman Within*.

"Your responses will come from the heart," said Gina. "So, we won't discuss anything before the recording."

"I understand the heart thing, Gina," said Denise. "But suppose I don't like what I've said? Would you remove or edit that out?"

"Yes, of course."

Moments later, Gina introduced Denise on camera. "She's my former boss's beautiful wife." Ten minutes into the recording, Gina asked, "I can't pretend I know what it is to lose a hubby in the fashion my former boss left, Mrs. Kanya. I want to know what you tell your children every morning. You know, that your hubby, their dad, isn't coming home? Or that he's dead?"

Denise had no intention of being uncooperative. But suddenly, she felt as if she was giving too much personal information to the public. "Why do you keep referring to my husband as 'hubby'?"

"Are you taking issue with that term, Mrs. Kanya?" Denise wiped a tear from her cheek. "I'm sorry, madam. Your husband was my boss. I knew him, too, and I miss him."

"Really? Do you know what it is to lose your husband, one you loved with all your heart, and you don't know if he's dead or alive, living with…?"

"Living with?"

Denise shrugged.

"Madam, we're on camera, and I apologize. Let's get back to…where were we? So, are you open to closely examining the circumstances that led to him leaving you, say, with a therapist? Why should a man walk away from a woman who's as beautiful, highly educated, and articulate as you? Three weeks ago, on this program, we heard how our guest, a lady, talked about how women can molest men emotionally. Emotional abuse. So, while women do not possess the physical strength that men have, they can use psychology to mess up men."

"Gina, are you suggesting that I emotionally abused my husband and drove him out of my life, his children's lives, and out of his native land?"

"I'm not suggesting that!" To Denise, Gina sounded unbelievably combative. "I'm merely saying that…"

Denise stood up. "Gina, I knew it was a mistake for me to come here."

"I'm sorry."

Outside, by the building's main exit, Denise told the corporation driver that she would find her way back home.

"No, madam," said the driver. "Don't worry about her. She is a crazy woman."

As the car approached the main road, Denise said, "You mean you already heard what happened in there?"

"No secrets here, madam," said the driver.

Denise pondered the question she had always wanted to ask: Was Patrick having an affair at the office? If there were no secrets at the television station, wouldn't the driver know? But wouldn't asking that question lead to more rumors?

"Tell me, sir," she said against her better judgment, "did you know if my husband was friends with any of your women here?"

"Only Miss Gina, madam."

Denise scratched her jaw. She wished she hadn't asked. But when the driver stopped the vehicle at her home, he said, "Only Miss Gina knows about every rumor, madam. Too many bad rumors at station. Mr. Kanya, he was a good man. I know you, you're very beautiful woman, madam."

As she watched the television car drive away, again she saw the man next door peep through a vent in the curtains.

The boys were not home. On the dining room table, a note read: *Mom, I took the boys to the cinema.*

Denise had a quick bath. She got in bed and berated herself for agreeing to discuss her husband on television. She should have listened to Rebecca. But soon, sleep came, and she was only awakened by Alice and the boys, who got back home just before dusk.

Soon after she had reluctantly risen from the bed, Denise stood by the living room window, where she listened to her children's chatter and laughter as they stood in the small verandah of the house, waiting for a car Alice said was going to take her "home." Someone had just used the toilet, and the stench from there had spread to the living room. She opened the window to let the air in and braced herself for a meeting with the MacKinnons. She would not mince her words when they came to pick up her daughter.

"Guys, listen," Denise heard Alice say. "I left school. I'm a housewife now." Denise saw her daughter touch her tummy. "You have a nephew inside there, boys."

"Cool," said Junior. "And his name is going to be Patrick, *not* Chris. Then we can go back to our nice house in Meanwood."

Denise wished she would just disappear from the surface of the earth. Maybe, like Patrick, she could find a way to escape the vagaries of life? She could go to Britain. South Africa. It was sad to see Junior looking so elated at the news of having a nephew soon.

Alice pointed at a wooden roof beam that crudely stuck out, the work of a job not done right by a poorly-paid hand. "You see that wooden thing?" she asked. "I hate it. I hate this house, too. It's like it's going to fall on me and kill me."

"Are you going to die?" Junior sounded alarmed.

Denise opened the window wide. "Alice, you don't say things like that to your brothers."

"I'm not superstitious, Mom," Alice retorted. "Just because people talk about things doesn't mean those things will happen." A car stopped in front of the house. "That's my ride, Mom. Bye."

Alice embraced and kissed her brothers. Denise was disappointed not to see the MacKinnons in the car.

That night, as Denise stayed awake in bed, she admitted that she had lost her only daughter. Since Patrick's departure, Alice had moved out and become pregnant and arrogant.

She thought about the many things she could do to get out of poverty. But first, she had to admit that she would never see Patrick again. She could start a nonprofit organization on abandoned wives. Who could she approach for help? She remembered the women she was with at the university who had become big names in the nation. Even though she worked for a bank, Lisa Daka-Tau was the chairperson of a nonprofit organization that empowered women in all areas of life. Hazel Omei had become famous for being the attorney of choice for women's causes. But both women carried a big sin: they had slept with Patrick while he was engaged to her. For that reason, she wouldn't go to them for help.

She remembered that Lisa, who could persuade her husband, Norman Tau, to pay Patrick's terminal benefits, was her biggest adversary. During a beauty contest at the university, everyone believed Denise was going to be crowned queen. Everything was going fine until Denise objected to wearing too much makeup from the sponsors of the pageant. "She won't win this, this stubborn girl!" she had overheard one of the organizers say. Lisa won the pageant, and the two girls were never to see eye to eye again.

It was 4:00 am, and Denise got out of bed. From her nightstand, she took out a photo album and turned the pages: Each one of her children as a baby. Patrick, herself, and their kids are in several photos, everyone saying, "Cheers!" She put away the album and searched her phone. Videos of Patrick and the many text messages they had exchanged before he left and while he was in the US.

"Oh, darling," she whispered. "Whatever happened to you, I want you to know that we miss you. If you are dead, I hope you died a painless death, and that you were given a respectable funeral. If you're still alive and well, I hope you can forgive me if I'm the reason for your absence." She sobbed and dried her tears, only to begin crying again. "But I hope you're happy, sweetheart. We all wish you well. Please, come back to us. I'll always be your good, faithful, black woman. Rebecca told me she thinks you're eloping with a white woman. I know she's wrong, sweetheart. I know you better than she does. I'm your wife and always will be."

Again, she couldn't hold back the tears, but when she heard someone at the bedroom door, she quickly dried her tears with one of her bedsheets. Junior came in. Denise thought she had locked the door.

"My friend say mommies can't sleep when the husband is dead."

Denise thought about what to say to her son, but within seconds, Junior was asleep. She lifted him, took him back to the boys' bedroom and tucked him up in his bed.

She got back to her bedroom, feeling exhausted. Sleep slowly caught up with her, and Patrick was smiling at her, and she wasn't amused. He made love to her, and she told him marrying him was the biggest mistake she had ever made. He laughed. He was laughing at her, so she hit him in the face, and her left arm hurt.

She woke up, and her left arm was still hurting.

She thought about how much she had loved Patrick from their university days. He was every woman's dream. Tall. Handsome. Athletic. A great demeanor. She remembered how jealous she would feel whenever she saw him share a joke with a female classmate.

Eventually, the bright Southern African summer sun was up. She needed someone to talk to about starting a nonprofit. So, she dialed Rebecca's number.

"Why do you call me at three in the morning? Dee, could my brother be gay? Maybe he left you to marry another man. Have you ever thought about that? Anyway, you called. You want to hear me say it's okay for you to find yourself a man?"

"Sister Rebecca, how can you be so cruel to me? It's not three in the morning, and it's not right to treat me this way."

"You called me at three the other night. Hey, I wasn't cruel to my brother to make him leave. Go on and find a new man. Isn't that what you wanted when you made sure he never came back? Who cares? You miss it so much, go get it."

"Why must I deserve this, Sister Rebecca?"

"You must know what you did to him for him to run away from you."

"No, I don't!"

"Don't raise your voice! Well, did he tell you that I told him not to marry you? I said you were much, much, too, too old for him. A man always marries a woman several years younger than him, and not the other way round. Maybe he ran away from bad sex? I've heard that beautiful women are never good in bed."

Denise felt warm tears drop to her cheeks, and she let them fall to one of the pillows Patrick had used for years. She had used those pillows since he hadn't shown up at the airport. "He loved me." She started to sob. "We loved each other very much. We had great sex."

"I know, I know," Rebecca said. It was obvious that she, too, was sobbing.

"You may not believe this, but in my entire life, I've slept with only one man. I don't intend to sleep with another."

Rebecca blew her nose and said, "Just like you said, I don't believe you, of course. Okay, Ben, let me talk to Denise first. Dee, I don't think you understand what I'm going through, losing my little brother. I understand your pain, too. But please never wake me up at this hour again to cause me so much emotional pain. Patrick's disappearance is like your flesh being cut off from you and dumped at sea, so you never see that part of you again." There was a pause. Denise didn't want to aggravate the situation, so she chose to remain silent. She heard Rebecca blow her nose. Denise removed the cellphone from her right ear and looked at the receiver. The line was dead. She thought about calling Rebecca again. No, if she did, she would utter the wrong words. Between Rebecca and her, Denise would always choose to be the mature one.

CHAPTER 32

Patrick stood before the big mirror in his bathroom, the haircutting kit Aretha had bought for him from Amazon and a small mirror his only tools. Cutting his hair according to the photo on D'Angelo's driver's license wasn't much of a challenge, for he had cut his sons' hair and his own many times before. D'Angelo was slightly shorter than him, so the height would not pose a problem. What Patrick couldn't do anything about was to change his dark complexion to D'Angelo's light skin like Denise's. Next, he sat at the study table by the window and practiced D'Angelo's signature.

The following day, Patrick spent hours taking notes as D'Angelo narrated his childhood tales at Ramstein Air Force base in West Germany, where his father was stationed.

"When you get a job and you do your tax returns," D'Angelo concluded, "I'll claim all of them. That's what we did with the other African guy who stayed here last year. He was happy with that, and left when he got married." Patrick didn't care about tax returns. All he wanted was a job. "Try to learn to speak like an African American. The other guy didn't speak well like you. He said back home, he spoke French or African. But he did well."

Patrick had already thought about his accent. "That's no problem. I know you people have laws not to discriminate against people with disabilities. I will not be speaking. I'll have a throat ailment that has taken away my voice."

"What?" D'Angelo's mouth opened wide and stayed that way for a little longer than Patrick expected. "What kind of guy are you? But hey, if you get caught, I'll say I don't know you. You hear me, my man? *You* stole my license from my mother."

By the end of the day, both Patrick and D'Angelo were exhausted. Patrick concluded that D'Angelo was a good man.

In the evening, Patrick walked up the hill to the main road, counting the cars that were parked in front of the homes. He had counted more than a hundred when he heard a male voice behind him.

"You good?"

Patrick turned to look behind him. He had seen the small Latino man before. On some occasions, the two had waved and smiled at each other. He lived in the house across the street, and he seemed to be a pleasant man, probably full of humor, his big eyes telling Patrick that he was hungry for friendship.

"Me, Julio," said the man. Dressed in work clothes, Julio seemed to be slightly younger than Patrick. "I see you other husbands for Ms. Aretha?"

"Another husband? Ah, you mean, she's my wife?" Patrick chuckled. "No, me, not husband to Ms. Aretha."

"So, in bed, she good?"

"No, no…" Patrick forgave the man's lack of social skills. He looked too human, too simple, too unpretentious not to mean well.

"No good? But she look good to me. Nice?"

"My name is Patrick. I'm renting a room from Ms. Aretha. Understand?"

"Ah! I see. She good?"

Even with the communication problem, the two men spoke for a long time while they walked in the neighborhood. When they parted, Patrick felt he had met someone to whom he could relate. Julio was a simple family man who had set his sights on the American Dream. Patrick wished he could feel that way towards the United States, too. Unlike Julio, he wasn't in the country to make a living out of choice, no. If he had a choice, he would go back home.

That night, Patrick had a nightmare.

He was standing barefoot on one side of a river. In the water, he saw snakes and crocodiles swimming together in harmony. On the other side of the river, Denise and the kids stood on the white sands of the bank and desperately waved their hands.

"It's okay here, Patrick," Denise shouted. "Please, cross the river."

A large snake got out of the water and opened its mouth...

"You gotta problem?" Aretha was pounding Patrick's door with fists.

"What time is it?" he asked.

"It's two in the morning and you were screaming. I'm worried about you."

"I'm okay," Patrick said. His neck hurt badly.

"Patrick, did you kill somebody over there in the Motherland? I hear there, too, there's black-on-black violence? I saw that *Hotel Rwanda* movie." She paused. "I know I need the rent money, Patrick, but I don't want trouble from the white man's FBI. And I can't keep you in my house if you don't tell me the truth."

"I'm good. It was a political thing." He wished he would stop telling lies about why he hadn't gone back home. "I mean..." But he knew it wouldn't be wise to tell Aretha the truth.

"Ah! I never heard you speak like that before. You always say 'I'm fine,' like you being white?"

He stayed awake long after Aretha had left his door. He had failed his family, and he hated himself.

Given a choice, Patrick would have stayed in bed because he hadn't slept well. But he just couldn't sleep.

He ate his usual breakfast of oatmeal with sugar and yogurt, while memories of his family weighed him down. The breakfast arrangement he had with Aretha wasn't working because the landlady always woke up late.

"Let me tell you something you don't know about dreams." Patrick was startled. He hadn't seen or heard Aretha place herself at the foot of the staircase, wearing her usual blue dressing gown that sometimes exposed her yellow thighs.

She got to the dining table and sat down, facing Patrick. With a smile, she looked him in the eye and said, "You look exhausted. Always sleep yourself eight hours. Did you know that videos are as old as the human race? Even dogs and cats, they carry videos in their heads. Dreams are cheap videos. They're hostile and annoying. So, don't be scared of cheap videos when you go to bed. Hey, did I tell you someone wants to hire you?"

Patrick had heard Aretha say that before. He was ready to work as D'Angelo, but where was the job?

CHAPTER 33

A woman's scream woke her up. Above the ceaseless rumbling in the sky and the pattering of rain against her window, she heard children crying. She rushed to the boys' door. It was locked. She didn't want to wake them up. Better if they didn't know what was going on in the neighborhood. Back in her room, she stood by the window until the wailing had stopped, even though the dogs continued to bark. Maybe she needed to buy a dog? But how would she feed it?

The rain was gone when the sun came up, and someone was knocking on her front door. It was a police officer. She knew she hadn't committed a crime, so what was he doing there?

"Madam, we're investigating a rape and robbery," said the officer. "Last night, did you see anyone looking suspicious here?"

"Last night?"

"Yes, several men raped a woman while her children were looking. That house over there." The officer pointed in the western direction.

"Sorry, officer, I just heard screams."

"That's what everybody says. No one saw anything."

After the officer had left, Denise sat at her small dining table and noticed that her fingers were shaking. She was surprised that the police were investigating the crime. They never came when her goods were stolen from her stolen home. If it rained again that night, she could be the next victim.

She didn't want to fail as a single mother, no. She had applied for jobs—as a teacher in Botswana and at a local international school, as a personal assistant to the managing director of an international bank, as a secretary to a transportation executive who was a fellow woman, and an administrative job at the Zambian Parliament.

Only one prospective employer had responded— "you lack teaching experience," and she was running out of money.

The sound of the phone startled her, and she answered it without even looking at it.

"I'm not coming home."

She tapped her fingers on the table and wondered for how long she would be able to continue paying the phone bill. "Alice, I'm too tired to talk."

"One burden off, Mom," Alice said jubilantly. "Your favorite white boy Alex and I are getting married."

The room seemed to be swirling around her. "Child, you're only a child..." It was as if someone had hit the top of her head with a brick. How was she to react to that? Her only daughter, the one Patrick wanted to be a journalist, had left school to marry another child like herself. Slowly, she stood up, and her knees felt so weak, it was as if she had lost half the strength in her legs.

"What do you mean, child?"

"Mom, what do you mean, what do I mean? You got married, and I'm getting married. And stop calling me 'child.' I'm going to be a mother."

"Do you and this young man know what you're doing, Alice?"

"Mom, do you know what Dad is doing? Do you know what you're going to do next? Do you have a plan to get out of your mess? Do you even know you're in a mess? I know I sound like Chris, but he's my brother."

There was a knock on the front door. Denise wasn't expecting a visitor. Again, without thinking, she found herself opening the door. It was Wizzie, the family's former gardener. Hands in pockets, he stood not far from the door.

"It's not very good to open like that," said Wizzie.

Over the line, she heard Alice say something inaudible.

"Alice, we've got to talk," Denise spoke into the phone, but Alice had cut the line. "Wizzie, what a pleasant surprise! Are you still staying at the house?"

She hadn't seen him since the afternoon she went back to her former house to salvage whatever she could after the burglars had raped Martha, the former maid.

"No, we left months ago. But you don't open the door before you see the person. That's dangerous. You heard about last night?"

She didn't like Wizzie's attitude, who, for the first time, was speaking to her with his hands in his pockets. "Yes, I heard, and thanks for the advice, Wizzie. Please come in."

They sat at the dining table, across from each other. Wizzie seemed to have gained self-esteem, but his cologne was still repellant.

"So, where do you live?" she asked. "Ah, before I forget, there's a man who keeps staring at me."

"A man?" Wizzie snorted. "You, you're a very beautiful lady." Denise saw that Wizzie was gazing at her, and she felt uncomfortable. "Boss, he shouldn't have left you like that."

"Well, Wizzie, human beings are human beings."

"I moved to the next house."

"Next door? The yellow house?"

"Yes, yes," Wizzie spoke with an air of bravado.

So, Wizzie had moved into the house the kids had wished the family had moved in; the one she had heard had better amenities than the one she occupied, but the one she couldn't afford?

"That's a good house," she said.

"The bank, they paid big for looking after your house," Wizzie said as he glanced around the house Denise was so ashamed to call home. "So, I bought house in the shanty compound. But yellow house was mine before. I have two houses." He showed her two fingers. "When Martha and me, we stayed in your servant's quarters, we saved money to buy a house. We used to joke at each other." He laughed like he was the happiest man in the world. "Like we pretended we had a house rent to pay every month. So, I put my money under the mattress, she put her money under the pillow. No rent."

"That was very smart of you. So, are you the man behind that curtain?"

He gave her a curious look. "I like you. I watch out for your safety."

"Thank you. I like you, too. You and your wife are very good people."

She didn't see his arm dart across the table like a viper, but she knew that touching her arm was extremely offensive, disgusting, nauseating, and repulsive.

"Excuse me?" she said, pulling her hand away and springing to her feet. Her nostrils twitching, and her heart beating faster, she wanted to hit her former servant with something. Anything. How dare Patrick let her status sink this low? How dare he…

"I'm sorry," Wizzie said and stood up. Quickly, he headed for the door. "You said you like me. Forgive me."

"Wizzie, I don't…I don't want us to be enemies. We're neighbors again. Please, Wizzie." There was a burning in her throat. She wanted to spit and vomit. At the same time, she knew she couldn't afford to break down in Wizzie's presence, so she turned to face away from the front door, even as she heard him close it gently.

He was gone, and she crossed the room to the door, where she stood still as if she had lost her ability to move. Moments later, Wizzie's wife, Martha, appeared in the window, carrying a large bowlful of cabbage on her head. Denise opened the door, calling, "Martha!"

Martha veered toward the front door and put the bowl on the porch. "I want to apologize, madam," she said.

"Not your fault," said Denise. "Men will always be men. Look at what mine did to me. Come in."

"So sorry. Me, I'm in much hurry. I didn't come to say we came to the house with yellow wall. Always busy, busy at the market."

The two women sat in the living room and talked at length.

"So, are you making money selling those vegetables?" Denise finally asked.

171

"Yes. You want stand at market. I get you one? Small profit, madam, but profit. But they want you to be ruling party member." Martha raised her hands. "No opposition party member, no."

"A market stand?" asked Denise, as if she hadn't understood what Martha meant — *You have become one of us.* "Yes, please, Martha. You'll show me how to do the business?"

The telephone rang, and Denise angrily looked at the number. It was a strange one, but she answered it. After all, she had responded to several job ads.

"Hi, girl!"

"Is this…Lisa?"

"Girl, give me a week or so. I'll get you a job at the bank. I promise, girl."

Did Denise really want to work under Lisa? "I'd be grateful, *girl.* I don't know how to thank you."

"Don't, till you get the job. Sorry, I'm on a short break. Will talk later."

"It was nice of you to…"

The phone was dead. Denise knew then that when your husband leaves you, and you are broke, it's not you who chooses when people speak to you and when to end the conversation. Rebecca was not the only one who had perfected that rule.

"I go now, madam." Martha, too, was ending their conversation.

"I'm glad you stopped by," said Denise.

Martha opened the door, and Denise saw her former maid lurch over and clutch her abdomen. A guttural sound followed, and Denise rushed to the door. What would people say if Martha died in her house?

"Martha, what is it?"

Martha seemed to have lost her voice. Denise saw that Martha's bowl of vegetables was gone. Denise remembered the days when Martha and her husband depended on her and Patrick for their livelihood. If Patrick hadn't left, Martha wouldn't need to carry a heavy bowl of cabbage on her head. She wished she had the money to help Martha regain what she had lost. But as things were, it was probable Martha had more money than Denise.

"I'm so sorry, Martha," said Denise as Martha dejectedly walked towards the yellow house.

CHAPTER 34

Christmas was approaching, and Patrick had missed a month's rent, but Aretha said she understood. He would pay her when he got a job.

Hungry and dejected, he ambled down the stairs. He didn't believe in miracles. He had to find a solution to his crisis soon. Still, though, going back home hadn't become an option.

"Patrick, you should eat something," Aretha said from the dining table, the aroma of the food on her plates making Patrick salivate. On several occasions, he had turned down Aretha's food offers as he didn't want to get into deeper debt.

"I'm okay, Ms. Aretha," said Patrick.

"No, you should eat," Aretha said, and she rose and strode to the kitchen.

"Seriously, I'm not hungry."

"Oh, yes, you are!" Aretha insisted, and already, she was preparing a meal for him. "Sit down."

Patrick had no choice. He had to eat something, or else his body would stop functioning soon.

"Did I tell you they're hiring seasonal staff at the supermarket?" Aretha put the plate of food on the table. "I spoke to someone in HR. You know I used to be an HR director?" Aretha laughed, and Patrick sat down. "Do you celebrate Christmas back home?"

"Many people do, but I don't."

"So, you're a Moslem? This is not a Christmas meal. Look, pork. Eat."

The following day, Aretha drove Patrick to a supermarket in her red 1976 Cadillac Seville.

"You like the car?" she asked, and he nodded. The car was clean inside and out. "D'Angelo sold it to me for one dollar after he bought that truck. Did you see me over the weekend? No. My friend and I, we was flying over North Africa. I fought there during the Second World War Two. I was the only female colonel." She looked at him with a broad smile. "Do you know that if you was a slave, you'd be a breeder?"

Patrick had no idea in what context Aretha was referring to him as a breeder, so he chose to remain silent. He was getting very concerned about Aretha's state of mind.

Welcome Supermarket was a national chain whose slogan was *We Sell Everything a Kitchen Needs.* From kitchenware to groceries, Welcome Supermarket had it all on its shelves.

Aretha led the way to the back end of the store, and in a long passageway, a young female associate said the HR manager was not in the office.

"She knows about you," Aretha said. "I spoke to her. If she says she don't know you, just come back home, Patrick. Remember, you lost your voice. And if you do a good job, they will hire you permanently. It's up to you. You know how to get home? It's a five-minute walk from here, that way." She pointed in the wrong direction. Patrick had walked that distance before, and on each occasion, it had taken him no less than twenty minutes to get home.

Patrick sat on a bench, not far from a set of computers. Watching Aretha leave reminded him of his first day at school. Both his parents had escorted him to the classroom, and he felt vulnerable after they left. But he had survived the day, and he was confident he would survive his first day at the supermarket—that was if Aretha had secured him a job.

For half an hour, associates kept passing by, and none said a word to him. Just as well. He wasn't ready to put the notebook and permanent marker on his lap to use yet.

"D'Angelo?"

He looked up.

"I'm Cicely from HR," a black lady introduced herself, and they shook hands.

Patrick almost said, "Pleased to meet you," but he remembered he was supposed to have lost his voice. He nodded.

Her tiny office had no door, just a wide entrance. "Sit down," she said. "Your mother told me about your situation." She winked at him. "Don't mess up, D'Angelo," she whispered. "I've helped you people before. My first husband was African. I understand what it means to be black *and* African, *and* an immigrant. It's hard even for us who are American."

He applied for the job on a PC, and soon after, his future section manager, a young white woman took him outside the store. "They call me Olivia," she said. "We work outside, rain or shine, snow, heat, all the above," she said, her body movements synchronized perfectly with her melodious voice, and Patrick kept nodding. "You'll join a group of three other cart pushers who work rotating shifts."

After making Patrick clock in—a concept Patrick wasn't familiar with—Olivia led Patrick outside.

"Leroy!" Olivia called out. A young man abandoned a train of shopping carts and hurried toward Patrick and Olivia. "Meet your new teammate."

Feeling breathless, Patrick stared at the young man. Except for his age, Leroy was the spitting image of the son he had abandoned back home.

"Patrick, Leroy is going to be your trainer," said Olivia. "Leroy has one story after another to tell all day, so beware of that." Olivia laughed uproariously. Studying the parking lot for the first time as an associate, Patrick was surprised to see how large the area was. Some carts needed to be collected from long distances. "Leroy, your friend here, he has a voice problem." As she turned away, she mumbled, "God, they never warned me they were bringing me a movie star."

Leroy waited until Olivia had left before he said, "She likes you, man. Your a movie star, man."

Using his notepad and a permanent marker, Patrick wrote: *I'm no movie star.*

As the day progressed, Patrick learned that to get along with Leroy, he had to agree that the supermarket's management team was incompetent and racist. Leroy also spent long work periods in the restroom, leaving Patrick to do most of the work. "Don't work too hard," was Leroy's way of justifying his transgressions.

The work wasn't as easy as Patrick had expected—*just pushing carts*—but it was doable. Ironically, it was slightly more challenging than pushing D'Angelo's self-propelling lawnmower. Instead of customers leaving shopping carts in designated stations, they left them scattered all over the parking lot. Patrick's task was to assemble the carts, hook them to a powered cart mover and steer them to a place near the entrance to the store. At thirty-two hours per week, with a wage of $8.50 per hour, Patrick reckoned he would be making about two hundred dollars a week, so he would be able to pay his rent and even save a little.

One afternoon, after a long day at work, Patrick was leaving the supermarket when he saw her. Except for her age—she was slightly older—the woman who was pushing a buggy towards a white Cadillac Escalade was a Denise double. His stomach tightening, he watched her remove her shopping from the buggy. He watched her put the shopping in the trunk of her vehicle, one or two bags at a time. He watched her close the trunk and gently push the buggy to the nearest cart corral. Was nature trying to tell him something? Leroy resembled Chris, and now, he was looking at Denise's double?

Minutes later, he punched out and walked home, his head hurting. He missed his family. He missed Denise in bed, in the kitchen, and he missed the kids. He missed the African sun, the languages, and the rainy season's petrichor.

He was the only person walking, so he allowed himself to sob without restraint. But soon, he was in Aretha's subdivision, and he calmed himself.

"*Hola!*" Patrick looked behind him. "Hi, how are you, Julio?"

"Ah, you good man. Remember my name?"

"Julio. That's an easy one."

"Ah, my friend. I see you at supermarket," said Julio. "Is good job?"

Patrick was in no mood for small talk. All he wanted was to get to his room and sleep, dream bad dreams about his family and wake up the next day and go back to work. "Yeah, it's a good job," he said.

"So, I hear, you from New York, yes?"

"Yes."

"Okay, you do me sometimes good," said Julio.

"Good sometimes?"

"Ah, like something." Patrick nodded, prodding Julio to go on and say what he wanted to say, for Patrick wanted to leave. "I say, so you marry my wife, she get papers." Patrick shook his head and laughed. "You see my wife in window? My wife, you don't like? She no good?"

Patrick looked up. A Latino woman was standing behind the bedroom window of Julio's home.

"Me, already married," said Patrick.

"Ah, to Ms. Aretha?" Patrick nodded. "Good, good. Me, don't know much. But joking only."

Patrick liked Julio. He was the only man from the neighborhood who had ever spoken to him. He also loved the way Julio spoke English. He reminded him of the way Maxx and Martha spoke. Denise would have said that all the three had a problem with the use of auxiliary verbs and articles.

"Okay, I go now, my friend," said Patrick. "You, me, we speak tomorrow."

"Good man, you."

When Patrick got home, Aretha was preparing a meal in the kitchen.

"Do you think you'll manage this job?" she asked. "You look very tired and sad."

"I whisper and use my notebook," said Patrick. "My biggest challenge is to ensure that I don't speak aloud."

"Good," she said. "You'll be able to pay the rent. And I want you to feel comfortable in this home and in this country. I didn't go out today. The police are shooting every black man they see."

Patrick got to his room and sat on the bed. He accepted the fact that just like Aretha faced some mental health issues, he too needed to resolve his survival issues. He needed someone to confide in, someone who would understand, without judging him, why he could not go back home. Someone trustworthy, but certainly not Pastor Gawo.

CHAPTER 35

Denise sat on her twin bed, her chin cupped in her hands and her cellphone on her lap. For days, she had avoided doing it. Just how could she bring herself to say what she had to say?

She dialed the number. "My sister, I don't know how to say this, but we can't pay the rent."

She heard children's voices outside, and she knew those were not her boys playing. Chris and Junior rarely left their bedroom on the weekends.

She didn't like Rebecca's silence, for it kept her guessing. She was glad that she hadn't told Rebecca that the family could no longer afford more than one decent meal a day. Sometimes, their breakfast consisted of sweet potatoes taken with black tea.

"Listen, girl," Rebecca sounded cold. Denise wanted to hang up, but did she have a choice? Her sons were Rebecca's nephews. "It seems to me like my boy isn't coming home."

"But how do you know, my sister?"

"Let me talk, Denise. You can't afford to be arrogant. Listen, you didn't tell me about my niece. She's pregnant, and she tells me you were mad with her. What?"

"Sister Rebecca…"

"I haven't finished," Rebecca snapped. "Did Patrick leave because you two had problems in bed? Tell me. Correct me if I'm wrong, but whenever I saw him, he looked like the only bull in the kraal."

"Sister Rebecca, you keep asking about that. Let me say it one more time: Patrick and I had *no* problems in bed. You remember your niece saying at the meeting that we used to quarrel at night?"

"Yes, Denise. That's why I laughed." Rebecca chortled.

"Then you know that we had a good, noisy time in bed. He would always ask me to lower my voice."

"I don't need the details, Denise. But what I'm saying is…okay, go on. Are you there?"

"Yes, I'm here."

"I don't believe you can't get a job. You have a university education. You're a single woman, and you're still very, very beautiful even by my very high standards, so why don't you make use of that beauty? Lots of rich men would hire you just for looking good, pay well for…"

Denise hung up, sprung to her feet, and within seconds, she was in the living room. Her breathing labored, she sat at the dining table for a long time before Junior came out of the boys' bedroom. He headed for the kitchen, from where he emerged with a glass of tap water and sat on the other side of the table. To Denise's surprise, Junior gulped the water down. Her poor boy had never liked drinking water, let alone tap water. "It has no taste, Mommy," was his usual argument.

"Mom, are you sick?" asked Junior. Denise nodded. "I'm sick, too." Denise touched her son's forehead. He had a fever. "My friend at school, he said, don't worry, you have your mother, no father. His mother, his father, they all died."

"I'm so sorry to hear that, sweetheart."

"We saw our furniture, Mom,"

The boys' bedroom door opened wide. Chris came out and pulled a dining chair, the scraping noise it made on the concrete floor making Denise overly edgy. She was grateful her boys understood why she could no longer serve three decent daily meals at that table or provide bottled drinking water.

"It's true, Mom," said Chris. "What Junior said? We saw our furniture next door."

"Yellow house?" Denise whispered. The boys nodded. "The bastard! I'm sorry. What furniture?"

"The stolen furniture, Mom," said Chris. "Uncle Wizzie. He has it in his house."

"Are you sure?" Denise asked, and her phone rang.

"You called, and I'm here," Rebecca was at the front door.

Denise glided to the door, opened it and shouted, "How *dare* you say I should become a whore!"

"I didn't mean that," Rebecca said calmly. "I'm just suggesting that with your great looks, you could easily get a great job."

"No, Rebecca, you said any man could pay..."

"Again, you're being unnecessarily argumentative, and in front of my nephews. Boys, go out and play." Chris and Junior reluctantly dilly-dallied to their bedroom. "I was in the neighborhood, and had already brought groceries for myself, so I'm giving them to my nephews. And again, beautiful women have influence over men who matter. That's what I meant. You have a good education. Analyze, understand simple things, Denise. Be strong."

"Are you going to ask them, Mom?" Chris was standing behind the partially-open boys' bedroom door. "About the furniture?"

"No, my dear. That furniture is sold to anyone who has the money to buy it from any furniture outlet."

"What are you two talking about?" asked Rebecca. "Come on, you didn't even say Hi! to auntie. Close the door. Mom and auntie are talking adult issues. I said the groceries, Denise." She sat on the sofa. "In the car."

As she picked up plastic bags of groceries, Denise wished Rebecca had given her the money instead of giving her groceries. Did Rebecca not consider her good enough to know what the family needed?

She put the groceries in the kitchen, and when she got back in the living room, Rebecca said," How are you doing for utilities?"

While Denise wondered if her sister-in-law's mood swings had anything to do with bipolar disorder, for the first time, she saw a relationship between Rebecca's gruff behavior and Big Maxx's lack of civility. Both could be cantankerous and annoying, and yet they could be very nice and kind.

"If I can't find a job, I'll start some business of some kind," said Denise.

"Business? No, start an NGO, girl. You were at school with Susan. Well, she started an NGO, and now, she's swimming in money." Rebecca put an envelope on a side table. "Money for your rent. One month only. Your landlord can go to hell if he insists on three months. What I said on the phone? Forget it. It's just tough girl talk, that's all."

"Thank you. I worry about the boys, Aunt Rebecca. They come from school, eat whatever there is to eat, and they find refuge in their tiny room. There's no more laughter in this house. Chris never says a word unless he's talked to."

"They'll get over it. I remember the day our parents brought baby Patrick home," Rebecca said, looking at her fingernails. "I was five, and he was a day old. It was getting cold, and it rained that day, in late April. Yes, I remember the rain. He was wrapped up in blankets. I was jealous. It was like, he's here to take my place. And yet I loved him so, so very much." She covered her face in her hands. "Patrick has always been my little boy. It's me who told him to read journalism at the university. I've been his mother since our parents passed on. And about our parents, well, that's another story."

"I know about your mother," said Denise. Rebecca stood up and dried her face with a hankie. "I don't want to talk about my mother. But, you know, I'll never stop waiting for Patrick until I see his grave. Let his boys stay in their rooms if that's their choice."

Long after Rebecca had left, Denise was still standing in front of her house, thinking about how to start a nonprofit, when five men in their early twenties appeared. They stood in a line across the road and stared at her.

"What can I do for you, gentlemen?" she shouted. She was scared, and she wished she had just gone back into the house and closed the door, but she thought it necessary to show courage.

The boys walked lackadaisically towards her. The sun was bright, and there were people everywhere. She hadn't seen Wizzie since the day he offended her, but she hoped he was home. Wizzie would protect her.

The boys got close, stood at attention, the way soldiers did, and one of them spoke softly. "We salute you, madam. Your beauty belongs to Hollywood, not here. Me, I promise, I can make you happy. Where is your husband?"

"Are you seriously expecting an answer?" she asked.

Above the laughter that followed, another boy said, "Sorry, madam. Ignore this joker. He's mad. Me, I'm Bonaventure. We can protect you."

Denise was sure she had heard that voice before, but she couldn't remember where or when. Her shoulders squared, she said, "Protect me? From what?"

"You don't know?" said the boy who had spoken first. "Boys in this compound want you bad. We can protect you free for one month. After that, we start charging. If you have no money, we can talk."

The other boys, except the serious-looking one who had introduced himself as Bonaventure, laughed. Denise looked steadily at each one of them. Bonaventure was strikingly handsome. She looked at her feet, and suddenly, as if they were not expecting her to challenge them, they walked away. She committed the name 'Bonaventure' to memory. It was the way Patrick remembered people's names. *You say the name aloud many times,* he had told her.

CHAPTER 36

Life scared her, for lying in bed facing the ceiling without engaging in useful thought was becoming her daily routine. She feared that one of these days, she would have a nervous breakdown.

For days, Alice hadn't returned her calls, until that morning, when she showed up to pick up her brothers and take them out. Denise had seen that Alice's tummy was big, but was there any point in talking about it? She wished she dared to call the MacKinnons and talk about Alice's situation.

The boys were back home, and Junior came to her bedroom and lay next to her. "The chicken was very, very nice, Mom," he said. "But me, I'm sick, Mom."

She touched his forehead. His temperature was high. "We must take you to the hospital."

"No, Mom, I don't want an injection. And I want to vomit."

Denise had no money to take her son to a good hospital. She didn't even have money to hire a cab, for soon after Rebecca had given her the money, she had paid the rent.

"I'm going to see Uncle Wizzie to see our chairs," said Junior. He was already closing the bedroom door behind him.

Denise picked up her cellphone and looked at it for a long time before she called. "Sister Rebecca, I'm sorry, but I need transport to take Junior to see a doctor."

Rebecca was home an hour later. "My nephew can't go to a public hospital, no!" Rebecca screamed from the front door.

As Rebecca's vehicle approached the private hospital of her choice, Denise felt exhausted. Suddenly, everything seemed to move in slow motion, and the sounds of the world felt like a muffled song without lyrics. The Italian-owned hospital surroundings and its interior were beautiful, and Denise feared that she wouldn't afford the hospital bill.

Junior was seen without a long wait, and the doctor ordered labs. After a long wait, the doctor said Junior had malaria, so he put him on treatment.

The bill was forbidding, but Rebecca settled it in cash.

"Say thank you to Aunt Rebecca, Junior," said Denise.

"What for?" Rebecca shouted.

The trio had been in the vehicle for a few seconds before Junior started to scratch his back and arms. "They're biting me, Mom," he said. "Can you see them? I don't want to die lie daddy."

Denise got in the back seat and sat next to her son. She held him tightly in her arms, even though she felt so tired, she wished she would cry and die. "Don't worry, baby," she whispered. "They won't bite you. Mum is here."

"But they're biting me, Mom," Junior hissed. He continued to scratch his arms, neck, and scalp. "They hate me."

Rebecca turned off the ignition. "We can't take him home like this, girl. He's hallucinating. Let him stay overnight for observation."

"No, Aunt Rebecca. I'll take care of him. He's very hot, but the medicine should be working soon. I know how to bring the temperature down."

"If it's the money you're worried about, it's nothing, Dee," said Rebecca, and she turned on the ignition.

It was past midnight when they got back home, and as Rebecca headed for her kitchen door, which Solomon held open for her, she said, "Be strong, Denise."

"Yes, I will."

Back in the warmth of her bedroom, Denise soaked several wet bath towels in cold water and wrapped them around Junior's naked body. It was a trick she had learned from her parents as a child. The temperature would go down soon.

"Mom, when are you going to collect our chairs?" asked Junior.

Denise didn't want to think about the furniture. It was maddening to imagine that Wizzie and Martha could steal from her, she who had been so good to the couple for many years. She was worried about her son's health, and she was angry with Patrick for leaving the big task of parenting to her.

Before long, Junior was fast asleep, and Denise felt even more exhausted. She slept next to her son, and without taking a shower.

In a dream, she found herself walking in a botanical garden alone, and a butterfly landed on her right eye. Appearing from nowhere, Bonaventure opened his mouth and swallowed the butterfly. He took her to a nearby bush and made love to her.

She was awakened by the sound of her cellphone. She didn't know what time it was, and she ignored the call. She sat up and took off her shoes.

She was thinking about how she and Patrick used to listen to soft rock music and Maxwell when the phone rang again. It was Norman. She let the phone ring until it stopped. Why was he calling her so late in the night? On the other hand, he was the man who could decide whether she could get Patrick's terminal benefits. Maybe out of the money, she could buy a plot in the compound, build a house, start some business—she had no idea what business—and accept that this was where the family belonged.

She heard a car screech to a halt a few houses away. A while later, a loud sound startled her. It was as if someone had dropped something heavy close by. She tiptoed to the window and peeped outside. Not a single movement. Her heart raced. How come there were no sounds of cars, and no dogs were barking? As if to respond to her inquisitiveness, she heard gunfire in the distance. There was nothing uncommon about that. Congolese music started to play in the distance. Dogs were barking, and soon, she heard someone whistle close to her house, followed by another whistling from a distance. Distant laughter followed, and she felt safe. A car passed in front of her home, followed by another. Life was back to normal. Again, she toyed with the idea of owning a gun. But how much would it cost, and what would she do with it? Kill somebody, or let burglars use it to kill her?

She looked at her cellphone. It was 2:15 in the morning, and still, she couldn't sleep. Had Norman called by mistake? She picked up the phone and returned his call. He answered on the first ring.

"Thanks for calling, Denise." Patrick's former boss sounded flustered. "It's your friend, Lisa." He sniffled. "We were involved in an accident. The gun…it…it went off." He started to weep.

"What?" asked Denise. "What accident? Talk to me, Norman. Please!"

"I'm at ER, Denise. Why did your friend insist she should drive? It was my fault. It was my fault."

"Norman, be calm! Please." Denise sat up. She remembered one student newspaper stating that it was *"difficult to decide which one between Denise Neo and Lisa Daka, and in that order, is the most beautiful girl in the university, followed by that crazy future lawyer, Hazel Omei."* Denise heard a crashing sound. Was someone trying to break into the house? She scurried to the window and peeped outside. No movement. "Is Lisa okay?" she asked.

"Denise…she's…your friend is dead."

"Oh, Norman, I'm so sorry to hear that." She gaped at the curtain, and suddenly, she was crying.

Norman started to cry, too.

Denise peeped through a gap in the curtains again. Outside, the gusty wind menacingly hit the roof, and she was scared.

On the phone, she could hear people talking in the distance. "Norman, can you hear me?" There was no response. "Norman?" She cut the line and frantically searched her contact list until she found Lisa's number and called it. *"Hi, Lisa Tau here! Please leave a message."*

Lisa, her nemesis, was gone. Lisa, who, despite their relationship, had promised to get Denise a job, would no longer be urging Norman to cut Patrick's terminal benefits check. She forgave Lisa for the transgressions of their youth. They were all adventurous then, and Lisa was too beautiful for any man to resist. It was Patrick, the man very few women could resist, that she couldn't forgive for what he had done in their adulthood.

It was Saturday morning, and it was Alice's eighteenth birthday. Junior was fast asleep in Denise's bed, and his temperature felt normal, so Denise decided to sleep in, but soon, excited voices woke her up. From her bedroom window, she saw a large crowd in front of her house. With her heart in her mouth, she rushed to the front door, kicking several items with both feet in the process.

She opened the door, and an invisible force more powerful than she had ever experienced hit her deep in the chest.

CHAPTER 37

Back home in Patrick's country, even though the temperatures sometimes reached freezing point between May and July, the winters were mild. The nights in Patrick's room were getting colder, so he bought a duvet.

Aretha was in the kitchen, a can of Coca-Cola in one hand. "I'll give you an electric heater," she said. No pleasantries, just straight to the point. "But you have to turn it off as soon as you fall asleep."

"Yes, ma'am, I'll remember to do so as soon as I fall asleep."

She smiled at him and said, "If you see the ambulance, tell them I'm tired of waiting."

"The ambulance?"

"I can't drive in the night, so I called the ambulance to take me to church."

Patrick looked at his phone. Eight in the evening. He worried about Aretha's worsening weird behavior. What would she do next? Burn down the house? Drive her Cadillac into an eighteen-wheeler?

Unhurriedly, Angela took another swill from her Coke. "Want some?"

"No, I'd rather drink water," he said.

"No, no, no. Water has no taste."

"I know," he said. "I know you love Coke, but taking it with every meal, starting with breakfast is bizarre."

"You've been watching me?"

"No."

"So, how do you know?" she asked. "Who are you?"

Patrick hurried up the stairs and got to his room, where he lay in bed, facing up. On his phone, he found YouTube and listened to Maxwell, followed by Matchbox 20, and tears filled his eyes. Every day, his life was becoming more unbearable, his blood pressure rising, and his neck hurting, and yet he couldn't see a doctor. Finding shopping carts in the parking lot, hooking them together, arduously pushing them to the bays, and cleaning them in the cold, left him exhausted at the end of every shift. At times, he took a leaf from Leroy's advice and hid in the bathroom, where he sometimes shed tears.

"What am I doing here?" he said aloud. He had no one to talk to, for the only friends he had—Nicholas and Kezia—were always working, and D'Angelo's health was deteriorating. He hadn't seen Julio in weeks, and besides, was Julio a friend or someone he had spoken to only twice? He knew he couldn't go back home, but was his decision to stay in America the only, or the best, option he had?

Work the following day was physically demanding. He clocked out a few minutes early, even though he knew he would get in trouble, but he couldn't stand being at work any longer. He got to the staff breakroom door, and the next thing he knew, someone was shouting at him. "Better look where you're going, big man!"

It was a young black man, almost as bulky as himself, and he looked agitated.

"I'm sorry," said Patrick.

"What, big man?" the young man laughed and slowly clapped his hands. "You just spoke, man." Addressing everyone in the room, he said, "His broke voice, it's back, man."

His mouth dry, Patrick felt sweat in his armpits, and with shaky limbs, he scurried away from the door and headed for the front exit of the store.

"D'Angelo," someone called behind him. It was a fellow associate, someone whose name he didn't know. "Tell me the truth. I heard you in there. The cafeteria. Are you African or Haitian?"

Patrick took his notebook from one of the back pockets of his jeans, opened it, and using a permanent marker, he wrote in big letters: *LEAVE ME ALONE, BROTHER. HOMESICK.*

"Hey, they will find out soon," said the man. "I mean, just tell me the truth. Maybe I can help."

Patrick stopped and turned to look at the man. He had seen the man many times, and he looked like the kind of man he could trust. He wrote in his notebook: *LET'S GO OUTSIDE.*

Outside, the man said, "So, you have a voice. Why are you not using it? Okay, okay." The man looked at the dark sky as if to seek wisdom from his ancestors. "I can guess." He smiled and looked Patrick in the face. "You don't want people to know you can talk. Why? Someone is going to find out soon. From a distance, I see you talk to customers in the parking lot."

Patrick was scared. Was this a trick? Had his manager, Olivia, asked the man to spy on him?

"My name is Sonko. I'm from The Gambia, Africa. I work in fresh foods. Maybe I can help."

It took a few minutes for Patrick to verbally explain his position.

"I started my life like you," said Sonko. "You know the answer to that, brother? I can find you a woman to marry. She's not beautiful, but she's cheap. I mean, affordable. Just five thousand dollars."

"Brother, I don't have that kind of money," said Patrick. "Besides, I'm still married, and if nothing works for me here, I'll leave."

"Leave and go where?" Sonko looked surprised. "You just said you were a politician, and they wanted to kill you. They don't play back there, brother."

"Actually, there's more to it than that."

"Okay, save some money and come back to me. Hey, it's good to hear you talk. I didn't know you were African. You look so American. A Denzel Washington like you, brother, you'll have no problem finding a beautiful woman for a real marriage."

"Promise, brother, that this is strictly between you and me."

"Me?" Sonko pointed at the skies. "No one will ever know."

It was cold and Patrick hadn't heeded Aretha's advice to bundle up. He had hoped he wouldn't have to spend money on warm clothing. But...

And there she was again, standing by her Cadillac SUV.

Denise's lookalike.

"My brother?" Patrick looked behind him. An elderly white man, his dirty hair touching the shoulders, held up a paper with the note: *Homeless*. "I'm hungry."

Patrick thought about Denise and their kids. He believed Denise had found a great job, and the kids had never gone to bed on an empty stomach. "Here, brother," he found his wallet and pulled out a ten-dollar bill.

The old man looked at the bill. "I have no change."

"I don't need it."

CHAPTER 38

Lying in bed, Denise was exhausted and hungry. Her mouth was dry, and the taste of bitterness made her want to spit. She looked at the phone. Three in the afternoon. Had she been sleeping since morning? Suddenly, she remembered it all, and she started to cry, the sobs making her body shake violently. It couldn't be true. How could it be?

She calmed down, found her voice, and called the boys. She needed to see them alive, and it was okay for them to see her cry. She wanted to see them cry, too.

None of them responded.

The sight of her daughter's body hanging from a roofing beam on the tiny balcony of their home made her shiver. She recalled the sharp pain in her chest, followed by… Nothing. She would never forgive Patrick for the crimes he had committed against her family. At the university, she had seen many boys she considered would have made good husbands. She had chosen Patrick instead.

She would never see her daughter again, or the grandchild she had carried. She wished she had told Alice that she would be happy to be a grandmother to a child who would probably never know his or her grandfather.

She shook her head. She feared her life was about to come to a stop like a car that has lost its engine. She had to fight hard to fend off the mental paralysis she felt rushing in. She sat up, and suddenly, she feared that she had become incontinent. The inside of her thighs was wet.

Slowly, she put her right hand there.

"What?" she cried out.

She was certain the slimy matter she felt hadn't come from her body. She brought her right forefinger close to her nose, and she knew that someone had raped her. Unwilling to admit it, she got off the bed and examined herself carefully. Yes, that was semen between her thighs.

"Bonaventure...Bonaventure! I'll kill you," she whimpered. Her vision was blurred, there was a humming sound in her ears, and she fell to her knees.

She cursed the day she met Patrick. Some bastard had done that to her because Patrick had left her, and because of that, the family lived in that compound, and her daughter had taken her life. She closed her eyes, the anger, the anguish, and a craving to find and kill the person who had violated her making her body shiver again.

What would her parents say about Patrick if they were still alive? "He's a good boy," she imagined her father say. "He's just gone bad."

Who had killed Alice? Where did Alice find the energy to get the two bulky building concrete blocks from wherever and place them on the balcony, put a wire rope around her neck and hang from the roof beam on the porch? Denise had taken in all those details in that moment of crisis.

She heard excited chatter outside. She stood by the bedroom window and saw two police officers armed with automatic weapons kick and hit a young man in the head, the ribs, all over the body. The young man pleaded for forgiveness, and the crowd simply looked on. The torture went on until the young man lay still on the ground.

There was a loud knock at the front door. Denise remained still. She didn't want to see anyone.

"Denise, you have to be strong," Rebecca said from the bedroom door. "The door was open, and that's not good. I should have come back earlier to check on you."

Denise sat on her bed and wondered if she should tell Rebecca about the semen between her legs. But who cared? Her daughter was dead, and that was what mattered. If the rapist had made her pregnant, she would know what to do after burying her daughter.

Denise and Rebecca sat on the bed.

"I took the boys home," Rebecca spoke softly, and with tenderness. "They're not eating, they're not talking. I hear someone called the police, but the bastards said they had no transport. No transport? How many police cars are sitting idly at State House, guarding a man who has brought this economy to its knees?" Both women sniffled. Rebecca rubbed Denise's back with one hand. "I'm sorry I'm almost shouting. A young man called Bonaventure used his cousin's Land-Rover to take Alice's body...sorry...to the mortuary. He's a ruling party cadre, but he did a good job, for once. What kind of society are we?"

"Did the boys see their sister's...?" asked Denise.

Rebecca was silent for a long time. "I hear none of them shed a tear. They just...*looked*."

Denise wished her boys had cried. They should have cried.

"The only thing Junior said to me when we got home was he wasn't going back to school. I asked why, and he said a classmate had told him his mother was a bad woman who had chased away his dad, so his dad had killed himself in America, so Junior came from a bad family. I think you should move in with us, Dee. Uncle Ben insists. Leave this compound. Now."

A long silence followed. All Denise wanted was to be alone, and, perhaps, just die. There was nothing more to say about her predicament.

"Denise, are you listening? You should be strong. You're the man of the house now. This business of fainting when your kids need you is no good. I'll host the funeral at my home."

Denise started to sob again. She concluded that if she ever saw Patrick, she would kill him.

CHAPTER 39

Denise and Rebecca drove to the MacKinnons' home in Olympia Park. Denise hadn't been to the area in a long time, and the sight of the house next door, where she and Patrick had raised their first two children, almost brought tears to her eyes. Once more, she concluded that Patrick was dead. The man she had married would never have deliberately caused her so much pain.

She hadn't seen the MacKinnons in many years, but in their early seventies, the couple still looked strong, and they were as friendly as always. Alex, their only child and the boy Alice said was the father of her child, said he was devastated by Alice's death.

"I've loved sweet Alice since I was..." He looked at his hands. "I don't know. She's the only girl I ever loved, the only girl I ever slept with, I swear."

"We don't need the details," said Rebecca. "Tell us what happened on the night of Alice's death. You know I was in law school?"

Denise liked Alex. He was strikingly handsome and looked dependable. No wonder, her daughter had fallen for him. Denise also believed that Alex was the only man Alice had ever slept with, just like Patrick was the only man she had ever consented to, even though Rebecca didn't believe that. Traits like those run in families.

"Late at night, we had a disagreement," said Alex. "Sweet Alice didn't want to disturb our parents, so she took a taxi. She said she wanted to see her mum. I tried to stop her."

"Go on, son," Alex's father said when his son looked down, speechless.

"I...I..." Alex stammered and broke down.

"There's no point," Denise said.

"No point in what, Denise?" Rebecca sounded upset. "He has to tell us..."

Denise wanted to be alone and cry. She stood up, and Alex's mother showed her to the guest toilet, where she sat down and cried. She stood up, washed her face, and whispered, "Be strong, girl."

She got back to the living room, and her tea was cold. Alex had left.

"We've discussed at length what needs to be done," the senior MacKinnon announced. "I've insisted to Rebecca that my family will meet all the funeral expenses, from food, the coffin, the grave lot, all that. And again, my wife and I are very sorry both families have lost such an angel."

Denise was pleased when she and Rebecca didn't say a word to each other as they drove back to KK Square.

Like every African funeral, Alice's was a public celebration where mourners came to Rebecca's home to share their life stories, eat, drink and socialize. The burial took place at Leopards Hill Memorial Park, and Denise wasn't surprised to see the multitudes of people who had come to bid farewell to a young lady who had lived for barely eighteen years to the day. Alice was a socialite in her own right.

Denise found it disturbing that neither Chris nor Junior shed any tears at the graveside. Alex, though, cried nonstop. She wished she would urge the boys to cry. Had their father's presumed death hardened their feelings to the extent that another death in the family meant nothing to them?

During the past few days, Denise had pondered over what kind of argument Alice and her lover had that had led to her death. According to Rebecca, Alex had said Alice just wanted to be with her mother. But Rebecca had also said she had heard rumors about Alice's death ranging from Alex saying he didn't know if he was the expected baby's father to Alice taking her life because her father's ghost had told her to do so. All nonsense, of course, Denise had concluded.

Denise, the boys, and Aunt Rebecca were the last to leave the grave, and soon after, it rained so heavily, everyone was soaked to the skin.

"It's her way of erasing her broken history," said Rebecca. Denise didn't comment.

Days after the funeral, Denise was still waiting to hear Rebecca repeat her invitation for her and the boys to move to the guesthouse. When the invitation didn't come, she asked.

"I made the offer, but you never answered me," Rebecca quipped.

Junior was very happy to hear that he, Mom, and Chris were moving to Aunt Rebecca's place. "Can we move today, and Alice can now come?" he asked.

"How about you, Chris?" asked Denise. "Aren't you happy we're leaving this place?"

Chris stared at the roof.

CHAPTER 40

The family's new home was a guest quarters Rebecca had just built. It was by far more comfortable than the KK Square house. Rebecca's residence had a six-foot- security fence with a guard at the gate, and Solomon, Rebecca's houseboy, who lived in the servant's quarters that was adjacent to the guesthouse, was very courteous to Denise.

As Denise arranged the furniture in her new residence, she pledged to find her own home soon. No one would give her a job, of course, so she would be self-employed. She wished Alice was still alive, as a decent home like the guesthouse would have given her a good reason to visit more often.

She vowed never to cry over Patrick again. A new home meant a new beginning.

She apportioned the larger of the two bedrooms to her sons. The living room was separate from the dining room, and the bathroom, which had hot running water, was located far from the kitchen.

But a new home didn't mean her nightmares were over. On her first night, she dreamt about Patrick, Alice, Norman, and even Bonaventure.

The morning after moving into the guesthouse, Rebecca took Denise to the supermarket and paid for the family's groceries. "I'll not always be there to buy you groceries, Dee. You better find a job soon, girl."

"I understand," said Denise as she sat in the passenger seat, ready to go back home. "And the rent? How much is it going to be?"

Rebecca put her fingers on the ignition switch for a long time. "You really think I'm a devil, don't you?"

"I just want to know."

"You're my brother's wife, the mother to my only nephews."

The two women turned to hug each other, and both broke down.

When Rebecca's vehicle stopped in front of the main house, Solomon asked Denise not to remove her groceries from the trunk.

"He's a good boy," Rebecca said after Solomon had left with the groceries, and the two women didn't disembark from the vehicle. "But stay away from him, you hear?"

"What do you mean?" asked Denise. She took offense. Did Rebecca believe she was that kind of woman?

"He's thirty-seven, and his wife is Melody," Rebecca explained. "She's such a beautiful girl, she could do better in life. I hear she's twenty-five, but you know, some of these people don't even know when they were born. Look at her three kids. It's like they never heard of birth control."

Denise had known Solomon for many years, and she knew that he was no ordinary domestic worker or house servant like Wizzie. He dressed so well that a stranger would mistake him for a blue-collar worker. That morning, she had heard him run around the servant's quarters.

On Rebecca's insistence, the boys didn't go to school for a week after Alice's funeral. "They have to learn to mourn family," Rebecca insisted. After that, Rebecca made arrangements for a man to ferry the boys to and from school every day, and she met the costs.

Meantime, Denise continued to look for business ideas. Her home area was the nation's major producer of rice and fish. Maybe she could venture into that? But did that mean buying the fishnets, hiring fishermen, or merely buying fish from fishermen in bulk and reselling in the big cities? How much money would she need to get started?

She was surprised to see Rebecca at her home one afternoon. Over the past weeks, Denise had learned that being Rebecca's tenant came with some challenges. Rebecca was a typical case of now-she's-friendly-now-she's-not.

"I want us to go out, girl," Rebecca said and sat on the sofa. "It's comedy night at the playhouse tomorrow."

The following evening, Rebecca was energetic and chatty as the two women drove to the prestigious Lusaka Playhouse.

Rebecca talked about her marriage. "I consider myself unmarried but not single because Uncle Ben is an alcoholic. He needs help."

During the show, Rebecca said, "It's good to see you laugh, girl. Get a job and claim your life back."

Denise felt guilty. Rebecca was probably tired of looking after the family, hence the reference to her need to get a job. And maybe she had responded to too many jokes with such boisterous laughter, her sister-in-law could have been offended. After all, Denise was supposed to be mourning both Rebecca's brother and niece. Denise wanted to apologize. Instead, during the rest of the show, she guarded against expressing happiness.

They did not get back home until midnight. As she walked to the guesthouse, Denise looked behind and, through the kitchen window, she saw Solomon cutting a chicken with a large knife. An hour later, she was retiring to bed when she heard a baby cry above the muffled voices of a man and a woman. She believed Solomon and his wife had differed over something. Well, whatever reason had made Patrick leave her, the couple had reached a stage in their marriage where they never quarreled.

When she called the HR office at Patrick's former workplace the following morning, the lady who answered said, "I'm sorry, Mrs. Kanya, but we wrote to your husband, informing him that he had been terminated for desertion."

"Yes, I read the letter, and it said the issue of terminal benefits could be reexamined," Denise argued. "Mr. Norman Tau said so, too."

"Are you aware if he's dead, Mrs. Kanya?"

"Could you say that again, madam?"

"I'm sorry. I shouldn't have said that, but we'll get back to you if circumstances change."

Twice that morning, Denise called Norman's cell number, and he didn't pick up.

The day was turning out to be miserable when she received a call from a kindergarten principal who wanted to give her a job interview. Denise couldn't remember applying for the job. She didn't know a thing about teaching toddlers. But if the job was available, she would learn to do it, and do it well.

She called Norman again. This time, he answered.

"I was calling about my husband's terminal benefits, Norman." Denise felt it was time to take off her gloves and fight for her children's survival. "The HR people say they can't pay me."

"Well, I haven't been to the office in a while, but I believe whatever the HR people said was the company's position. But as friends, I'd say, Denise, let's meet again. Same place? For lunch? I'm sorry I couldn't attend your daughter's funeral. Lisa died tragically about the same time that your daughter died. And I'm sorry about your child's death, of course."

"I'm sorry to hear about your loss, too. And you forget you called me that night."

"Uh, I did? Yes, maybe. So, tomorrow, Denise? Lunch?"

"I have an interview tomorrow, about midday," she said. "Maybe you could take me there and wait for me? That way, I won't bother my sister-in-law with the burden of giving me a ride every so often."

"Sounds like a plan, Denise. And another thing..."

"Yes, Norman?"

"I'll tell you tomorrow."

She looked forward to meeting Norman again, for she believed he held the key to her future. As the second top executive at the corporation Patrick had worked for like a horse since he left the university, Norman could make things happen and direct HR to release Patrick's terminal benefits. If the check was good, Denise's life would change forever.

She convinced herself that a lunch appointment with Norman was just that—a business meeting, not a date. Looking forward to the meeting, she found it hard to concentrate on the house chores. She even entered the boys' room without knocking, where she found Chris, standing by his bed, naked.

"I'm sorry," she said and slammed the door. Like his father, Chris had become big.

CHAPTER 41

"Don't I know that man?" asked the bespectacled woman who sat behind a large desk in the school office. "Is he your husband?"

"No, madam," said Denise. "He's a...a friend."

"A *friend?*"

"Sort of. He was my husband's boss."

"Your *ex*-husband's boss?" the stocky, wig-wearing lady who was the school's proprietor chuckled. "You sure seem to be close. I saw the vehicle stop. You spoke for a long time, laughing. Of course, you didn't kiss, but I'm old enough to know when I'm looking at lovers."

"No, we're *not* close!"

"May I remind you that we *don't* shout in my office? You're here begging to teach my kids, and I will not take kindly to candidates who can't control their temper."

Denise hadn't noticed that she had been shouting, but she realized that she was standing up and breathing heavily. "I'm sorry, madam." She sat down.

"So am I, and you don't have to sit down. We have no vacancies. Besides, we hire only morally straight teachers at this school. Teachers who know their place in the school and have the patience not to lose their temper."

Denise remained seated and calmed herself down. "Madam, I need this job. *Please.*"

"Shouting again?" The woman pointed at the door.

Denise knew she hadn't shouted again. She stood up and walked to the door, where she stopped, looked at the woman behind the desk, and said, "Madam, I'm not what or who you think I am."

The stocky woman picked up a pen and started writing something on the piece of paper before her.

"That was quick," said Norman when Denise sat in the passenger seat of the Lexus SUV. "Hey, what's the matter? If you were white, your face would be as white as snow."

"I'm okay," said Denise. "They filled the position this morning."

"Then why call you?" Norman shouted, his lips twitching. He opened the driver's door.

"Where are you going?"

"To tell them they just can't treat you like shit," Norman shouted. "They should have called and advised you not to come. Bastards!"

"Please, Norman!"

Norman slammed the door, started the engine, and they drove away.

"I think you should fill in an application at the television station," said Norman. "Not that we have any openings, but it's always good to have an application in the HR office."

"I'm not qualified to work anywhere."

Norman extended his arm toward Denise, but he didn't touch her. "You could learn."

"No, too many memories, knowing Patrick used to work there." There was a long silence. "Norman, don't you have friends? People who could hire me? I could make a good PA."

"Hey, I'll try. Look, Denise, you're lovely, lonely and I'm lonely. Can we go somewhere together for the weekend? We could go hunting. I'm not being fresh, I can assure you. I had a lot of respect for Patrick, of course." Norman's voice rose. "I hunt the duiker, antelope, whatever you call them. Small animals. I have several guns, Denise. I could teach you how to shoot without missing."

Denise wanted to believe that Norman had a lot of respect for her husband. Everyone who knew Patrick had a lot of respect for him. "I don't know. I'm not sure I could do that." If she had a choice, she would have asked him to stop the vehicle and drop her right there. She would walk home, even if that took hours. But she accepted the fact that she no longer had too many choices in life.

Denise was surprised to see how quickly she and Norman got to the restaurant. Her mind had been wandering in distant places, trying not to think about the judgmental school owner, about Norman's lack of respect for her, and about what Patrick could be doing at that very moment if he was still alive. Of course, Patrick was dead, she concluded.

As they got inside the restaurant, Denise remembered her rivalry with Lisa at the university. Although Lisa had made herself available to Patrick during their university days, Norman's late wife had tried to get her a job just before she died. Was that a way of saying sorry?

They had been standing by the entrance to the restaurant for probably a few minutes—Denise feared she was losing her sense of time—when she heard Norman say sternly to a waiter, "I'll not sit anywhere, sir. The last time me and this beautiful wife of mine were here, we sat at that table over there."

"Your wife?" said Denise, and she was glad the words had come out softly.

"I'm sorry, Lisa, I thought…"

"Denise, Norman. I'm Denise. But I understand." Denise looked across the room. Two happy-looking couples were sitting at the table where she, Norman, and the late Lisa had sat the last time they were there.

An elderly staffer approached and cleared his threat. "I couldn't help overhearing your conversation, sir," he said, "but unfortunately, that table has already been taken."

"Do you know who I am?" Norman snapped.

"Please!" pleaded Denise. "Will you take me home, please?" She wanted to sound civil because, after all, she needed Patrick's benefits check.

The younger man, the one Norman had been so rude to, led them to a table.

"I hate sitting this close to the entrance," Norman hissed, but Denise noticed that he was beginning to calm down.

As they were sitting down, Norman touched Denise's right hand, and she quickly moved it away.

"Hey, I'm sorry." Norman smiled and cracked his knuckles. "Patrick said something to me in confidence the day before he left." Denise wished she had turned Norman's invitation down. "You know, we were real buddies, Patrick and I. He was my righthand man. He told me he wasn't going to come back home. I thought he was joking, so I didn't press him, but he said you and him were having problems."

Feeling exhausted, Denise said, "Sir, I don't think Patrick ever said those words." Norman didn't look at her. "Why do I get the feeling you're taking advantage of me?" She stood up. "Please, sir, don't ever call me again."

"I'm so sorry, Denise—I mean, Mrs. Kanya. I really shouldn't have told you about it. Look, it was boys' talk, that's all."

"Please, take me to my former home."

"Denise, please, sit down. Please!"

Although Denise believed she was hurrying toward the exit, Norman got there first, and he opened the door for her.

She gave him the directions, and as they stopped at Denise's old home in KK Square, Norman said nervously, "If you could get out quickly, please. This is a dangerous place."

Denise was fidgeting with her purse—a means to annoy Norman—when she saw Martha come out of the yellow house with a big bowl of wares on her head.

"Denise, please forgive me," Norman said quickly. He got out of the vehicle, walked to the passenger door, and held it open. "Things have been hard for me since your friend's death."

"I understand, and I forgive you." Of course, she would never forgive Norman for lying about Patrick. She stepped out of the vehicle and waved at Martha, and Norman's vehicle backed up dangerously, and soon, it was speeding away, leaving a cloud of dust behind it.

"You are back, madam?" Martha said excitedly.

"No, I'm waiting for my former landlord. He wants to see the house, and I give him the keys this afternoon. I have to clean up a bit."

"Aah, madam, I can help clean, but I have to go to market," said Martha. "I can come inside house in two minutes."

Seeing that there was no furniture in the home, Martha said she could make some tea at her house. "The way I use to make tea for boss."

"Not to worry," said Denise. They stood in the middle of the kitchen.

"Madam, someone bother you? The new boss with good car?"

"I'm not well."

"Maybe malaria. I know my friend, her sister is nurse at big private clinic. She can give injections that work. You remember, madam, the one who gave you injections when Alice, she died?"

"Gave me injections?" asked Denise, her eyes wide open.

"You don't remember? You were in bad shock. I see you sleeping there, outside, so I take you inside to there." Martha pointed at Denise's former bedroom. "So, I asked my nurse friend, what do we do? She gave you injections to sleep."

"She did?"

"Then I go to market for business, so I ask Wizzie, he stay with you to protect you." The room began to blur around Denise, and she feared she was going to vomit. "Aunt Rebecca, she took the boys."

"Thank you for your kindness, Martha." Denise's right hand stretched out until it found the wall to lean on. "You and your dear husband."

"Do I call nurse for injections now, madam? Or you go to hospital?"

"No, I'll be all right. Thank you. Just tell me one thing. It's okay if you don't want to talk about it. How are you coping—you know, after you were raped by those men?"

"Me, madam? Raped by those men? When?"

Denise looked blankly at Martha. "Don't worry about it."

As soon as Martha had left, Denise rushed to the toilet and vomited. She knew why her periods had been erratic since Patrick left; she had stopped taking the pill. She repeatedly hit the toilet seat until her fingers and knuckles hurt.

CHAPTER 42

He was in the parking lot of the supermarket, walking home, when he saw her again. He had never seen someone who looked exactly like Denise, so, as was the case before, when he had seen her, he unashamedly stared at her like a child. Her Cadillac Escalade was parked in the usual place, by a big tree, and she was putting her shopping bags in the trunk. She was so beautiful, he imagined touching her hand would be like touching Denise's. The beauty of her small feet was tantalizing, and he recalled how, when they were students, he loved to kiss Denise's toenails, which were always painted a bright red, and how he massaged the silver ankle bracelet she wore for many years.

He wondered why the woman who looked just like his wife came to the store alone. Was she married with children? Divorced? If widowed, what did the husband die of? Not AIDS, hopefully. Could she be looking for a man? He knew he had no chance of winning a good woman's heart again.

Hands in pockets and deep in thought, Patrick walked home slowly, thinking about Nathan, the driver who died in that car crash, the one that could have taken his life as well. Well, Nathan was a free man. But Denise? What had happened to her?

He wished he could physically take himself into his past. There, he would walk slowly and observe every moment, stopping whenever he saw a red flag. When did he acquire the cheating trait? Maybe it was in his DNA? From his father's side? Why did he lie that he would buy his family presents and go back home to remodel the master bedroom, a gift he had promised to give Denise even when he knew he wasn't going back? Did he know who he was?

As he kept walking, he recalled that several times, he had counted the number of turns he had to make before he got home from work. Twelve times. He didn't remember turning anywhere that day, and yet he was home. He didn't remember feeling cold, either. He hadn't seen Julio in a while, and he wished he could talk to him again.

He was about to take a shower when Aretha called. "Are you at work?"

"No, I'm home."

"Good. I don't know where I am, Patrick. Can you help?"

"What do you mean, you don't know where you are? The sun is up and bright."

"I'm on the road, but I don't know where I am."

"I have no idea where you are. I don't drive. I don't know this city."

"I been calling D'Angelo, and he don't answer. Can you talk to our neighbor? The girl on the right? You know Chantelle. I know she don't work today. Give her the phone."

Patrick wished he would free himself from the prison walls he had built around himself. He could fly back home. But what would be the consequences of such an irrational decision? As he reluctantly got dressed, he thought about Aretha's neighbor. She was a pretty, short, black woman who kept her hair short like a man's, and she was about his age. Was that her name? Chantelle? Once, he had said good evening to her, but she had not responded.

Moments later, he knocked on Chantelle's front door, and to his surprise, she instantly opened it and invited him inside.

"What's happening in the neighborhood?" she asked. It was hard to believe Chantelle's house had the same floor plan as Aretha's. Chantelle's living room looked much bigger than Aretha's. "Take a seat."

"I'm sorry, I have an emergency, Ms. Chantelle."

"Call me Chantelle, Patrick."

"You know my name?"

"You said you had an emergency."

He sat in a leather chair and handed his phone to Chantelle, and for half an hour, he heard Chantelle give directions to Aretha. Then finally, he heard his landlady scream, "I got it now! Yes, I can see Windy Hill Road."

Chantelle shook her head, cut the line, and handed the phone to Patrick. "I don't think she fully recovered from that head injury."

"Ms. Aretha had a head injury?"

Chantelle shrugged. "If she didn't tell you about it, then you won't hear it from me." He liked her relaxed attitude and her broad smiles. "I see they have very handsome men over there in the Motherland. Would love to go there someday."

"I have to go," Patrick said. He didn't want to get entangled in a relationship with a neighbor. Unless, of course, she could help him get the papers he needed to stay in the country?

"She was a good artist, actually," she said, as if she was searching for the right term to use. "She painted this one." Chantelle pointed at the painting on one of her walls. It was the same kind of painting of market women in Africa which hung on Aretha's walls.

"Aretha painted that?"

"Uh-hah!"

"Good night," he said. She didn't say a word, so he left.

Aretha got home an hour later. She knocked hard on Patrick's door and said, "Hey, I'm going to cook, so join me for dinner. Is that okay? You won't need to pay."

"I'll be honored, Ms. Aretha."

Patrick wasn't the only guest at Aretha's dinner table. "My friend Delores," Aretha said, and the other woman continued to stare at him. "She's a retired Pre-K assistant teacher. Sit down, you two."

Delores was a big woman with a handsome face. Probably in her early sixties, her dark complexion made her large eyes look like shining stars in a clear night sky.

Forks, knives, spoons, and plates of food covered the dining table, and the smell was inviting.

"So, this is *the* Patrick I hear of every day?" asked Delores.

"Yes," Aretha laughed as she spoke. "*The* man."

"Looks good, actually," said Delores, her voice husky and deep like a man's. She could have been a great lead singer in a jazz band, Patrick observed. She stood up and rushed to the kitchen, where Patrick noticed that she didn't pick up anything, but when she came back to the table, she sat in a chair directly opposite Patrick's.

Aretha took a swig from a Coca-Cola can. "Have some," she said, and Patrick shook his head.

"He wants to keep his great body great," Delores said and chortled.

Patrick felt uneasy. The comments, the body language. He wasn't interested in the big lady, no. Besides, her bright yellow wig was off-putting. But the cornbread with meatloaf and pork chops were very tasty, even though all he wanted was to go to bed and think. He listened to the women's chatter about police brutality towards black men, racism, and a new Denzel Washington movie about a guy named Roman.

"I love Denzel," he said, not only to be seen to be a part of the family but also because he liked Washington.

Delores's eyes opened wide. "You *love* him? Did you hear that, Aretha?"

Patrick stood up. "I like him," he said, his voice slightly raised. There was silence as he climbed the stairs. They would wash the plates, thought Patrick. He wasn't the kind of man the ladies seemed to think he was.

He was awakened by a knock at his door. He ignored it.

"Are you okay?" It was Aretha.

Grudgingly, Patrick wrapped a duvet around his body and partially opened the door. Wearing a gown, Delores said, "You're more handsome than Aretha tells me."

"Excuse me, Ms. Delores..."

"We got lost," Delores whispered. "Aretha kept insisting she knew where we was going. I said, no, Aretha, this ain't the way. We ended up in Chattanooga, Tennessee, honey. But why am I talking about irrelevant things?"

She got closer to the door.

"I'm glad you found your way back home, Ms. Delores, but if you'll excuse me, I'm so tired, I need to sleep."

"No black man gets too tired for the action, honey," Delores said and chuckled. She pushed the door slightly and put her right hand on Patrick's left shoulder.

"I'm sorry," Patrick said and gently closed the door.

"You was right, Aretha," Patrick heard Delores say. "Tell the brother to come out of the closet." She laughed and clapped her hands for a long time. "*I love Denzel.*"

Patrick remembered three of his most trusted subordinates dying of AIDS. He remembered the sores. The greying skin. Thinning hair. Above all, the stigma that came with it. He knew that over the years, there had been remarkable advances in the treatment and care of AIDS patients. But he would never take the risk of sleeping with any woman.

Patrick closed the door and got back to bed. But he couldn't sleep. He needed to apologize to Ms. Delores. After all, she was Ms. Aretha's guest.

Hours later, he woke up from a nightmare in which he had failed to rescue his kids from drowning in a large river.

CHAPTER 43

Denise found what she was looking for in the pharmacy section of the supermarket in the small shopping complex near Rebecca's home.

"Which one between these two is better?" she asked the young man who had just been dispensing medications to a customer.

The young man looked at the boxes, and with a straight face, he said, "Both."

Denise chuckled. "Problem with having a teenage daughter. I sure hope I'm wrong."

"I understand."

The kids were still at school when she got back home, but still, she locked the bathroom door, and with her fingers shaking, she took the test. She breathed heavily, wrapped the test kit in a shopping bag, and walked to the back of Rebecca's kitchen door. The garbage bin was full, so she lifted a few small bags from there and pushed her bag further down the bin.

Later that night, Denise was alone in the living room, thinking about what would have happened had the results of the pregnancy test been positive. She was certain she would have gathered enough courage to take her life. Just how could Wizzie, Martha's husband, make himself the only man, other than Patrick, to sleep with her?

Someone was at the front door, and she wished the world would leave her alone. "Who is it?"

"Just open, girl. Open!"

Rebecca came in and glanced around the living room, as if she was expecting to see a man hiding behind the curtains. She wore no makeup, and for the first time, Denise saw a thin line that ran from her sister-in-law's left cheek to just above her left eye. Was the scar a result of a war between her and Uncle Ben?

"It's a good place, Sister Rebecca, and I'm so grateful to you for accommodating us."

"Forget it, girl. Where are the boys—my nephews, where are they?"

"In their bedroom, as usual, watching TV, playing games, maybe," said Denise. "The boys have become..." She shook her head vigorously.

"What? Junior has malaria again?"

"No. But the kids are now a poor image of their past."

Rebecca beckoned to Denise. They sat next to each other on the sofa.

"Maxx told me what happened at the school, Denise." Rebecca was gracious enough to speak in low tones. "If you really need a job, I think you should forget your pride. A woman like you can move mountains."

Denise gasped. How could Norman tell Maxx about the school incident? "Girls do what they have to do to find shelter, put food on the table. Which is why I came here. Maxx wants you back at work. And girl," Rebecca leaned over and whispered, "you need a job, remember? So, get laid."

"What did you say?" Denise felt a pounding sound in her ears. She was about to stand up when Rebecca burst out laughing.

"You heard me. Get laid. If my brother is still alive, then I don't know who he is. Maybe he's not my blood brother, even. He must have been switched at birth. He doesn't deserve you. Lay Maxx if he wants you. Marry Norman if he wants you. Lisa is dead. Change your name. Will you do me that favor?"

"Would you, yourself, marry Maxx?"

Rebecca stood up and headed for the door, where she stopped, and without turning to look at Denise, said, "Be careful how you dispose of trash. Solomon was trying to make room for more trash in the bin when he found the pregnancy thing."

Denise felt terror creep up her spine. "I can explain, Sister Rebecca."

"I don't care," said Rebecca. "Just marry him." She closed the door gently behind her. Outside, Denise heard Rebecca speak to Solomon.

For a long time, Denise sat on the sofa, feeling emotionally drained. She was mad with Rebecca for her audacity to suggest that she should sleep with any man. She needed Rebecca to listen to her story about being drugged and raped. She was mad with Patrick, too, for pretending to be such a nice guy for all those years, only to leave her in the lurch. She remembered how he used to do the dishes sometimes and promise he would be doing so until he had bought a dishwasher. He was the man with a thousand and one things to get done at work, and yet he always came home with a smile, a new joke. Was that all pretense?

She got in bed, only to remember that she had not locked the door after Rebecca had left. She got to the door. Rebecca and Solomon were still talking not far from her door. She went to bed and cried herself to sleep until she was awakened by a loud knock on her window.

"Uncle Ben is dead, madam," said Solomon.

"Dead?" There was a tight feeling in Denise's throat. It was just after midnight, and like Patrick, she always slept naked. She dressed quickly and hurried to the main house.

"He's just asleep," Rebecca said through the driver's window of the Range Rover. "Too much drink, as usual. Go back to sleep, Dee."

Ben was sprawled on the rear seat of the vehicle. "Please, let me come with you."

"I said go back to sleep," Rebecca retorted.

The night guard opened the security gate and Rebecca drove away. As Denise walked back to the guesthouse, she saw, through the kitchen window, Solomon washing plates.

She got back to bed but couldn't fall asleep. It wouldn't look good if Rebecca came back from the hospital and found her not waiting. She was amazed to see to what extent a woman would go to prove to the world that she was married. After Patrick had left the way he did, Denise concurred with people who believed that the institution of marriage was overrated.

It was 4:00 am, and Denise was awakened by the slamming of a door, followed by a man shouting, and a soft-spoken woman responding to the verbal onslaught. She got to the living room window and looked at the main house. In the kitchen window, she saw Rebecca turn off the kitchen light, and her phone rattled. A text from Rebecca read: *Uncle Ben was fed intravenously and discharged. Nite.*

Denise got back to bed. Again, she couldn't sleep. Was the loss of her husband more painful than the loss of her daughter? She couldn't tell.

In the morning, she called Maxx.

"My good girl!" Maxx was in high spirits. He always was. "Your good sister Rebecca, she tells me everything. When are you starting job?"

"How about now?"

"Denise, I tell you, you're the *bestest* in the world. Better than Tina Turner, that Bassett." He chuckled. "You see, I didn't go to school much, but I know superstars. The pretty ones." The laughter was irritating.

Denise spent the rest of the day racking her brains for how best to deal with Maxx. She would go back to work, all right, but practically, how would she ward off his advances by building an invisible but impenetrable wall around her?

Knowing that she would have a job the next day, she asked the boys to escort her to the stores. Junior was excited. Chris found more than one excuse not to come.

Although Christmas had never meant anything to Denise and Patrick, the children always expected gifts because their friends received presents on that day. At the store, Junior chose a pair of school shoes for himself, and a shirt for Chris, while Denise picked up a few groceries.

"Is that the total?" she asked, looking at the cash register.

"Yes, madam," said the female cashier.

"I'm sorry," Denise spoke softly. "Can you take out this chicken...the tomatoes...the biscuits? Yes, how much does that come to?" The cashier pointed at the cash register. "Sorry, but I can't afford that."

"Wait, madam," said the cashier, and the red light above her came on.

Moments later, an elderly man came laughing. He listened to the cashier explain the problem at hand and said, "Okay, give her a ten percent Christmas discount."

Denise looked behind her and saw several people leave the line. She wanted to apologize, but she knew those people still wouldn't have forgiven her for delaying them.

"I still can't afford that," she whispered.

The elderly man left to attend to another red light.

"Excuse me."

Denise turned her head. Norman was approaching fast, almost pushing people aside.

"My fault," Norman addressed the cashier. "I told my wife I would be here on time. Put everything back in."

He took out a bank card from his wallet, and Denise considered it unwise to protest, as that would cause a scene. "Thank you," she said.

Norman swiped his card. "I'll be in the next store, honey," he said and kissed her left cheek.

She watched him walk away without looking back. He had saved the day, of course, but at a cost. How dare he call her his wife and kiss her in public?

She felt Junior's fingers tighten around her dress, and she did her best to hold the tears back, but they still fell to her cheeks.

"Don't cry, Mom," said Junior, and he broke down.

"Don't cry, honey," she said and sniffled while people looked on, some of them whispering to each other.

Outside the supermarket, Denise looked for Norman. She was grateful when she didn't see him. Her only fear was that Junior was going to tell Chris that he had met Mom's new husband.

CHAPTER 44

Patrick was at the front door, ready to leave for work, when Aretha, who was in the kitchen preparing a meal, said above her daily symphony of falling objects, "How it works is, when you're on disability, you can only work a few hours." The water stopped running in the sink. "D'Angelo. He's applied for disability."

Thinking about D'Angelo made Patrick's heart palpitate. Was the brother HIV positive? No, it wouldn't be right to pose that question to Aretha, who approached and said, "Disability. That means *you* can no longer work long hours. Hey, I had a video in my head last night. Lots of black folk, like in the Motherland, standing in a long line, and this white guy says he's going to cut off our heads. He says, 'Who wants to be the first to die?' and I raise my hand. He says, 'Why?' I say I don't want to see black folk being killed. So, he says, 'You be the last to die.' Ah, you in a hurry, Patrick?"

"You could write comedy, Ms. Aretha."

"There's nothing funny about black folk being killed by a white man," she said with a sense of seriousness. "You too young to remember Steve Biko, Mandela, Cabral, and all those black heroes?"

"I gotta go. Ma'am, I understand you were an artist once?"

"Patrick, my son won't be able to bring your check here every week."

"I understand."

"So, the new arrangement is that you go to D'Angelo. He write a check to me, I cash the check and give you cash. But Patrick, you pay me twenty dollars for gas. You understand that?"

"Sounds fair, yes."

Through the transom window, Patrick saw a man get off a truck in front of the house across the street. The man crouched by the driveway, and moments later, he walked to the front door of the house and knocked. A woman wearing pajamas instantly opened the door. Patrick couldn't hear what the two were saying, but they seemed to be engaged in a fierce argument.

"She don't pay her bills – water, electric, gas, cable," Aretha laughed. Patrick saw that she was watching the spectacle through the kitchen window. "They've disconnected her water. At long last."

"I'm so glad you pay your bills, Ms. Aretha."

"You think I'm ghetto like her?"

As the meter reader walked to his truck, the woman threw shreds of paper after him. The man calmly stood by his truck as a school bus stopped by, its red lights flashing. Every time Patrick had seen that bus, it had stopped at the same spot and at the same time. The driver's efficiency, even in the presence of heavy traffic, reminded him of his television days. Despite the absence of sufficient equipment, every project was delivered on time. He missed the challenges of his job.

"I didn't mean it that way, Ms. Aretha. You know that, surely."

"Oh, yes, you did!" Aretha sounded very upset. "Me, I'm like her? She don't even pay her homeowner association."

"I apologize."

"And Patrick, do you prefer men to women?"

As Patrick searched for an appropriate response, Aretha hurried past him, and in a moment, she was walking upstairs, laughing.

Half an hour through his work, Olivia, said, "I'm reducing your hours from thirty-two to fifteen a week."

Patrick stood still, his mouth wide open. He wasn't going to ask why. What if the argument got heated, and he spoke aloud?

The parking lot was full of cars, and people were walking in and out of the store. He wished she would walk away. Instead, she stood still and watched him pull and push carts.

"Some people say you're as handsome as Elvis Presley, D'Angelo—hey, I didn't say that, okay?" Olivia looked at her cellphone. "But you're sluggish. If you don't improve your work performance in a week, we may have to find a replacement. So, you can go home now. Come back tomorrow, same time."

As Olivia walked away, like someone who had just admonished a disobedient child, Patrick saw *her* again.

Standing not far from him, Denise's double was staring at him. "I heard that," she said, her shoulders slumping. "I see you work hard every time I come here. But I'm disappointed. Why didn't you say something?"

She sounded so sexy, so civil, so educated, Patrick believed she would be an instant hit on television. "I need the job," he said.

"I detect an accent. Jamaican?"

"No, African."

"Ah, Nigerian?"

"Not every African is Nigerian. Zambian. Know where that is?"

"Of course. I teach African American Studies at Emory." For an awkward moment, they stared at each other, and Patrick was scared. He didn't want to fall in love. "Take care now."

Licking his lips, and his heart throbbing, Patrick watched the lady's white Escalade drive away.

Across the parking lot, Olivia was looking in his direction. He berated himself for not asking for Denise-lookalike's name. Doctor Johnson, Brown, Jackson? And was she looking for a man? Getting a green card through her would be close to finding a replacement for Denise. But could anyone replace Denise?

He wished he could spend more time at work than at home. Staying home meant nursing a wandering mind that would take him into the past and eventually push him to commit suicide. Life had become a burden too heavy to bear.

He thought about D'Angelo as he walked slowly to the back of the store, where he would clock out. The last time he saw him, D'Angelo had lost a lot of weight.

He got home, and Aretha's car was not in front of the house. When he didn't see the car the following morning, he knocked on his landlady's bedroom door. There was no response. The next day, he left for work, hoping nothing had happened to Aretha, for he couldn't contemplate the consequences of her death. The police would pick him up for questioning.

Leroy was hooking carts to form a train when Patrick got to work.

"We've got to work faster, man," said Patrick.

Leroy turned around and gave Patrick a stare, and suddenly, Patrick was afraid.

"The bitch ain't here, man," said Leroy. "I told her, some of the hooks, they broke, man." He pointed at the carts and took several steps away as if he hated what he was working on. "Hey, I notice, the way you behave, sometimes you think you the boss? Were you some kind of manager at KFC, man?" Patrick felt better. Leroy hadn't noticed that he had spoken when he was not supposed to be able to speak. "I heard the bitch, she tell you to go home yesterday." Leroy was never excited, and when he spoke to Patrick, he always did so slowly. Patrick had realized long ago that Leroy couldn't decipher the difference between speaking to someone who was hard of hearing and one who had merely lost his voice. "Man, they arrested them last night. Five guys. Never knew their names, man."

"They who? What did *they* do?"

"Immigration, man. ICE. They ain't cool, man. They were illegal. Cashiers and them. Hey, your voice! It's back!"

A humming sound threatened to render Patrick's ears obsolete. "It comes back sometimes," he whispered.

"Better take some whiskey, bro."

"I will."

Working the shift when Olivia was away made the job Patrick hated more bearable. It was a busy day, and the shift ended without incident. As he walked back home, he wondered what he had achieved that day. Nothing. He needed to be a man again, go back home and confront his demons.

He opened the front door, and Aretha, sporting a navy midi dress and a jacket, was sitting comfortably on the sofa. Patrick interpreted the permanent smile his landlady wore to be a sign of comfort and achievement. She had told him that she earned both social security and a disability.

He got to the foot of the staircase and asked, "Did you go away somewhere, Ms. Aretha?"

"I was in Africa," she responded instantaneously, innocently. "Checking on my gold mines." She laughed boisterously. She stood up. "Going to Walmart now. That's where my friends find their soulmates." She laughed again. "Not soulmates, come on! A boo. You know a beau? Young people don't understand that's just a guy you have a good time with, then you get rid of him because he don't mean much to you."

"Wish you well, Ms. Aretha."

Again, she laughed. "I like it. You beginning to speak like a black man."

That night, Patrick couldn't sleep. If ICE, the immigration police, had come to the supermarket the previous night, they would be back to arrest more people that night. Someday, they would come during the day while he was working, and they would arrest him and deport him. What he needed was a big plan that would give him permanent residency and get a good job and a house. Maybe Denise's double could do that for him? What if he asked her? She was nice to him that morning.

The following afternoon, Patrick had worked only two hours before Olivia told him to clock out. In the evening, someone knocked on Patrick's door. A beautiful woman in her late twenties hovered in the doorway.

"I'm Makeba," she said. "Your landlady's daughter."

Makeba was lighter-skinned than her mother and her brother, which made sense because the siblings didn't have the same father.

"Of course, come in," said Patrick. He showed her the chair by the study table, while he sat on the bed. "I thought your name was Nubia."

"I prefer Makeba." She ran her fingers through her dreadlocks. She seemed to be the carefree type.

"Makeba. Who gave you that name?"

"Dad. He was a prominent member of the Black Panther."

"You know what it means—Makeba?"

"Yes. Greatness. Just like Miriam was a great singer, a freedom fighter, Carmichael's wife. So, Patrick, tell me the truth. Mom is very fond of you. Are you sleeping with her?"

Patrick frowned.

"Why not? She's a beautiful black woman."

"And one who is a quarter-century older than me, and one I'm not married to."

Her eyebrows shot up. "Why does that offend you? Maybe there's some truth in it? And what's this about being married and not sleeping with another woman? Is it a truly African thing? I understand you told Delores the same thing."

Patrick remembered Aretha telling her that Makeba was an associate professor in anthropology at Emory. Was it possible she knew Denise-lookalike, who said she was a professor in African American studies at Emory?

"Hey," she stood up. "It was nice talking to you."

"No, sit down," he said. "Please?" She sat down. "I worry about your mother sometimes. She says weird things." She gazed at him with half a smile. "She told me the other day that she used to be an African king's horse, and that she was there when the white man came to raid the palace for slaves. She used to own diamond mines in Africa, but the white man stole them from her, but yesterday, she said she had gone to Africa to inspect her gold mines. She told me she was sentenced to death in Florida, but she knew some secret African numbers that made her escape death. Have you seen her canned foods? Some of it expired three years ago. She told me that canned food doesn't expire and that the white man who makes it simply wants to produce more and make money."

"Nothing new there," Makeba laughed. "Yeah, it's just getting worse, maybe. I'll check the canned foods out and throw away the bad."

"I think you should be visiting her more often."

"I'm busy." She stood up and headed for the door. "But thank you."

Patrick's phone rang, and Makeba left.

"Patrick, my brother." It was Nicholas. "Sorry I didn't return your calls. Kezia and I would be honored to have you for lunch and dinner on Sunday."

"I'm not sure if I'll be working, but maybe I should come, brother."

"Good. We'll pick you up early Sunday, then. We go to church."

As promised, the couple came to pick him up. Just seeing Kezia made his heart beat faster. She was so beautiful, Patrick wondered how and why she had chosen Nicholas, who was far from being good-looking, for a husband.

"You look good," said Nicholas.

"I don't feel good, *mzee*," said Patrick.

"His Kiswahili is improving," Nicholas addressed his wife. Kezia looked detached. "I hope he has found a Kenyan lady." They all laughed. "The pastor says he's worried about you, given what you told him as the reason why you're here."

"And what exactly did he say was the reason for my being here?" asked Patrick, a headache instantly attacking him, and his mouth rapidly drying up.

"Everything, brother."

Kezia said, "Sweetheart!" Patrick could tell that Kezia was warning her husband about something.

"Oh, yes, I forgot something," said Nicholas. "But do we need to go back home, Kezia?"

"I'm sorry, but I have to ask my sister," said Patrick. "I need some blood pressure medicines. Atenolol, maybe."

"I'll speak to a doctor friend," said Kezia.

"You two are still *friends?*" Nicholas asked angrily.

"Nicholas, I haven't spoken to Dr. Johnson ever since. But that's hard because we work together. I'll ask Karen, our nurse practitioner."

"I don't want to get you in trouble," said Patrick.

"No, no, no," said Kezia. "I can help."

The couple talked about some of their experiences in America. "It's hard to adjust to a life that gives you little time to share your life as a couple," said Nicholas. "Like back home, weekends are free."

"Yes, we're always working," said Kezia, suddenly sounding vibrant.

"The immigration people," said Patrick. "I hear they picked up many people at my store. I can't sleep."

"I'm sorry to hear that," said Nicholas.

"Maybe he should leave work, Nicholas," said Kezia, sounding anxious. "He can stay with us. We have such a big house, and we can't get someone to rent the basement."

"Kezia!" There was an edge in Nicholas's voice. "Couples discuss things like those in private."

Kezia made a clicking sound. She looked behind at Patrick, and their eyes met. Patrick knew he had to stop feeling the way he did toward the woman whose husband had been so kind to him.

"But tell me," said Patrick, "what exactly did the pastor say about my coming here?"

"He said politics," said Kezia. "That you journalists are an endangered species in Africa. Isn't that why you didn't go back?"

Patrick felt a sudden relaxation. Still, he wondered if the pastor had told the couple the real reason why he had not gone back home. "I sometimes don't even want to think about it," he said. If the pastor had told the couple the truth, they probably wouldn't have picked him up.

Nicholas turned to glance at Patrick. "Is there another reason why you couldn't go back home?"

Clasping the back of Kezia's seat with both hands, Patrick felt shaky in the limbs. He had always known that telling the pastor the truth was the second biggest mistake he had ever made after doing what he had done back home which made it impossible for him to go back there.

"Oh, looks like we can't park here," Nicholas spoke to himself as he looked around the large church parking lot. "Too many cars belonging to the good servants of the Lord. Thank you, Jesus."

CHAPTER 45

Denise woke up early and prepared to leave for work. She thought about telling the boys that finally, she had her job back, but she changed her mind. What if Maxx hadn't changed into a good man overnight?

It was 8:00 am, and Rebecca was still in her night clothes. "I will take you later," she said, standing at the kitchen door of her massive mansion. Denise had not seen Uncle Ben since the night Rebecca had taken him to the hospital.

At 9:30, Rebecca was making her face in the car. "I'm so late," said Denise.

"Who says?"

"Maxx expects his staff to be at the office before he walks in. That's seven-thirty."

"That's okay. I spoke to him today. You're not just an employee, girl. You're something special to him."

"What exactly does that mean?"

"Denise, don't shout. It simply means I spoke to him to treat you right. He won't bother you. Just apologize to him."

"Apologize?"

"You know, girl, the most important thing happening to you today is that Maxx is giving you a well-paying job, a job I don't have, myself. A job thousands of qualified people can't have. So, apologize for walking out of a great job."

"Thank you," said Denise. "Before I forget, are you aware that Solomon and his wife have a problem?"

"What kind of problem?"

"I think the wife lives in fear. She avoids talking to me, and the other night, I heard him scold her." You know, like he was talking to a child?" Rebecca chuckled. "Did I say something funny?"

"Every marriage comes with loads of MP—Marital Crap, or MAP, *Masipa A Poho* in our language. BS in English. And maybe that's why my brother left."

"How is Uncle Ben?" Denise changed the subject. She and Patrick didn't have marital crap, but she didn't want to pick up a quarrel with Rebecca. Aunt Rebecca had so far been very supportive of the family.

Rebecca laughed again. Denise didn't like that, so she inquisitively gazed at her sister-in-law. They drove in silence for a long time, and Rebecca used that opportunity to shout obscenities at other drivers, even though her window was closed, and she was the one in the wrong.

"Denise, Uncle Ben, he's always drunk," Rebecca said at last. "Now, let me let you in on a small secret, my dear, provided you tell me your little secret about the pregnancy kit. Okay, you know we built our house, no mortgage, and I pay the bills, Uncle Ben drinks and sleeps. I don't remember the last time he touched me. So, I turned to the nearest store for supplies. Guess who? King Solomon's mines, of course. So, don't think you're the only one with problems in this world."

"What?" Denise felt lightheaded.

"That's why I dress him well. Girl, that boy is good, big, strong, and loyal. And that worthless wife of his? She knows about it, but what can she do? Can she do without the money I pay Solomon?"

Denise was glad she didn't have to respond to that, for the car had stopped by the entrance to the large office complex Maxx was said to have built without taking a mortgage.

"I'll find my way back."

"No, Denise, I'll tell Maxx to drop you home. You two must get to know each other better. And remember to stay away from my Solomon."

Denise opened the car door.

"Before you go," Rebecca said, making faces. "Now that I've told you my secret, tell me, what's your secret?"

Denise got off the vehicle. "Must everyone have a secret?"

"Everyone has a secret, honey."

"Like your brother? What's Patrick's secret that you know about, but you won't tell me...Why am I even saying all these things, Aunt Rebecca?"

Denise slammed the car door behind her and entered the building. As she opened the office door, Matilda Chanda looked excited and said, "The new girl was fired yesterday. She was a bitch. I'm glad you're back, Ms. Denise."

"Thanks, Matilda."

From the doorway, Denise wasn't surprised to see new and expensive furniture in her office. It was a statement from Maxx that she was welcome to a new beginning, one of respect and expensive taste. She still wasn't sure, though, if all would be well this time.

Looking behind her, she said, "Matilda, is everything okay? I mean, between you two?"

Matilda dabbed her eyes with a hankie. "Just didn't sleep well last night. Mosquitoes. I need the job."

"Looks like none of us has any choices, no."

Denise sat at her desk and thought about all the things she could do with the coming paychecks. Rent a good house in a good area, away from Rebecca and her Solomon. Solomon! She shook her head slowly.

She was going to buy new furniture. Get a car note. It would take months before she got all those, of course.

The door opened wide and violently. Wearing a bright yellow suit and red shoes with a red tie to match, Maxx closed the door behind him. A large black feather adorned his white hat. Denise fought hard not to laugh.

"Come to my palace, Mrs. Denise Neo Kanya," Maxx shouted, beckoning.

The furniture in Maxx's office had been upgraded from leather to what Denise believed was super leather. Maxx's English hadn't improved, but he spoke about the need to keep strong family ties. "Many, many years ago, there were many girls, but I choose you to be in my office. You know I pay you best salary in transport industry?"

Still not sure where the conversation was leading, Denise listened attentively. Any wrong move from Maxx, and she would walk out of the office, and this time, for good. Maybe Maxx was a good man, after all? Maybe she shouldn't have left her job in the first place?

"Lady Rebecca," Maxx laughed. "Like Lady Gaga? She told me very sad story. She gave you her guesthouse, but not for long. I tell you, Denise, I will find you house to buy. I have plenty houses. I sell it to you at zero. Something wrong?" Denise shook her head. Five minutes back at work, and already, she was seeing a red flag flying. Maxx buying her a house? "Good. Don't be like many people who do plenty things without too much take care. Tell Matilda to come here. I want to break news."

Denise stood up, and Maxx lit a cigar using a gold lighter, the one he showed off to every visitor to the office. At a time when everyone had become civil enough not to smoke in the working place, Maxx always did. After all, this place was his palace.

"If she's not here, check toilet. She likes toilet. Too much food, that girl." He laughed.

Matilda wasn't at her desk.

In the ladies' restroom, Denise heard someone sobbing behind a closed stall door.
"Matilda? Is that you?"

The door opened slowly to reveal Matilda sitting on the toilet seat, her puffed eyes red as fire. The floor around her was littered with sheets of toilet paper.

"I'll be all right, Ms. Denise." Matilda coughed, as if she was trying to dislodge something big from her throat.

"My goodness, how can I help?"

"Nothing. I'm tired of this job, Ms. Denise. I'm tired. I'm a married woman, but Mr. Maxx..." Matilda took a deep breath. "I've been sleeping with him." She resumed sobbing.

Her heart palpitating, Denise said, "You have been *what?*"

Denise's cellphone rang. It was Norman. What a time to call. "Hey, I was wondering if you could escort me to Livingstone for the weekend?"

"Me?" Denise wished she could tell off Norman. But Norman held the key to her future. He could order his staff to write Patrick's severance check.

"I swear, I won't touch you. Separate rooms."

Matilda was still sobbing, and Denise wanted to shout, *Leave me alone!* Norman was still on the phone, after making a pass at her because Patrick had abandoned her. Maxx was waiting for her and crying Matilda in the palace, where they would hear the big news.

"Is that a joke?" she said and hung up. "Matilda, we must talk."

The main toilet door opened, and three of Maxx's many teenage daughters trooped in.

CHAPTER 46

Patrick was awakened by the loud thumping of the front door downstairs. He looked at his phone. Three in the morning. Usually, he would be insomniac at that time, but that morning was different. So far, he had had a good night's sleep. He stealthily walked downstairs and got to the kitchen window. Several officers with the letters "POLICE ICE" on their top coats stood in the garden, watching Aretha's second-floor windows.

His heart pounding, his knees wobbly, he remembered the immigration raids at the supermarket and wished he had not missed that flight back to his family. He made no noise as he climbed the stairs until he sat in the study chair in his bedroom. He thought of calling Nicholas. But what would the Kenyan brother do? Maybe he too was illegal.

He would have to plead with Aretha to hide him. Maybe she would let him stay with D'Angelo or Makeba for some time. But D'Angelo, wasn't he dying of AIDS or cancer? Given a choice, Patrick would die of cancer, not AIDS.

It was all his fault that he couldn't go back home. Maybe the time had come for him to be deported back home and face the music. Or he could give cash to Aretha and ask her to put it in her bank account and buy him a one-way ticket. He would apologize to Denise and tell her the truth, and maybe she would understand. No, no, no! He shook his head. Neither Denise nor anyone he knew would understand. He just shouldn't have done what he did.

He was startled by a loud knock on his door. "It's immigration," said Aretha, and he was mad with her. Why did she speak so loudly? He rushed to the door and opened it. Aretha was already heading down the staircase.

"Please, Ms. Aretha, I..." he whispered, but she didn't seem to have heard him, for she kept walking downstairs, taking her time.

He got back to his room and looked around. He started to pack his belongings. Clothes. Shoes under the bed. Would they torture him? Would they let him keep the cash he hid under the mattress? And back home, would he get a job as good as the one he had before?

Downstairs, Ms. Aretha was talking to someone in low tones. Patrick feared that the police would shoot Ms. Aretha and claim it was him who had killed her.

He waited.

Finally, he heard the front door close and the lock click.

Aretha hobbled up the staircase and shouted, "They came to the wrong door," and in a matter of minutes, he heard her snore.

He couldn't sleep after that, and at long last, when the sun came up, he found Aretha in the kitchen.

"They got them," said Aretha.

"Who?"

"The police. You know that small Latino man who was crazy for me? Julio? They took him, his family away."

"I know Julio, Ms. Aretha."

He remembered Julio asking him to marry his wife. Was America that good that people from all parts of the world would do anything to live in the land of jail time and unaffordable healthcare?

Patrick didn't feel like leaving home but had to go to D'Angelo's home to collect his check. Julio's arrest had shaken him to the core. He and Julio had one thing in common—living illegally in America, and in fear. He was worried about D'Angelo's deteriorating health, too.

It was Saturday and not as cold as Patrick had anticipated, so he dressed casually. He called for a cab, and Aretha was surprised when it arrived an hour later.

"The white man, he expects everyone to buy a car from him and buy gas, Patrick," she said amusedly. "Tell my son to be strong."

Like Julio, the Latino cab driver spoke very little English, but he found his way to D'Angelo's home without trouble.

"Please wait for me," said Patrick. "I won't be long."

Sitting on an old sofa that, in Patrick's opinion, ought to have been thrown away years ago, D'Angelo looked a sorry sight. The foul smell of garbage in the living room made Patrick wish he was back home in his ship-shape Meanwood house. Patrick took the garbage out and offered to vacuum the house.

"The vacuum don't work, bro. Not really broke. Just a little problem with it." D'Angelo's wheezy voice was almost a whisper. He had lost more weight, and his hair was falling off. "Tell you what, bro? You're a good man. My mother comes here, she don't make the offer to clean up. I don't have children of my own, but I have a nephew who's like a son to me. Lives in Florida. Hey, did you play my numbers?"

Since D'Angelo had stopped venturing outside his home, Patrick had been buying lottery tickets for him at the supermarket. Sometimes, D'Angelo expressed disappointment when his numbers didn't win. At other times, he simply said, "I won't need money in my grave."

They sat in extended silence.

"You never talk about your dad," Patrick spoke.

"He was a good guy." D'Angelo turned on that faraway smile of his. "A tough military man. Like many of us black men, he died in jail." He paused and wheezed. "There's something clever about you I haven't figured out. Listen, do you intend to live in this country?"

Patrick gave himself some time to think before he said, "I don't know."

"Just from what I seen, bro, you're too soft for this kind of life. You gotta learn to be hard to survive. I hear the other day you denied a good woman a good time. Delores?" D'Angelo chuckled and a bout of coughing set in. "She's a beautiful black woman. I always like wanted her myself, but my mother, she wouldn't let me. Shit! Even my mother, she likes you, bro."

"*Your* mother?"

"Hey, you never talk about your family."

Patrick rose. "It's a long story, but I have to go. The taxi is waiting."

"Can you talk to me about Africa sometime? You know, we hear of dangerous snakes, lions, stuff like that. How do the niggers over there manage that?" He chuckled.

"Well, I guess your ancestors..."

"No, don't say that. My ancestors didn't come from the jungle. I'm American. I wouldn't go there because I value my life. Just want to hear about it—if you see what I mean."

"Well, your mother said she was once an African queen."

"My mother is a special woman. You know that."

A bottle of sleeping tablets and another of Hennessy sat on an old side table. Next to that was Patrick's check, which was already signed and ready to be deposited in Aretha's bank account.

"You...you..." D'Angelo stuttered and coughed. "I got some sleeping tablets for you. Some for blood pressure, too. Just remove my name from the bottles. Told my doctor I had accidentally thrown mine in the toilet." He laughed for a long time before he started to cough again.

"Thanks, brother," said Patrick. "I appreciate you. When we started working together, I thought you were devoid of feelings. I was wrong." He wondered what would happen if D'Angelo died. Would he still be able to work?

D'Angelo closed his eyes. "*Devoid.* Do you always use the white man's big words in the Motherland?"

Patrick picked up the check and the medications and hurried outside. The cab was still waiting.

Patrick got in the back seat and said, "Okay, here is what I want to do..." He realized that the cab driver was black. "What happened to...?"

"He was called, and they sent me to wait for you," said the man with a southern African accent. "He has an immigration problem."

Patrick ignored the chest pain that had been bothering him for some time and said, "No problem." He went on to outline his plan. "All I want, brother, is to find a friend. A female friend."

The driver cupped his chin in his right hand.

CHAPTER 47

His heart pounding in his chest, Patrick sat in the back seat of the stationary cab for half an hour, two cars away from a white Escalade. For weeks, he had studied the lady's shopping routine. He was glad the lady had not broken her routine that morning. He would wait for her to come back to her car, even if that meant spending half his week's wages on the taxi fare.

"The name Hove, is that your last name?" Patrick asked.

"Yes, Goodson Hove, Junior," said the cab driver. "I'm originally from Zimbabwe."

"What a small world! My name is Patrick Kanya. From Zambia."

Goodson turned to face Patrick, and the two men shook hands. "You Zambians, you people, you mean so much to us. I wasn't born at that time when the white rebels under Ian Smith unilaterally declared independence from the British and introduced apartheid in Southern Rhodesia. My parents, like many blacks, they fled the country and came to Zambia. That's where I was born and raised. My father was a man of great wisdom. When my country became independent, he stayed in Zambia. Dad, he will retire next month as a highly respected judge. You know, brother, I didn't listen to him, so when my country, it became independent, I went to Zimbabwe. You see me now, I drive a taxi in a white man's land. Like Ian Smith, President Mugabe, he forced everybody out of the country."

Patrick would never forget Judge Hove and the television news story and how, it was rumored, it had incensed the honorable judge.

"Of course," Patrick said, and he heard a relentless knock at his window.

"What are you doing in the cab?" she asked.

With the fury of a caged animal, Patrick stared at Aretha, who wore a broad smile. "I'm going somewhere."

"I want you to use your staff discount and buy me bananas."

To Goodson, Patrick said hastily, "I'll be back. Just watch that Escalade."

Goodson nodded and Patrick walked briskly toward the supermarket, Aretha scurrying behind him. It was still warm, but the sky was overcast. He hoped it wasn't going to rain. "Just bananas?" he asked.

"Just bananas, Patrick."

Leaving her standing near the self-checkout, Patrick hurried to the fresh produce area and hastily collected ten bananas. He got to the checkout, and Aretha said, "The bananas ain't right. Can you get the big ones?"

"Ms. Aretha, the cab's waiting."

"Why are you whispering, Patrick?" Aretha laughed, and Patrick gave her an angry look. "Something wrong?"

He hadn't seen Denise-lookalike in the supermarket. Had she left already? How could Aretha be so unfair to him? He rushed back to the fresh produce area and replaced the bananas with large ones.

"I like them big," said Aretha while Patrick paid for the bananas.

"Two dollars fifty," he said.

"Give me the receipt," Aretha said.

Patrick gave the bananas to his landlady and rushed toward the exit.

He was panting and sweating when he got to the cab, and Goodson was fast asleep behind the driver's wheel. The Escalade was still parked where he had left it.

Patrick waited for another fifteen minutes in the back seat of the cab before she appeared. He concluded that Americans' shopping habits were very predictable.

"That's the lady," said Patrick, the sight of her making his heart palpitate.

Goodson yawned and said, "Ah, I see why. She's beautiful beyond measure." Goodson seemed to be the reserved type, and he wore a cap that reminded Patrick of Andy Capp, the comic strip his late father never failed to read first before he read the rest of the daily paper. That, and the soft sound of Southern African music that came from the cab's hidden speakers made Patrick feel nostalgic for his home and his late father.

"You say your wife looks like her?"

"Almost to every detail."

Goodson chuckled. "You don't know about that, brother. So, why not just sleep with your wife?" Patrick didn't answer. "You know, an American taxi driver wouldn't do this. But I trust you. That's one good or bad thing about us Africans. We're too trusting. Look at what the white man did to us, but we still talk to him."

"Do we have a choice, bro?"

Denise-lookalike leisurely put her shopping in the back seat, and soon, the Escalade was driving away.

Goodson was an experienced cab driver. Not even once did Patrick lose sight of the Escalade, and yet Goodson allowed one or two cars between the cab and the Escalade.

Patrick had spent hours thinking about what he was going to say to her. *You look like my wife.* So what? And where is she? *In Africa.* Why isn't she with you? *Bad politics.*

They were on Alpharetta Street in the city of Roswell, and the Escalade suddenly slowed down. Goodson stopped the cab. With unmatched expertise, Denise-lookalike embedded the big SUV in a tight parking space. She came out of the vehicle and without looking behind her, walked hurriedly away. A car horn startled Patrick. Goodson found a parking space and apologized to the other driver, who gave him the finger.

"Racist," Goodson muttered.

"I have only cash, brother," said Patrick.

"Just give me whatever you can," said Goodson.

It was only then that Patrick realized that the cab meter had not been running all the time.

"Won't you get in trouble?"

"No, I won't. I sympathize with a man who's in love. Besides, you people did so much for us."

"Seriously?" Patrick was in a hurry to leave, for Denise-lookalike was approaching a corner. He didn't want to lose sight of her.

"I was in love once." There was melancholy in Goodson's voice. "Very much in love. Until I found her in bed with my uncle, a ruling party activist, a ruffian, a terrorist. There's nothing I could do, brother. Ruling party cadres were so powerful during the Mugabe days, you could die if you challenged them. Go on, she's hidden by that building. I don't want your money. Your people, you taught me that life is more important than money."

"I don't know how to thank you."

Patrick got out of the cab, and the sky was dark, the cold wind menacingly hitting his face. He still didn't know exactly what he was up to, and if it was right. He hadn't left his wife and family to get married to a stranger. Rather, it was to run away from what he had done, something that would soon hurt and haunt him even more.

He saw her when he got to the end of the building, and she was still just as irresistible, but suddenly, he feared she would call the police and claim he was stalking her. But did she see him at the supermarket?

She hastened her pace. It was as if she knew she was being pursued. Or did she want to make sure the dark clouds above didn't surprise her with a heavy shower that would leave her short hair wet? Okay, all he wanted was to hear her voice again, even though she didn't sound exactly like Denise.

He walked on, and the more he looked at her, the more resemblance between her and Denise he saw. He glanced behind him. Goodson's cab wasn't in sight. Through the large windows of a Lucky's Burger and Brew restaurant, he saw her. She was walking toward an unoccupied table. Was she waiting for her husband?

He was a few yards away from the entrance when he felt something annoying and vengeful in his left eye. pulled his eyelid down and let go. It felt better. He remembered Grandma Alice. She used to blow air into his eye, and the force of the air often removed the offending item. Well, Grandma Alice was dead, and he was there to fend for himself.

Denise-lookalike was seated and seemed to be studying the menu. Suddenly, he felt guilty. He was still deeply in love with Denise, and here he was, pursuing a total stranger.

He entered the restaurant, and not far from her table, he stood still, wondering if he should walk over to her and tell her that she looked like his wife. He was aware that she was aware he was staring. He quickly looked to his right.

"Do you live here?" she asked.

Four women sat at the corner table next to Denise-lookalike's. And Patrick couldn't believe what he was seeing.

Dr. Emily Ramson.

CHAPTER 48

Ten minutes, and Matilda, tears in her eyes, and Kneelex tissue on her lap, didn't seem to want to leave Denise's office.

"I don't have a choice," Matilda spoke at last. "My husband hasn't worked in a year. He has a degree, but he can't find a job."

"I understand," said Denise. For as long as Maxx didn't come in looking for his secretary, Denise would let Matilda sit there and cry. Everyone needed a shoulder to cry on.

"I can't even go home to cry there, Ms. Denise. My husband will be asking why I'm not at work."

"I'm sorry," Denise said, and Matilda reluctantly stood up and left.

A few minutes later, Denise heard Matilda talk cheerfully to a visitor. She concluded that it was what all poor people had to do if they wanted to avoid being homeless and hungry.

There was a lot of work to do, and Maxx seemed to have forgotten about his wish to announce the big news.

"I take you home?" Maxx eventually appeared in Denise's doorway, just when she had picked up her bag, ready to go home.

"No," she said. Someone is giving me a ride.

"Another man?"

"No. My sister-in-law."

Maxx didn't look convinced, but he let Denise pass by and leave. She took a cab home and entered Rebecca's house through the kitchen. Solomon, the servant, was placing pieces of chicken in a large pot.

"Madam Denise is here, madam," Solomon said without looking at Denise, who studied the man with great interest. She couldn't imagine Rebecca in bed with him.

"Come in, come in!" Rebecca shouted from the living room.

Wearing a dressing gown, Rebecca was sitting on a sofa. "Sit down," she said, and suddenly, she seemed to realize that her thighs were over-exposed, for she rearranged the gown to cover her fully.

"I'll not take much of your time, but I thought I should tell you about Norman."

"Norman Tau?"

"He's invited me for a weekend in Livingstone."

"Now you're talking," said Rebecca. "Sit down. King Solomon?" she shouted. "Make us some tea." Denise sat down. "Livingstone, eh?"

A city to the south of the country, and at the border with Zimbabwe, Livingstone was named after Dr. David Livingstone, a Scottish explorer and Christian missionary who had paved the way for the conquest of Southern Africa by Britain. The city was popularly known as the nation's "tourist capital." Not far from the city's business center, the waters of the mighty Zambezi River, the fourth-longest river in Africa, fell into a 335-feet precipice, twice the height of the Niagara Falls, to create a noisy opera Denise's people called the Mosi-Oa-Tunya, or 'The Smoke That Thunders,' which the missionary had named 'The Victoria Falls', and was later classified as one of the seven natural wonders of the world.

"Who doesn't want to go to Livingstone, girl?" Rebecca asked. "I'm almost tempted to ask you to take me with you, but…Hey, he likes you, not me. Go and marry him. I'll take care of my nephews while you're away. Have some good sex."

Denise's chest tightened. "I can't believe you're saying that."

"What I said is what you wanted me to say, isn't it? Don't misunderstand me, girl. I simply want you to be happy. Look, Patrick? You know why I hate him? It's because he ran away from you. Hey, Solomon, are the tea leaves running away from you?"

"No," Denise said and rose. "I'll have no tea."

"Suit yourself, but sit down."

A resentment toward her sister-in-law bubbling inside her, Denise sat down.

"Aren't you going to tell me who has been sleeping with you in my guesthouse?" asked Rebecca, teeth tight together. "And don't tell me it's Solomon."

"I was raped," Denise retorted. "On the day Alice died. Someone drugged me, and Wizzie took advantage of me."

Rebecca studied her fingernails. Denise suspected that her sister-in-law didn't believe her story.

"I'm sorry to hear that. So, tomorrow, I'll take you to the Planned Parenthood Center. Yes, Denise, they're confidential. You'll test for HIV, for STDs."

"Thank you, Aunt Rebecca."

This time, Denise left the massive house through the front door. She didn't want to face Solomon, whom she believed had been eavesdropping on her conversation with Rebecca. She walked briskly to the guesthouse, and several times, she stumbled, but she was determined to get to her room before she broke down. Rebecca and Solomon! Had Denise become so outdated, so conservative over the months Patrick had been away, that she couldn't find anyone who seemed to think like her? How come Rebecca didn't see anything wrong with Norman inviting her to Livingstone for the weekend? Wasn't Norman asking her for a date? But then wasn't Rebecca sleeping with her houseboy? Wasn't Matilda sleeping with Maxx? Okay, Matilda saw something wrong with that. So, maybe Denise wasn't the only one who was crazy.

She didn't sleep well that night, and the following morning, she was so tired, she wished she would stay in bed. But it was Friday, and Maxx didn't like his staff reporting late for work on Fridays. "You want longer weekend?" he often screamed on Mondays. "Go forever weekend."

She got a cab and got to work early, and Matilda looked cheerful. Denise hoped she would have a chance to advise Matilda to learn to defend her dignity. Denise had stood up to Maxx, and she was given her job back. She could never see herself sleeping with Maxx. Never.

Her heart went pit-a-pat. She hadn't told Norman that she was not traveling with him to Livingstone. She hoped he would understand. She picked up her phone and called. Norman answered on the first ring.

"It's like you were watching your phone," she said, and she heard him laugh.

"I was about to call," he said curtly. "To tell you that I have changed plans."

"Oh, you have?" Denise wished she hadn't said those words.

"Yeah. Instead of going to Livingstone, we have booked two rooms…Uhm, they call them tents over there. Tents. We leave first thing tomorrow. We'll spend one night at the Victoria Falls River Lodge, on the Zimbabwean side."

She wanted to stop him, but he had the cheek to go on as if he was talking to a toy he had bought on Amazon. Norman wasn't asking her for anything. He was telling her what the program was. She was still in the slow process of recovering from her daughter's death, for goodness' sake. "So, I'll pick you up early. See you then"

Norman had hung up, and Denise was befuddled. Maybe it was the way things were supposed to be; someone sort of running her life to show her the way to happiness? But was there such a thing as the way *things are supposed to be*? What did that mean? That Patrick had left her for any man to abuse her?

On her desktop, Denise googled the Victoria Falls River Lodge. The rooms there were highly-priced, but she knew Norman could afford that. Maybe she needed to go? Didn't Norman say he had booked two rooms? That meant they would be sleeping separately, unless, of course, that was a trick.

She would decide later in the day.

"It's a nice office, Denise!"

Denise looked up. Rebecca was dressed to kill. How did she come in, unannounced? Where was Matilda?

"I talked to someone about those tests I told you about." Rebecca sat down. It was as if she owned the office.

"Uh, yes." Denise wondered if Rebecca and Norman had connived to do the test so that Norman would be sure he didn't catch a disease. She wasn't going to Livingstone to sleep with him. But the tests. What if she had contracted AIDS? Then maybe she would have a good reason to take her own life, for she couldn't imagine herself living with the disease and dying slowly with the shame that came with it.

The two women drove to a private clinic in Emmasdale Suburb, where they were quickly ushered into a small treatment room. A nurse gave a form to Denise.

"No, no, no!" Rebecca grabbed the form and tore it into pieces, which she scattered on a bed. "What's this crap? I'm paying for top confidential."

The nurse said, "My fault." She smiled. "Madam, we need your urine, blood, and a mouth swab."

An hour later, as the two drove home, Rebecca said, "This Wizzie man is clean, girl. No HIV, no STDs? Are you sure it was him or Solomon? Because Solomon is clean."

Denise managed a fake smile.

For the first time in a long time, Denise slept well that night. Knowing that Wizzie hadn't infected him with an STD was good news. Early the following morning, she called Norman and said, "I'm ready when you are."

Her bag sitting by the door, Denise told the boys that she would be away at work and that they would be sleeping in Aunt Rebecca's big house.

"I want to come with you, but I want to sleep in the big house," said Junior.

The telephone rang. Norman was at the gate, and Junior was on the verge of tears. There was a loud knock on the front door.

"Come on, open the door," Rebecca shouted. "You can't make him wait, girl."

Junior rushed to open the door, and Rebecca hugged him.

"Denise?" Rebecca said, "This is great. You're wearing makeup for him!"

Denise wasn't going to let Rebecca spoil her day. Surely, she hadn't gone overboard with her makeup.

"Come with me for breakfast, baby," Rebecca said, and Junior looked pleased. "Where's Chris?"

Denise got to the gate, and the guard saluted her. She was always embarrassed by that, but that's what Rebecca wanted.

Norman didn't come out of the red Land Cruiser double cab pickup he was driving. Wearing shades and looking disoriented, he signaled to Denise to put her bag in the back seat. She was tempted to say it was him who was supposed to put the bag in there, and that she wasn't coming. But she needed Norman to pay Patrick's terminal benefits, so she obeyed, opened the passenger door and sat in the passenger seat. While she was sure she didn't like Norman, she was certain she liked the smell of new leather seats.

Without saying a word, Norman pulled his shades down, and the trip began.

"Have you had forgotten how to speak?" she asked.

"Yes, sometimes I do forget how to say words in any language," he said pleasantly.

After being on the road for five hours, the couple had not even covered half the 230-mile trip between Lusaka and Livingstone. The problem was that Norman stopped many times to either pee or buy a snack. Denise wondered if Norman was diabetic, but she didn't ask. He made her laugh and she suspected he must have googled the many jokes he told so well. Several times, he said, "Again, if you don't mind, I want some quiet to reflect on things."

Denise liked that because she too wanted time to think. Besides, both had lost their loved ones not so long ago.

"Tell me, what's the dirtiest part of one's body?" he asked.

"What a question," she said. If the question was meant to be a joke, she didn't like it.

"Now, don't say it's what I think you're thinking," he said, and she wished he would change the subject.

"It's your mouth," he said triumphantly, reminding her of Junior.

"No, Norman, it can't be."

Norman slowed down the vehicle and turned his head to look at Denise. "Well, would your body be filled with all that shit if it wasn't for the mouth that put the shit in it?"

She nodded, and she didn't like the joke.

"If we have a flat tire, you're going to change it."

"Why me?" she asked.

"Because I can't do three big things at the same time—driving, changing tires, and being the man."

They laughed together, and for a moment, she felt close to him. The next moment, she wondered if she was doing the right thing, even when that thing had Rebecca's approval. She just wasn't ready for a relationship. So far, during the trip, Norman had not said a word about Patrick. That was the way Denise wished it to be.

"Do you know how many years the human race has been on this earth?" he asked.

"I think I know that one. Six million?"

"And how many graveyards are there?"

"No one knows that one, I'm sure."

"Makes me wonder how come we're not running out of burial land." He cleared his throat. "Go to church?"

"No, and I never discuss religion."

"Same here."

"Then case closed," she said with finality.

They finally got to Livingstone and headed south. From miles away, Denise saw the famous spray of water rising into the sky like smoke and forming a rainbow. They got to the falls, and it was the first time she was seeing them. She couldn't believe the magnificence of the falls, and she wished she could bathe in them naked with Patrick by her side and relocate to the city of Livingstone.

She was too scared to escort him as he crossed one of the gorges to an island, using the narrow Knife-Edge Bridge that was constantly bathed in water sprays.

They got to the Zimbabwean side of the Zambia-Zimbabwe border at the Victoria Falls Bridge and an immigration officer asked for their passports.

Denise felt a powerful force squeeze her heart. "I don't have a passport," she whispered to Norman. She never had one, and the last time a close family member used a passport to cross borders, he had never come back.

"I didn't know there were people living normal lives without passports," Norman said, and Denise felt slighted.

"You can take a chance on the other side, director," said the immigration officer.

Denise felt a little dizzy as they drove slowly on the high bridge that divided the two countries that were once part of the Rhodesian federation with Malawi. She avoided looking on the sides, and soon, they were at the Zimbabwean immigration post.

Norman pulled the tough-looking immigration officer to one side and said, "What's your name, sir?"

Denise heard the officer say, "Sam."

"Look, Brother Sam, we told your friends on the other side that we were just looking around. Look, the borders between African countries were delineated by foreigners—the Europeans. That was in Berlin, Germany, in 1864. Otherwise, we're one people." He raised his voice and continued, "Why do we have these borders?"

"You're right," said another immigration officer who seemed to have been eavesdropping on the conversation. "For instance, my parents ran away from white supremacy in the 60s, so I was born in Zambia. You can go, madam. Just make sure you're here after lunch tomorrow. I'll be here."

For the first time, Denise understood why Norman was a director. While she was impressed by his power of persuasion, she wished immigration had turned her away. She would have spent the night on the Zambian side, while he probably would have proceeded to Zimbabwe. She saw him as a powerful man who made things happen. Would Patrick have managed to do what Norman had just done? But if Norman was so persuasive, how come he hadn't facilitated the issuance of Patrick's terminal benefits?

Norman didn't gloat about his great performance at the border, and when they got to the lodge, she loved what she saw.

The lodge seemed to be an extension of the river, but away from the water.

He escorted her to her tent. "I hope you love it here, Denise," he said.

Of course, she did. Her room was an airy tent with a ceiling made of river reeds, giving it a true and inviting African feel. The bed was massive, and a mosquito net dangled from the ceiling. From where she stood, the freestanding tub looked as if it was floating in the river.

"I want you to be happy, Denise," he said politely, and he seemed to mean it. "My tent is not far from yours." He sounded tired, and he wasn't going to harm her, she concluded. He was a gentleman. If he tried to harm her, she would scream and cause a scene. In his position, he wouldn't want to make headlines on Zimbabwean television. "I'll go to my tent now and give you time to get ready, for we have a river trip to make before it gets dark."

The sun was still up when he came for her, and they went on a boat cruise to an island. It felt strange to be the only black couple on the boat—well, they were not a couple, but she suspected everyone thought they were. She could tell from their accents that some of the tourists came from the United States. She hated thinking about the United States.

Although Denise had seen wild animals before each time she drove from Lusaka to her western hometown of Mongu, it was the first time she was seeing elephants and other animals on a conducted tour. She wished Patrick and the kids—all the three of them—were there to see what she was seeing.

"I love these innocent creatures," she told Norman, and a couple that had introduced themselves as the Whittinghams from the south of England agreed with her.

"I hunt them, Denise," Norman said dolefully. "I hunt them, I kill them, but since your friend's death, I haven't killed a single living thing. I don't even touch my guns."

It was dark when they got back to the lodge, and he suggested they have dinner before they went to their tents. "Is that okay?"

he asked, and although she would have preferred to clean up first, she nodded a yes.

She ordered butternut soup, to be followed by pork fillet. "Add anything you consider good enough for a hungry woman," she said.

The main meal came, it was so huge, she wasn't able to eat even half of it. She wished she would have a to-go box for her kids, but Chris and Junior were hundreds of miles away from the natural beauty around her.

"I'm not used to full meals," she told Norman, who had ordered the same meal as hers.

"Is it lack of appetite or…?" he asked naively.

"The money, Norman," she said. "Life has been hard since…" She didn't want to talk about Patrick. She wasn't there to have great fun, of course, but neither was she there to talk about negative things.

It was hard to watch half the meal being taken away to be trashed. Yet again, she agreed, on Norman's insistence, to have dessert. It was vanilla ice cream, and suddenly, she felt tears rolling out of her eyes. Norman looked concerned. "Is it something I said, Denise?"

"No," she said and dried the tears. "Just thinking about my kids. I know they're eating well tonight from Aunt Rebecca's table. She's a good woman."

"No doubt," he said and touched her hand. She didn't ask him to remove the hand because she didn't want to cause a scene. Besides, Norman meant well. "Rebecca, we took the same course in our freshman year. Oh, Rebecca was a tough nut. Kind but a straight talker."

He walked her to her tent, and she felt a little uncomfortable when he came in and sat down, uninvited.

"I hope you had a great day," he said. There was fatigue in his voice.

"Yes, a great day, thanks," she said. "But I'm so tired, I'd love to have a shower now."

"Ah," he said and stood up. "A gentleman knows when it's time to leave."

"Good night, Norman."

He didn't say goodbye. He just turned to face the door and left.

He had said that his tent was not far from hers, so if there was trouble in the night, she would call him. She had a hot bath, and she was tempted to call Rebecca, but that would have meant speaking to her children. She decided to go to bed. The pillows were so comfortable, she wondered if she should ask the hotel staff where they had bought them.

For hours, she couldn't sleep, though. She felt uncomfortable because she had overeaten, and she knew her kids would have loved the food. She shouldn't have come with Norman, as that meant she was cheating on Patrick. Also, she feared that soon, Norman would be at the door with a plausible excuse to be in her tent at that late hour in the night.

She waited. What game was Norman playing? Didn't he want her? Then why did he bring her there at such great expense? Of course, she wouldn't have let him in. But it would have been…almost good to know that someone higher in society than Wizzie wanted her.

She woke up in the morning feeling good. Norman hadn't made a demand on her, so he gained her respect.

He didn't come to her tent, which was good. Instead, he called and asked when they could meet for breakfast.

"Did you sleep well, Denise?" he asked when they met. "Great dreams?"

She remembered then that she had dreamt about Patrick warning her not to sleep with Norman. They had a fight, and she couldn't remember how the dream ended.

"Remember, we have to get to the border after lunch," she said. "Sam will be there to help us."

"Don't worry about that," he quipped. "What can they do to you? Stop you from entering your own country?"

They didn't say much to each other during breakfast or the short trip to the immigration post at the Victoria Falls Bridge. Sam was friendly and asked them to visit Zimbabwe again. "But remember to bring your passport next time, madam."

Hours later, when the vehicle stopped at Rebecca's gate, again, Norman didn't come out of the SUV to help her with the bag. Instead, he said, "I'm glad you didn't catch a disease, Denise."

Denise got to the gate, and the guard opened it for her.

In Rebecca's living room, Junior was playing a video game and didn't seem too excited to see his mother. Rebecca was eager to hear what had happened, so she invited Denise to the garage, where the two women sat in Rebecca's vehicle.

"I called Norman last night, but he didn't pick up, so I didn't call you. I took it you two were at it. After such a long time, Denise, it must have hurt, right?"

"I'm not that kind of person, Rebecca," said Denise. "Besides, I didn't catch a disease."

"He said that?" Rebecca looked and sounded upset. "Okay, so, you two didn't sleep together? Well, I guess sleeping with Norman would mean you, girl, cheating on my brother."

"I'm not that kind of woman."

"Okay, I'm disappointed Norman opened his big mouth but didn't propose. Maybe what they say about him is true. Do you know if he's a man?"

"How would I know?"

Rebecca seemed to be thinking deeply. "I want you to listen carefully," Rebecca said with a great sense of seriousness. "You should court Maxx. Don't sigh heavily like that, Denise. It's a strategy. You don't have to sleep with him. He's an old man, he works hard, always tired. Just be his woman, for goodness' sake. He will pay you well."

"I'm tired..."

"No, you can't be too tired to listen to your landlady, Denise. It's the reason Maxx gave you a job and putting myself in his shoes, I entirely agree with him. You don't get the good things for nothing in this world. Look, I'll always be your sister-in-law. I give you the go-ahead to court Maxx. If Norman is the kind of fool that can take the most beautiful black woman to the most expensive hotel in Africa and not demand sex, then he's not man enough to deserve you. So, go for the man who will give you a good time and the money."

Denise opened the passenger door of Rebecca's Range Rover, got out, and started to walk to the guesthouse.

Rebecca was right behind her. "Denise, let's be realistic. You know, girl, I built this guesthouse using my entire savings so that I could collect rent. I already have someone waiting to move in and pay me good money." Denise stopped walking, allowing her sister-in-law to catch up with her. "My future tenant is smart, handsome, and he's single, girl."

Denise could tell that his sister-in-law was slightly inebriated. "Go ahead and evict me, Rebecca."

"You know I will. My tenant is ready to move in next week." Rebecca sauntered away.

The next day, at the office, Denise tried to be as positive as she could. If Rebecca were to evict her and keep the boys, she had no doubt her kids would enjoy a more qualitative life in their aunt's house. In which case, it would not hurt them much if Denise took her life.

CHAPTER 49

Although she had shaved her head, Patrick was sure the person he was staring at was Emily. Had she lost her hair due to her illness? Where he came from, women usually shaved their heads when they lost their husbands. The mere sight of her stirred deep inside him, though. She was just as attractive as the last time he saw her.

She and three other women were seated at a corner table, and one of them was talking rapidly while the others laughed. He hadn't had company like that since he came to America. He took cautious steps toward the table, away from Denise-lookalike. The laughter ceased as the women returned his gaze. He stood next to Emily, unable to move, not knowing what to say as she looked up. Looking into those sparkling, large, sexy, green eyes gave him a hollow feeling in the stomach. Why hadn't he met her before he met Denise? In his days at the university, many American students came to study a subject or two for one semester. Many dated local students. Why hadn't she joined them?

Suddenly, he was conscious of his looks. For more than a year, he had lived a thrifty life, so his jeans were worn, and his T-shirt and top were craggy. He couldn't remember ever polishing his steel-toe shoes.

Emily excused herself, stood up and headed for the exit. Feeling like a child who had to go wherever his parents went, he followed.

Outside, it was cold and drizzling. She was standing not far from the entrance and close to a group of four white young men who were overly excited about the rain. One of them spread his arms wide, looked up in the sky and danced.

"Anne May told me you hadn't left," she said, and he was still in love with her voice.

"Oh, she did?"

"Your ticket, sir, wasn't used." She wasn't looking in his direction as she spoke, and time and again, she passed her left hand over her scalp. "Let's make this quick, okay? Mary Anne is my colleague. She lied about me quitting my job. I took a two-week vacation to avoid meeting you." She spoke fast. "I wasn't HIV positive."

Patrick feared he was going to collapse. "You mean...you're not positive?" His mouth was dry. He needed a drink. A Coke. If Emily was serious, he was free of the killer virus.

"Can I finish talking, sir?" He nodded. "I've been testing every so often, just in case *you* had AIDS, not me. I'm negative. But I was angry—very angry, in fact, with you when you let that...whatever...break. You shouldn't have done that. And yet I enjoyed what we did. The fact that I didn't attack you violently then confirmed one thing, that I was falling for you and frighteningly so. You told the class how happily married you were, so by telling you I was positive, I thought you'd hate me and keep away from me. I wanted you so badly, and yet I needed to stay away from you. Make sense? That's why I wrote that blackmail note. To scare you."

They were getting wet, and he was feeling hot and disorientated. He didn't want to cry, for that would be a sign of weakness. What he knew to be certainly wrong was that because of Emily, he had abandoned his family.

"Can we sit down somewhere?" he asked. "Maybe in your car?"

"In my car?" she chortled, shrugged, and looked around her, the buildings, the roads, the cars, and the people witnessing the occasion without being privy to the harsh words that shaped the drama. "No!"

He could feel his energy levels running low. He needed a fizzy drink. He remembered the note that had fallen off his door that last morning of the first phase of the workshop. He had suspected Kamili, the Tanzanian, of writing it. He remembered how he had missed the plane back home because he believed he was HIV positive. He wasn't worried about his own infection. It was the knowledge that he had infected his innocent wife that had bothered him most. He wouldn't have survived the pain of seeing Denise suffer because of his infidelity. How would he have handled the stigma that would follow? When he made the decision not to go back home, what he had in mind was the memory of his subordinates who had died from AIDS. How the disease had decimated their bodies to a mass of sores, their skins turning gray like ash. He had feared that he was going to look like them. Maybe Denise would even die before he did. What would he have told her when she discovered they were both HIV positive? He couldn't have accused her of cheating on him. He was convinced the answer, selfish as it was, was to run away from his family.

He stole a glance at the restaurant and imagined Denise-lookalike sitting alone at her table. "Are we going to talk in the rain?"

She looked him in the face. "What's there to talk about? You think we're lovers? And yes, I love the rain, don't you? You don't know a thing about me, sir."

He wanted to touch her, feel her smooth skin and ask her not to address him as 'sir.' He hoped he would hear her say he had meant something to her even for a second. That he should leave Aretha's home and move in with her. That she would find him a job, a better job than the crappy one he had at the supermarket.

"What are you waiting for? I've given you the good news, sir. Now, leave me alone." She looked at the skies. The rain was beginning to let up. He wanted to curse her, to tell her that she had lied to him, but suddenly, he was yearning for her again, and he couldn't understand why. He wanted to ask her if it was true she wasn't HIV positive. After all, hadn't she lied to him before?

"Don't get me wrong," she said. "You were the man I yearned for and yet couldn't keep." She raised her voice: "And of course, I was wrong to think you were a smart guy."

One of the four young men standing by stepped forward and said, "Excuse me, lady. Is this handsome guy giving you trouble?" The man's friends laughed.

"No," she said. "This guy made me pregnant and I couldn't find him, so I aborted."

Patrick rubbed his forehead. The man who had posed the question shrugged and looked away. It was as if he was embarrassed, and yet Patrick saw him smile as he stole a glance, first at Emily, and then at him before he rejoined his friends.

"I wasn't protected when we...did what we did," she hissed. "Sir, in that workshop, I taught you the right way to use a condom. You were so stiff, so rough, so big, so sweet!" She chuckled. "How could I keep a child who would never see her father?"

Patrick felt so helpless, he wanted to scream for help. But help from whom?

The drizzle suddenly turned into a downpour, and the boys who had been standing by trooped to the restaurant. He too wanted to take cover somewhere, as he could not afford to fall ill, and yet Emily didn't look bothered about standing in the rain. Without a word, she walked away, crossing the street, sheets of rain pounding her shapely body, and he knew he couldn't make her come back. Was it true she had carried *their* baby, Junior's younger brother?

She got to the other side, where she opened the driver's door of an old, blue-and-white VW Bus Camper. She jumped in and drove away.

He was wet and cold, and he couldn't see through the large restaurant windows due to a mist that had covered the glass. Across the road, he saw a couple walk hand in hand under one umbrella. He wondered if one of them was cheating on the other.

Slowly, he found his way to the restaurant. He didn't look to see if Denise-lookalike was still at her table. Instead, he walked to the restroom, where he locked himself in a stall and sat on the bowl without checking to see if it was clean or not.

"Denise, my darling," he whispered between sobs, the lump in his throat hurting. "Denise! Alice, my baby! Chris! Oh, Junior! Please, forgive me. I'm such an idiot, a fuckin, fuckin idiot! I don't deserve you."

He cursed Norman for making him attend the workshop. Had someone else gone in his place, he wouldn't have met Emily. Emily. He hated her.

He had no idea how long he had been in the stall, but someone was knocking softly on the door.

"Are you okay in there, ma'am?"

It was a lady's voice.

Patrick sniffled. Drying the tears off his face with a tissue, he stood up and opened the door. A tall, big, black lady gave him a surprised look. "I'm sorry. Just received news of my baby's death," he said.

"I'm sorry to hear about your loss, sir, but this is the lady's restroom."

CHAPTER 50

Denise entered Matilda's office.

"He's in a bad mood," Matilda whispered. "He just walked past with his ugly friend, Teddy. Not even one stupid word from his big mouth."

Denise knew the Teddy Matilda was talking about. He was a short, shady character who never took off his shades. She suspected was a drug dealer. And yes, he was annoying and as ugly as sin.

"He wants to see you in the palace, Ms. Denise."

Denise hated it when Maxx was going through a bad phase in life, and add to that, he had Teddy in there. People with a big ego problem were dangerous when they were not winning, so to win, they always found a fall guy. She knocked softly on Maxx's office door and entered.

"Don't sit down," Maxx shouted from behind his desk. Teddy turned his head and winked at Denise, who stood by the door, ready for a fight. "Close the door. I have decided I give you a house to stay. You alone, no children. Don't be the impossible, Denise, because when it comes to Big Maxx, every woman must come."

"Yes, yes!" Teddy said with great excitement. It was as if his friend had just announced a major discovery on one of Jupiter's many moons.

Feeling goosebumps all over, Denise feared she was going to piss in her pants. She pressed her thighs together to avoid a spill.

"I have promoted Gilbert," she heard Maxx say. "He's your driver. Whatever you want, where you want to go, to buy whatever. Gilbert is the one."

Denise stood still, trying to focus on her situation. Even though Uncle Ben had intervened, Rebecca had said she wanted Denise out of her guesthouse by the end of the coming week.

Both men were watching her, and she heard Maxx say, "Good." He pointed at the door.

Denise turned, and as she gently closed the door behind her, she heard Teddy say, "I want this girl bad," and both men laughed. She ignored Matilda's inquisitive expression and dashed to the restroom, which was down the hallway. She locked the stall door and, like Matilda before her, she shed tears.

Denise had known Gilbert Zulu for a long time. He was the guy who drove an SUV that was replaced by a new one every year, and his job was to do errands for Maxx's concubines. From midmorning to evening, Gilbert delivered groceries and picked up whoever needed transportation among Maxx's many families. There was a time when Denise and Matilda used to agonize over Gilbert's itinerary until Gilbert told them he enjoyed his job. That was the man who had been *promoted* to the position of Denise's driver.

She calmed down, and in a few minutes, she was ready to face the world.

"Madam, I want to talk to you." Gilbert was waiting in Matilda's office.

"Come in," said Denise.

"The boss told me I show you your new home."

Denise wasn't going to give in to Maxx's sexual demands. Never. On the other hand, Rebecca had said she wanted her out of the guesthouse. She had no idea where to go next.

Gilbert was a chatty man, so Denise did most of the listening as her driver related stories about the daily adventures of his job. "You know what I think, madam? Some of those children, they are not children of the big boss, sure. They don't look like him, but he just accepts one after another, and then another."

Denise watched the heavy traffic and the city buildings. How did things get to this?

"Gilbert, let's go back to the office," she said. "You'll go in, pick up my belongings and bring them to me."

"Madam, wait," said Gilbert. "See the house first."

"I don't want to see it!" she screamed.

Gilbert behaved as if he hadn't heard her. He stepped harder on the gas and kept driving. Twenty minutes later, Denise felt like peeing again.

She couldn't believe what Maxx had done.

CHAPTER 51

Patrick lay in bed, thinking about what Emily had told him. Just outside his door, Aretha was talking loudly to someone on the phone. "Black people, black people!" she said, and in a moment, he heard her walk down the staircase, laughing.

He recalled the drama at the first phase of the Eastern and Southern Africa Media Managers on HIV-AIDS Reporting Workshop. It was his super boss, Norman Tau, who had insisted that the head of production, and not any one of his subordinates, should attend the workshop. In Patrick's opinion, he was too busy to be away from the office for so long, and at a time when the board wanted him to produce a paper on the department's restructuring. But Norman was not the kind of boss one disagreed with.

The workshop took place at Lilayi Lodge, a luxurious resort located half an hour's drive from downtown Lusaka. The resort's thatched and red-brick chalets were surrounded by tall trees and well-kempt gardens, and the surrounding wildlife ranch boasted of various animals, including large ones such as the zebra and the giraffe.

When the participants first gathered in the conference room, Patrick was disappointed to see not a single black face among the three Americans who had traveled from Atlanta to conduct the workshop. Workshops were about giving jobs to people.

A Caucasian woman with a shapely body, and in her mid-thirties, introduced herself as Dr. Emily Ramson. "Call me Emily, folks." She chuckled and ran the fingers of her left hand through her long hair, which was neatly tied into a ponytail. Her saggy pair of jeans and a loose checked shirt gave her a boyish look. "Yes, just Emily. A Ph.D., not MD. Okay, cool. I work for the workshop's sponsors, Southbound Hands, an Atlanta-based nonprofit dedicated to providing health initiatives to developing nations."

She introduced her colleagues. The elderly, reserved woman was Dorothea Hall. Emily wrote the name on a dry-erase board.

"You mean 'Dorothy,?" Patrick asked.

"No," said Emily. "Let me see." She drifted close to Patrick. "What's your name again? Patrick. Good." She smiled broadly and her green eyes gave him a lingering look. "Dorothea." Dorothea sat still, her face expressionless as if she wasn't the moment's center of attention. "Pleased to meet you, Patrick," she said and walked back to the front.

Charlotte was the twenty-something intern who smiled a lot.

"Folks, I have no doubt you'll all enjoy these facilities," said Emily. "A great place, this."

Patrick concurred. He looked forward to devouring the pecan nut pie he had seen on the day's menu.

"Coming to Africa the very first time, and we all love it. We actually got here a few days ago, and our first trip was to Victoria Falls. I'd never heard of it before I knew I was coming here. Truly a natural wonder."

Patrick's view of American society was that one in every three Americans was obese. None of the three was. Emily was petite. Dorothea was tall and slender. Only Charlotte seemed to need to lose a little weight.

It was his turn to introduce himself.

"The name is Patrick Kanya. Mind you, my last name means 'light,' so I am visible everywhere I go." There was laughter.

"Even in the night, so no hiding under a condom," said a male voice behind him. Judging from the accent, Patrick concluded it was the gentleman from Kenya Broadcasting Corporation.

"No hiding," said Patrick. "I'm the head of television production at ZNBC. After this workshop, I hope our viewers will watch lots of documentaries on HIV-AIDS. At a personal level, my wife and I have three beautiful children, two of them in their youth, so I see trouble coming." There was prolonged laughter. "I guess I'll have to talk to them about condoms soon. By the way, I met my wife, Denise, at the university. We have been happily married for sixteen years, but our firstborn is seventeen."

"I see an accident there," said the man from Kenya, and again, there was laughter. "Accidental accident."

After everyone else had introduced themselves, there was excitement when Emily announced that the second phase of the workshop would be held in Atlanta a few months later, if not earlier.

By the second day of the workshop, Patrick had made friends with Peter Obong'o, the Kenyan. Patrick observed that Emily spent a lot of time at Peter's desk, always bending over to look at how he was resolving the many quizzes the participants worked on. On several occasions, he saw her place her hand on his shoulder. That didn't surprise him, for Peter and Emily had one thing in common: affability. Patrick believed that he wasn't the only one who had noticed Emily's affection toward Peter. How could she be so reckless?

"By a show of hands, let's see how many of you have been to the US, folks," said Emily.

Five out of nine hands went up.

"Okay, Patrick, tell me which city and state," said Emily.

"I raised my hand by mistake," Patrick said amidst laughter. "I was hoping you wouldn't see me."

"I got you!" she said.

The workshop participants were heading for lunch one afternoon when Kamili, a colleague from Tanzania, said to Peter, "She wants you, brother."

"Who?" asked Peter.

"Emily. I sit directly behind you, and I see everything."

"She's welcome," said Peter, chuckling. "The African bull never rests, condom or no condom."

"I would be cautious," said Kamili. "I could be wrong, but she may want a taste of Africa. You know the saying among European female tourists—*once in the heat of Africa, you never want to go back to cold Europe.*"

Peter turned to face the Tanzanian. "I'm a married man, brother," he said. "That means I'm married to only one woman.

And you're wrong. Emily is just a friendly girl, that's all. She's here to talk about HIV-AIDS, remember?"

As Patrick admired the well-tended gardens, he saw a man carrying a suitcase from one chalet to the one next to his own. He wished he could have a garden as beautiful as the one at the lodge, but the problem was that the city council's water supply was erratic.

In the dining room, Patrick shared a table with five other workshop participants, among them Kamili, the Tanzanian, and Peter, the tall, lean, boisterous, and prematurely balding Kenyan.

"Look at that," whispered Kamili. He was looking at one corner of the room where two female staff members were talking in low tones.

"They could be talking about you, my good friend Patrick," said Peter. "Even I, who is a fellow man, can tell you're very handsome."

CHAPTER 52

The SUV had been at the gate for five minutes, and neither Denise nor Gilbert had said a word.

The pounding in her ears ceaseless, and her fingers gripping her purse, Denise whispered, "Be strong, Denise." Aloud, she said sheepishly, "Why is your boss doing this to me, Gilbert?"

"The boss told me not to tell you. Surprise."

"My husband and I, we worked hard," she whispered. "We built this house, and we lost it...when...after my husband died in America."

"I'm sorry, madam." Gilbert still couldn't look in Denise's direction. "Maybe you just go inside. The house has changed. The boss, he made changes."

She didn't want to go beyond the gate, and yet she did. A short man was watering the garden, which, she admitted, was more beautiful than when it belonged to her. In one corner of the property, a water tank stood on a high steel frame.

The front door looked sturdier than the one she had left. It wasn't locked, so she stepped in.

Gilbert was right. The house had been renovated to very high standards. The living room smelled of leather, reminding her of Norman's vehicle. Norman! How come he hadn't called recently? Was that a way of telling her that he wasn't ready to direct accounts and HR to write Patrick's last check?

Everything in the kitchen, from the stove to the cabinets, was new. Denise opened the hot water tab and washed her face.

Oh, the memories.

The master bedroom bathroom had been done just in the manner he and Patrick had wished it to be remodeled. How did Maxx know about that? Ah, yes. Leaving in a hurry, she had left the master bedroom extension drawings in the house.

She sat on the king-size bed and cried. In this very room, she and Patrick had created the best memories of their life. "I have to be strong," she whispered and counted one-two-three and got off the bed. She had seen enough.

Denise could tell that even Gilbert had taken offense to his boss's scheme, for he said nothing when they drove back to the office.

In Matilda's office, Denise asked, "Is your boss in?" Matilda looked startled as if she had been half asleep.

"Yes."

Denise entered the palace without knocking and stood steadily before Maxx.

"You like it," said Maxx, looking pleased.

Denise decided not to burn any bridges, so she calmly, and without meaning it, said, "It was very kind of you to rent the house for me, but it just brings too many memories, sir."

"House rent?" Maxx barked.

"The one you're renting for us in Meanwood. That was our house, my late husband and I. We owed so little to the bank, but they still took it away from us."

"No, I bought that house. So, no rent."

"You *what*, Maxx?"

"Don't get cross. Angry. I bought it from that bank."

"But you knew it was my house."

"Bank was selling. There was no buyer, they plead for me to buy, so I buy it."

"And you want to play with my emotions and give me the house as one of your concubines?"

"Your what?"

"*Concubine.* Your sex slave." Maxx rose and walked around his desk. He stood close to Denise and tried to hold her right hand. "Don't touch me!" she screamed.

She found herself sitting on the sofa. She hadn't planned it; the tears just started to well up in her eyes, just as Matilda was entering the office with a tray full of snacks.

"Go, go!" Maxx barked.

As Matilda made a hurried U-turn, her tray hit the door, scattering everything on her tray on the carpet.

Matilda went down on her knees and hurriedly picked up everything. Denise waited until Matilda had wiped the place clean and left. She looked around for an object she could use to kill Maxx. She didn't see any. From her purse, she took out a hankie and blew her nose into it. She used the same hankie to touch her face, stood up, and unlike Matilda, she pulled the door hard behind her. A pity, there was no crashing sound because the door was padded. The story was that whatever noise was made behind that door could never be heard by anyone outside *the palace*.

In Matilda's office, Denise sat in one of the visitors' chairs, and once again, she felt like a stranger in that building.

"Ms. Denise..." Matilda started to speak.

"No!" Denise hissed. She stood up. "No more stories from you."

She got to her office and collected the few personal belongings she had on the desk—a photo of her husband and the kids, workshop attendance certificates, and pens. She was sure that as a fellow woman, Rebecca would understand why she was leaving work. She remembered that it was Rebecca who had made the right connections for Patrick and Denise to buy the land where the couple had built their home, the home Maxx had just offered to her in exchange for sex.

Carrying a box full of her items, Denise came out of her office, and Matilda stood up. "Say nothing, Matilda. I don't know how you do it, how you survive here. I'm not coming back."

Matilda remained standing.

Outside, in the parking lot, Denise heard Gilbert's SUV engine start. She continued to walk at a speed she knew she couldn't sustain for long.

"Madam?" Gilbert spoke softly. His window was down, and the vehicle was moving alongside Denise. "You can't walk in the cold, madam."

Denise didn't feel the cold of late April. Her wish was to just keep walking away from Maxx. The following week, she would catch a bus and cross the border to neighboring Botswana. There, she would apply for a job, face-to-face with a school principal. After all, she had a bachelor's in education.

Gilbert convinced her to get in the SUV. They drove in silence and stopped at a supermarket, where Denise took her time to do some shopping. By the time she got home, it was late afternoon, and Gilbert said he had missed several appointments with his boss's families.

"I wish you well, Gilbert," she said. "I hope you don't get fired."

"Thank you, madam."

Rebecca was not home, but Uncle Ben, who looked pale, was in the living room, wearing pajamas and drinking Gordon's London Dry Gin straight from the bottle. "You look happy, Derby," he said, his speech slurred.

"*Denise*! Yes, I'm very happy, Uncle Ben."

Denise headed for the door. At the guesthouse, Junior was asleep on the sofa. She didn't disturb him.

Sitting on her bed, she took a deep breath and made the telephone call she had for months avoided to make for a good reason.

"Institute for African Women in Law, how may I direct your call?"

"I need to speak to a lawyer," Denise said. "But not Ms. Hazel Omei."

"I'm sorry, but Dr. Omei is the only lawyer we have today, madam. If you could call, say, next week?"

"No, I will speak to Dr. Omei then, please. Tell her it's Denise Kanya."

She didn't know that Hazel had obtained a doctoral degree. So, as she waited to be connected to Dr. Omei, she regretted turning down an offer from her university to be enrolled in a staff development program that would have seen her go abroad to study for two graduate degrees and come back home to teach. How could she leave Patrick, the father of her child, the man she was destined to live with forever? A doctoral degree would have guaranteed her a job.

"Hey, Denise! Any news about my boyfriend?" Hazel sounded delighted.

"*Your* boyfriend?"

"What happened to that campus sense of humor, Denise? Look, pretty busy right now, but why don't we have lunch? I'll pay. Tomorrow?"

"Tomorrow? That's fine."

She got to the living room, and Junior was still asleep.

"Wake up, son, you won't be able to sleep tonight," she said. Junior mumbled something about being hungry. "Why didn't you make yourself a sandwich? And where's Chris?"

"I don't know, Mom. Chris don't tell me everything."

"Don't ever speak like that to me," Denise shouted. "*Chris don't tell me everything*, that's not English. Is that what they teach in government schools?"

"Mom, even the driver...the driver looked for him."

"And the driver left without him?"

"I don't know, Mom. Me, I'm just hungry."

"It's not *me, I'm just*...Oh, forget it."

Denise searched the guesthouse many times before she realized that her elder son couldn't be anywhere there. She rushed to the main house. Rebecca was still away from home, and Solomon said Uncle Ben was sleeping. "The driver told me, Chris, he wasn't at school."

Denise called Rebecca. There was no response. She walked to the main road to look for a cab. Half an hour later, she got on a minibus and found her way to Chris's school. It was getting dark, and the silence on the school campus was eerie. She moved from one classroom block to another, until she heard someone say, "Looking for what?"

It was the night watchman.

"Are there any students around?"

"Madam, students, they left long time ago."

"Sir, do you know Chris? Chris Kanya?"

"I don't know students, madam. Me, I work in night."

Denise insisted on searching every classroom and restroom. Chris wasn't there. Knowing that there was no point in her reporting her son's disappearance to a worthless police system, she walked in the dark to the nearest hotel, from where she hired a cab.

Rebecca was at the guesthouse, showing a smartly dressed couple around the home.

"I have to speak to you, sister," Denise demanded.

"We have guests, please," Rebecca spoke with a great sense of formality. "Rodwell here wants his girlfriend to move in. I've told them you'll be leaving in two weeks."

Her throat feeling tight, Denise rushed outside. She didn't want Rodwell, who was in his early thirties and very good-looking, and his forty-something girlfriend to see the frustration in her face.

"Come back in, Denise," Rebecca called. It sounded like an order; a landlady calling her tenant who was about to be booted out of a house she didn't deserve to live in because she wasn't paying rent.

From the doorway, Denise saw the couple enter her bedroom.

"You'll like the other room even better," said Rebecca a moment later, when the trio was back in the living room. "It's bigger, but that's my nephews' room. You'll view it after they have left."

"It's okay," said Rodwell. To Denise, he said, "My girlfriend is pregnant, so I want her and my baby to have a good home, and we very much love this place."

The couple spent a few minutes in the kitchen and the bathroom before Rebecca led them outside. Denise slumped into the sofa, and for the sake of her younger son, she tried hard not to cry. Where could Chris be, and how come Junior seemed not to be worried about his brother's absence? Where was the world coming to? And where was the man she had married for better or worse?

There was a loud knock on the front door. Rebecca walked in. She sat in her favorite chair. "He's so handsome, I almost came, just shaking his soft hands," she said excitedly. "He seems to be doing well as a chemist. But I don't care what he does, girl. Drugs or no drugs, as long as he pays the rent, that's fine by me. He offered two thousand US dollars a month. That amount can only come from dirty money."

"Sister Rebecca, your nephew is missing."

"What?"

The door opened wide. Looking almost sober, Uncle Ben stood totteringly in the doorway. Denise took a closer look at Ben this time, and she thought he looked frail and much older than his age. He had a long beard that was graying, a mustache that made him look like a clown, and his clothes needed laundering.

"What are you doing here?" demanded Rebecca.

Ben stood still. "I heard what…what you…said," he stuttered. "Uh, you," he pointed at Denise, his righthand forefinger quivering. "You, Derby, and your kids will stay here until your husband comes, uh, back. Do you hear that, Rebecca? This woman here is your husband's, uh, brother."

"Husband's brother?" Rebecca asked mockingly.

"I don't care what I said," Ben roared, almost losing balance in the process. "How can you be so cruel to your own blood? These boys are your nephews."

Rebecca rolled her eyes.

"And I'm coming with you to find your missing boy."

"Were you eavesdropping on us?" Rebecca asked angrily. "You're spying on me, Ben?"

CHAPTER 53

Rebecca told Denise to tuck Junior in bed in the main house. She called a number and spoke to Chris's headmaster.

"He's the principal, but he doesn't know if Chris was in school today," Rebecca said, looking astonished.

"He's an administrator," said Denise.

"So? What's he paid so well for if he doesn't know if my nephew was there today? Tell me, what does he know?"

Denise could feel her heartbeat in her ears. She remained calm, unlike her sister-in-law who was kicking objects in her sight and pressing numbers on her cellphone.

"So, he was in class, right?" said Rebecca, and finally, she sat on the sofa. "Thank you, thank you." To Denise, she said," That was the teacher of his last class. Chris was there."

"Girls, we must file a missing child report with the police," Uncle Ben said from the doorway leading to the long hallway in the sleeping quarters.

"You know the police are worthless, Ben," Rebecca quipped. Ben raised his hands above his head as if he couldn't believe what he was hearing. "Okay, I'll call."

Looking all focused and dignified, Uncle Ben said, "Call the hospitals, too. As for you, Derby, your son, you two sleep in this house."

Denise spent most of the night hoping to hear that Chris had arrived. Could he have taken his own life like his big sister? She didn't care where Patrick was. Patrick was dead to her. As soon as Chris was found, Denise would take that trip to Botswana and find a job.

A moaning sound made her sit up. It was 2:30 am. A woman's voice, followed by a man's. So, Uncle Ben could still play the game? She closed her eyes, feeling lonely and wishing she had a man. A few minutes later, she heard a door open. She got to the window and looked outside. Solomon was heading for his quarters.

She couldn't sleep after that, and the night was long, but the sun finally came like it always did. At the breakfast table, Denise watched Rebecca and Junior enjoy their fried eggs and sausage. She would not eat anything until she had found her son.

"Denise, did you admonish Chris?" asked Rebecca. Denise shook her head. Except for the time she had slapped the late Alice, she had been soft on her kids since Patrick's disappearance.

The home telephone rang. Rebecca rushed to answer it and listened. "Oh, thank you, sir. I'll be there. Girl, the principal is keeping Chris in his office."

Denise and Rebecca got to school thirty minutes later, and the headmaster left his office so that the two women could speak to Chris in private.

To Denise, Chris didn't look remorseful. It was as if he was ready for war. "I just spent the night at my friend's place, Mom."

"You think this is funny, Chris?"

"No, Mom. This life is not funny. It's just that...I don't know."

"He's sorry, Denise," said Rebecca. "You won't do it again, will you, Chris, my dear?"

"No, auntie. I won't do it again."

"Chris, listen, listen, child," Denise didn't know whether to celebrate or cry. She had found her child, which was a great thing. But Chris's behavior was unbecoming. He was uncouth, uncaring, plainly stupid. *I just spent the night at my friend's place!* Since when? On whose authority? "You know, I'll deal with you when we get home." Chris stared at his mother, then at Rebecca, as if saying, *Aunt, looks like Mom doesn't understand what I said. Can you interpret for her?* "And to make sure you don't behave foolishly again, I'm not leaving school till I get you home."

Denise was starving, so she and Rebecca had lunch at a nearby restaurant. When they all got back home later in the afternoon, Rebecca took Denise to the side and said, "Don't be hard on him. The boys are going through a traumatic experience, losing their sister and the father they loved so much, and they don't know if he's dead or eloping with a strange woman in a foreign land."

"I will."

In the guestroom's dining room, Denise made Chris sit across from her at the table, while Junior rowdily searched for something to eat in the kitchen.

"I want to hear only the truth, Chris."

"I said it won't happen again, Mom."

"And you won't tell me where you spent the night?"

"No, Mom."

Her hands shaking, Denise stood up. "I've never whipped you before, but today, I will."

"No, Mom, you won't do that."

"*What?*"

"I'll run away, and you won't catch me. That's why Alice died, right? And Aunt Rebecca? She's evil." Chris's lips twitched. "I *hate* her, I hate Solomon."

Denise got to her bedroom and slammed the door behind her. She lay in bed, facing the ceiling. The audacity of her son, the way he spoke so softly and confidently, made her mad. Chris seemed to be the reincarnation of her late sister. Where had she gone wrong? And had Rebecca been so careless, even the kids knew about her relationship with Solomon?

Slowly, the bedroom door opened and Chris stood in the doorway. "Exactly why Dad and Alice left," he said softly. "So, you want me to kill myself? Are you going to answer me, Mom?"

"Mom, I'm hungry," Junior shouted from the kitchen.

"Wait a minute, Junior. I'll be right there. As for you, Chris, I want you and me to go to the main house, and you, me, Aunt Rebecca, we'll talk. *Now.*"

CHAPTER 54

Patrick remembered the last three days of the first workshop.

It was late in the night, and Patrick had been sitting alone in his chalet, performing his nightly chore—talking to Denise and the kids on the phone.

"Thanks, darling, see you soon."

"I can't wait to see you, sweetheart," said Denise, and Patrick heard a soft knock.

"Who is it?" asked Patrick, and he stood up. To Denise, he said, "Good night, sweetie. It must be my friend Peter."

Patrick cut the line. The lodge had been entirely booked for the workshop, so everyone on the premises was a colleague from the media. Earlier in the evening, Peter had come to his room, and the two had talked for hours. Maybe Peter had forgotten something in the room?

Wearing a gown, she stood just outside the door, the usual sweet smile covering her pretty, boyish face.

"I, uh, I was in my room, feeling cold…and…you know? I didn't know it ever got cold in Africa. May…I…come in?"

He showed her in, and she made straight for the bed, where she sat down and gave him a naughty stare.

"Please, close the door," she said, and he obeyed. "I'm your neighbor now. There was something in my, uh, other room. In the, uh, ceiling. A gecko, perhaps? The truth is, I was having dreams in there. So, my assistant, Charlotte, said we could exchange rooms."

Had Patrick been listening, he would have asked what a gecko was, and she would have told him it was a lizard. But this was no time to ask questions.

"Come here, Patrick." She pulled her gown up to expose her thighs and put her left palm on the bed beside her.

He took one short step towards the bed, and the phone rang. It was Denise. He ignored it.

Kneeling before her, he found himself between her open thighs. She caressed his short hair. Rubbing. Stroking his temples.

He heard her labored breathing. The world began to spin around him, and it felt like a place to which he had never been, but one he should always have been to. Hazily, he saw her undress him and slip his penis into a condom. He knew what they were doing was wrong, but he had neither the energy nor the will to stop it. He was still on his knees, and she sat on the bed, and she was so, so warm, he was drowning in everything about her, wanting her whole body to be a part of him. Outside, the wind rattled tree leaves and whooshed against the thatched roof. It was a rollercoaster that did a full circle in a matter of minutes.

"What?" She was off the bed, hovering over him, her eyes red. In one hand, she held a used condom. "You!" she exploded. "I've spent the week telling you how important it is never to break a condom, and you ignore the rules?"

He felt a thickness in his throat. How could he do this to Denise, to his family?

"You know what, sir? I'm positive. Yes, HIV-positive. That's why I joined this nonprofit. To fight the disease. And that's why I gave you a condom."

He looked at her red face and wanted to vomit and ask her to leave. He had betrayed his wife, and nothing could upstage the guilt he felt. Nothing could undo the wrong he had just done. She slipped on her gown and left.

He felt as if a heavy weight was placed on his chest. All his married life, despite the many temptations, especially after he became a manager, he had been faithful to Denise. In one careless moment, he had eroded the achievements of two decades to get to this. He was a cheater, and he was going to infect his wife and kill her.

The following day, he wanted to leave the workshop. But he wasn't at the lodge on his own time. Norman expected him to complete the training. Given the choice, he wouldn't attend the official closing ceremony in the evening, which would be followed by a social gathering that would go on until midnight. He didn't want to be there, and yet he didn't want to go home and face his wife. Soon, he would have to tell his wife that he had contracted

HIV, which to him sounded like a death sentence. He thought about the stigma that came with that status. Being HIV positive meant that one had been unfaithful to his or her partner. How would Denise take it? Not only Denise but the kids, the family, the journalism fraternity?

In the conference room, he said nothing. Emily didn't talk to him, either. During the last hour of the workshop, she passed close to his desk and surreptitiously placed a piece of folded paper on his desk. He pushed it under his folder, and minutes later, he read it: *My phone number in the US inside.*

The final ceremony started with the issuance of certificates of attendance. Patrick's Kenyan friend, Peter, received a standing ovation when he walked to the front to collect his certificate. When snacks were served, accompanied by music, Patrick's colleagues took the floor. Patrick didn't dance, and Emily ignored him. That was the way he wanted it.

The workshop officially ended at midnight, but it wasn't safe to drive that late in the night. The rate of car hijacking, especially at traffic lights, had been high recently.

Back in his room, he had just finished speaking to Denise on the phone when there was a soft knock on the door. "Who is it?" he asked.

"It's me."

He opened the door, just enough for him to tell her to please leave. But no. How could he stop her from coming in? She stood in the middle of the room, and he left the door ajar.

"Close the door," she said. He didn't move. "About last night, it was a mistake. And it wasn't your fault the condom broke. You're a big guy, stiff and...you know?"

She walked past him to the door, closed it, and locked it. He wanted to protest. No. She was already in bed.

"You and I are already infested. So, what do we have to lose?" she asked.

The reasonable human part of him told him to plead with her to leave, but the foolish male side propelled him to the bed. He loved the smile before him that revealed large incisors, like

Denise's, which shone like falling snow. No living man could resist that. His hands went all over her body, feeling the curves, the warmth of her youthful, white, smooth skin, the feel of her long, loosened hair. Perfect. He looked into her green eyes. All he wanted was to drink her like sweet wine. To be inside her and stay there forever.

Their tongues met. He ran his tongue over her teeth, the way he did with Denise. Her warmth engrossed him without shame, it was as if he was immersed in a sea of gold, lavishly splashed with Namibian diamonds and Zambian aquamarine.

Outside, he heard the trees sing, their leaves rattling just like the previous night. Up above, he believed, the moon, like a daring spy satellite, must have been gazing at the revolving earth and the chalet and smiled.

And when it was over, he wanted to tell her how much he wanted her again, but not how scared he was. Tomorrow, he would be compelled to make love to Denise. Pretty Emily, with her HIV-positive status, had turned him into a timebomb.

He let her sleep in his arms. The whole night.

The following morning, Emily woke up first. They had made love two more times before sleep swept both of them into a deep sleep.

"Why didn't you tell me the sun was up already?" she asked.

She left, and after a quick shower, he put on a polo-collar T-shirt, a present from Denise. *You look more handsome than Tiger Woods,* he remembered Denise saying the first time he wore it. He also put on a pair of long khaki pants and white Nike tennis sneakers. He was ready to face the world and, later, his wife.

He was scared.

As he opened the door, a sheet of white paper fell to the doorstep. It was wrinkled at one end. He picked it up. In red capital letters, a computer-generated message read: *TWICE, I SAW HER LEAVE YOUR ROOM AT NIGHT. ONE CARELESS STEP AND THIS WILL BE ALL OVER SOCIAL MEDIA. YOU OWE ME.*

His hands shaking, he took a few steps back into the room and read the note again. He searched for a hidden message, a concealed dialect, and a distinct voice that would make him identify the author of the message. Okay, everyone in the workshop had access to a computer and the laser printer at the back of the room. So, anyone could have written the note. If someone saw Emily come out of the room, it must have been someone who was in the immediate neighborhood, probably someone whose chalet was opposite his own. It couldn't be Kamili, the Tanzanian. Kamili would have nothing to gain from blackmailing him. It was probably one of his fellow countrymen. Or lodge staffers.

He put the note under his armpit and walked to his Jeep Cherokee. In the distance, Emily and his workshop colleagues were chatting and hugging. He folded the note and put it in a little bag in the glove compartment. He had said goodbye to Peter the previous night, and that was all that mattered. He turned the ignition and headed for the city.

Lusaka's CBD, or Central Business District, was quiet that early on a Sunday morning. He parked the Jeep near a shoe store on Cairo Road.

He thought about how he was going to face Denise. He had never cheated on her since they got married. He remembered, in his freshman year, dating Hazel Omei. A year younger than him, Hazel came from a neighboring village, and he had known her since childhood. Reading the same courses, they often sat at the back of the lecture theater, where she touched his manhood under the desk. After he met Denise, ending his casual affair with Hazel had been more challenging than he had anticipated. Denise had always suspected that his affinity for Hazel had continued, even when that was not the case. Hazel was hurt, and after she had enrolled in law school, she had left a note in his pigeonhole: *To legally go after guys like you.*

An hour later, he got home. Denise and the kids sat in the living room and listened to him narrate some of his experiences at the workshop. "So, my new friend, Peter, is from Nairobi, Kenya," he said.

"Can we go to Nairobi, Daddy?" asked Junior. "We go to see your friend. Daddy, never, never go away, okay, my daddy? Or I go with you. Leave Chris and Alice with Mom."

"Okay, I hear you, son. Except..." He saw Junior's twisted-up face.

"Okay, Junior," said Denise. "Dad will go away again."

"I don't like that, okay, Mom?" said Junior, frowning and standing up, as if he was ready to leave for some better place, away from Mom.

Patrick lifted his son and put him on his lap. "Daddy loves you, okay?"

"Yes, Daddy. I love you, too. And do you love Mom and Alice?"

"Yes. And your brother, too."

"Oh, no, Daddy, Chris beats and pinches me and takes away my toys when you're not here. Please, never leave me. Mommy is always at work, and I get scared."

"Okay, I promise."

"Liar!" said Chris.

"Did you hear that, Daddy?" asked Junior.

"Okay, Chris, please don't ever bully your little brother," said Patrick. He couldn't concentrate on anything, but he saw Junior smile, exposing the two large upper front teeth all the kids had inherited from their mother. The boys were so handsome, he feared they would soon be in trouble with the girls. As for his beautiful daughter, Alice, he suspected it was just a matter of months before she started trouble. He wasn't sure if she wasn't dating anyone already.

Patrick couldn't stop daytime from turning into evening, and eventually, it was Sunday night, and as Denise was working the following day, she went to bed early. Patrick sat alone in the living room, staring at the television set without following the programs his teams had produced while he was away.

It was long after midnight when he planted his body next to hers.

"Two weeks is a long time, baby," said Denise. She touched his right shoulder, and he almost let out a scream.

"I'm just...Honey, I'm so, so very, very tired. Can it wait?" He wished he could tell her about Emily, the pretty woman who had given him the infection of death. Okay, there were many people he knew who had been diagnosed with HIV two or more decades ago, and they seemed to be living happy lives. Magic Johnson, for instance. No, he wouldn't tell her about it. Maybe he would tell her later, or maybe he would find a way around the problem. Or maybe, a few weeks later, he would get tested. But what was he to do, in the interim, to avoid sleeping with his wife and infecting her?

He stayed awake all night in her arms. And not even once did he manage to get it up.

CHAPTER 55

Saturday morning and Patrick hated the fact that he was working in the afternoon. Although he wasn't hungry—he rarely was—he opened a packet of raisin bran and poured some into a big mug. "Shit," he hissed after rummaging through the many boxes and packets of food in the refrigerator. The warning on his two-percent milk gallon read that the milk had expired a week earlier. He poured the milk into the sink and helped himself to a small portion of Almond milk. He had no taste, but still, he ate, and quite hurriedly.

As he walked the three miles to D'Angelo's place to pick up his check, he thought about his next move. He accepted that he was a bad man because it was wrong to abandon his family. Was it too late to undo the wrong?

As usual, D'Angelo lay on the timeworn sofa. His hair was getting thinner, and his face was covered in sweat.

"Your door wasn't locked," said Patrick. The room was getting filthier, the foul smell getting more offensive.

"I'm dying, my friend," D'Angelo chuckled, his voice a mere whisper. "I don't fear death. It's the moment of dying that scares me, bro, not death."

"I know."

Patrick would have loved to clean the room, but the last time he was there, the vacuum wasn't working.

"I don't wanna live long," moaned D'Angelo. "I don't want my mother to suffer, looking after a big guy like me. Hey, you heard about my nephew's death, right?"

"Your nephew?"

"Yeah, my dad had three children, two not with my mother. There was my sister, there was my brother, and his son, he was killed by a cop down in Florida, right at the border with Georgia."

"I'm sorry to hear that."

"Yeah, the boy and I, we're tight. I raised him like my very own when his dad was incarcerated. I gotta go say farewell."

"But you're not in a position to travel, D'Angelo."

"I drive my truck, man. I gotta go. Mum isn't coming because that wasn't her grandson." D'Angelo seemed to be getting more tired as he spoke. "Was hoping you'd come with me even if you don't drive the truck. You know, see beautiful Florida? I'm gonna miss Florida when I die, bro."

"Yes, I'm told it's beautiful down there. So, why don't you live there?

"Brother, I have to be close to my mother and take care of her."

"I understand. But I'm working today."

"I hear you, bro. Gotta pay your rent."

That afternoon, Patrick worked like a dog. He wanted to inflict pain on himself. Talking to Emily had changed the way he saw himself. He believed he was living a lie. And he had told lies before. One of them was hinting to Denise that there was a spy at the first workshop. It was frightening to know that not only was he a liar, but that he was still attracted to Emily. He didn't understand how he could be in love with both Denise and the woman he hated at the same time.

Later in the day, Patrick and Leroy were hooking shopping carts when a white, blonde, and lean woman who was standing by a sports car said to Patrick, "What's your name, son?"

"Patrick."

She seemed to be in her early sixties, and even though she wore sandals, she was tall, the skin of her small feet looked smooth and clean, and her painted toes long and slender. She blew smoke through her small nostrils and said, "I come here often, and I love just sitting in my car and gazing at you." She got close to him. "If you want to see what a good woman can do for a handsome man, you come with me."

Patrick felt a tingling in the chest. "I'm sorry, I'm on the clock."

"Honey, I promise you wouldn't need to be on that clock ever again if you came with me. My husband is away as usual. Business, he says. Huh!" She continued to stare, then threw her cigar to the ground and squashed it with her sandals. "Anyway, you can't say I never tried." Her thin lips pressed together, she hurried to her car and recklessly drove away.

"Man, you crazy?" Leroy's mouth was open wide. "That white woman, man. She's got bucks. Everyone here knows her, man. Multi-millionaire, man. That car, man? It's a 2017 Porsche Cayman, man, and she smokes Ashton cigars, man."

"How do you know all those details?" asked Patrick.

"She told me, man. I've always wanted her to invite me home, but she likes tall men. I keep telling you, you're a celebrity, man."

"I'm not that kind of person."

"Okay, then who are you? D'Angelo?" Leroy was shouting, and Patrick was getting irritated and panicky. "Okay, my man, you just told that woman your name is Patrick, you pretend you don't have a voice, and you pretend to speak with an accent. Who are you, man? You can't hide from the FBI, man. Did you kill your wife or something?"

"Leroy, please!"

Leroy gave Patrick a stare, shook his head and swaggered away. Patrick continued to pull, push and hook the buggies with renewed energy. As Leroy disappeared into the store, Patrick knew that he was in trouble. Was Leroy going to talk to Olivia? He wished he would run. But where to? Now that he knew he wasn't HIV positive, he wanted to go home. But could he?

CHAPTER 56

He remembered, a few days after the first workshop, deciding he was going to get tested for HIV. He had driven to the Planned Parenthood Association testing center on Church Road. Too many people around, so he had driven to Champ Zambia on Chikwa Road, where he parked his Jeep and waited for an opportunity to go in. He had left, only to slow down as he passed the Corpmed Medical Center. He had proceeded to TuneMe Center on Twin Palms Road, where he had sat in his Jeep for an hour before he concluded that testing was not a good idea. The social media wouldn't be kind to him if word got out that he, Patrick Kanya, had appeared at an HIV testing center not to inquire about making a television documentary on HIV testing facilities, but to be tested. Although he had stopped appearing on camera, many people still remembered him from his days as a television news reporter. His subordinates would be seeing him differently. In a protracted civil war, Denise would be asking questions and probably leave him.

He had driven away.

It was two weeks since Emily had told him that she was HIV negative, and Aretha told him that he didn't need a social security number to be attended to at a county clinic. "You want to see a psychiatrist?" she asked.

"No," Patrick laughed. "Just not feeling well."

The reception hall of the clinic on County Services Road in Marietta was full of men, women, and children of all ages, colors and sizes.

"I'd like to take an HIV test," he said to one of the people at the reception desk, a bearded, hard-faced elderly white man. *You have to look confident,* was Aretha's advice. *You're not Latino, so they won't suspect you're an immigrant.*

The lady behind the man at the desk gave Patrick a startled look. The elderly man kept a straight face while he gave Patrick the directions to the testing area.

Upstairs, at another reception desk, a woman asked for his name. He stood still, his heart pounding in his chest. Suddenly, he realized that giving his name to the woman would mean revealing his whereabouts to the government.

"A moment," he said and pressed his cellphone against his right ear. "Hello, David?" He pretended to be listening. The woman at the reception desk smiled at him. "Okay, okay, David, don't panic. I'll be there in, uh, ten minutes?" To the woman, he said, "I'm afraid I have to go. What time are you closing today?"

He didn't hear the answer, for he was in a hurry to implement Plan B.

The county's public transportation system wasn't equal to London Transport. It didn't go everywhere in the cities, forcing many people to buy cars. Patrick waited for fifteen minutes before the CobbLinc bus came. It felt good to be on the bus again that day, for it made him feel that he belonged to the community. No one asked for his name, or why he was on that bus.

The previous night, he had googled where to go, in case he changed his mind about doing business with a government agency.

At the reception window of the testing center, a young Latino woman walked him through the process and finally said, "It's fifty dollars, and the test we do here is as reliable as any other."

Half an hour later, he was sitting before another woman, this time in a small room. "I'm looking at the results for the first time now." His mouth dry, he watched her open the envelope before her. The process reminded Patrick of the paternity television shows Aretha watched often. Was Emily negative? Did she carry his baby?

"Congratulations, sir, you're negative. You said you have a new love? I wish you two well."

His right hand pressed to his heart, he stared at the woman. He wished he would hug her and kiss her and tell her that because of what she had just told him, his life would never be the same again. Why did he believe Emily? Why wasn't he bold enough to take the test at home? When he was the head of production, he always insisted on his staff checking the facts. That was the culture he had brought with him from the newsroom. How did this particular problem escape his scrupulousness? Had he known that he was HIV negative, he wouldn't have left his family.

"Are you okay?" the woman asked.

Patrick nodded and headed for the door.

When he caught bus No. 15, there were very few passengers on board, and he sat alone in the back seat. He got off the bus at a public park, for he didn't want to get home early and answer questions from Aretha. *So, what did the psychiatrist say?* he could hear her ask.

When he eventually got home, Aretha greeted him with, "You look tired and troubled." She was pacing her kitchen, possibly waiting for her lover.

A pity, he couldn't share the news about his HIV status with her. Instead, he asked, "Ms. Aretha, I've always wanted to ask you about that cat."

"The black one?" she asked instantaneously.

"I see it walking from door to door as if it's searching for something."

He noticed that Aretha had already prepared her meal, for well over two dozen spoons, folks, and knives were in the sink.

"Really, Patrick?" she grunted. "You must be the only one who doesn't know."

"I don't understand."

"That's not a cat. It's a robot." She laughed, covered her face in her hands, paced the kitchen, opened the hot water faucet, closed it, then suddenly wore a serious expression. "A spy robot. The white man painted it black so black folk can relate to it. It goes knocking on different black people door spying on us."

"Really?" Patrick's eyebrows shot up.

"Are you serious? Black America, wake up! You don't know about the white man's spying cats?" Again, she laughed. "Ah, can you go away until I call you? My boyfriend is just around the corner, and we want to make noise."

Patrick looked at the dining table. A meal for two. Aretha's best wine glasses. Her best cutlery. A bottle of red wine. Two large bottles of Coca-Cola. It wasn't the first time Patrick had seen that welcome party paraphernalia laid for a boyfriend he had never met.

"I was reading about the human stomach today," Aretha said calmly. "It's full of foul air, chemicals, and stuff. Hot stuff, like high temperature and spices." She passed by Patrick, got to the front door, peeped outside, and shook her head. "I was thinking, if you force your head down your stomach, you know your nose would peel off? You'd be blind, Patrick. The chemicals, enzymes, they eat up all your eyes. You come out of there a dead man."

Patrick was not amused about having to leave home, even temporarily, for he paid rent on time. He smiled and headed for the staircase.

"I was talking to you," she said.

"Yes, I know," he stopped to face her. "The stomach is a very dangerous part of our bodies."

"No, it's not. Without it, we can't eat. Hey, did you hear about my son?"

"Yes, he told me he was leaving for Florida. He asked me to come with him, but I couldn't."

"You *couldn't?*"

"I was working."

"You couldn't escort him after all the good he done for you? Well, my D'Angelo, he died last night in Florida. I hope he ate something before he died. That's why I was telling you about the stomach. Be careful what you eat."

"Ms. Aretha, did you say D'Angelo is dead?"

She smiled and said, "Did you know my first husband reared chicken? He was here last week."

Patrick was thinking about what he had done to Denise, to their kids, about the HIV test, and the late D'Angelo. The brother was no more in pain. But how was he to continue working on a dead man's identity? And was Aretha's mental condition getting so bad that her son's death didn't seem to bother her?

He pledged to move out soon. He had to find a way to make amends with the family he believed he had already lost.

CHAPTER 57

He was at the foot of the staircase when Aretha startled him with her hearty laughter. He didn't know she was home.

"Why do you look so agitated?" she asked from the dining table.

"Nothing," Patrick retorted.

"This is America, Patrick." Again, she laughed.

Patrick wasn't sure he liked the way Aretha laughed, but he knew she was an innocent lady who meant no harm, one who had given him a home, and one from whom he had learned a lot about black America.

"From my childhood, I know when someone has drunk my milk."

Patrick felt wobbly in the knees. He admitted that he was everything a bad man could be. A cheat, a liar, an adulterer, and one who had abandoned his family. But never before had anyone accused him of being a thief. "I'm sorry, Miss Aretha. I meant to tell you. I'll buy you two cartons. Mine had expired."

"But I told you, Patrick, food never expires until it has gone bad. That's what grandma used to say."

"I'll remember that next time."

"You don't have to replace it, no. I get my milk free from some crazy pastor's church." Aretha burst out laughing. "I mean, the guy's like crazy-crazy."

Suddenly, Patrick wasn't feeling hungry, so he got back to his room and called Nicholas again.

"Sorry, brother. Your sister and I have been so busy, we missed your calls."

That evening, the couple picked Patrick up, and Kezia prepared *ugali* with vegetables and charcoal-broiled beef steaks. After getting used to Aretha's small home, the couple's dining room looked even bigger than before, and Kezia was stunningly beautiful. He couldn't understand how such a striking woman ended up marrying Nicholas, who was certainly not an attractive man.

"And how is Brother Pastor Gawo doing?" Patrick asked in the middle of the meal. The couple exchanged secret glances. They never did a good job of silent communication, Patrick concluded. "Did I say something wrong?"

"No, brother," said Nicholas. "It just shows that we haven't been seeing each other as much as we should."

"Tell him the truth, Nicholas," said Kezia, and she looked down at her food.

The trio had been using their hands to eat, just like most people did back home in Africa. Nicholas picked up a fork and jabbed it into a chunk of beef. He breathed in heavily. "The man of God, Pastor Gawo, had AIDS," said Nicholas. "To avoid embarrassment, the stigma, he went back to his village, and..." He forced the chunk of meat into his wide-open mouth.

"He killed himself," Kezia said matter-of-factly as if she feared that her husband would omit that important part of the story. "Yes, back home, where he's not known as a man of God but a mere child of the village. And yet AIDS is no longer a problem in this country. Problem was, he had pneumonia, dysentery. I think he started taking his regimen late. In my opinion, he should have stayed. Why be ashamed of a disease? No one knows how he got it."

Patrick remembered telling the pastor the true version of the story behind his stay in America. Although he couldn't recall every detail, the pastor's reaction had surprised him. *Go back to your family,* Pastor Gawo's words echoed in Patrick's ears. Patrick remembered Gawo dismissing Patrick's claim that AIDS was a serious disease, one that came with a stigma, but that it was a common ailment that God could easily cure.

"Brother, are you here?" Nicholas sounded concerned.

"I'm sorry to hear that," said Patrick. "That time I spoke to him in the church, did he know he had AIDS?"

"Nobody knows," said Nicholas. "People keep secrets, brother. It's the only way to survive human wrath. Why do you ask?"

"But he's a pastor. He should have told me."

Nicholas allowed himself to swallow the food in his mouth before he said, "He didn't have to, brother. You don't tell a stranger that you have AIDS. Besides, pastors are human. Okay, they're extraordinary people. They're in the business of telling motivational stories. In the process, they lie or cover some truths." As if he was surrendering to fate, Nicholas raised his right hand. "Survival."

They ate in silence. Nicholas and Kezia.

"Eat, brother," said Nicholas.

Patrick started to eat.

"Brother, do you see yourself going back home soon?" asked Kezia. "Don't you have a new government there?"

"No. But I have a confession to make."

The couple stopped eating, and Patrick told them why he was in the United States, and they listened without interruption. "I didn't want to see my wife suffer. How could I face my children, my sister, everyone? Anyway, I'm glad I tested negative. Because I was a public figure, I was scared of taking the test back there."

"That wasn't a good thing to do," Kezia said, gasping. She looked at her husband as if she was asking him to agree with her. "Pastor Gawo told us about your AIDS. We sympathized because he didn't tell us how you contracted the disease."

"The pastor told you what I told him in confidence?"

Kezia's mouth twitched, and her hands quivered. "You don't get it, do you?" she hissed. "It's not that he told us about it. The point is, *you*, sir, cheated on your wife!"

Nicholas cleared his throat. "Let's be calm." He picked up a knife from the table, and Patrick noticed that, like Kezia's hands, the knife was quivering, too. "There're times when I used to question some of the things Gawo used to say. So, when he told us about you, Kezia and I prayed to our God Jehovah that he was lying." He looked at Patrick. "I thought you were a gentleman."

"Same here!" said Kezia. And as if she had seen a venomous snake, she stood up and took several quick steps away from the table. "You can't do that to your wife, to your children!" she retorted, her eyes wide open and her nostrils flaring.

Nicholas drew in a deep breath, stood up, got close to his wife and held her by the shoulders. He said something in Kiswahili that Patrick suspected was equal to *"let me talk to him alone,"* for she started to walk away, and then she looked back and said, "I don't want him here, Nicholas. I remember how he used to stare at me when he was living here. Did he want to give me the disease?"

"Kezia!" Nicholas raised his voice. "Let me handle this, man to man."

"Get him out of here, Nicholas!"

"I'm so sorry, madam," Patrick whispered. "I was wrong."

CHAPTER 58

After the three of them had abandoned their half-eaten meal, Nicholas drove slowly, to the chagrin of some drivers who were behind him. Patrick berated himself for thinking that telling the truth to the couple would free him from the lie he had lived with for over a year. But no, the couple hadn't even given him a chance to wash his hands after using them to eat their meal. Kezia was right to behave the way she did, though.

"I agree with my wife," Nicholas finally spoke. "You don't abandon your family for any reason."

Rubbing his palms along his thighs, Patrick wished that Nicholas, the only person he could call a friend in America, would forgive him and assist him to get another job as he could no longer work because D'Angelo was dead. But Patrick had neither the courage nor the time to say that because after what looked to him like an endless trip, Nicholas's Mercedes had stopped next to Aretha's Cadillac.

"Thank you," said Patrick.

Nicholas grunted.

Patrick watched the Mercedes drive slowly away, and all he wanted was to be alone and not meet Aretha on his way up to his room, where he would cry himself to sleep.

Aretha's storm door was locked. Patrick knocked and called, and he could hear Aretha's landline ring until it stopped.

Half an hour later, Chantelle, wearing a loose truck suit, came out of her house and said, "Locked out as usual, neighbor?" Patrick nodded. "Come and wait in here."

Patrick wanted to say no, he didn't want to be seduced, but he concluded that not every woman was after him. Inside her living room, Chantelle showed him the sofa, and as was the case the last and only time Patrick had been in that room, he felt safe and warm.

She offered him a drink, and he declined. Again, she talked about her desire to visit Africa. "I'd love to see the animals."

"Yes, when you visit the national parks. I hope you'll be open to meeting the people as well. Most of them look like you."

"I'm sorry, Patrick," said Chantelle. "I'm stereotyping. We grew up hearing negative narratives about what they called the Dark Continent."

There was a loud knock at the door, the type one would expect from the police. Patrick decided that if the immigration people were there to get him, he would gladly accept the punishment that came with the crime of family betrayal.

"That's Aretha," Chantelle whispered.

Wearing a nightgown, Aretha stood in Chantelle's doorway and smiled. "I'm so sorry. I didn't know you was out."

"You can stay a little longer, Patrick," said Chantelle.

"I'm afraid I'm not feeling very well," said Patrick.

In his room, Patrick stayed in bed for hours, but sleep never came. On his phone, he googled news about Zambia: ruling party youths harassing opposition party members, one tribe pitted against another. He had never told Aretha that, like her, a black woman living in America, he too was considered a minority in his home country. He shoved the phone under his pillow and tried to understand himself better. Maybe he could find a good reason to justify everything he did, from sleeping with Emily, leaving his family, his overwhelming desire for Kezia, following Denise-lookalike, only to find Emily, losing his friendship with Nicholas, to sleeping in that creaky bed. What exactly went on in his mind that day when he did not board the flight back home? And Denise, what exactly did she think when he didn't show up at the airport? Was she seeing someone? Oh, if only he could find even a small piece of evidence to show that she had cheated on him. He would justify everything he had done.

And did Alice go to the university?

When he fell asleep, he had the same dream he had many times before: Denise and the kids were on one side of a river, and he was on the other side, and he couldn't reach them due to the reptiles he saw in the water.

In the morning, he knocked on Aretha's door and asked her to call the supermarket. "Tell them I'm not to work today." It would be the first time he was calling out.

"Your phone not working?" she asked nonchalantly without opening the door.

"I have no voice, Ms. Aretha."

She abruptly opened the door. "What happened to it?"

"I lost it, remember?"

"But you know I'm mourning my son."

"When is the funeral?" he asked.

"What funeral?"

Patrick pulled away from the door and got back to his room, where he lay on the bed, staring at the ceiling. Outside, someone was using a noisy leaf blower. He had done that job before, and it was easy. He thought about calling Nicholas to apologize. No. The couple wouldn't forgive him. The friendship he had lost could never be revived.

Hours later, he wasn't hungry, but he went downstairs to the kitchen to look for something to eat. He needed the energy to continue living and go back home to apologize to his family. Each of the three clocks, the one on the stove, and one on each of the two microwaves displayed a different time. He concluded that the time must be close to 8:00 pm.

Through the window, he saw the red sun between the tall trees behind the line of townhouses sink like a dying, burning ball. He was scared of the night, which, like a hooded hunter, was approaching fast. Insomnia. The nightmares in between. He wished he would die with the sun, but unlike the master of light, he wouldn't wish to resurrect.

But he had to go back home.

CHAPTER 59

It was a quiet evening, as usual, and the boys were in their room. Denise was about to go to her room when she heard a loud knock at the front door. It was Solomon, a large tray full of food in his hands.

"It's from madam," he said and, without being invited in, he passed so close to Denise that she was tempted to grab his shirt and tell him to leave. He headed for the dining table, where he placed the tray, and without a word, he marched out.

"Tell madam, thank you."

"No need, Dee," Rebecca said from the door.

She hadn't spoken much to Rebecca since the day she had walked out of her job. But when they did, it was Denise doing most of the listening as Rebecca urged her to marry someone before she became homeless.

"Am I welcome, girl?"

"Why not?" asked Denise. "It's your house."

They both sat down in awkward silence.

"Talking about which. Remember that young man I showed the house to? His woman wants to move in. As you know, business is bad, and I need the rent money."

"I'll do my best to find a place, Sister Rebecca."

"Denise, be strong and practical. It's one thing to talk about doing something, but quite another to..."

"I know!" Denise suddenly realized that she had just raised her voice. She thought about asking Rebecca for a loan to enable her to travel to Botswana to look for any available job.

There was a prolonged silence before Rebecca said, "Will you ever tell me the truth why Patrick walked out on you, because I'm not that dull, Denise. You know I could have made a very good lawyer if I had chosen to. I know that Americans have a problem keeping tabs on immigrants who are in hiding. But when someone dies, the body can't hide. That means my boy is still alive."

"Isn't it obvious that my husband abandoned us because he hates me?"

Rebecca was quiet for a long time. "Why did you take so long to tell the truth?"

"Because I thought you knew that he and I never spoke for ten years."

Rebecca stood up. "Sarcasm is not my thing."

"Please, the children," Denise whispered.

"I don't care!" Rebecca glided to the door and turned to give Denise an angry look. "You will pay for this in the next few days, Denise! I swear. I want you out of here by the end of the month. I'll keep my nephews. Find a job, find a man, I don't care what you do."

Rebecca slammed the door behind her. For an hour, Denise remained seated, tears in her eyes. She was glad that the kids hadn't come out of their bedroom when their aunt exhibited those tantrums like a spoiled child. Yes, she knew, even without being reminded, that she had to find a job.

She put the food on the table in the refrigerator and got to her bedroom. From under the bed, she pulled Patrick's old briefcase and put it on the bed. She rummaged the case and took her school certificate out. Then Patrick's university certificate. More documents followed.

"Where is my university degree?" she whispered. She needed to make copies before she left for Botswana. Yes, she was going to show Rebecca that even she could get a job.

Her fingers kept working, and she felt something. It was a side compartment with a concealed zipper. She undid the zip, put her hand in it, and pulled out a folded white sheet of paper.

TWICE, I SAW HER LEAVE YOUR ROOM AT NIGHT. ONE CARELESS STEP AND THIS WILL BE ALL OVER SOCIAL MEDIA. YOU OWE ME

She read the note again, and it didn't make sense. Who was it addressed to? She put it on the side and continued to look for her diploma.

Again, she read the note. It must have been a script idea. Patrick always came up with little plots which later became big television dramas. But why was it the only paper in that concealed compartment?

The telephone rang, and she was incensed to see it was Norman calling after midnight.

"Norman, what is it?"

"Can we have lunch tomorrow?"

Norman never seemed to care if Denise sounded angry, very angry, sad, or very sad over the phone. He always said exactly what he wanted to say. Maybe that was because he yielded so much power at the television station, he had learned not to listen to anybody? Maybe she could take a leaf from that and make things happen only her way?

She said, yes, and during lunch the following day, Denise found herself telling Norman, a stranger, about the disagreement she had with Rebecca the previous night. "I'm likely to be homeless soon," she concluded.

His left hand covering his forehead, Norman looked at the plate of food before him and said slowly, "Patrick and I were discussing dilemmas the day he told me about the marital problems you two were having."

"Please, don't say that to me again. Patrick and I had no problems."

"Okay, okay," Norman said, looking steadfastly at Denise. "The problem we have here is that we can't find Patrick. That's a dilemma. We can't resolve dilemmas, but we can manage them. How much reading do you do, Denise?"

"Norman, a woman in my circumstances can't find the time to read. I used to read a novel a week before I found myself in this shit—excuse my language."

"I understand. So, we have a dilemma, unsolvable, but we can resolve your multifaceted problem, which is no shelter above your head, joblessness, and of course, loneliness." Norman paused. "May I suggest we get married?"

Her facial muscles tightening, she said, "What?"

The couple at the next table turned to look at her momentarily. She was short of breath, and she wanted to go to the bathroom and pee. She looked at Norman. As if he hadn't just uttered an abomination, Norman seemed to be enjoying his meal.

"What do you mean?" she lowered her voice. "That sounds like a business proposal, not a marital one."

"Okay, Denise, will you marry me? I'm lonely. Does that sound better?"

Denise saw the sadness in Norman's face, and she knew that he meant what he had just said. She wanted to stand up and leave, though. Or maybe she could give the issue some thought and get back to him with an appropriate, more civilized answer the following day? Married? And to, of all people, Patrick's former boss? She thought about Patrick cheating on her with Lisa. Maybe, to get even with Lisa, she could marry Norman? But, hey, Lisa was dead.

"We could live together, Denise. Out of choice, Lisa and I had no children. I could adopt your boys and learn how to love children. Why? Because I'm crazy for you. Always have."

"What?" was all Denise could say.

"About sex and other things? When a man loves a woman, everything she wants to be put on hold can wait. We'll have all the time in the world to ourselves to do whatever pleases us after we're married."

There were only a handful of people in Norman's favorite restaurant, and Denise wondered if the couple at the next table had heard his plea and her uncalculated responses.

"Can you drop me at the KK Square open-air market after this?" She didn't want to hear about the proposal again. She wouldn't even discuss it with Rebecca. Rebecca! Suppose it was Rebecca who had asked Norman to make that proposal? Rebecca and Norman were contemporaries at the university.

"You haven't answered me, Denise." Norman chewed his lower lip.

"And you haven't given me time to think."

"Okay, let's go!" he stood up, put some bills on the table, and headed for the exit.

Denise looked at the food on the table. Her kids could do with that, but that was okay. The food wasn't meant for them. Besides, the food Rebecca had given them was enough food to last a few days.

None of them said a word until Norman stopped the vehicle at the market and said nervously, "Am I safe here? I mean, this is a bad neighborhood, and this is an expensive vehicle. Let's say I pick you up in an hour. You could walk to the main road, right?"

She nodded, and as she watched Norman's vehicle drive away, she wondered if he believed she would marry him.

"Nice car!" Denise turned sharply to look into the eyes of a young man. "You scared me, Boyd!"

"Not Boyd. Bonaventure."

"Yes, of course. You promised to protect me."

"You moved, madam, and I got a job."

She studied his jacket and tie. "I'm happy for you. Where?"

"A security company, madam. I'm their kind of accountant. Is he your new husband? I'm jealous."

"My husband? No. Yes, we moved out. Look, now that I have seen you, I want you to be honest with me." She could tell she had Bonaventure's full attention. "Why is that man always saying bad things about you? I mean, really bad things."

"Your boyfriend?" There was an urgency in Bonaventure's voice.

"No, the man in the yellow house. Next to where I used to live. He certainly hates you. He saw you and your friends talking to me the other day, and he said such horrible, horrible things about you, I can't even repeat them. He said he was going to report you to the police, and if the police didn't do anything about it...Look, I can't say more. Tell me, are you boys engaged in crime?"

"Madam..." With a stooped posture, Bonaventure looked down.

"Sorry, maybe I shouldn't have...uh, I have to go."

She walked toward the market, and when she looked behind her, Bonaventure was standing still, looking at his shoes.

Denise found Martha sitting on concrete blocks behind her wares of boiled sweet potatoes, yellowing cabbage, boiled peanuts, and dry fish. "Good to see you," Martha was excited. "Boss not back from America?" Denise shook her head slowly. "I say you see witchdoctor. Witchdoctor can help bring my good boss here." Martha stood up. "Sorry, madam, nowhere to sit that is very good. But sit here." She pointed at her concrete block seat.

Denise remembered the two concrete blocks under her daughter's dangling feet.

"No, actually, uh, actually..." She wondered if it would be right to tell Martha that her husband, Wizzie, had raped her. How would she react? Tell her husband, who would deny the accusation and cause a scene? "Martha, I was, uh, just passing by to see you. How's your friend, the nurse? The one who gave me the injection."

"Oh, you want other injections?" Martha looked concerned. "She is not my friend. My friend, her friend's sister." Martha chuckled. "It's like sister-sister-sister. Unfortunate, she died last week."

"She *what?*"

"She gave somebody injections."

A bearded, gray-haired man appeared from behind Denise and picked up a dry fish from Martha's bowl. "How much?" the man asked while he examined the fish. "Oh, no good." He threw the fish back in the bowl and walked away.

"Here, I get used," said Martha. "Some people? Very rude. Ah, the nurse with sister-sister. She gave injections to people. Two people, they died after injections, so the police, they were looking for her. She took her many injections. She died."

"You mean she committed *suicide?*"

"Yes, a suicide."

"I'm sorry to hear that."

"Why do you ask, madam? You want injections?"

"No. It's just that she did me a very good favor, giving me those injections, so I wanted to see how I could repay her. Sorry, in a hurry, I have to go."

Denise was disappointed. She had wanted to hear from the nurse exactly what had happened on the morning of her daughter's death.

"Madam, you want a fish?" asked Martha.

"No thank you, and I have to go."

Outside the market square, Denise called Norman. He didn't answer, so she caught a minibus cab and got home an hour later. She found Rebecca working in the flower garden.

"You should have called, Dee." Rebecca threw the garden fork in her hand into a wheelbarrow full of weeds. "Let's have some tea."

As the two were sitting in the living room, Rebecca said, "You know I would have come to pick you up, girl."

"Pick me up?"

"It's a small world, Dee. I hear Norman proposed, and you said yes. Congratulations. He said he waited for you at the market. But why didn't you eat his lunch?"

Denise felt a pounding in the ears. First, Bonaventure had thought that Norman was her new husband. She hadn't taken offense. Then Rebecca was telling her that Norman had told her some big lie. She took offense.

Solomon brought a tray of assorted snacks, which he arranged meticulously on a coffee table.

"White sugar or brown sugar, madam?" Solomon addressed Denise.

"No!" Denise shouted. She was short of breath. She wanted to run. Norman had a big mouth, and she hated Rebecca and her Solomon.

"Leave us alone, Solo," Rebecca ordered.

Solomon left, and Denise apologized.

"Calm down," Rebecca spoke softly. "I know too much is happening right now. This marriage thing, girl, it could change your life forever." She poured a cup of tea for Denise. "You better have some bread, since you didn't eat. First things first. I can arrange a divorce lawyer and a judge. For that, we don't need to follow any silly procedures."

"Who's getting married?"

"*You*, of course. Do you know how many women would love to marry Norman after that slut of his passed on? What's the name? Lisa."

Denise wished she would leave, but Rebecca was her landlady.

In just over an hour, Denise had told lies to both Martha and Bonaventure, and Norman had told a lie about her to Rebecca. She had been rude to Solomon, too, a man who had been polite to her until the previous night when his body almost touched hers.

"Thanks for the tea, but I have a headache," said Denise, and she wasn't lying. She left and tried to get some sleep, but a pounding headache made her fear she was developing a migraine.

She didn't sleep well at night, either. Had she become a liar? Was Patrick a liar? Was he still alive or was he cheating on her at that very moment?

Early the next morning, Rebecca called. "Girl, did you and Norman talk?"

"No."

"Okay, he called me. Said we should give you some surprise of some sort. I'm going to arrange things for you."

"Sister Rebecca, I don't want to marry Norman or anybody. I'm still married to Patrick."

Denise listened in trepidation as her sister-in-law laughed as if she had taken a large dose of an illegal substance.

"He says as his wife, you won't need a job, girl. If I were you, I'd marry him. Look at you, you can't find a job. You need a home. My tenant is moving in next week."

"I'll not marry him."

There was a knock at the front door. Denise opened it and Rebecca entered, her cellphone still pressed to her ear.

"We need to talk like adults, Denise."

CHAPTER 60

For days, Denise agonized over the undue influence Rebecca was putting on her to marry Norman. Norman himself never called. In Rebecca, he had a committed, persuasive representative who spoke to Denise several times a day, outlining the marriage plan and stating with which lawyer she had spoken and when.

Denise rarely slept. Only when the kids went to school did sleep come, but not for long. She took pain pills, but that didn't help. She wondered if Rebecca needed the rent money she would be collecting from the young drug peddler named Rodwell so badly that she would marry off her sister-in-law to any man.

A week had passed since Norman had proposed to Denise when she realized that her dream of getting a job in Botswana was an impossible venture. Starting a new life in a foreign country, and at her age, would be quite a challenge. Besides, there was no guarantee that anyone in Botswana would give her a job when no one in her own country did.

She called Norman.

"So glad to hear from you, Denise," he said. "Have you considered our proposal?"

"I will marry you, yes," she said. "But on condition that..."

"We don't do silly things?" he chuckled. "Agreed."

Her hands shaking, she cut the line and put the cellphone on her bed. What had she just done? Was she crazy?

Not long after that, Rebecca was at the front door.

"Okay, girl, first things first," Rebecca seemed to be in no hurry as she sat down in the living room "The matter of the dissolution of the matrimony between Denise Neo-Kanya and Patrick Watae Kanya will be heard in chambers tomorrow," she announced delightedly. "In-camera, girl. That means away from the public eye."

Denise wished she was made of the same material as her sister-in-law.

That night, Denise did more crying than sleeping. The boys knocked on her door, and she didn't open it. She felt as if she had been sold, just like some of her ancestors, she believed, had either been sold or stolen by slave raiders who marauded the land that made modern Zambia from their base in the port of Lobito in modern Angola.

She dreaded the coming of the new day, for the divorce case was coming as early as 9:00 am.

"Don't worry," Rebecca said as the two drove to the Magistrate Court Complex on Hibiscus Road. "The magistrate is an old friend from university. Besides, this is legal. For more than a year, we, as a family, have searched for a Patrick Kanya, and we can't locate him."

Outside the courthouse, after the marriage had been dissolved, Norman led Denise and Rebecca to his red Toyota Land Cruiser. It was the first time Denise was seeing Rebecca and Norman together, and she could feel the good vibes between them. Were they lovers once, she wondered?

"Here," Norman said, handing a cellphone to Denise. "A new phone and number, a new life. And you can drive my car until I buy you one." He dangled a set of keys before her.

Tears in her eyes, Denise said, "I'm sorry, but am I allowed to drive your company car?"

She was finally a single woman, and it didn't feel right. When she married Patrick, she, and not him, was serious about the vows they made. For the first time, she hoped that Patrick was dead. If he wasn't, she would never be with him again.

"It's not my official car," said Norman. "Yes, it's yours now."

"What do I do with the old phone?" she asked.

"Hey, lose it, okay? Give it to Charity, uh, Chris."

"Denise, take it!" ordered Rebecca.

Denise accepted the phone. "No, not the car," she said, and Rebecca didn't look too pleased.

"I've booked a suite at the Intercontinental on Haile Selassie Avenue," said Norman. It was as if he was oblivious to Rebecca's presence. "You and the kids can stay there until you all move in with me."

"But I haven't said just because I'm divorced, we're moving in with you," Denise said politely. Rebecca walked away to a not-too-distant spot, where she stood still, facing the courthouse. Denise knew that her sister-in-law was still listening to the couple's conversation, though. "I haven't been with a man in a long time." What would her boys say if she told them she was marrying their father's former boss or any man at all? She wasn't even going to tell them about the divorce. "I'm...uh, not sure if I could marry you."

"Yes, you *will* marry me," said Norman with irritating arrogance. "Didn't Rebecca tell you? That guesthouse is no longer available."

Rebecca joined the couple. "So, now that you're no longer my sister-in-law, you can find yourself a new home."

"Hey, is collecting rent all you really care about?" Norman asked, and Denise knew that was said in jest.

"What are you going to do, Norman?" Rebecca sounded displeased. "I got you the girl of your life. You married Lisa because Denise wasn't available."

"What? Is that so, Norman?" asked Denise, not believing what she was hearing.

"Denise, I'm giving you two weeks to move out."

Rebecca and Denise drove home in silence, and they didn't speak to each other until the third day when Rebecca again went to the guesthouse to show Rodwell and his girl around.

"So, when are you moving, madam?" asked Rodwell.

"Tonight," said Denise, and Rebecca's mouth dropped open.

Denise stood still, listening to Rebecca and her new tenants making plans about the guesthouse. As soon as the three had left, she called Norman. He answered on the first ring. She remembered a time when she used to call him about Patrick's terminal benefits, and Norman would never answer the phone.

"I'll marry you, Norman," she said.

"Of course. I knew you would come to your senses."

"There will be conditions, though."

"Yes, I understand. I'm not ready to violate you, so to speak, darling."

Did he call her 'darling'? "Norman, will you let me talk? One, you will give me and my boys a roof over our heads."

"Denise, I…"

"Two, we will not live like a couple until later. I have no idea when 'later' will be." He will accept those terms, she concluded. If it was true that Norman had been in love with her all these years, she and the boys would be getting out of the guesthouse soon, and on her terms.

"It shall be done."

A few days later, Rebecca arranged a private ceremony presided over by an elderly deputy registrar of marriages. Rebecca and a chatty man Norman introduced as a cousin witnessed the ceremony.

"Since you insist, and to prove to you that I'm a gentleman, I'll let you go home," Norman said. "Come when you're ready, or when the guesthouse is no longer available."

Denise and Rebecca drove home as if they had just quarreled.

"I knew the registrar many years ago when he married one of my cousins," Rebecca spoke at last. "Now, girl, we don't tell the boys about any of this shit." Denise closed her eyes. "Again, let me ask you. Suppose Patrick appeared today, would you marry him?"

"No. Do I know what diseases he has contracted over there, sleeping with all sorts of women? What if he has AIDS? Besides, anyway, I know he's dead. And you know why I married Norman? You forced me to, so I did it for my boys. I know they won't be happy, but they need shelter over their heads."

"No, girl, I didn't force you. Norman told me he made you pregnant in Livingstone."

With clenched fists, Denise hit the glove compartment of Rebecca's SUV. "That idiot! I told you we never slept together."

"No, girl, he told me you were great in bed, so I keep wondering why Patrick left you. Denise, I also knew about your rivalry with the late Lisa. You won."

"How do you know about Lisa?"

"Don't shout. Patrick. He liked Lisa very much, and Lisa liked him, and Norman knew."

As Rebecca's vehicle approached home, the security guard was closing the gate.

"Who was here?" Rebecca asked the guard.

Holding Junior's right hand, Solomon rushed out of the main house. "Madam! The police Land-Rover. You see it?"

Junior started to cry.

Denise quickly got out of the vehicle. "What is it, Solomon? Honey, what's going on?" She put her arms around her son, the way a chicken protects its chicks from the prowling hawk.

"They came here and put handcuffs on Chris," said Solomon breathlessly.

"What?" Rebecca said as she was coming out of the vehicle.

"The police say his friend, she had the gun, and they stole from a supermarket in town," Solomon gesticulated.

Denise felt a hollowness in the stomach. A gun? A girlfriend? Chris? "Sister Rebecca, I have to..." How could this happen to her? "Thank you, Solomon. Thanks. Rebecca, I have to go. Which station, Solomon?"

"Why do you say, *I* instead of *us*?" Rebecca barked, only to calm down. "You can't handle this one alone, Denise. Call your husband."

"Patrick is not here, Sister Rebecca." Denise was choking from sobbing, and her eyes were red.

"Norman. Norman has connections."

Norman didn't pick up the phone, and for hours, Rebecca used the landline to speak to people Denise had either never heard of, or to whom she thought her sister-in-law would have no access because of their high political status. Unfortunately, Denise couldn't follow the conversations because the phone had no speaker.

"I want you to get some rest," Rebecca said at last. "They intend to charge my nephew with aggravated robbery. That offense is unbailable."

"Oh, my God," said Denise.

"Don't go there, girl. Where was God when they took my nephew away?" asked Rebecca. "I hear that after school, Chris accompanied his girlfriend to a supermarket, where the owner, a national of Greek origin, was shot in the stomach. The gun used in the robbery belonged to the girl's parents, but Chris, they say, is the one who pulled the trigger."

Junior had long fallen asleep on one of Rebecca's sofas, and it was Denise's turn to cry again, this time, uncontrollably. *Chris has no girlfriend,* she wanted to scream. *He knows nothing about guns. He just lost his sister. His father is dead.*

"Tears won't help us, girl, but feel free to cry." Rebecca impulsively threw a box of Kleenex tissue at Denise. The box fell to the floor, and Denise ignored it.

Looking dazed, Uncle Ben appeared from the bedroom. Denise stopped crying. She could not believe what she was seeing. Wearing pajamas, Uncle Ben had lost so much weight, his full-fledged Afro was unkempt, and his big, oily nose was the most prominent part of his face. He staggered until he collapsed in the nearest chair. Rebecca slapped him gently across the face, trying to get him to come to, but without success.

"He'll be okay, girl," said Rebecca. "I'm used to this stupidity. Go get some rest. We'll deal with this Chris thing tomorrow. Leave Junior here. I don't want you disturbing him with your crying." She broke down, and it was Denise's turn to comfort her sister-in-law.

That night, Denise couldn't sleep, so when Norman finally called at 3:00 am, she quickly answered the phone. "There was an urgent issue at the station," he said. "My newsroom boys carried the wrong story. Now, listen, darling. Rebecca told me everything. I'll speak to some people in high places this morning. Everything will be all right, I can assure you. All these politicians owe me. I run the newsroom, Denise. I make them and break them at will."

Denise didn't mind Norman boasting, as long as he got her child out of jail.

When, eventually, Norman left Denise alone, the questions that nagged her were: was getting married the right thing to do?

Would Norman treat her kids well? Norman and Lisa never raised a family. Denise had heard that it was him, and not her, who was to blame, and yet Lisa had been subjected to many unnecessary and expensive surgeries. Just as she feared that Patrick was dead, she saw the possibility of her son being sentenced to death. In which case, would Rebecca look after Junior? Would Junior survive the trauma?

CHAPTER 61

Denise had just married Norman when, on the other side of the Atlantic Ocean, Aretha knocked on Patrick's door.

"Are you off today? I'm buying heavy stuff, and I need you to come with me to the store."

Patrick had hoped he would spend the whole day in bed undisturbed. He remembered the wealthy woman at the supermarket who had asked him to escort her to her home. Maybe he should have taken the bait and become financially independent?

"I'll come with you, ma'am."

Aretha drove to several stores, where she bought groceries and a step-ladder. As Patrick dutifully put the shopping in the Cadillac's ever-so-clean trunk, he wondered if Wizzie was still working for Denise.

They stopped at Walgreens Pharmacy, where Aretha picked up some off-the-counter pain medications. While she joined the line at the cashier's, Patrick waited for her by the main entrance.

Patrick's phone started to ring, and at the same time, Aretha was shouting, "Patrick, do you have five dollars on you?"

"Listen, my man." Leroy was on the line. "I have a coat for you here. Some white woman—yeah, remember the one with the Porsche? She wants you to keep it. Expensive stuff, man. But listen, trouble here, my man, trouble."

"Trouble?" Patrick asked and wondered who had given Leroy his number.

"Patrick!" Aretha called again.

"Listen, I hear they know about your voice, man," said Leroy.

"D'Angelo?" several people turned to look at the woman who had called.

Patrick felt sweat cover his face. Standing between him and Aretha, Olivia was staring at him, arms akimbo. "Let me call you back," Patrick whispered into the phone.

"No, D'Angelo, it can't wait, man," said Leroy. "It's urgent, you know what I mean?"

His hands shaking, Patrick hung up and arrogantly said, "Do I know you?" He hoped he had sounded convincingly African American.

Olivia snorted. "I have always suspected there was something funny, uh, weird about you. I see you talk to customers in the parking lot. Who are you?" She turned to face Aretha. "Did you call him Patrick?" Turning to Patrick, she said, "D'Angelo?"

"She's got the wrong person," Patrick addressed no one in particular. "I don't know of no D'Angelo, man."

Aretha seemed to have found the five dollars she needed a while back, for she had already paid and was heading for the exit.

"Okay, let's talk outside," said Olivia. "Maybe I can help."

Patrick's chest hurt, and he feared he was going to piss in his pants.

Outside, the afternoon sun was blinding him, but he managed to see Aretha's Cadillac quickly reversing out of its parking space. He ran towards the Cadillac and tried to open the passenger door. It was locked. He knocked hard on the window, and a loud car horn startled him. The pain in his chest was getting intense. If he had a heart attack, he would refuse to go to the hospital, for there, he would be arrested and deported. He thought about Denise…

The Cadillac had stopped. Behind it, the driver of a red SUV shouted through the window, "Are you crazy?" Patrick opened the passenger door of the Cadillac and hurled himself in. He looked behind. At the pharmacy door, Olivia stood still, cupping her eyes, as if she was studying the Cadillac's tag number.

"Who's that crazy woman?" asked Aretha with annoying composure.

"Olivia. She's my manager."

"She say she don't know you," Aretha laughed. Patrick shook his head slowly. "White women are like that. They like a handsome black man, and when you turn them down, they become vindictive. I keep telling you that. But since she's your boss, that's retaliation. I was head of HR. I know about these things."

"It's not her fault, Ms. Aretha. I'm to blame. I have to leave."

"You've found a place?"

"I have to go home. To Africa."

"But you just paid your rent, and I can't refund you. I spent some of it on my son's funeral. You know that."

They stopped at a railroad crossing, right behind an SUV, while a long train passed.

"What's he doing?" said Aretha after the train was gone. "The motherfucker ain't moving."

"The hazard lights are blinking, Ms. Aretha. He must have a problem with the car."

"Do you know how much an Escalade costs? A hundred thousand. Black folk, they broke, but will still buy a Cadillac. A car like that, it never breaks down."

Patrick saw that there was a long line of cars behind them. Soon, a car came from behind and passed by Aretha's car. Another followed, and yet another.

"Shit, I must go," said Aretha. "This motherfucker must be high on something."

She reversed the vehicle a little and turned the wheel like a professional driver and drove past the Escalade.

They had been driving for a few minutes when Aretha adjusted the rearview mirror and said, "You see what I been telling you? Blue lights."

With a clenched jaw, Patrick said, "Please, stop and be polite to the police. Do you think they're going to ask for my identity?"

"I'm looking for a spot to stop. One where there'll be witnesses."

By the time Aretha stopped the Cadillac, Patrick feared he was going to pass out. It was the first time he was experiencing a police pullover. He internally cursed Aretha for inviting him to escort her on a shopping spree that didn't need a man to lift the few items she had bought.

"You see, Patrick, he's taking so long to come out because he wants reinforcements. Maybe they're planning on shooting us."

"Please, be polite to them," Patrick pleaded.

Aretha laughed.

Finally, a young male cop appeared at Aretha's window. "Put your hands on the wheel, ma'am. You know you drove on the wrong side of the road?"

Patrick looked straight ahead, making no body movement.

"No, young man, that vehicle in front, it was in a breakdown. I had to drive around it like the others."

"May I see your driver's license, please?"

Patrick didn't see Aretha take out her driver's license, but he heard her say, "There!" He wished she would be polite and be mindful of the possibility of him, and not her, getting into trouble.

"Will be back," the officer said and walked back to the patrol car.

Suddenly, Patrick felt extremely weak.

"He's in training, I can tell," said Aretha. "Black America, wake up!"

Patrick wished Aretha would shut up.

"I keep telling you about these things. Now you know about spying black cats. Did you see all those cars that went before us? They were white drivers, and this motherfucker, straight from high school, he don't stop them. I could just drive off, Patrick. But they may shoot you. You're a black man, right?"

Minutes later, the young officer was back at Aretha's window. "I'm gonna give you two tickets. One for not stopping at a stop sign…"

"Young man, I stopped behind that Escalade." Aretha sounded combative, and Patrick, this time looking down, felt his stomach contracting.

"You say that to the judge, ma'am. The other ticket will be for driving on the wrong side of the road."

"Officer!" Aretha shouted. "Check my driving history. I'm a proud black woman who obeys the white man's laws."

"Ma'am, you say that to the judge."

Patrick was relieved when the officer handed two tickets to Aretha and even wished her a great day. But when she drove slowly, Patrick feared they would be stopped for obstructing traffic, and this time, the police would ask for his ID.

"They always do my people wrong," Aretha said, as if she was speaking to herself. "They hate black people that's smart. Did you see that? But you don't fight racism with racism. You know who said that?"

"I don't," said Patrick. He realized how ignorant he was about the black American experience on American roads. Since he moved to Aretha's place, all he had known was to walk to work, work like a horse, eat very little, go to bed, and have nightmares.

His phone rang.

"Answer that," Aretha said agitatedly.

"Look here, brother." It was Sonko, the African coworker who had been nice to Patrick from day one at the supermarket. "Please, listen to me. Leroy gave me your number. He says you refused to speak to him. That's not good, brother. Let me advise you because I know about these things. If you come here…you know ICE? They're immigration people. They will arrest you. I can still help."

"Thank you, brother," said Patrick, and the other man hung up.

"Who the hell is that?" asked Aretha.

"Someone at work."

For the first time since his arrival in the US, Patrick really wanted to go back home. He would get home unannounced and hope for the best.

CHAPTER 62

He lay in bed, his neck hurting from the pillow he had never gotten used to for over a year. With D'Angelo dead, he could not see himself going back to work at the supermarket. His airline ticket had expired, of course, and his passport would expire in a week. Sonko had told him that immigration in Atlanta wouldn't bother him at the airport if he was going back to his country. He used to think of himself as a smart man, but living in a foreign country had shown him that he wasn't. He was going back home. He couldn't live in fear, in poverty forever. He was HIV-negative, after all. He would tell Denise the whole truth and apologize.

Aretha knocked hard on his door and announced that her man was coming to visit, so, could he go away for a few hours? "We want to make noise," she said, and that reminded him of Denise. He and Denise used to make so much noise that sometimes he feared the kids used to hear them.

He wasn't happy that he had to be hounded out of bed, but did he have a choice? He got downstairs, and Aretha was intently watching the front door.

"Ms. Aretha, I have a problem." He just had to say it. She didn't turn to look at him. "I need help." She got closer to the door, pulled the curtain in the transom window and peeped outside.

"Be a natural woman, Aretha," she whispered to herself. "He'll be here soon."

"Ms. Aretha, please."

"I told you, I'm waiting for my man. What do you want now?"

"Maybe I should ask you later?"

She finally turned to face him and smiled. "I'm sorry, but this guy gets on my nerves. No, let's talk now before he gets here."

"I want to give you some cash."

"You know I can't say no to that," she laughed. "But for what?"

"I give you the cash, you put it in your account and buy me an airline ticket to Africa."

She seemed to be thinking about it. "Sounds illegal to me. You saw how that young white police officer threatened my life. So, you're serious about leaving?"

"Are you going to help me or not?"

"I don't want to get involved. You know, Trump he's watching all black people, especially people like you and me."

"Thank you for your honesty, Ms. Aretha."

"I know I said the rent agreement was from month to month. But you should have given me time to arrange things. Can you find me someone to rent your room? You know, my son, D'Angelo, he use to give me money when his company was doing well."

Patrick excused himself, passed close to Aretha, opened the front door, closed it gently, and stepped outside. His shoulders hunched forward, hands in coat pockets, he walked to the cul-de-sac, made a U-turn, and kept walking. There was no second car in front of Aretha's house. Did Aretha have a boyfriend, or was that aspect of her life imaginary?

Patrick wondered what had happened to Julio and his family. Were they back in Mexico, or were they still at a detention center? He wished he had known Julio better. He would have listened to the man's stories about living in the country illegally, constantly looking over his shoulder. What was it like to live in Mexico? What had motivated him to come to America?

He searched his phone for recent calls. There were more than a dozen calls he couldn't recognize. He hadn't saved Sonko's number, so he called one that had come at a time when he thought Sonko had called. No. It must have been a telemarketer's number. He walked on and made four more calls. None was answered by someone he knew.

Like Denise before him, he made a difficult decision.

"Hello, my brother!"

What a relief. Patrick hadn't expected that kind of response. He quickly explained his predicament.

"Oh, that's no problem, brother. In fact, Kezia and I were talking about you last night. We said, why do we go to church if we can't appreciate a brother's problem? If Adam, our ancestor, could be deceived by Eve, surely, all God's children can make mistakes. A moment. Just a moment...Okay, I'll call you back, brother."

The line was cut, and for the first time in a long time, Patrick smiled. He had underestimated his friendship with the Kenyan couple. Nicholas and Kezia were the typical family found in an African village. They were trusting and kind.

He walked on, going back down to the cul-de-sac. Still, only the Cadillac stood in front of Aretha's house.

The telephone rang: *Scam likely*, the message on the phone read. He answered it and said, "You idiot!" and the call ended. He was about to put the phone in his coat when it rang. It was Nicholas.

"I had to speak to your sister first. And, brother, to show remorse for judging you, we'll pay for your ticket. We have always wanted you to go back home and tell your wife the truth. That's what I would do, brother. You'll need whatever little money you have when you get home. I know how it is over there."

Patrick sat on a pad-mounted transformer near the road and broke down.

"What's the problem, brother?" asked Nicholas.

"You...you are more than a brother. I never thought you two would ever talk to me again."

"I don't understand you, Brother Patrick. All people—Africans, Europeans, Asians—we're all related, brother. We all came from Africa. Give me a minute."

Patrick heard footsteps, which were followed by distant voices before Nicholas came back on the line and said, "Your sister wants you to come home tonight."

"Even after what my sister said about me staring at her?"

"My wife never tells untruths, Brother Patrick. But man to man, I understand. We forgive you."

"I don't know how to thank you."

"Okay, I'm working tonight—you know the kind of jobs we do here. I'll be leaving early. I hope you sleep well. Your sister will be here, in case you need anything. So, get ready."

He heard Aretha's laughter as he opened his bedroom door. He locked the door and hurriedly packed his belongings. He wouldn't need the two pairs of frayed jeans and the shoes he had used at work. The one case he had brought with him from home and the clothes in it were all he would take with him. He heard Aretha open her door, and he rushed to open his own.

"I'm leaving tonight, Ms. Aretha."

She kept walking down the stairs, and he felt bad. He understood her position. She needed the rent money, especially after D'Angelo's death.

An hour later, Kezia was at Aretha's front door. Aretha invited her in and all the three of them sat in the living room. Patrick did his best not to stare at Kezia. She was still stunningly beautiful, of course, but he now saw her as a sister.

"You'll be all right, Patrick," said Aretha. "You know, black people always meet again in the great Kingdom of Africa. And you?" She addressed Kezia. "I've never seen a black woman as beautiful as you. You remind me of..." she laughed as she clicked her fingers. "Don't you think she's extremely beautiful, Patrick?"

"Oh, thank you," said Kezia.

"Patrick is a good man, and you'll make him a good wife. Please, take care of him."

"I will, and thank you," said Kezia with a smile.

"Do me a favor," Aretha lowered her voice. "Can you find me someone to rent your husband's room?"

Kezia nodded. "I'll try, auntie. I will. Please, give me your number."

Aretha quickly wrote her number on a piece of paper.

"Thank you," said Kezia as she put the piece of paper in her purse, and there was a loud knock on the front door.

"That should be him," Aretha said and she rushed to the door. "My man. I told him you were leaving, Patrick."

Aretha opened the door, and a black man wearing a yellow utility vest, a piece of paper in his hand, said, "We just disconnected your water."

"I'm afraid we have to go," said Kezia.

"The stuff I tell you about the white man, it's real, Patrick," Aretha laughed.

The drive to Smyrna wasn't what Patrick had feared it would be. He felt at ease as he sat in the passenger seat of Kezia's SUV, the very first time the two had been alone together in a vehicle. He wasn't looking forward to spending the night alone with Kezia in the big house, though: *Your sister will be here, in case you need anything.* What did Nicholas mean by that? He had heard about an African tribe that allowed a man to invite his brother to sleep with his wife. He didn't think Nicholas and Kezia were that kind of people, no. But why had Kezia not told Aretha that she wasn't his wife?

They got home, and Kezia took Patrick's case upstairs. When she came back down, she was wearing a grey, tight-fitting tracksuit and a silver necklace with a large, sparkling cross dangling from it. It was the first time Patrick had known Kezia to be chatty. As the two watched television news, Kezia talked positively about the politics back home in Kenya. She wanted to know about the political situation in Zambia. She talked about the Trump presidency, too, but she stopped when Patrick didn't respond. He had no desire to discuss politics.

He gave her a long stare and said, "How did you manage that?"

"Manage what?" she asked.

The dimples in her cheeks were killing him. He feared she had probably heard the tremor in his voice. "Speaking like an American." He touched his lower lip.

"Oh, practice," she said mischievously. "Back home, I was a teacher, not a nurse. So, when I went to nursing school here, I listened to the instructors, the students, the patients talk, watched TV, practiced, and practiced like a good student. Brother, anything you want, you can get. I want to be a doctor someday."

"You're very smart, Kezia," he said. Just saying her name made him tremble, and he felt an aching hollowness in his stomach. "You'll be a doctor soon." He took a deep breath. "I'm sorry, sister, but I'm...I'm attracted to you."

He closed his eyes, expecting Kezia to smack him across the face and ask him to leave. Instead, she chuckled. "Temptation," she said at long last. "You, brother, as a believer, you know it goes all the way back to our ancestors, Adam and Eve." He opened his eyes. She was staring at him, laughter in her eyes. "I felt the same about you the very first time I saw you, my brother in Christ. Even Nicholas said to me, 'What a handsome brother!' That day you came here with Brother Peter, I couldn't sleep that night." She giggled.

Patrick wanted to stand up, get close to her and hold her.

"But I prayed about it," she said. "And the Lord spoke to me about it. When I heard about the reason why you are here, well, that made it easy for me to let go of my feelings. You know, your brother is a good man, and he unfairly accused me of having an affair with my boss, Dr. Johnson. Can you keep a secret?" Patrick nodded. "Brother Nicholas has erectile dysfunction, and he gets easily agitated and suspicious of everything I do. My movements. My phone calls. And yet he, too, has been tempted before. What I'm saying is, a man like you can tempt any woman. Let's pray about it, brother." She got on her knees. "Come, hold my hand. Both hands." He got closer.

CHAPTER 63

It was mid-morning, and Uncle Ben joined Denise and Rebecca in the living room. To Denise, Ben looked frailer and much older than the previous night, but he spoke with poise.

"So, you want to see your son in jail, and they say no?" he asked. "Five times?" Denise nodded. "All I need is a good haircut, and I'll ensure you see your son today, tomorrow, the day after."

After a nerve-racking hour of waiting for him to get ready, Uncle Ben got in the back seat of Rebecca's SUV.

"We start with police headquarters," he gave orders, and the trio drove in silence to the Zambia Police offices on Government Road.

For two hours, Denise and Rebecca waited in the car. They talked about Chris and Alice, and what must have been going on in Junior's head. None of them mentioned Patrick. When Rebecca said she wanted to go in and fetch her husband, in case he had fallen asleep in some waiting room, Denise said, "I would give him time, my sister. He seems to know what he's doing."

Moments, later, Uncle Ben appeared. To Denise, he looked more alert than when he left.

"The director of public prosecutions, the director of legal aid, the commissioner of prisons, they're all junior lawyers to me," Uncle Ben boasted from the back seat. "We're going to see the attorney general, another junior lawyer."

It was another hour before Uncle Ben came out of the Fairley Road offices and said without fanfare, "Tomorrow, you, Derby, you'll see your son."

"Who are you calling Derby?" Rebecca asked.

"I tried to get you, Rebecca, to be included as a visitor, but hey! They say Chris is a dangerous man. What do they know about my little nephew? Small men without brains!"

"Thanks for all this," said Denise. Tears filled her eyes, and Rebecca patted her right thigh.

"He's my nephew," Uncle Ben said nonchalantly. "Every episode of your life, ladies, is a classroom. You stack up knowledge with each class. I stacked up in law school. Now, look at me, I'm the best husband in the world."

"You have a great sense of humor, Uncle Ben," Rebecca said sarcastically.

"Tell me, Derby, what one thing can human beings never stop doing?"

"I don't know, uh...Living? No. Breathing."

"You can stop breathing for a few minutes, Derby. It's thinking!" said Ben with bravado. "We're always thinking. Unfortunately, most of that amounts to naught. As for you, my dear Reb, all those things you do behind my back, are they funny?"

The car slowed down, and Rebecca looked straight ahead. "What things, Ben?"

"You really want me to mention them in front of Patrick's wife?"

Denise wished she wasn't in the vehicle, but it was a little pleasing to witness Rebecca lose a battle. She stole a glance behind her. Uncle Ben had either fallen asleep, or he was feigning it.

As usual, Denise did not sleep well that night. She was eager to see her son. Sleep finally came, but at 6:00 am, and soon, she was dreaming that Chris had been sentenced to death. An hour later, she was awakened by Solomon, who had come to take Junior to the vehicle that took the boys to school Monday to Friday. Junior left without a word, and soon after that, Denise broke down.

Rebecca and Denise got to police headquarters at 10:00 am. Rebecca stayed in the vehicle, and Denise, dressed in all-black, was ushered into a small room on the second floor. When her son, escorted by an armed paramilitary officer,
finally walked in in handcuffs, she found herself rising and standing still. Chris was still wearing his school uniform. Had he even had a shower since his arrest? His Afro seemed to have become even bigger in a matter of days. He had vowed never to cut his hair until his father was found. The officer left the door

partially ajar and stepped outside, but the muzzle of his gun still showed in the door.

Denise noticed that her son was gazing at her. He was expecting her to free him, of course.

"It's not your fault, Mom," said Chris. Her little boy sounded like a grown-up man already. "Don't cry. Are you listening, Mama?" He hadn't called her 'mama' in a long time. Denise told herself to be strong. "I killed the businessman because my life is worthless without Daddy." Denise wiped tears off her cheeks. How could the son she loved so much, the bubbly boy who wrote such meditative hip-hop lyrics, suddenly become the stranger she never expected to meet? How could he be so brave and calm about his fate? How could he say he couldn't live without his father? Was his father there when the family buried Alice? When they lost the house and had to move from house to house? When he and Junior were enrolled in public schools? When they had only one meal a day? When her boss, Maxx, wanted to sleep with her?

"It wasn't my gun," she heard her son say. "It was my girlfriend's gun, and I pulled the trigger, yes, and I killed the Greek."

She wanted to ask him when he started dating this girl she had never met, but that wasn't important. The big issue was that her son was telling the police that he had pulled the trigger.

"Mama, are you listening? I could have stolen some food for you and Junior, Mama, but I didn't. I just can't wait for the judge to kill me next week."

"Listen, Chris, listen," Denise said and sniffled. Her son kept gazing at her, and it made her feel uncomfortable. Chris was never like that. Although he used to talk a lot, Chris was a shy boy—especially after his father's departure. She wished she had spent more time with him, with all the three of them, talking to them, counseling, leading them into a safe future.

"I'm listening, Mama."

They sat on hard chairs, facing each other, a large table separating them.

"It doesn't work like that, killing you next week. Never talk like that, Chris." She wished the table was small enough to allow her to touch her son. "Son, it wasn't you. Besides, the businessman is still in a coma."

"Oh, they said I killed him. I want to die, Mama. I don't tell lies, remember? You and Dad telling never to lie?"

Denise wanted to tell his son that his father had lied to the family when he said he would be coming back home with gifts. That wanting to die by killing another person was the daftest story she had ever heard. "Are they looking after you well, my child?"

"Yes, Mama."

"I tried to bring you some food, but they... They told Uncle Ben that I couldn't."

"I'm not hungry, Mama. There's this guy." Chris hesitated. At long last, he looked down. "He brings me food."

"What guy?"

"I don't know his name. Tall. Handsome like Dad. I know it's fast food he brings, but he pretends it's from his home. He puts it on nice plates with spoons and forks. Like those we used to have, the ones we sold when we moved out?"

"What's his name?"

"He gets very angry when I eat very little. I'm never hungry, and he's always angry in a manner that's bad, Mama."

"Is that one of your songs?"

"No, Mama, this is no joke. I'm serious."

"This man, could he be a policeman?"

Lifting his eyebrows, Chris whispered, "Mama, before I die, can I change my last name to your maiden name? Please, let me die as Chris Neo. I hate your husband, I hate his sister. I hate Wizzie, too. He stole our chairs. Junior had written his name behind one of the chairs, and we saw it."

"Listen, Chris, if you want to come back home, you..."

"Have you found a house, Mama? I don't want to come to that evil woman's house. And Solomon?" The door opened wider and the police officer came in. "Time up," he said.

"Officer, I hear someone comes to see my son, and yet I wasn't allowed to see him."

"This boy is crazy," said the officer. "No one comes to see him. And you're seeing him now. So, what's the problem?"

"I love you, Mama," Chris said from the door.

Later that evening, Rebecca again brought food to the guesthouse. Junior devoured his portion, but Denise said she had no appetite.

"Have you heard about your Wizzie and Martha?" asked Rebecca. "Some boys broke into their home. The fool that he is, Wizzie escaped, leaving Martha to be raped and brutally killed." Denise slumped back into her chair. "The thing is, everyone in the neighborhood knows who did it. They saw this boy and his gang. His name is Bonaventure. But they're party cadres, so they won't be arrested. Good night, Junior. Go to bed now. Mom and I have things to talk about. And it's bad manners to stand by the door, listening." Bonaventure? Denise sat still in a stooping posture, watching her son close his bedroom door without saying good night. She remembered the night her Honda was stolen. How could she not tell any earlier that it was Bonaventure who had called out her name?

CHAPTER 64

He hadn't set foot at the airport since that fateful day when he didn't catch his flight back home, and he wished he would drop dead.

"No one is going to arrest you," Nicholas reassured him again.

Kezia had said that she had not paid for the ticket. Her friend Keisha, who worked for Delta Airlines, had secured a buddy ticket for him.

Nicholas stood close to him at the check-in terminal. He punched in his ticket number, and the boarding pass came out. At the luggage desk, he booked his case straight to Lusaka, Zambia, and he hugged Nicholas, who smiled all the time.

He joined the TSA security-check line, and after twenty minutes, an officer looked at his passport and his boarding pass and waved him on. "Take off your belt, your shoes..." He didn't hear the rest, for he was doing what everyone else was doing. Soon, it was his turn to go through the body scanner. There was no drama, and before long, he was following the directions to the underground train.

Soon after he had boarded the Delta Airways Airbus A350 for Johannesburg, a member of the cabin staff upgraded him to premium economy. "The name is Keisha," she said.

"Pleased to meet you," Patrick said. "Kezia told me all the bad things about you."

Keisha smiled. "If you need anything, call me."

He slept most of the time, dreaming mostly about Denise and the kids, about Kezia and Nicholas. When the captain announced that they were about to land at Johannesburg's Oliver Tambo International, Patrick couldn't believe that during the entire twenty-two-hour flight, he had visited the restroom only once.

Under normal circumstances, he would have rejoiced to land on African soil after being away for so long. But suddenly, he was wondering if going back home was the right thing to do. He was tempted not to take the connection flight to Lusaka, but putting on his old hat that hid half his face, he felt empowered to board the flight. With that hat on, no one would recognize him. He declined everything he was offered to eat or drink.

What was he going to say Denise? To Rebecca? Alice? Chris? Junior? Uncle Ben? Norman? To everybody? What lyrics was Chris working on at that very moment? And Junior? If someone asked Junior, where's your father? *I don't know.* What's your father's name? *Daddy.*

He closed his eyes, but no sleep came.

The flight landed at Lusaka International, and he braced for trouble. He saw that everyone was in a hurry to get their check-in baggage and leave, and someone behind him said, "Sir, may I pass?"

The line of passengers moved at a slow pace, and he wished he would never get to the aircraft's exit. Finally, he faced the country he had foolishly refused to come back to, and his stomach rolled. He hesitated and almost stepped back into the aircraft, but he knew that wasn't allowed. He remembered Kezia, two nights back, telling him to stay calm and focus on what needed to be done. "Crying won't be one of the right things to do," she had said. "Put one hand on your chest, the other on your forehead. Pray."

Putting his trust in the old hat that concealed half his face, he got to customs and immigration and showed his passport.

"You're in the wrong line, Mr. Kanya," a lady said sweetly. "Returning residents stand in that line, but it's okay. Take off your hat, please."

Patrick looked around. He obeyed, and the lady gave him a long look. "You kinda look familiar."

She stamped his passport and handed it back. A close shave, he thought.

He put the hat back on and got to the carousel, where he waited for his luggage. Several people gave him close looks before they minded their own business. His luggage came half an hour later. So far so good.

He didn't want to concentrate on what happened that afternoon when he didn't show up at that very airport. Instead, he would concentrate on what to do next. That was what Kezia expected him to do.

While calling Nicholas to ask for a ticket was an act of extraordinary bravery, he believed the call he was about to make was the most difficult ever. "I'm looking for a phone," he said aloud, waving a ten-dollar bill in one hand. "I'll pay you."

A young man grabbed a young lady's phone and gave it to Patrick. The young lady said, "What?" and laughed. "Ten minutes only."

His hands shaking, he dialed her number.

She answered on the second ring.

"It's me," he said.

"Am I supposed to know Mr. It's Me?" she retorted and cut the line.

He called again. "Please, don't hang up."

The line was dead.

He called again, three times, and she didn't answer. He called again, and she said, "If you call me again..."

The owner of the phone said, "That's too many calls."

Patrick clumsily took another ten-dollar bill and gave it to the young lady. Her companion snatched it off her hand. The two laughed and watched Patrick speak into the phone.

"It's Patrick!" he said.

"Patrick? Patrick who?"

"It's me. *The* Patrick."

"Yes, you sound like him, but..." There was a pause. "You mean, *my* Patrick?"

They spoke for three minutes, and the owner of the phone said, "Sorry, we have to go. We hired a taxi."

"I'm at the airport, yes," he concluded, and she said she would be there to pick him up.

His heart fluttering like a tattered flag in a heavy storm, he found a seat in the foyer and placed his luggage on the spotless floor. His body slouched, and his hat fully covering his face, he remembered an old Zambian song about a man who had crossed the southern border and lived in Zimbabwe for many years. When the man came back home, all he had was an empty suitcase, and all his relatives had long passed on.

CHAPTER 65

He must have fallen asleep, for when he looked up, she was standing before him, looking down, as if she wasn't sure it was him.

She dropped to her knees, and they embraced and cried together.

"You're still as handsome as our father," she said, sniffling. "I'll take your hand luggage."

They were in the Range Rover, and she held the steering wheel tightly. He was certain that the only time Patrick had seen his sister shed a tear was when their parents died.

He waited for her to calm down before he said, "You kept your promise, didn't you?"

Rebecca sniffled. "I was tempted, but I didn't tell Denise or Ben. Aren't you going to ask about your children? What kind of father, husband are you?"

"I was giving you a chance to calm down."

"Honestly, I'm very disappointed. I used to be so proud of my little boy, I would boast about him everywhere I went. One day, I used to think, he'll be in Norman's position. Then he'll be CEO. Used to think you were smart. Really smart." She turned her head to face him. Her eyes were red. "I was wrong. Okay, I'll take you to a place where I can hide you until the coast is clear. You know, you better have a good explanation for what you did."

He was glad there was no drama. Rebecca had always been the wild one, and he, the cool one. He had feared her all his life. And now, he had given her a good reason to find fault in him. What defense did he have?

About six miles from the airport, in the suburb of Chelstone, the vehicle stopped at a motel. "I'll pay for the room. Three days and nights, that's all."

At the reception desk, a young man with big eyes said, "Sir, they said you were dead."

Patrick remembered Olivia and said, "I don't think you know me." He was so tired, he feared he was going to collapse.

"Oh, yes, I know you, Mr. Patrick Kanya, even with that hat on. You were my boss at ZNBC. I was in marketing. You've lost weight, sir."

Rebecca took the man's right hand and led him outside. A few minutes later, the two came back in, and none of them said a word.

Patrick's room was clean and airy. He slumped into bed. The pillow felt good—much better than the one in Aretha's room. Given a choice, he would sleep, but Rebecca was staring at him from across the room, waiting for him to exculpate himself.

"I paid Big Eyes stroke Big Mouth so well, he won't talk for the next three days. Are you hungry?"

"I've missed our T-bone steak so much."

She ordered room service.

"I'm eager to meet my family, but I'm scared, sister. Will they welcome me, forgive me?" He wanted to say more. But what was there to say?

They talked for half an hour before the food came. None was eager to eat, and two hours later, the food on the table untouched and cold, Patrick finished narrating his story, one detail after another, as if he was rolling out a red carpet for the FBI chief to walk on before his arrest.

"I never told you this, Patrick, but marrying Denise was the best thing you ever did," Rebecca said calmly. "She's a strong woman." She sniffled. "She took a lot of shit from me, and I love her. And of all the things you've done, leaving her was the most foolish. Total idiocy. You don't deserve her."

"I know, sister. But I was faithful to her until the very end. I didn't tell you that Kezia and I..."

"Shut up!" Rebecca snapped. "Have some respect. You can't discuss sex with me. Because of your foolishness, you no longer have a family. Maybe you still have me, I don't know. Listen! Where do I start from? Denise remarried."

Was the room spinning, or was Patrick imagining it? Denise remarried? He feared that he had lost his only sister's sympathy. He looked at the knife on one of the plates and feared she was going to use it to put him out of his misery. "I...I don't...blame her." He sniveled and wiped tears off his face. "But who's this...this guy? I...I can't believe she could do that."

"She couldn't believe it when you dumped her like stinking shit! She married Norman, you fool!"

"Norman?"

"Your boss. Norman."

"What?" he screamed. He felt as if the knife on the plate was already in his stomach, and Rebecca wasn't pulling it out but turning it clockwise. Denise, the love of his life, had married that brute?

"I said listen, you fool! Alice got pregnant."

He thought about Emily and the baby she had butchered. "So, I have a grandchild?" He was unwilling to stop crying, and Rebecca let him do so until he stopped.

"No."

"Did she go to the university?" He broke down again. "Oh, Denise! Tell me it's not true, Rebecca."

Rebecca was silent for a long time. "And this one is hard. Very hard. Alice is dead."

Patrick tried to get off the bed. Instead, he fell off, weeping uncontrollably, and this time, Rebecca also wept. Together, they cried and ignored the hard knocking on the door. Because of the pleasure of a few moments, he had killed his only daughter, the child he had named after his maternal grandmother. He wouldn't blame Rebecca if she killed him.

Finally, Rebecca blew her nose into a hankie, and the knocking ceased.

"She...died...during delivery?" His voice was a mere whisper.

"No." Rebecca helped him get back on the bed, where he sat. "She took her own life."

"But why?" he shouted and started to cry again.

"Patrick, I had nothing to do with it, okay? *You* killed her. She committed suicide because of *you.*"

Patrick stopped crying.

"Is everything okay, sir?" a man asked outside.

Rebecca shouted, "We're okay. Leave us alone!" She shifted on the loveseat and cleared her throat. "She killed herself while she was carrying the poor baby. And one more. Chris was arrested and charged with armed robbery and murder. He pleaded guilty, so he could get a life sentence. He told the cops he couldn't live without his dad."

"Please, don't say that to me." Patrick feared he was losing his sight. He touched his face, his eyes, his ears. He could hear his sister talk, but her words were muffled.

"Okay, you fool. What am I supposed to say? Tell you lies? You want to hear that everything is okay? Okay, then hear this, our house was repossessed by the bank."

It was an hour later when Patrick realized that he was sprawled on the floor and that he was not in his rented room at Aretha's place.

He remembered Rebecca and the room service. *The French fries and the T-bone steak on white plates. Vegetables…*

On a private-owned television station, a newscaster was reporting that former ZNBC head of television production, Mr. Patrick Kanya, who had been feared dead for more than a year, had been spotted in Lusaka. "Although an immigration spokesperson could neither deny nor confirm this, an insider, speaking anonymously, confirmed that Mr. Kanya arrived from Johannesburg this afternoon."

He saw the two plates of food his sister had ordered. He saw that the steak knife was sharp enough to give him the satisfaction of a lifetime. He picked up the knife.

Hours later, a motel staffer found him lying in his blood-drenched bed. Someone called the police and an ambulance. The first group of people to arrive on the scene was a score of radio and television crews and newspaper reporters.

That evening, Rebecca let Junior spend the night in the main house while she spoke to Denise at the guesthouse.

It was midnight, and Rebecca said, "For the sake of my nephews, you have to learn not to cry forever. Be strong and good night."

CHAPTER 66

Dressed in the only white business suit she had, Denise climbed a long staircase at Lusaka's University Teaching Hospital. She watched men and women turn their heads wherever she went, and that was exactly what she wanted. Visibility. The fact that people still saw her as an attractive woman.

The floor of the surgery ward on the second floor was sparkling clean, but still, the smell of iodine and disinfectant compelled her to stop momentarily to adapt to the environment. A haggard-looking nurse at the nurse's station said, "It's not visiting time, madam."

"Sorry, I'm Mrs. Kanya. I called before…"

The nurse lowered her gaze. "I'm sorry." She led Denise to Patrick's bed, which was enclosed in blue curtains on metal rails whose white paint was scaling.

Denise felt great discomfort from the harsh rays of the sun that escaped into the room through gaps in the curtains in the large window facing the east.

"Mr. Kanya?" the nurse said and gently touched Patrick's shoulder. "Your beautiful wife. She's here."

Denise stared at Patrick. He lay still, facing the window. She steadied herself, unwilling to collapse, physically and emotionally.

"What?" Patrick asked, as if he had just been propelled out of a nightmare. Slowly, he seemed to recognize her.

She heard the nurse's fading footsteps, and she fought hard not to cry. The sight of him brought many memories, and she was getting overwhelmed. Still, she could effortlessly put one of the many pillows on his bed over his nose and push. Or she could remove the two tubes that fed him with liquids from the bottles that dangled above him. But he was the killer, and not her. He had killed their daughter—*her* daughter. Patrick didn't deserve to be called a father.

She extended her right hand until it touched his good wrist. She sniffled and coughed. "I was gullible enough to marry a total stranger."

"I can't believe you're here, sweetheart," he whispered. "I'm so, so sorry."

"You'll be alright."

"I'll spare you the pain of asking, sweetheart," he said.

"Never mind. Rebecca told me everything last night. I rarely watch the news nowadays, but I don't think she exaggerated anything."

"I'm sorry," he said, and they awkwardly stared at each other. "I couldn't use a condom because the last time I did was that time at the university lakes, remember? When we were almost caught by security?"

She shook her head. "It's hard to remember anything nowadays." She chuckled. "You should have told me. I would have known what to do. Get a divorce. Get support. Maybe I'd have forgiven you. Just maybe."

"I'm guilty. I feared I had passed the disease on to you, and I didn't want to see you suffer."

"That was selfish. And maybe you should have committed suicide at that time, instead of subjecting us to all this pain of not knowing if you were dead or not." She didn't want the anger she had tried to hold back to take control of her. " Why did you come back?" She had no desire to cause a scene. She wasn't that kind of person.

"I tried, Denise. I don't know how people manage to do it. Suicide? It's not easy. How our daughter managed that…"

"Don't say it." She had calmed down. "Don't ever mention our daughter's name. Never!"

The nurse brought a metal chair. Denise sat down close to the bed so that her face and Patrick's were barely a few feet apart.

"I understand you…remarried." She kept staring at him. His breath was so foul that she feared she was going to vomit. "Please, don't leave me. I don't have no AIDS."

"An Americanism." Her nostrils twitched. "I know. Rebecca told me."

"I never touched anyone while I was away."

"I know. Rebecca told me."

A long silence followed. "Patrick, chances are, our son will get life. That's why I came here. Just to let you know that I hold you accountable for that. Chris...he changed completely after you left."

She hated him, and she wanted to see him suffer, to be remorseful, but all she saw was...arrogance? It was as if he considered himself *the* victim.

Only the previous day, she had seen Chris again, and while she cried in his presence, her son never shed a tear. The little boy she loved so much had become a man in front of her eyes. She wanted to tell Patrick how Alice had died a very painful death, and how their grandchild must have suffered, too. But what was the point?

"Do me a favor, sweetheart," he sounded strong. "Pull that curtain and open the window for me. I need some fresh air."

"Do me a favor, too, Patrick," she said sternly. "Never call me 'sweetheart.' Never."

"I understand, sweetheart—I mean, Denise."

She sat still for a long time before she stood up and walked to the window. The window lock wouldn't budge. She pulled the curtain to one side and put more pressure on the lock. The window opened, and the fresh, cold breeze that flowed in made her relax a little. She looked at the ground below. There was no grass but red-brick grounds that were blighted by a green mold arranged in irregular patterns.

"I don't know if I'll ever see you again," she said without turning to look at him. "I'm a married woman now."

She opened her purse and took out a folded sheet of paper. It was the blackmail note Emily had written and left on Patrick's Lilayi Lodge door.

"Denise, I'm really sorry. I apologize for everything."

"You apologize? And you think that will bring our daughter back? Make our boy a free man?"

She put the note on Patrick's bed, close enough to his free hand so that he could pick it up and read it. She knew she shouldn't have come to see him. She turned and fled the room.

In the large hall that separated three wards, she saw people, some chatty, others weeping, walking hurriedly in both directions; some coming in, others leaving. She could quickly walk away forever and pretend her ex-husband wasn't there.

Or she could go back to his bed and nurse him.

CHAPTER 67

To the east of the hospital was Prospect Hill, one of the city's affluent suburbs. Unknown to Denise, Norman had a house there, not far from the hospital wire fence that had several holes in it, and through the holes, people to come in and out without going through the security gate.

Using her new phone, the one Norman had given to her, Denise dialed a number.

"Hi, sweetheart!" Norman responded on the second ring.

She took a deep breath. "It's me. Mrs. Denise Kanya. I want a divorce."

"That's a good one," Norman laughed. "So, where are you, my darling? Look, about Chris, I think we'll have to find a better lawyer. That Hazel girl is a politician, not a lawyer."

"I'm at the hospital, surgical ward, nursing my husband. I didn't have a chance to tell you, but I'm pregnant."

"*Pregnant?*"

Denise pressed the power button.

She could no longer hold back the tears, so she dashed into the nearest ladies' restroom. She hated telling lies and public bathrooms, but she had to cry in private. Of course, she wasn't pregnant.

She avoided stepping on the patches of water on the floor, and eventually, she got to a stall. It was filthy, and the door lock was broken. From her purse, she took out a makeup mirror and touched her face with a little makeup. She was surprised to find a whole roll of toilet paper. She pulled sheets of it and cleaned the toilet seat. She hoped no one would come in, and she cried. Memories of Matilda crying in the toilet made her realize how she, herself, was just a common woman among many who suffered the same fate of male dominance and poverty.

Again, unknown to her, back in Patrick's ward, at that very moment, Patrick sat up in bed. He painstakingly freed his hand from the two IV tubes. He got off the bed, and one unsteady step at a time, he got to the open window. Behind him, Norman, dressed in military fatigues, pulled the blue curtain to one side.

Patrick turned, and the two men angrily stared at each other.

"You…!" Patrick said, and suddenly, he felt dizzy. He was so tired, all he wanted was to get to the window and jump—or go back to the bed and die.

"Patrick," Norman spat out. "You'll not have my wife just because she still carries your fuckin name." He pulled out a South African Vector SP1 pistol from one of the large pockets of his pants.

Three bullets hit Patrick in the chest. His hands shaking, Norman looked at the gun, stuck it in his own mouth, and pulled the trigger.

At the same time, Denise left the restroom. In the hallway, she saw people running and heard them yelling. This was the hospital, one the public had nicknamed *the departure lounge*. She ignored the hullabaloo. Things happened there all the time.

Her phone took time to come on, but she noticed that she had missed several calls from Norman, and another she considered very important.

She called the important number.

"Talk to me, Denise, where are you?" It was Hazel Omei, the nation's most dreaded lawyer and one of Denise's foes from their university days. "Sorry to hear about Patrick, but listen. Good news. We got your house back. Maxx didn't contest the claim. A lot of corruption in this country, Denise. Come 2021, and we'll change the government. You can move in soon, and without paying any loan arrears because Maxx paid those."

A man who was running away from the surgical ward shouted, "A gunman!"

"Aren't you excited to hear about your house, Denise?"

"Wait a minute. Let me call you back."

"No, even greater news, Denise. Is this the right time to talk?"

Denise looked around her. People were still running, some of them screaming. "Say it quickly. I hear there's a gunman." Two armed police officers ran past her. "I heard gunshots." She was panting.

"Well, I hear gunshots everywhere in this city every day."

The phone pressed hard against her ear, Denise headed for a door and opened it. It was a little room full of cleaning materials. She entered the room and closed the door. The stench was unbearable, and there was no light.

"Okay, I won't be long," Hazel spoke calmly. "Let's start with Chris. Norman thinks there's a chance. I don't know what he means by that. You know how things work in this country. You know Norman, of course, Patrick's boss, the late Lisa's guy. I know you're in a hurry, but one more thing. If you are watching Breaking News, you should be seeing Maxx Mandallo's look of shame. The Big Maxx. Who says he can't be touched? I got him arrested." Hazel sounded like someone who was gloating before her foe—which was what Denise had always considered her to be. A foe. Hazel had tried hard to get Patrick from her. Denise wished Hazel had succeeded. "Maxx is in jail right now. Corruption, extortion, you name it. No judge will consider his bail today, I hope. That's him and his twelve accomplices from the banks. Some reporter is referring to them as Maxx's Disciples."

"Maxx, arrested? I've got to go."

"Yes. For years, Maxx was bribing bank staff to sell him bank repo houses at a song from widows. Already, I've received death threats. You know me, I'm not scared."

Denise feared she was going to pass out. The stench in the room was getting too strong for her lungs, and she needed to leave.

"One other thing, Denise. Hey, did you know that the house in Meanwood was in your sister-in-law's name?"

"Hazel, I have to go," Denise said and cautiously opened the door.

"Okay, okay. The title was in Rebecca's name."

Denise came out of the little room, panting, and her phone rattled. A text message read: *Mrs. Kanya, thanks for your application. We have two senior openings, one in the editor's office, the other, administrative. Please call me back. Ken at Parliament.*

"What?" she whispered and looked up. A large crowd stood still in silence, looking intently at two nurses who were speedily wheeling a gurney from the surgical ward.

"Mrs. Kanya..." one of the nurses, the one who had earlier given Denise a chair to sit in, shouted.

"Patrick!" Denise screamed. She looked on, unable to move. Partially covered in a blood-stained blue bedsheet, Patrick was loosely strapped to the gurney and seemed to be in danger of falling off. "What did you do to him?" She screamed again, and as she started to run, she didn't feel her new phone drop to the floor. All around her, people started to speak excitedly. "What did you do to him?"

The nurses kept wheeling the gurney while Denise ran alongside it.

"No, Mrs. Kanya, please!" the nurse who had spoken earlier said. "No!"

Denise caressed Patrick and kept running along even as the gurney picked up speed.

"Don't die, Patrick," she whispered. "Please, don't die. The boys, Patrick."

By the time Denise and the nurses were approaching the entrance to an operating theater, Denise's suit had become a blend of bright red and white colors.

"Tell me he'll be all right, please. His boys need him."

The gurney disappeared into a double door, and a nurse dressed in blue took Denise to the side. "I think it would be advisable for you to wait outside, Mrs. Kanya. Please."

The wait wasn't long. The nurse in blue came out of the theater and said, "I'm so, so sorry, Mrs. Kanya."

"No, please...Okay, okay. A lady will come here." Denise sniffled. She felt numb in the limbs. "Her name is...is Rebecca. Rebecca Kanya. She's my sister-in-law. Please, tell her to look after her nephews."

The nurse winked constantly. "You can't do that, Mrs. Kanya. Please. Your family needs you."

Denise hurriedly walked to a long corridor whose concrete wall rose only to her chest. Beneath the wall was another level, and the redbrick ground seemed to be beckoning to her to join it.

SIX MONTHS LATER

Holding Junior's fingers tightly with her left hand, Denise felt the wind sway her flared skirt until it covered her son's face. She had lost fifty pounds, her eyes were sunken in their sockets like a famished war victim's, and all her clothes had become too big for her. Junior, on the other hand, had gained weight to dangerous levels, making him look many years older than he was. She was glad the lady from social welfare had stopped coming to see Junior. *Are you sure he's not suicidal?* the officer used to ask.

As far as the eye could see, old and new flowers encased in clear plastic bags fluttered on graves like buntings.

"Let's get down, son," she said, her voice tiny and hoarse, and together, they clumsily knelt before Patrick's grave. She adjusted the dark glasses she never took off in public and removed a leaf that had landed on her shaved head. She wished she could say a prayer for Patrick's soul. But no. What purpose would that serve? She used to think that she would revert to Christianity after Patrick's death, but after all the grief she has had to bear, she was even a stauncher nonbeliever.

She wished there was a third grave—one for her first son. In one of the shortest murder trials in the land, Chris, being a minor, was sentenced to life imprisonment instead of death by hanging. The name of the judge, Denise had vowed never to forget. Judge Goodwin Hove. Not even Chris's lawyer, Hazel Omei, could explain how the case was disposed of so expeditiously. It was only after Chris was found dead in his prison cell that the news media started to ask questions. Okay, the Greek supermarket owner had died at a South African clinic a month after he was shot in the abdomen. Why was Chris's girlfriend, who had confessed to plotting the robbery with some unknown people, been acquitted? Connections? One of the girl's uncles was said to be a big fish in the ruling party.

Denise had been so devastated, she had declined to see Chris's body. Acting against Rebecca's advice, Denise had given the state the go-ahead to bury her son.

As if on cue, mother and son rose at the same time and moved to the next grave. Rebecca had been lucky to find space to bury Patrick next to his daughter.

Connections.

"Sleep well, Alice," Denise whispered. "We'll see you again next week."

Mother and child got to the taxi that had been waiting close by, and the driver wanted to know where to next, and Denise said, "The Great East Road campus of the university, sir."

No one spoke as the taxi negotiated turns, and sometimes, potholes, and when they got to the parking lot near the graduation square, Denise said, "We won't be long, sir. I won't run away. As usual, we'll pay."

Mother and child walked in silence to the dining room complex near the imposing university library building. Denise hadn't visited her alma mater in a long time, and the abundant evidence of dilapidation of the premises was embarrassing. They found their way to the entrance to the lower dining room. Behind that door, Denise had first spoken to Patrick. Memories of their good times made her sad, but she soon composed herself. She didn't want to disturb Junior. As she remembered her friends, she wondered why Gertrude had denied the truth about Patrick being institutionalized when they were students together. The truth was that soon after Patrick had cheated on her with Lisa, Denise had called off the relationship. For weeks, Patrick had pleaded for forgiveness. To attract her sympathy, he had washed his books in water. Denise had put her foot down. She could not marry a cheat. It was not until Patrick was institutionalized for depression that Denise had forgiven him, and he had quickly recuperated.

In her room, Patrick had knelt before her and said, "I'll forever owe you, sweetheart, and I have a confession to make. The woman you knew as my late mother was only my stepmother. Dad abandoned my mother when he met the woman you met. My mother died years later in a mental hospital."

The cab driver was pleased to see Denise and Junior come back.

"Take us to ZNBC," she said.

"Yes, madam. Now I remember. I saw you on TV!"

Again, no one spoke during the short drive to the television company. Like Chris, Junior had become a recluse and rarely looked in Denise's direction.

The taxi stopped at the security gate, and Denise took her only son's hand. Junior had become a small child again, always waiting to be told what to do. She stood by the driver's door and paid the fare in cash.

"A tip, madam?" asked the driver.

"Sorry, I have no extra money."

She remembered the good news, a rare occurrence in her life. Only the previous night, Rebecca had said that if Denise dropped her smoking habit, she and Junior could stay in the guestroom for as long as was necessary because, in Rebecca's own words, "No one will give a job to or marry someone who is just a heap of bones, a skeleton." Maxx still owned the Meanwood house, as the matter was before the courts, and Hazel didn't seem to be doing a very good before the honorable judges.

She took a pack of cigarettes from her purse, and with shaking hands, she opened it and took out one cigarette. She spat to the ground, and as the cigarette fell next to her saliva, she crushed it with her shoe.

"Will this do?" Denise showed the cigarette packet to the driver. She decided she would stop smoking, a habit she had started soon after Patrick's funeral. What she couldn't understand was why Patrick's death had touched her much more than her own children's. Even Rebecca, who was Patrick's blood relation, had recovered from the loss of her only brother. It was Chris's death that seemed to haunt Rebecca, for she had never ceased to blame herself for failing to get her nephew out of prison.

"Thank you, madam," said the taxi driver, and surprisingly, he looked quite pleased.

They were in the HR office, and the secretary asked, "How may I help you, madam?"

Denise found that strange because she had been to the office before. She grunted. "Sorry we're a little early, but we have an appointment to see the new head of HR."

The secretary looked at the PC screen before her. "I'm sorry, madam, but Ms. Stevenson is expecting someone now."

"Mrs. Kanya?" asked Denise.

"Yes."

"I'm Denise Kanya, and this is my son, Junior."

Her mouth wide open, the secretary gave Denise a long look. "Of course. And the lawyer is here already."

Denise was ushered into the main office.

"Sue Stevenson," a lady with a pleasant personality, and in her early thirties, introduced herself. Sue, whom Denise considered to be very pretty, wore an Afro the same way Denise used to wear hers when she was in high school, and Angela Davis, the former civil rights activist whom her elderly history teacher was very fond of, was her hero. "Sit down, please."

"Sit down, Junior," Denise said, and Junior sat at the edge of the chair nearest to his mother's. Denise felt a tear run down her left cheek. What could she do to bring life back into her only child?

"This is Mr. Desmond Wina," Sue introduced the formally dressed, short, and serious-looking man with ears like Obama's. Desmond gave Denise a stare before he looked away. "I won't speak for him. But here's the thing." Denise liked Sue. Affable. Freewheeling. A large black belt on khaki pants and a deep green men's shirt with brown buttons that looked like plums. Denise had no doubt that the young lady had a great family, lived a great life, and had a great future at the television company.

"Now, Mr. Patrick Kanya." Sue sighed and consulted a bulky file. "There were benefits he should have been paid after deserting. Vacation, personal days. He seemed to be the kind of man who never went on vacation. I have a check for you for that." She leisurely pushed a check to one side of her desk. "I'll ask Mr. Wina to speak for himself."

"Mrs. Kanya, first, let me say how I got here," the short man spoke like someone who would do anything to sound like an educated Englishman on BBC World. "I'm your husband's lawyer, by the way. We got your number from your husband's records, we called, and you never picked up the phone. We contacted this office, and that's how we learned that you would be here today." Denise had never liked short men. "We were classmates and great friends. It's been half a year since your husband's death, and we had some family members claiming his estate."

Denise knew everyone Patrick called a friend or relative, but she was not in the HR office to argue with anybody, least of all, with a learned gentleman. "Do you have some tissue?" she asked.

"Of course," said Sue, and she pushed a pack of Kleenex tissue across the table. "I'm sorry, I didn't mean to be rude."

"No problem," said Denise. She half rose, picked up the Kleenex box, and with shaking hands, she quickly pulled out a handful of tissue and spat in it.

His feet jiggling, Desmond gave Denise a hard smile and said, "In his last will, prepared by our firm some five years ago, he left his entire estate to his wife. That means his farm, the milk cows, the beef cattle, the big house in Prospect Hill and four others, one tractor, the lot. They're all yours." He finally saw it fit to smile.

Denise wanted to stand up, pick up the check on Sue's desk and leave. She would put the money to good use. Although Rebecca had become a good friend, Denise still wanted to find a place she could call her own. She needed to remain seated for a few more minutes more, though, for she felt so weak, she feared she was going to either throw up or pass out.

"Are you following, madam?" asked Desmond. "Can you make it to our offices tomorrow afternoon? I'll be in court in the morning. We're located in the Woodlands area, at the roundabout." Desmond put a business card on Sue's desk.

"I'm sorry," said Denise. "I'm tired, and I need to leave."

"I understand," said Desmond. "Like I said, I wasn't only his lawyer but his friend as well. So, finding his marriage certificate, and authenticating it at the registrar of marriages, came as a shock to us all at the firm." Denise listened attentively. "He never told us he remarried. Madam, the terms of the testament were clear—that his wife would inherit everything. His wife is not mentioned by name. And as far as we know, you're the only woman he was married to at the time of his death."

"Excuse me, Ms. Stevenson, but is this real?" Denise asked. "It sounds like a TV drama to me." She attempted to stand up.

"Your husband, the late Norman Tau," said Desmond with a sense of accomplishment, "he had cash at the bank. Three vehicles. Norman was a shrewd businessman, and I wonder why he kept a job. He was worth almost a million US dollars, madam."

Denise stole a glance at Junior, whose eyes were closed, and she feared he might fall off the chair. She was glad her son was not following the conversation.

"And his terminal benefits were very good, of course," said Sue, who picked up another check from the bulky folder and put it on top of the other check. "A hundred thousand US dollars plus. Of course, because he committed suicide, he forfeits his company's life insurance money."

Denise was getting upset. She was tired of being pursued by Norman's ghost. Three times since his death, two detectives had been to see her. They wanted to know how come she married Norman so soon after Lisa's death. Was she seeing him while Lisa was still alive? Was she aware that Norman couldn't perform in bed, a condition that led to serious disagreements between him and Lisa, and that earlier on the night of her death, Lisa had been seen in the company of a man who also died a mysterious death a week after Lisa's death, and that the police believed that Norman had caused both deaths?

"No!" Denise yelled and stood up. She grabbed Junior by the arm. "Let's go, my darling. I'm not here to inherit anything. Look, Ms. Stevenson, it wasn't a marriage. It wasn't even consummated. Do you understand, Sue?"

"Mama?"

Her hand clasped to her mouth, Denise went down on her knees before her son. "Baby, was that you calling me mama?"

"Get the money, Mama."

Behind her desk, Sue stood up and intently watched mother and son. Desmond looked on, his face bland.

Denise sobbed at her son's feet. "Ms. Sue, he hasn't said a word since his father's death. Six months. He cried night and day until he lost his voice. He whispers sometimes, of course."

"Get the check, Mama."

Her hands clasped by her chest, Denise stared at the thick carpet. Minutes passed before she took in a deep breath and said, "For you, my only child, I will." She sniveled. "For you, my only son. Just for you."

Made in the USA
Columbia, SC
29 May 2022